Chaotic Energy

Stephanie Yeboah is a British–Ghanaian body image advocate, multi-award-winning content creator and freelance writer with nearly a quarter of a million followers on Instagram. She is the author of *Fattily Ever After*, her 2020 memoir, and is passionate about centring plus-sized bodies in TV and literature, especially within the categories of romance and romantic comedies. Stephanie currently lives in south London.

Instagram: @stephanieyeboah
www.stephanieyeboah.com

Chaotic Energy

Stephanie Yeboah

TRAPEZE

First published in Great Britain in 2025 by Trapeze,
an imprint of The Orion Publishing Group Ltd
Carmelite House, 50 Victoria Embankment
London EC4Y 0DZ

An Hachette UK Company

The authorised representative in the EEA is Hachette Ireland, 8 Castlecourt Centre,
Dublin 15, D15 XTP3, Republic of Ireland (email: info@hbgi.ie)

1 3 5 7 9 10 8 6 4 2

A CIP catalogue record for this book is
available from the British Library.

ISBN (Hardback) 978 1 3987 2186 9
ISBN (Export Trade Paperback) 978 1 3987 2187 6
ISBN (eBook) 978 1 3987 2188 3
ISBN (Audio) 978 1 3987 2189 0

Printed in Great Britain by Clays Ltd, Elcograf S.p.A

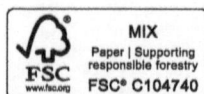

MIX
Paper | Supporting
responsible forestry
FSC
www.fsc.org FSC® C104740

www.orionbooks.co.uk

*To my best friend, Uwa, who knows me better than
I know myself.
It's a shame we both didn't know about the Google
Reverse Image search tool back then.*

Chapter 1

It was 3.30 a.m. on a warmish May morning, and I was sitting in the reception of King's College Hospital, waiting with bated breath to find out whether the medical staff had been able to dislodge a vibrating bullet from my best friend's arsehole.

As someone who considered themselves to lead a fundamentally boring life, I could see the humour of my current situation: being woken up at midnight by a frantic call from my best friend Jean, who went on to tell me – in extreme detail – that he had somehow stuck a 'bullet' sex toy far enough up his arse that neither he nor his midnight companion could get it out.

'Have you tried sharting it out?' I suggested between my badly muffled guffaws as he hyperventilated down the phone.

'Temz. Now ain't the time for gags. I'm having a crisis here! Can you please, please meet me at A&E? I feel like I'm gonna blow up.' I hear a firm beep as he hangs up on me.

Despite needing to be at work in under six hours, I slid on an old Nike tracksuit and power-walked my way down Denmark Hill to the A&E department. I had my keychain alarm and a heavy-ass empty candle jar (Jo Malone's Pomegranate Noir, of course; I'm fancy) to hand in case some randomer felt like causing trouble while I walked alone.

I texted Jean to let him know that I'd arrived and took a vacant seat in an empty corner of the waiting area. As I was scrolling through one of my Instagram accounts, swiping through all the spam messages and bot follows that seemed to have overtaken the platform of late, one of the profiles that had recently followed my page caught my eye. Something told me to click on their photo to see their full Instagram page:

@RubesCubes 445 Posts 13.8k Followers 902 Following
Ruben Alexander he/him Follows You
Freelancer in Tech // I like to sing sometimes // Add me on Twitch – @RubesCubes5
Music: info@RubenAlexander.com
For Tech Consultation Inquiries: RubenA@InnovativeTech.com

As I scanned his page, I realised that I was gazing at one of the most beautiful men I had ever had the fortune of laying my eyes upon. He had this gorgeous mahogany skin that almost looked as if it were glowing; probably owing to him adorning himself with the finest of cocoa butter straight from the coast of Ghana itself. He had a perfectly spherical, shiny head and cheekbones so sharp one could probably cut glass with them. His eyes were small, yet bright and inquisitive, and framing his symmetrical lips was a finely trimmed, full beard.

'Oh, honey, I am FOLLOWING you, OK?' I breathed to myself as I hit the follow button and proceeded to look through this stranger's account for the next hour; I needed the entertainment. Given the circumstances and given my shit track record with men at the moment, I needed all the eye candy I could get right now.

Three and a half hours, three KitKat bars and two diabolical coffees later, Jean appeared from the triage ward, looking pained and embarrassed, but with a slight coy air about him.

'Not gonna lie, that was probably the most action I've had in two months, Temz,' he said, giggling, as we hugged and made our way outside the hospital. He had a slight limp, and would groan anytime he stood up straight. It took every fibre in my being not to get my camera out and record a video of him to post on Instagram.

'Jean, how on Earth? Who on earth . . . Just . . . *why*?'

'Girl, it's not like I haven't done this before – d'you remember when we all went to Heaven and I kinda disappeared for about fifteen minutes?' I nodded. We had been at the nightclub celebrating Jean's new work assignment, which would have him travelling across Europe on location for a photography project. 'Well, there was this rando who was selling these little sex-toy bullet things by the bar and I bought one, and so Mike and I decided to test it out in the toilets – and, honestly, sis, it was amazing.'

I shook my head as he continued, 'Anyway I thought we'd try it out again tonight, and well, chile . . . I guess it was a case of misjudging the distance once it went in, cause I'm pretty sure I shouldn't have been feeling a vibration around my lungs.' Jean screamed out in laughter as he booked his Uber. 'Thank you so much for coming, though, babygirl. You truly are a gentleman and a scholar, and I appreciate and loves ya.' He mockingly tipped an imaginary hat as I curtsied and playfully offered him my hand to kiss. Jean then glanced down to the empty candle jar in my hand.

'Erm. Sis? What's this for? I know you're all "Woowoo" and everything, but I don't think smoking the bullet out woulda worked, to be honest.'

'First of all, you're very welcome, sir, but next time, I'd appreciate you doing this at a more reasonable hour when I can actually get a few minutes' nap in beforehand. And secondly,' I retorted, tossing the candle jar between my two hands, 'I'm a single Black woman walking through Camberwell in the early hours of the morning; your girl's gotta stay strapped at all times.'

Jean tried to stifle a laugh before flinching in pain slightly. Hopefully the meds would kick in soon. 'Only Artemis Owusu would think about attacking someone in the middle of the night with a Jo Malone candle. Not even an Aldi or TK Maxx one you know. Bougie bitch.'

Typical Jean to get into a situation like this. I love the guy and he's a fucking fabulous mate, but I do sometimes feel more like his caretaker than an actual best friend.

Jean (pronounced 'jawn' like the 'gen' bit in 'genre', as he likes to remind everyone) is the first of my two best friends in the whole world, and the way that we met is a tale I always delight in retelling.

Five years ago, I was on a disastrous first date at the Telephone Exchange bar in London Bridge, trying to figure out how to get out of it. I had met the guy on Tinder, and as he approached the bar and caught a glimpse of me – all five feet six inches and eighteen stone of me – I saw the light slowly leave his eyes. He approached with a strained smile.

Throughout the date, I could tell he was uncomfortable with my appearance and wanted nothing more than to leave. I ordered a pasta puttanesca with a side of garlic bread and the side-eye he gave my plates could have cut glass, or coke, which I presumed he was also high on at the time. Whenever I shifted my dress in my seat, he scoffed and shook his head. He then proceeded to wax lyrical about the online workout classes he took each morning, asking me if I'd be 'keen to get the YouTube link too?' I would rather suck a denim vest through a straw while having my taint waxed then wake up at the crack of dawn and emulate fitness influencers with Brazilian Butt Lifts completing bleep tests.

'Nah. I'm OK, thanks, mate. I already have a gym membership, can't you tell?' I flexed my arms in jest. He stared blankly at me, not getting the joke. Yep, an absolute write-off.

If I weren't so used to guys acting this way on dates, I would almost be offended. I started dissociating and turning my eye towards the other patrons in the bar after the Tinder Date Guy asked me whether I would 'be eating all of that' for the third time. After ten minutes, someone had caught my eye. A tall, slender-looking man, sitting alone in one of the booths across from us. He had deliciously supple, smooth, caramel skin peppered with light freckles, a jawline that could cut glass, bouncing black curls that framed his handsome face perfectly, a wickedly devilish smile and the biggest most beautifully shaped cloudy-grey eyes I'd ever seen. He was, for all intents and purposes, absolutely stunning; like a porcelain doll of sorts.

What's more, I noticed that he was noticing me too, looking up every few minutes to smile at me with a cheeky glint in his eye. This carried on for the next half an hour until my date had to go to the bathroom. He never came back. Crushed and slightly drunk with absolutely nothing left to lose, I decided to sexily saunter across to this mysterious stranger and try my luck.

'I noticed you noticing me,' I slurred, 'and I just wanted to put you on notice that I noticed you back.' He laughed a hearty, deep guffaw that sent tingles of pleasure through each of my orifices before proceeding to tell me that he was, in actual fact, trying to make eyes at my date. I let him know that he had actually left already.

'You're very cute too, though, sis, and fuck him for leaving like that halfway through. He didn't deserve ya. I'm Jean, by the way, pronounced "jawn", as in "genre",' he drawled, as he held out his hand for me to shake.

'I'm Artemis, but everyone calls me Temz for short,' I mumbled sloppily.

'Artemis? Well, OK, I see you, Goddess! Love to see it and lovely to meet you. Now, let's get a few more rounds in.'

I always used to feel a tinge of embarrassment when stating my name for the first time, because for some reason, people never expect someone who looks like me to be called something like that. A whole dictionary of perfectly reasonable names and my parents had to go and name me Artemis of all things. It's not that I don't like my name, it is beautiful, and being named after a Greek goddess was always going to be pretty cool; it's just one of those names that gives off intense 'Main Character Energy', I suppose. I guess that's what you get when you have two parents with a love of Greek mythology and fine art: bougie for no reason.

Jean and I had a few drinks that night accompanied by incoherent tales about our lives, and when it was time to go, I lazily booked an Uber back to my place and we ended up sleeping together. We remained sex buddies for about five months or so, and in all that time I had only really seen him as a good friend, so it was a pretty cool arrangement for me. We ceased the sexual part of our friendship when we both started dating other people, but we've remained the best of friends ever since.

A mere two-and-a-half hours after my A&E excursion, I clambered groggily out of bed and started getting ready for work, with the sweet melodies of Sam Cooke blasting in the background serving as my early morning soundtrack. I started off each morning doing the same thing: I stared at myself in the mirror for a few minutes; traced my bumps and curves with my hands, and my thighs that displayed a myriad of small, moon-like craters of cellulite I had tried so desperately to get rid of as a teenager.

My eyes casually flickered over the other markings on my

thighs, secretly self-inflicted during my lowest moments but which I eventually came to accept and love. My small 'Gye Nyame' Adinkra tattoo, signifying my Ghanaian heritage, stretched over my expanding ribcage, now resembling more of a Rorschach blob than an ancient African symbol.

I opened up my journal and wrote a list of the awesome things I liked about myself today:

1. We are fans of the big lips today. No filler for me!
2. My kinky curls look fabulous and bushy this morning, though they could do with some leave-in conditioner, tbh.
3. My legs look a bit leaner, I suppose. Note: ask PT about weighted lunges!
4. One of my back rolls is currently holding my thong in the right place above my hip. We love God's strongest soldiers.
5. The stretchmarks have a slightly golden hue this morning, like thunderbolts. Not mad at them.

I put my journal away and hopped into the shower, thinking about this morning's chaos with Jean, as well as wondering what fuckery I was going to have to put up with at work today. I daydreamed of a Pret A Manger cappuccino to relieve the gross fatigue and exhaustion I felt as I hurriedly got ready for work.

'Artemis, babes? Just a quick one. Can I pull you over to remind you about all the shower stuff?' my flatmate Natalie called from her room, and the hairs on the back of my neck instantly rose up as I went into flight-or-flight mode.

'Nat, I'm gonna miss my train – is this something we can chat about when I get home?'

Upon hearing me reply, Natalie peeked her head of voluminous blonde curls around her bedroom door and glanced at me in a manner that let me know that she was approaching her final Karen form. *I don't bloody have time for this . . .*

Natalie is one of a small group of people who refuses to call me by my shortened name, despite me insisting at every instance. She's been my flatmate for two years and she is – all hyperbole intended – an absolute nightmare, with a puffed-up superiority complex that can only come from a person who has grown up with immense wealth and privilege. But the rent is cheap and I still get to live in Zone 2. Swings and roundabouts, I s'pose.

I check my phone to glance at the time – seven minutes until my train.

'I just wanted to remind you of the time limits for taking a shower in the morning, Artemis. I know you're . . . you're a bit bigger than me and everything—' she shuffles as she looks down at the floor; I smile '—but I thought we agreed that we would keep it to under seven minutes for each shower? You were in there for at least twelve minutes, is all.'

I stared at her, considering my response. Do I keep it cute and tell her it wouldn't happen again? Or should I dress my answer up with a little bit of shade? *Decisions . . .*

'I'm sorry, Nat, I know you're not used to washing your body with a sponge, and that's probably why it takes *you* such a short time. But normally, in order to ensure the cleanliness of skin generally, a degree of exfoliation is needed, and this can sometimes take a little more than seven minutes to do. We'll chat later though, babe!'

I smiled sweetly and slammed the door on my way out, taking delight in seeing Natalie's incredulous expression as I power-walked through the park and into the station.

★

I cherished my daily train rides to work as it meant time to carry out the admin for the little side hustle I've had for a few months now – my lovingly and thoughtfully named Instagram: Say Aloe To My Little Friend (™ coming soon), where I write about all things houseplant-related.

I've already racked up around five thousand online followers over the last eighteen months, half of whom frequently send me a barrage of random houseplant-related questions which – me being ever the professional (by way of owning thirty-four houseplants and being lucky enough to live in a flat with south-facing windows) – I am able to answer with finesse and ease. It's my dream to one day be to houseplants what Nigella is to home-cooking.

I opened up the Instagram account and checked through today's selection of DMs:

@KatieB2016: Babes! I hope you're well. My Devils Ivy isn't growing and I need to know what I'm doing wrong xx

I respond:

SayAloeToMyLittleFriend: Hey my love, thanks for getting in touch! Trim the plant underneath the little nodes; it'll force the plant to grow longer over time – lemme know how it goes! Xxx

@BusyBumblebeexo: Hey Aloe, can you recommend the best soil to plant a cactus in? There's a weird smell coming from mine atm

SayAloeToMyLittleFriend: Hey! Any combination of normal potting soil, bark and gravel will work well for cactuses and succulents. Make sure you add loads of stones so the soil drains freely ☺

Ugh. I was such a natural. Perhaps horticulture could be my true calling.

@aeo8110: Click HERE for the chance to win an iPhone 14 Pro!!

I carried on scrolling through the various comments on my latest Instagram post featuring my collection of favourite succulents when I came across a comment that caught my eye.

RubesCubes: Damn, ma ... that's hella plants you got there. Impressive.

My encyclopaedic knowledge of US TV dramas and sitcoms kicks in, instantly letting me know that the owner of this comment may be from the West Coast of the US – more specifically, California. Even more specifically, the Bay Area. I briefly looked at the username and caught my breath: it was only Mr 'Fine-as-Fuck' RubesCubes himself, who had followed my account earlier. I smiled to myself as I quickly swiped back onto his full profile to remind myself of how just how fine he was:

@RubesCubes 445 Posts 13.8k Followers 902 Following
Ruben Alexander he/him Follows You
Freelancer in Tech // I like to sing sometimes // Add me on Twitch – @RubesCubes5
Music: info@RubenAlexander.com
For Tech Consultation Inquiries: RubenA@InnovativeTech.com

'Whew.' I breathed quietly to myself as I swiped through some of his most recent photos. I quickly flitted back to his comment on my photo, liked it, and replied:

SayAloeToMyLittleFriend: Ahh thank you, yeah I'm pretty awesome with plants tbh 😊

I scrolled through his grid posts, briefly dipping into a daydream where I imagined what our prospective kids would look like and which private schools they'd be attending, and liked a few of his photos before putting my phone down, trying to not obsess over whether the Adonis that was RubesCubes would comment back.

Unable to resist, I switched my Instagram account over to my personal account and found Ruben's again and with the aim of viewing his Instagram Stories of the last twenty-four hours. It seemed safer to do it on my own account as I didn't want to give him the impression that this random plant page was stalking him and being all weird. I'd have all the time in the world to stalk him privately, though. Then I had a sudden thought – before looking through his Stories, I quickly changed my profile picture to something more alluring. Fat chance he'd even click onto my profile to have a look at who's been viewing his videos, but on the off chance that he did, I wanted him to be greeted with a photo of me looking like an absolute snack, even if the rest of my profile was currently on private. I quickly sped through Ruben's IG Stories, all four of them. Him posing in front of the Golden Gate Bridge in San Francisco. A photo of the biggest, slimiest cheeseburger I've ever seen with the caption 'Beeftown's cheeseburgers are the best, make sure y'all check them out!' A portrait photo of him with a link to his SoundCloud account (which I made note to copy to my clipboard to peruse later) and then a final photo of him topless in bed with the caption 'Goodnight y'all'.

I lingered on the last photo for a couple of seconds, admiring his chest. He was broad and bear-like; slightly chubby yet toned. He had the kind of body that would be capable of giving a person the greatest hugs of all time, and somewhere deep down in my stomach I felt a sudden twitch of pure, hot lust. I had become – in that moment – obsessed. The fact that he could also sing only added to the allure. I needed more.

Suddenly remembering that I hadn't caught up with Jean since last night's events, I sent him a quick text as the train slowly pulled into Victoria Station:

Me: Babes! Just sliding through and seeing if all is OK? Hit me up if you need anything xx

Jean instantly hits me back:

Jean: I'm good babes, will call you this eve! Speaking of 'sliding through', I've been shitting non-stop since they gave me that enema at the hospital last night xx

I laughed to myself as I made a mental note to ask Jean later if he would mind reviewing my private Instagram page from a man's point of view, just in case I needed to tart up my profile with some thirst traps for when I eventually decided to follow Ruben on that account. Outside of dating apps, the majority of guys I've dated in the past have come from my DMs being slid into on Instagram, and I'm not about to ruin my current streak with this one: Atlantic Ocean be damned!

Chapter 2

Sent at 8.42 a.m.:

Artemis,

I have just booked a meeting for us at 10:30 in boardroom 3 for a last-minute pitch rundown for Maranette Clothing this PM. Please make sure to update the slideshow deck with their relevant social media statistics as well as any prospective content creators and journalists we could potentially offer them. I have left more notes on your desk.

Cheers,

Stephen

I finished reading the email on my phone while simultaneously juggling a pain au chocolat and a large cappuccino in my other hand as I speed-walked down Great Portland Street to my office: an absolute unit of a building on the corner of Margaret Street that overlooked all the other digital marketing agencies on the street. *Great.* Another last-minute email with work fluff more suited to a PR assistant than the head of content.

Note to self: speak to Stephen about me potentially getting an assistant.

My boss Stephen was – for all intents and purposes – wonderful at his job as a marketing director, but also scatty and very last-minute dot com, often to the detriment of the rest of the team.

I made it to my desk with seconds to spare, trying to stabilise my breathing to make the two flights of stairs I'd just climbed sound less like I'd just completed a twenty-six-mile marathon.

My role as head of content meant coming up with creative strategies and marketing plans for clothing and luxury retail brands wanting to expand their visibility online, in print and on TV. As someone who would often internally scrutinise and amend tube station billboards and magazine ad concepts during my daily commute like the apparent jobsworth I am, I took to the role like a duck to water. Despite it becoming a little boring, I enjoyed my job for the most part. The money was great and most of the people were cool.

My meeting with Stephen was a little chaotic, to say the least. We'd been trying to pitch Maranette, a huge national clothing chain, for months, and after finally being able to get a meeting in, Stephen had taken an almost neurotic approach to ensure that this afternoon's meeting went without a hitch. However, not only had I forgotten to include at least four key media contacts in my slideshow, I then accidentally knocked my coffee over the keyboard, immediately short-circuiting the laptop. This was shaping up to be an amazing day!

'Artemis, what's going on? Speak to me,' said Stephen, propping himself up on the edge of the table looking like a concerned social worker as I mopped up the keyboard, apologising emphatically. I was exhausted after last night's shenanigans, but I needed to get it the fuck together. I wasn't going to tell him that, though.

'I'm fine, honestly, Stephen. Again, I'm sorry about the laptop. I have a back-up of the presentation in my emails so it's all good. I promise you, I'm ready.' Today was my opportunity to show Stephen and the clients why I was so good at my job – today's clumsiness excluded, of course.

'OK, well, get yourself another coffee and I'll ask IT about borrowing another laptop. I know you're probably a bit nervous about today, but you've got this. The whole department believes in you! You're gonna slay this thing.'

Thanks, Stephen. 'Slay.'

I'll try to!

I decided to take an early lunch down Great Portland Street in order to prepare myself for the Maranette pitch in the afternoon, grabbing Claudia – my work bestie – from her desk on the way out.

Claudia Aoki is my day-one buddy. A safe space. An ally during times of distress, anxiety and sporadic freakouts at work. We started at Season Eight Digital around the same time, and I remember our very first introduction to each other with much fondness, alongside a tinge of embarrassment. Halfway through my induction, I had suddenly found myself overcome with a nervous bout of what I can only describe as the 'green apple splatters' (also known as The Shits). I spent approximately eighteen minutes in a random seemingly empty bathroom on the eighth floor relieving myself while singing several show tunes from my favourite musical, *Hamilton*. As I reached the climax of the song, a voice from a couple of stalls down from me suddenly arose out of nowhere: 'LAFAYETTE!'

It took another few minutes of digesting my shame before I came out of the stall and faced the person who would eventually end up becoming my best work friend.

'Babes, we've all been there. I, too, like to find an inconspicuous bathroom where I can shit and recite *Hamilton* to my heart's content. Hi, I'm Claudia, by the way.'

Thus began what would go on to be a beautiful friendship. We were also the only ethnic members of staff in our little department, making us bond even more as we spoke about workplace microaggressions and traded our traditional food recipe link over Slack, with me sending through some Ghanaian soup dishes while Claudia would link me to her favourite Japanese recipes. As well as being brilliant at her role as my number two in the office as content executive, Claudia's also an incredible listener who always makes time for me and my Series of Unfortunate Dating Events sagas. As someone whose relationship with her fiancé began long before the boom of dating apps, I've always treasured Claudia's perspective and advice when it comes to my online dating woes, even if she does view them from a place of mild interest.

I paid for my protein buddha bowl and latte and found us a seat at our favourite cafe on the corner of Great Portland Street and Mortimer Street.

'How did your date go last week by the way, babe?' Claudia asked, midway into devouring a ploughman's sandwich.

'Oh, him,' I mumbled, suddenly remembering the random Tinder date that cancelled on me two days after matching. The story of my life. 'The bastard ended up calling it off. To be honest, he referred to himself as a "Sapiosexual", and that immediately triggered my fight-or-flight response, so it was probably for the best.' That kind of talk always tends to give me the ick anyway. 'You would think it would be easier to just call yourself a dickhead.'

Claudia gazed at me incredulously behind her sandwich, raising her eyebrow in a way that even Dwayne Johnson would be proud of. 'Lord! Not "Sapiosexual"! That is, indeed, worthy of being considered a Capital Crime, Temz,' she whispered in a low voice in a tone that reeked of sarcasm. 'This is what you do, though, isn't it, Temz? You have a tradition of always going for guys you have nothing in common with! I'm not sure what it is with you settling for dudes that aren't on your level, but you need to snap out of it because you're a fucking catch.' And with that, Claudia took another bite of her sandwich and sipped her tea in a way that let me know she was subtly throwing shade.

She's right. In a perfect world, I would be this super empowered, super confident woman who doesn't take any shit from men, knows her worth and can march to the beat of her own drum, but in reality, I'm a somewhat-confident woman that dates random guys who either constantly mispronounce my name or date me because they think I'm easy. So yeah, I could kind of see Claudia's point there.

'All I'm saying is,' continued Claudia, now staring me dead in the eyes, 'you're an absolute hot spice, OK? You could have your pick of any guy you wanted if you really wanted to. If you just . . . I don't know, made an effort to actually look for someone nice. You always seem to think that it's about your weight or something, but I don't think it is at all – it's your attitude, babe. You're a – what is it you say all the time? Pong thang, so to speak!'

I grimaced at the last part of Claudia's motivational speech. *Note to self: stop teaching Claudia slang.*

'Um. I think you mean "Peng ting", Clauds.'

'Oh, yeah, that's it. Well, whatever "Peng" means, you're it, OK? And you're gonna smash the meeting this afternoon too!'

'Thank you, my love,' I replied, sighing. 'And uh, we'll work on your London lingo, OK?'

She was right. As I stared into the foamy folds of my pistachio latte contemplating my latest dating dilemma, I felt my phone buzz in my jeans pocket. I unlocked it to find that I had received a message on Instagram – and for some very strange reason, a small cluster of butterflies began to flutter in and around my diaphragm. Could it be that fine ass Mr RubesCubes himself? A slow grin spread across my face as I logged into my account, an action that didn't go unnoticed by Claudia.

'What – or should I say WHO – has got you grinning all thirty-two teeth this early in the morning then?'

'First of all, it's half past twelve, Clauds – your timing and navigation skills need work. Secondly, it's nothing; one of those spambots again.'

I wasn't in the mood to incur yet another lecture from Claudia, so I decided to keep RubesCubes to myself. Not that there was anything to hide. As I logged into my Instagram messages, I was annoyed to find out that I *was*, in fact, once again, the latest 'WINNER FOR A BRAND NEW IPHONE14 PRO!!!!'

Fuck's sake.

Chapter 3

Boardroom 3 had been booked out for two hours for what would hopefully be one of the best pitches of my career. At the height of their popularity, Maranette Clothing had been the go-to fashion brand for customers aged eighteen to thirty-five. They were a premium brand made popular by B and C list celebrities, as well as all the big fashion influencers, and their pieces were routinely featured in the likes of *Harper's Bazaar*, *Who What Wear* and *Elle* magazine. However, they'd had a string of publicity stunts gone wrong, culminating in a shockingly fatphobic Christmas meme post on their Instagram page featuring a plus-size woman starving herself to fit into one of the Maranette 'It' dresses with a caption underneath reading 'BY ANY MEANS NECESSARY'. Needless to say, that secured them a one-way ticket to Canceltown.

When Claudia informed me that they were taking meetings with agencies for new PR and marketing representation to help mend their reputation, I jumped at the chance to lead the operation. As a size 26 woman who finds it hard to source decent, good-quality clothing, I'd never been one to shy away from dragging brands for filth over their lack of representation, but I'd always wanted the chance to revamp dying clothing brands by sprinkling some *Fat Girl Magic* into the mix.

As the members of Maranette took their seats in the board-room later that day, I silently breathed in and out to get rid of last-minute nerves and made my way to the front to switch on the presentation document projection and introduce myself and the team.

'Thank you all so much for taking the time to visit our offices today. I'm aware that you are meeting with a host of other agencies, so we all appreciate you being here to listen to our pitch today.'

So far, so good. The presentation goes off to a great start, with me gesticulating and moving around the podium like the absolute boss bitch I am.

'. . . One of the main things we'd suggest is actually expand-ing your clothing range to at least a UK size twenty-eight. Statistics show that the average size of a woman in the UK is a size sixteen, so to us it seems counter-productive to only create pieces that exclude a vast majority of the audience you're trying to—'

beep!

Shit. I forgot to put my phone on mute.

'—target. Apologies for the interruption. In a bid to tackle the recent allegations of fatphobia and weight shaming that the brand carries, it would also be a good idea to issue a sincere apology in a non-defensive manner, acknowledging the mistakes made in uploading the memes, acknowledging that they were, in fact, fatphobic—'

beep!

'I'm sorry, guys, let me just put that on silent!' I announced, smiling weakly at the clients while grabbing my phone to turn it off. Right before the phone shut off, I spotted two new Instagram notifications from my newest crush of less than twenty-four hours, Mr Ruben Alexander. The butterflies returned yet again as I wondered how he had responded. Did he notice I'd watched his Stories from my private account? Has he even clicked on my profile? Do I have any outstanding follower requests on that account, and if so, would he be one of them?

A cough from the corner of the room quickly brought me back to reality. I put the phone on the table, deciding that the tension of waiting till later to read the message freely would give me something to look forward to. I resumed my presentation with a bit more pep in my step than usual.

'So, as I said earlier, alongside the apology, I think it could also be a great idea to arrange some kind of focus group, where you invite some of your plus-size customers alongside some notable plus-size influencers to sit down and give some feedback on the collection – like a focus group of sorts? This could be a great opportunity to place Maranette as the brand who cares about its audience and actually cares enough to action their customers' concerns without it coming across as virtue signalling.'

Out of the corner of my eye, I saw the creative director of Maranette nodding and smiling while taking notes, with the marketing director staring at me in awe, hanging on to my every word. I was on a roll, and they knew it.

'Given how popular your pieces are with the Gen-Z crowd, I would even go so far as to collaborate with a well-known plus-size influencer on a capsule collection to show your consumers that you do care about trying to be as inclusive as possible. It's important for clothing to be accessible to everybody, as style doesn't have a size. Take me, for example.' I paused and jokingly did a twirl, showing off my outfit, which was thankfully met with smiles and laughs. 'I'm a size twenty-six, and I for one think I dress fabulously! The plus-size style market in the UK is worth nine point two billion pounds, and worth two hundred and eighty-eight billion in the States, going to show that plus-size people are definitely spending money on pieces that not only make them look good, but feel confident in their bodies. I've drawn up a few recommendations of some influencers who I think would be a fantastic fit for the brand.'

I turned to the next PowerPoint page, smirking as I confidently made my way through the rest of the presentation without a hitch.

Upon returning to my desk, I saw a new email from Stephen:

Fabulous work with the Maranette pitch today, Artemis! We think you smashed it. We should be hearing their decision by EOP today, so thank you for all your hard work, Queen!

Quick side-eyeing of the use of 'Queen' aside, I decided to celebrate my little win with a caramel Frappuccino. Grabbing my purse, I skipped down the stairs, a feeling of immense joy overtaking me, accompanied by tiny fragments of pride.

Even though I was always heavily into being creative, as the only child of two Ghanaian parents I was expected to follow in my grandad's footsteps and become a lawyer. I switched to Marketing and Public Relations halfway through my law degree, to the absolute disgust of my parents – my mum in particular – who had by that point already made it her business to tell our whole family that I had passed the bar and was already practising Criminal Law, much to the delight of several dodgy uncles of mine.

That was, until I started bringing home gifted product samples from clients, which very quickly changed their minds about my career switch. A brand-new, top-of-the-range coffee machine and several premium skincare products have a way of doing that, I suppose. Suddenly it was all 'My daughter works for big big clients in New York!' and 'Abena, can you message Mark Zooterberg and tell him to unblock my account?' Parents, eh?

I picked up my coffee and was headed back to the office when I got a WhatsApp notification:

The Sisterhood of the Travelling Lace Fronts 🖤
Aneni, Jean, You

Jean: Babygirl, are we still meeting up at Prince of Peckham this eve?

The Sisterhood of the Travelling Lace Fronts is a WhatsApp group consisting of me, Jean and my other best childhood friend Aneni, whose mum is best friends with mine. The group got its name (a proud creation of mine) through me and Aneni constantly loaning each other our lace front wigs to wear on nights out. Most people invest in stocks, shares, handbags and Crypto, but Aneni and me? Wigs were our poison, and so in order for us to save and purchase the highest quality Peruvian lace front wigs, we'd put our money together, buy a wig ranging between £500–£800 and wear it on rotation. An unconventional, yet super useful, life hack. Another side hustle, if you will. After making friends with Jean, I added him to the WhatsApp group. Aneni and Jean's friendship is a tad volatile, to say the least, but I like to think that I'm the glue that holds us (and our wigs) all together.

Artemis: Yep yep if you're still down for it! I absolutely smashed my pitch at work today so I feel I deserve to consume as many alcoholic beverages as possible this evening, at the expense of you and Nen.
Aneni: Congrats sis! Happy for you. I'm coming but I'm gonna leave a bit early – got another date with Mr Man, lol

Jean: ... Prioritising dick over your best friend? Rah boy. Couldn't be me!

Aneni: ... ?

Artemis: Lol Jean pls. I'm sure it's not like that! See you both later x

Oh, yeah. Over the last three years, Jean had desperately been trying to get me to drop Aneni as a friend. It's not that she's a horrible person. She's a sweetheart for the most part. But she's also a typical Sagittarius (read: Sagiterrorist): aloof, rude and sometimes messy.

We'd been best friends our whole lives due to our mums being best friends as well as next-door neighbours, but growing up around her – especially during puberty – was, frankly, annoying. She is incredibly stunning, which is great and everything, but she never lets me forget it. Aneni has light-brown skin the colour of pine next to my deep-brown complexion. She has the kind of figure that the Beyoncés and Doja Cats of the world flaunt proudly: a hugely curvaceous shelf of a bum, and hips underlining a contoured, lean waist, complete with long legs, big boobs and small, almond-shaped eyes. On the plus side, Aneni and I balance each other out personality-wise; she's always been able to bring out the fun, somewhat passionate and spontaneous side of me, with me in turn being able to ground her and be the rational thinker whenever she develops a flair for the dramatic during a crisis. That's fire signs for you, I guess. Chaotic.

When I got back to the office, instead of going back to my desk, I grabbed my laptop and headed to the office 'breakout zone' (which in reality consisted of a couple of old sofas and some raggedy-looking bean bags artfully thrown in between a couple of large, tropical-looking indoor plants).

My phone rings and it's Aneni. I sigh, popping my AirPods in to take her call.

'Temz. What the hell is Jean's problem, man? I don't get why he still has an issue with me after all this time? Wasn't it all sorted?'

Sensing where this conversation would be heading, I took a seat on one of the kitsch, over-the-top loveseats and opened up a game of Tetris on my phone. Ladies and Gentlemen, Act I of the Aneni show was about to begin.

'Nen, I don't know what you mean,' I told her. 'You know how you guys are — it's all banter at the end of the day, so I wouldn't pay it any mind.'

I cleared the first three levels of Tetris while Aneni continued. 'But I don't get it. Even after everything that happened between you and me a few years ago, I've never been rude towards him, but he consistently sends out these cheap shots as if I can't see what's going on. He can't seem to move past what happened, and it's annoying. It wasn't even anything to do with him. Anyway, you know how much I love you Temz and I am SO happy that your pitch went well, but I did arrange this date a couple of weeks ago . . . I know you understand?'

Level 13 complete. I love Aneni, but she's never had the best listening skills; I've found that a bulk of my advice tends to go into one ear and out the other, so checking out mentally seemed to be the right thing to do, sporadically coming back to the conversation with an 'uhhuh' or a 'mmm yeah' just so she knows I'm still on the other end. Whatever beef that was still lingering between her and Jean needed to be sorted out between the two of them.

I was halfway through listening to her talk about her newest Sugar Daddy (or Glucose Guardian, as I prefer to say) dating arrangement when I realised that I never ended up checking my Instagram for the message that came in during the pitch.

'Hey Nen, babes, I'm happy for you and I would let you finish but I've got another meeting in two minutes. I'm sure that whatever's going on, we can sort it out later? I'll see you in a bit. Keep your head up and all that.'

I ended the call before she had time to respond; I would apologise to her that evening.

Chapter 4

RubesCubes: Yo Aloe, thanks for responding to my comment 😊. I'm a big fan of your page, by the way; over the last few months I've somehow turned into a bit of a Plant Dad and your Monstera hack posts have been helping a brother out greatly. I may slide into your DMs again in future and enquire about some more plant trouble I'm having.

I read the message four times before finally acknowledging that he had really sent it. I'm used to receiving lovely comments from my followers who are having various plant issues, but I'm not used to fine-ass men like this Ruben Alexander sliding into my DMs all willy-nilly. Don't get me wrong, I normally don't tend to dwell on or romanticise random attractive men if and when I come across them. On the topic of dating, romance and attraction, I have a robot-like ability to switch my hormones and emotions off when it comes to men I deem super attractive or interesting, due to automatically assuming that they would never be into me. As much as I believe I'm a great catch, a part of me has always acknowledged that body types like mine aren't normally the preference for the majority of the men I'd come across while dating.

But THIS guy? I'm not sure what it was about this random Instagram user from across the pond, but I haven't been able to stop thinking about him since I saw his comment earlier. I'm normally very level-headed, unfazed and logical when it comes to these types of situations, and realistically, I don't know him from Adam. But damn is this Ruben a little bit of me. AND he slid into my DMs? Little old me?

But maybe that's what it is. I haven't had the opportunity to romanticise someone in a long time. I haven't had the opportunity to be reckless and delusional, and I miss being in that chaotic frame of mind, even if said interaction has not one ounce of implied sexual, flirtatious or romantic intention.

I decided that the rest of the afternoon would be dedicated to me doing some 'client research', so I took my laptop and headed to one of the available smaller meeting rooms for some privacy in order to formulate my response to Ruben, as well as to go on a quick 'liking' spree of his posts so he knew I was at least interested in his content and not just his bear-like body:

SayAloeToMyLittleFriend: Why thank you so much, kind sir. I appreciate you taking the time out to message and I hope you're doing well! Please feel free to message me with any plant queries, and I'll happily try and help as much as I can!

Delete, delete, delete. Sounding like a customer service assistant was not the way to go.

SayAloeToMyLittleFriend: Heyyyyyyy Ruben!

Nope, too unhinged. Calm down babes.

SayAloeToMyLittleFriend: Hello Ruben ...

Maybe addressing him by his first name feels too personal, considering he doesn't know mine? After I quickly scanned a few websites for tips on how to create engaging replies, I wrote:

28

SayAloeToMyLittleFriend: Hi Ruben. Thanks for the message and I'm glad you like the posts! Love the fact that you've become a Plant Dad; we need more like you in the world. I'd be happy to give you some plant tips so just let me know when you're ready. Xx

PS Severe apologies for the 'liking' spree by the way. I realise I may have been a bit trigger-happy haha. Also – you sing? We love a talented King! I'll have to check out your stuff sometime.

Somewhat content with my response, which kind of sat within the 'pleasant-and-engaging-yet-keen-to-let-you-know-I've-been-preeing-your-hot AF-photos' spectrum, I pressed 'send' and busied myself with a bunch of admin housekeeping tasks for the rest of the day. I checked my work emails and answered a couple of messages from Claudia and Stephen, and was about to get ready to pack up and leave for the day more jubilant than when I'd arrived, when I received a buzzing notification on my phone.

I felt the tiniest flutter of butterflies. Surely he wouldn't respond that quickly? But also more importantly, once again, why on earth am I acting so giddy over a total stranger?

I stared at my phone, grimacing as I realised it was just a message notification from Tinder. I gave a subtle groan, and opened the app to respond to James, Jonty, Josh, or whatever the match's name was.

Temi, so what qualities do you look for in a high-quality man? I believe myself to be an alpha male, and of course I have specifications for the kind of female I would like to entertain, so I'm curious to hear yours. Speak soon, Joe

If I had a pound for every time I've been approached by these High-Quality Alpha Male type-guys, I'd be sunning it up somewhere in the Maldives with my millions. The kinds of misogynistic men I seem to attract always look as if they own a female-bashing podcast where they reminisce about the 'good old days' when women were barefoot and pregnant, and how they would hate for their significant other to make their own money due to it being against the natural order of things.

I swiped right to unmatch. Jim/Jonty/Whateverhisnamewas would have to take a back seat for now.

A couple of moments later, I get another ping on my phone – and this time, it *was* from Ruben. I instinctively clutched my imaginary pearls: we have communication, ladies and gentlemen!

RubesCubes: Hey hey Aloe 😊 Some advice would be great thanks, I'll try not to take up too much of your time though! I bought a snake plant last summer just to give my place a bit of life and well . . . I'm now fifteen plants in and beginning to feel a bit overwhelmed, haha. Appreciate you engaging with my pics too, you're sweet 😊 And yep I've been singing for a few years now – nothing serious or anything, I perform every now and again, but thank you so much! You gotta let me know what you think when you have the time. Have a great day.

I tried to hold back from dissecting his message too much, lest I ended up becoming completely obsessed. I was enjoying this little back-and-forth between us, though. One of the reasons why I probably felt so inclined towards this guy was because it's quite rare for me to engage in any kind of civil, proper conversation with a man who wasn't a family member – or Jean – without it immediately taking a weird, sexual or super flirtatious tone. It could also just be the case that he was incredibly hot, seemingly sensitive and emotionally intelligent (purely going on him being a Plant Dad of fifteen) and I was just horny.

I messaged back:

SayAloeToMyLittleFriend: Hi Ruben, I hope you're having a great Wednesday! Love the fact you're already super into Plant Fatherhood. ☺ From what I can see from your photos, your snake plant looks really healthy, so you must be doing something right, haha.

I checked out a couple of your songs earlier too; you have such a gorgeous voice! Something so old-school about it, I almost get a Donny Hathaway vibe. How long have you been writing music?

Send. I thought it was an OK-ish message. Polite, yet curious to know more, plus a little compliment in there to boot. As much as I loved talking about plants, a part of me wished that I could have hit him up on my personal account so that we could really get into some actual non-plant-related gist. To my surprise, I noticed that he had already read my message and was in the middle of typing.

RubesCubes: It's currently two-something in the morning over here, so I'm still waiting for my Wednesday to begin, haha. And thanks! Whitney is my pride and joy (I name all my plants) so I wanna make sure I'm doing right by her. Speaking of which, can you recommend a good fertiliser?

Also, DONNY HATHAWAY? Damn, that's such a huge compliment; he's actually one of my favourite singers! I'm humbled, thank you! I mostly do covers, but every now and again, a Ruben Original might slip through the net – depends on what I can find to inspire me, but I'd say I've been writing for maybe ten years or so. ☺

He named his plants? Clearly, he was on a mission to get me to fall in love with him. Making sure to curb my smile so it didn't appear that I was doing something other than work, I hastily texted back. A part of me felt bad for messaging him so

31

late his time, but there was also a very gassed part of me that loved the fact that he was choosing to speak to me at this time of night, too.

SayAloeToMyLittleFriend: Of course! My fertilisers of choice are any that contain magnesium, as it provides great nutrition for the soil. Fish blood is also great – albeit messy. You can pick up those online.

How/why are you awake so late? – Also, yes, you're giving Donny Vibes with that throat of yours. The ladies must love you, haha! I think it's so awesome that you've been able to carve a creative outlet for yourself to funnel your creativity – very commendable!

As we started to message back and forth, in the back of my head I wondered why we couldn't produce men like him in London. This was a pleasant departure from the 'what's good babes what u sayin'?' I was used to.

RubesCubes: Fish blood huh? Well, damn, you learn something new and gross every day! I'll make a note of that. I'm a bit of a night owl – slight insomnia and shit – so it takes a while for me to get to sleep. This is the time when I'm normally at my most creative, so I don't mind much, to be honest. Also, I'm such a homebody, I ain't entertaining any ladies with my voice!

A sexy, plant-loving, creative, bearded American man who also liked to stay in the house? I made a note to tithe 70 per cent the next time I went to church.

SayAloeToMyLittleFriend: I'm sorry to hear that you get insomnia. Damn, now I wish I knew as much about biology as I did plants so I could prescribe you something or share some advice! It's cool that you're able to create music as a result of it though. Who inspires you? Also, a fellow #TeamHomebody here, we love to see it!

RubesCubes: People are always surprised when I say I like to stay in the house, idk why. Also, that's sweet of you, ma, but I've had insomnia for so long that I don't even notice any more. As far as inspiration goes, Stevie Wonder, Musiq Soulchild and the aforementioned Donny are my icons. I remember when my Pops took me to the Fox Theater down here in Oakland when Stevie was playing a few nights out here when I was young, and I saw him on that piano singing his heart out? I fell in love with his voice, man.

SayAloeToMyLittleFriend: Great choices, Stevie is one of my favourites too!! It's incredible that you were able to witness him live. That must be such a great core memory to share with your dad. I'm not surprised people are surprised you prefer staying indoors; you give off 'outdoor energy'. Maybe it's the beard; it looks like it's been meticulously shaped and styled to be seen outside haha. So you're from Oakland in California, then?

RubesCubes: Yeah it's a dope memory with my pops for sure. And yeah, I live out here now. I'm originally from Georgia, but moved out here when I was seven years old with the fam. They all live slightly north of here in a place called Richmond, but I moved to The Town for work so now it's just me, Whitney, Reggie, Mae, Addie, Stevie, Mahalia, Ella, Diana and Sarah in my little apartment. I got six more but I won't bore you with naming the whole brood. ☺ Also, as for my meticulously shaped and styled beard, don't be a hater! My finely crafted beard and I stay in the house, eat cereal and watch TV on the weekends.

SayAloeToMyLittleFriend: First of all, ain't no hateration or holleration over here, I can assure you. You have a rather splendiferous beard. Georgia, huh? A southern gentleman! Also, damn, fifteen people? You must have one hell of a huge apartment haha — is the rent that crazy over there lol?

RubesCubes: Hah. You're cute. Those are the names of my plants! I told ya, I take this Plant Daddy job seriously. What made you develop an interest in plants? And what's the UK like?

SayAloeToMyLittleFriend: Daddy? More like 'Zaddy', no? *rimshot*. And the UK is cold, rainy and for the most part, full of miserable, sarcastic, passive-aggressive people (I'm including myself here), but hey, free healthcare, amirite? Why did you move from Georgia to California? And bonus question: what's your favourite meal, i.e. the meal you would have as your last supper on death row?

RubesCubes: 'Zaddy'? Lmao, I wish, sis, you're too kind!! The UK sounds ... fun, but from our convo you sound like a ray of sunshine to me so I'm not inclined to believe this description (for now)! Um, we moved cuz my parents lost the house and I had an uncle in Richmond who offered to put us up temporarily while they got back on their feet. We've been here ever since. My favourite meal? Mmm. It's gotta be my grandma's mac and cheese for real. Can't beat it. What's your favourite?

I could feel my heart swell slightly larger with each response. He seemed so open and talkative, and I loved it. Again, WHAT was stopping the men of the UK from being like this? I didn't want the conversation to end, but I was wary of the time, and Ruben seemed to be thinking the same.

RubesCubes: It's been great talking to you, Aloe. You've been a great distraction from my inability to sleep over the last hour, but I'm gonna try and squeeze in a few Zs now. I'll holla at you later — it'll be nice to know a bit more about you too. Night/morning!

I said goodnight back, closed the app and let out a sigh. In an attempt to mine as much information about Ruben as possible, I had been bombarding him with questions while being vague about my interests. I was conscious that I had been messaging him from my Aloe account. While I wanted him to be as impressed with me as I was with him, a small part of me somehow felt like our conversation would probably have hit a dull or awkward point if I were to direct him towards my personal Instagram page. Besides, I hadn't tarted up my profile with the proper thirst traps yet. I wanted this man to be WOWED by me when the time came for him to add me to his friends list.

As I fought my way to a spare seat on the train to Peckham for drinks with Jean and Aneni, I decided to once again check my Instagram for any message updates from Ruben, even though he would probably still be asleep. Then I had more of a look into his Instagram profile. Ruben was thirty-two years old (as per his birthday cake photo posted several weeks ago); a couple of years older than me, perfect. According to his bio, his tech work had landed him some huge clients: IBM! Microsoft! TikTok! He was also pretty popular with his music hustle too, I noted; no big surprises there.

As great as all of his tech work stuff was on his profile, I had a feeling that the 13.8k following he had amassed had more to do with his looks and singing ability than his tech skills. Who could blame them? He was fine as fuck.

I clicked onto his 'followers' tab and my thesis was confirmed – his following showed rows upon rows of very attractive, very slim women, some of whom he followed back. The comment section of his posts were filled with scores of women complimenting him on his songs and on his appearance, with some of them being explicit in their emoji usage. I didn't need to know that his voice made some of these women wet, thank you very much.

I was so deeply ingrained in my *CSI*-level-investigation into Ruben that I didn't notice the passenger sitting next to me huffing and puffing away as he squirmed in his seat. I put my phone back into my purse as the passenger muttered under his breath, 'Fuck's sake, lose some fucking weight, would you?'

'What was that, my love?' I replied loud enough that the passengers sitting opposite us could hear. Fatphobia used to upset me when I was younger, but after I realised that I had just as much right to exist and be the recipient of all the things others enjoy, I decided to instead choose violence.

'I didn't say anything, man,' the passenger muttered quietly as he opened his newspaper.

'Nope, I'm pretty sure you just told me to lose some weight,' I declared loudly as I turned to face him. I had a bit of an audience now, and I wanted a chance to be a little chaotic.

'No, I— I didn't say—' he started.

I continued, 'I just thought that was interesting because as someone who seems to be balding rather rapidly from what I can see, you don't see me staring at that cul-de-sac you call a hairline and loudly exclaiming for your hair to grow, despite it causing me visual discomfort. If you were uncomfortable, you could have moved to the plethora of available seats on the carriage, but instead you decided to stay and fat-shame me instead. Aren't you ashamed? Sad!'

I pulled my phone out and resumed my Instagram stalker activities while the man next to me squirmed for a few minutes, sighed and finally moved to a different seat.

A nice little win for the fats there.

Chapter 5

I arrived at the Prince of Peckham pub only to find Aneni at the bar trying to flirt with the bartender, who seemed to be having a slow evening and was taking the bait.

'Hey, babygirl!' I exclaimed as I crept up to Aneni and gave her a bear hug from behind.

'Stop, Temz! You're creasing my new Christopher Esber dress, I just got it this morning,' Aneni squealed before turning around to air hug me as if she were a royal visiting a sick patient in hospital. Like me, Aneni had a penchant for fashion, but unlike me, she had the sizable inheritance to purchase pieces from the *crème de la crème* of brands. She wore Alexander McQueen next to my ASOS. Jacquemus next to my Jasper Conran. Chanel next to my Converse, etc. She also had the body to carry it off, I suppose, but I've always favoured comfort over aesthetics, and have been a lifelong card-carrying member of the Kitten Heel Society for Weak Ankles. 'Anyway, congratulations on your pitch today! You're a fucking Queen and I always knew you'd smash it.' Aneni reached into her Saint Laurent Rive Gauche tote bag and pulled out a bottle of Moët.

'Ha! You know me too well. Thanks, sis,' I replied, as I took the bottle of champagne from her. We put our orders in with the bartender and made our way towards a free booth.

'So, how did the whole thing go? When do you find out the brand's decision?' Aneni asked, her head falling lazily to the side onto her outstretched palms.

'I low-key think I smashed it, but we'll probably hear back from them in about a week or so, once they've had meetings with other advertising agencies,' I said. It's not often I attain bragging rights over Aneni, so I was going to take full advantage of the fact. 'If everything goes well, there may well be a promotion in it for me, which would be dope as it'll allow me to save up a bit more to get my own place at some point soon, at last.'

'That's sooo amazing, babes. I hope it all goes well for you!'

I gave a smug smile and continued to sip my drink, noticing the increasingly tense energy in the air as Aneni soon fell silent. She tapped her long stiletto fingernails against the table, stopping every now and again to look at her phone, then briefly glanced in my direction, forcing a strained smile before going back to it. I couldn't quite call it, but the silence was unnerving, making me slightly uncomfortable. She could have at least pretended to be a bit happier for me. It frankly would have been easier if she said she didn't want to be here, instead of her being super awkward, but the weird vibes were soon broken by the shrill tones of 'OH THERE SHE IS. The great one herself!' filling the entirety of the small pub. Jean bopped over to our booth after ordering a drink at the bar and gave me a hug, completely ignoring Aneni.

'Jean,' Aneni breathed lazily, acknowledging him with a slight head nod. You could cut the tension in the booth with a knife.

'Nenz,' shot Jean pointedly while he stroked my hair. 'How are you?? Ready for your date and all that? You gotta go in a couple of minutes, don't you? It's a shame you didn't ask him to meet you here so we could assess him – or were you nervous that he'd fall for Temz instead?'

38

Aneni's eyes glanced scornfully over to Jean as he turned to me and laughed.

'Anyway, guys, guess what?!' I yelled a bit too loudly in a bid to intercept any impeding arguments. 'I had an utter hot spice message me on Instagram today and we are actually conversing. Conversing about all the things. And he doesn't seem weird. And I'm totally overthinking and romanticising the whole thing because I am devoid of affection and intimacy and I probably need to seek help.'

I leave some time for Jean and Aneni to process this information as I take a generous sip of the rum and Coke I ordered earlier.

Jean and Aneni blinked at each other in quick succession before turning back to me, mouths agog.

'Um, bitch, you better tell us who this new dick is, please and thank you,' Jean yelled at me jokingly, slamming his fists on the table. Aneni looked at me up and down, a huge smile on her face.

'OK, so obviously nothing has happened as of yet, but his name is Ruben and he works in tech AND he sings in his spare time and he's an absolute hunk of a man.' My fingers gently tap the side of my phone in excitement.

'Tech?' Jean scoffs, scratching the back of his head in what looked like disgust. 'Lord. Ruben is already giving "Living in his Mother's Basement" vibes, Temz. What's the tea? Where's the pic? I wanna see him!'

'OK, wait waiiiit, lemme find a good photo of him,' I laugh. I've barely spoken to this man at length yet, and yet I'm already soft-launching him to my best friends as if we're an official couple. By showing Jean and Aneni his profile, it somewhat validates our interaction. Besides, if I was going to try and flirt with this guy, I would need some help.

Growing impatient after a matter of seconds, Jean took my phone and started to swipe through Ruben's Instagram page. 'Leave this with me, Temz. By the end of the day we'll find out his job, how much he earns, his blood type, his National Insurance number and the Facebook profiles of all of his exes.'

I laugh as Aneni took the phone to have a look, with her eyes widening in what I assume to be approval and . . . is that lust? I took my phone back before she had any more time to dissect his profile.

'Um, don't you mean his social security number? He lives in America,' I said. Jean – ever the dramatic – proceeded to screech like a banshee.

'Oop! Not Artemis living her best life with her own American Boy, OK, then Miss Estelle. We love to see you divest! And he sings too? You found a good one, boy. I wanna hear some of his music. Does he do R&B?'

I'm glad I told them. THIS is the energy I needed for the confidence to continue texting him. I love it when friends enthusiastically support my delusion. 'Ha! Yeah, he sings soul and his voice is gorgeous – I'll send you his SoundCloud link in a bit,' I replied, grinning from ear to ear. I'd forgotten how fun crushes could be.

'Oh, wow, Temz, umm . . . are you sure doing the whole long-distance thing is sustainable?' asked Aneni, picking at her nails while looking at me with concern. I knew it. Since we were both old enough to date, Aneni has always had an issue with the guys I've gone for in some way, shape or form, as if she hasn't had her own relationship problems and fuckboys to deal with.

I squinted my eyes at her in response. 'What do you mean?'

'You know what these random accounts on IG are like. Are you sure he's not just messaging everyone?'

Jean looked up. Oh, bloody hell, here we go.

'Mm. I mean . . . being excited and happy for a friend is free, you know,' he said.

I'd had it. Tonight was supposed to be about me! My amazing client presentation! My man who–isn't-my-man-yet but hopefully will be once I formulate and devise a plan!!

'Guys. I'm actually sick of being caught in the middle of your shade-fest. You are both my best friends who have one major thing in common, in that you both love me, so let's do just that, and celebrate ME and how awesome I am, just for one night? Can we embrace and strategise about how we're going to get this sexy American guy to fall in love with me? Please? Can we do that? Thank you.'

I can sometimes have a flair for the dramatic. I'm not ashamed though. You cannot shame the shameless.

Jean gave a knowing look to Aneni then back at me, and scoffed, 'You're such a dickhead, you know that? You're lucky I love you. Congratulations about work, darling, and this Ruben guy is very fine! Now let's get the alcohol flowing, yeah?'

Aneni looked at both me and Jean in defeat. 'Fine. Let's get this party popping, my date starts in like thirty minutes and I'm already a little bit waved.'

'Perfect,' I said as I opened the bottle of champagne Aneni had brought. 'Jean, I need you to look at my IG profile and let me know if it's cute enough to take off private. From a man's point of view, if you saw my profile, would you wanna sex me up?'

Jean looked over at me pitifully and smiled the way a doctor does before giving you bad news.

'I'm obviously gonna be biased because I've seen you naked AND have sexed you up several times and you're fucking gorgeous. You're deffo "public IG profile pretty", if that's even a thing, but it's up to you, babe,' Jean replied, then took a sip of his champagne.

The rest of the evening went significantly better. After Aneni left, I ended up necking several rounds of champagne to celebrate my big day, and Jean and I completed an absolutely flawless rendition of the Destiny's Child's 'Lose My Breath' choreography when the song came on over the speakers. Eventually, I stumbled towards the pub's exit for some air.

While outside, I quickly opened up Instagram and was greeted with a message from Ruben:

RubesCubes: Hey hey Aloe. Hope you've had/(are having?) a good day. I ordered the fertilisers you suggested, so hopefully they'll be able to revive my plant children, haha. I really enjoyed our chat the other day, by the way . . . x

My eyes zeroed in on the single 'x' at the end of the message as I quietly smiled to myself. Our interaction had become such that casual written displays of affection were now being used? I absolutely loved this for me! I swayed slightly as I began to think about how to reply before ultimately deciding that sending semi-drunk texts back wasn't exactly the wave if I was trying to impress him. After reading the message again, I felt something hard land in the pit of my stomach. How much longer until he asked what I looked like? My stomach fluttered at the thought of that moment.

Deciding to indulge my curiosity, I took a cheeky gander at his Instagram page photos again, and proceeded to casually look through his follow list to get a good gauge of the types of women he perhaps found attractive – a little trick I tend to always do after adding a Tinder match on Instagram, just to see whether they genuinely were open-minded and into us thick women, or whether I was only matched as to be a part of some horny guy's fetish. Needless to say, the majority of the girls I would see in their follow lists would be of the slim, pale variety.

I scrolled down Ruben's list, and as expected (with the exception of people who may have been family members or friends?), his was full of what appeared to be Instagram models and certified 'Bad Bitches'. I gave an exasperated sigh. No doubt groupies or previous 'situationships'. The pit of woe and doubt in my stomach began to grow larger. Why was I suddenly feeling so insecure about this guy? I put my phone away and took a deep breath, shaking the thought. I looked just as good as the girls on his follow list – deep down I knew I did. And yet . . .

As I turned around to head back into the pub, my face collided with what I can only describe as an absolute unit of a chest, underneath a sprinkling of thick coarse hair.

'O-ho there! Watch out, beautiful,' a deep voice called out from what seemed to be a hundred metres above my head. I looked up and saw a set of teeth grinning down at me. 'Are you gonna stay entangled in my chest hair all night or what?' The man laughed as I realised my face was still resting on his chest. I jumped back and mumbled some kind of apology mixed with 'It's the twenty-first century, mate, who says "O-Ho?"', before feeling both my spine and stomach jerk at the same time and sprinting towards a nearby bush to throw up. 'Bushy Chested Tall Guy' laughed and came over to gently hold my hair back while I violently purged what felt like five pints of alcohol from my system.

'Err, thank you,' I muttered after the ordeal was done. I couldn't tell whether it was due to my inebriated state or my newfound sense of confidence upon seeing that Ruben had replied to me, but this guy was kinda cute in the right light.

'Don't mention it, and uh hey, sorry for touching your hair without asking you first; I just didn't want you to get sick all over it, you know?' Bushy Chested Tall Guy put his hands in his pockets, smiling down at me.

'I . . . uh thanks . . . um for being considerate,' I replied, part-drunk, part-surprised at running into someone already seemingly versed in the politics of touching Black hair.

'TEMZ, BITCH, WHERE ARE YOU? ELECTRIC SLIDE BAYBEEE!' rang the shrieked tones of Jean, who was in the doorway, the intro melody to 'Candy' by Cameo beginning to play in the background. He grabbed my hand and pulled me back inside the pub as I looked back at the bare-chested stranger, who smiled apologetically and waved as I slipped back into the pandemonium of the pub.

Chapter 6

The next morning, I found myself lying horizontally on my bed in last night's clothes, with my head bent over the side of my bed frame. The taste of bile rose in my throat, and my head was thumping a thousand beats a minute. My mouth felt dry and an intense wave of nausea came over me as I slowly slid down the side of my bed to sit upright and make sense of my surroundings. I groaned and held my head in my hands as I tried to piece together the remnants of last night. Suddenly out of nowhere, my stomach decided to give an involuntary heave and I made a run for it to the bathroom, almost knocking Natalie down to the floor as she made her way to the living room.

Yells of 'Artemis, what the fuck?? Are you OK?' provided the background instrumental to my chorus of upchucking into the toilet basin. With my eyes blurry and unfocused, my stomach gave way to an absolute onslaught of bile mixed with what I believed to be yesterday's lunch. It all decorated the toilet, Jackson Pollock-style. I could hear Natalie knocking gently on the bathroom door and mumbling faintly about something or other, but I wasn't in the mood for her drama right now. I managed to produce a few groans of acknowledgement, enough for her to eventually wander off.

I could already tell from the deafening throbbing in my head that this hangover was going to be a serious one. I flushed the toilet and crawled slowly back to my bedroom.

I threw myself onto the bed, grabbed my phone and saw six missed calls from my mum between 2 a.m. and 4 a.m. It was currently 5:15 a.m. My parents moved back to our family house in Ghana a few years ago to help take care of my grandparents, meaning I only managed to see them twice a year or so. Alarmed, given that Ghana is in the same time zone as the UK, I gave her a call back.

'Oh, Abena, Jesus is Lord! Why didn't you return any of my calls? I've been so worried about you!' My eyebrows raised at this sudden rare surge of affection from my mother.

'Erm, Mum, what do you mean? What's going on? Are you OK?' Was *Dad* OK? My mind began to race, waiting for my mum to spill whatever bad news lay ahead.

'Oh, so you don't remember calling me at two-thirty singing that stupid "Sweet Caramel" or "Caroline" or whatever, and shouting nonsense down the phone? I kept asking you to tell me where you were to see if I could call Auntie Frema to come and pick you up, but you kept shouting down the phone at me like you had no home training. Are you actually mad?'

As she was talking, I got a sudden flashback of Jean and me walking (or perhaps stumbling?) down Rye Lane with a bottle of champagne in hand.

'Oh . . . yeah, Mum, I'm sorry for disturbing you,' I said, wanting the call to end. I needed to text Jean so he could fill me in on the evening. 'Err, Mum,' I suddenly remembered something as I clutched my throbbing head. 'Did I say anything else weird or random to you at all? I might have had a glass or two of champagne to celebrate a good day at work.' I tried saying the last part in an upbeat tone.

46

'Abena, do I look like Siri to you? I wasn't up taking notes about your drunk babbling. Your grandad isn't feeling well so I was taking care of him through the night. So no, I don't remember. As long as you're alive, that's all I care about. You should also call your grandparents more, mmm? You know they aren't going to be here forever. Anyway, drink some water and sleep. Don't embarrass me, and don't harass my phone that late again unless you've died, do you hear me?' With one click, the phone went dead. Phone calls with my mum often turned into soliloquies, and for the most part, I've just learned to leave her to it when she starts one of her rants.

With a groan, I found the strength to get up and attempt to guzzle down some water. It had been so long since I'd drunk alcohol to this excess, all I could think as I made my way out of my room was, 'I'm never drinking again'.

Natalie – who also happened to be awake uncharacteristically early, considering she was jobless – managed to intercept my journey into the kitchen. 'Artemis, I have no idea what happened last night, and I hope you're doing OK, but it's just that you have a— a situation in the kitch—'

'Oh, Nat, to be honest my head's banging and I'm not really down for a telling-off right now,' I cut in, incredibly aware of my vomit-breath. 'I apologise if I've made a bit of a mess in the kitchen, I'll clean it up now, but I just need some water if that's OK?'

Natalie looked at me shiftily, darting towards me and the kitchen. 'Yeah, I get that, Artemis, but there's someone in th—'

I breezed past Natalie and blindly towards the cupboard for a glass when I heard,

'Oh . . . hey, Amy.'

Amy? At least get my name right, bro. I turned around, and standing by the fridge completely topless was a man looking at me with a wry smile on his face. I squinted and turned to Natalie, who put both her hands up as if to say, 'Hey, I tried to warn ya!' and practically sprinted into her bedroom.

My eyes scanned the figure in front of me, trying to make sense of who he was and why he was standing in my kitchen half-naked like some kind of hussy. He stood at around six feet four, with a wild 'Aldi-version-of-Jason Momoa' look to him. His rock-hard set of abs was covered with a light spray of coarse hair that grew thicker as it reached his chest. My brain unlocked another memory of last night. It was Bushy Chested Tall Guy. In my kitchen. Tucking into my pot of strawberry rice pudding. 'Umm . . . how – I . . . huh??' I spluttered, trying to be polite but also impatient and anxious over the events from last night. I managed to pour myself a drink of water, and turned to face him, drinking slowly while taking him in. Did I sleep with him? If so, go me, because homeboy was very sexy.

Bushy Chested Tall Guy clutched the area above his heart in mock disappointment, a spoon dangling sexily from his mouth. 'Ouch! I was that memorable, huh? I'm Anthony? We met at the Prince of Peckham last night. You nearly threw up on me? And, um, well I guess we eventually ended up back here.' I managed to unglue my eyes from his chiselled chest to meet his eyes.

'OK, so . . . um . . . we did sleep together then, I'm assuming, yes? I mean, it makes sense. I would absolutely climb you like a thoroughbred under normal circumstances . . .'

'Ha! Nah-uh, we didn't,' Anthony quickly cut in, holding his hand up and ducking out of my way. He flashed another wide grin in my direction as he put my empty rice pudding pot on the counter.

'Thanks for finishing that, by the way. It went off a couple days ago, I've been meaning to throw it out.' I smirked. 'Also, do you have a shirt you could put on? You're distracting me.'

His wolfish smile immediately turned into a grimace. Apparently it took me mentioning his half nudity for Anthony to suddenly appreciate the vulnerable position he was in, and he ran back into my room to get a shirt while I sat in the dining area, utterly perplexed. After this encounter, I knew that I'd be having words with Jean, seeing as our lifelong deal to always keep the other from making bad decisions while inebriated (with 98 per cent of the time it being me who looked after him) was broken last night.

Anthony came back into the kitchen, this time wearing a crumbled white tee and a biker jacket, shoes on, ready to go.

'Hey,' he sighed, avoiding my gaze all of a sudden. 'I didn't mean to cause any trouble for you or your roommate.' He glanced in the direction of Natalie's door. I didn't need to be a mind reader to know that Natalie's ears were probably pinned to it, trying to soak up every word of our conversation. 'But yeah, just to clarify again, we didn't sleep together. You still have your clothes on from last night. I mean, don't get me wrong, we were both into it and I think we could have if you hadn't fallen asleep halfway through, but rest assured that no intercourse took place.'

In my room, I could hear my phone ringing. No doubt Aneni or Jean trying to get through to find out the tea. One detail Anthony mentioned struck me. 'When you say halfway through, halfway through what, exactly?'

'Oh.' Anthony started shifting in his seat, his cheeks turning a warm red. 'Well, erm, we were making out for a while, but then you fell asleep, and I guess I must have passed out next to you too.' I felt my entire pelvis clench in excitement at the mention of this. Damn me for not being sober last night.

'I see,' I concluded, standing up and staring at Anthony, wondering what to do in this instance. I've had my fair share of one-night stands, but never actively fallen asleep halfway through a make-out session. Lord, the embarrassment alone was enough to make me want to climb back into bed.

A part of me was still willing myself to wake up from what was clearly some weird fever dream, but the other more chaotic side of me wanted to get his number and finish where we left off. Why not seize the day and all that?

'Well, Anthony, it's lovely to properly meet you, and I'm sure you have other things to be getting on with today, such as performing the walk of shame back to your place, but if you would like to take another stab at repairing your bruised ego, hit me up and maybe we could try again sometime.'

Anthony's eyebrows raised in amusement, almost as if he weren't expecting this response. It's a look I've grown accustomed to when it comes to quite a few of my conquests. The 'oh-wow-she's-so-confident-and-forward' look. The 'predator-becomes-the-prey' gaze. But that's always been me, I suppose. I like to get straight to the point, and like the saying goes, 'If you don't ask, you don't get.'

Anthony cocked his head to the side at me, sharing another wry smile before picking up my phone and tapping his number into it. He's bold himself, this one.

He stood up, stared at me momentarily before coming in for an awkward hug. 'I like a girl who knows what she wants. It's been a pleasure to share the past fifteen or so hours with you and I do really want to finish off what we started – it was fucking hot.' He kissed my hand and strode over to the front door.

The butterflies in my stomach twitched slightly at the knowledge that he actually wanted to sleep with me.

'Hey, it's Artemis, by the way,' I said, slowly starting to close the door behind him.

He turned around with a quizzical look on his face. 'Hmm?'

I repeated, 'My name. It's Artemis.'

The sly grin returned. 'Artemis. A beautiful name, fit for a beautiful goddess.'

He gave me a wink and walked outside as I closed the door behind him, jogged to my bedroom and opened up the WhatsApp group.

What in the fucking fuck just happened?

Chapter 7

The Sisterhood of the Travelling Lace Fronts ♥
Aneni, Jean, You

Jean: Oh, babes, you better get it in! That guy was hot!

Jean: Temz, babes, let me know when you get home pls.

Jean: TEMZ.

Aneni: What's going on? Is Temz OK? I just got home from my date.

Jean: Yh I think so. Temz gt in an Uber not too long ago with some guy – checkin to make suree she's safe. We endded up havin a bit too drink, sorry i'm still drunk lol 😬

Aneni: Ohhh for fuck's sake. Why would you let her go off with some randomer? You can be so irresponsible sometimes. Lemme call her.

Jean: Whatever, Aneni, as if you actually care abt her lmao. You shuld have stayed and partAY with us if you were rly about that life!!

I scroll the remnants of previous morning's WhatsApp messages, trying to piece together the events of last night. I'd received eight missed calls from Aneni and a couple from Jean. Bless them for being worried about me. I thought about – and quickly decided against – calling Jean now, knowing that our conversation would go on for hours, and I didn't quite have the energy or time for that right now. Instead, I texted back into the group.

> Artemis: Guys. There was a grown man in my bed this morning and I have no memory of last night. Can one of you make like Craig David and fill me in?
> Aneni: Oh, thank GOD. I'm glad you're OK (also, WTF?)! Umm well, I left you guys a bit early for my date, you remember that bit, right? It went really well by the way, he took me to Gordon Ramsay's restaurant near Chelsea, which was gorgeous, and we went to the theatre after! Anyway, when I left you both were already getting a little lit and . . . welp.
> Jean: Um, yeah, last night was v fun! You randomly started chatting up some rugged Jason Momoa-looking dude at the bar for like a full hour, leaving me on my lonesome, but it's all good. Did you get some??

I remembered none of these events whatsoever. I pressed on for more info.

> Artemis: A whole hour? I'm sorry, babes! Was I behaving? Lol. I didn't get into any shenanigans, did I?
> Jean: Oh, nah, I was a little tipsy but I made sure to keep an eye on you from a distance. We were mostly doing karaoke with a random group of girls by the bar, and then you were talking to Momoa boy. I slipped one of my AirTags in your bag btw. Safety innit?
> Artemis: Lmao bless you; a friend!!
> Aneni: lol.
> Jean: That's what real friends are for, babes!! Now . . . did you guys fuck or what? I'm waiting for the gossip pls.
> Aneni: . . . lol. Glad you're safe hun x

As Jean continued to fill me in on the events of last night in between taking shots at Aneni, I looked at the time and realised that I needed to get ready for my session at the gym with my newish personal trainer before heading to work. I suspected this new trainer was low-key fatphobic, but he was also high-key cheap, so I'd resigned myself to keeping my mouth shut. For now.

What I would have preferred would have been to spend the first half of the day in bed feeling sorry for myself, making up some random excuse in order to work from home. I felt like hell and really should have rescheduled my session, but I decided that a bit of fresh air and some exercise would probably make a better impact on the hangover than mooching under my duvet.

After putting on my new co-ord gym set that hugged every crevice and curve of my body – shoutout to those TikTok influencer stores – and packing my work clothes into my gym bag, I put my Afro (which desperately needed a wash) up in a loose bun, grabbed my bag, popped a couple of painkillers and walked down Denmark Hill to catch the bus to the gym. On my way, I grabbed a palm-sized slice of freshly buttered hard dough bread and a cup of Milo hot chocolate from a newly opened Ghanaian-Nigerian coffee shop located next to the bus stop, alongside a pastry for later. Could I have opted for a protein smoothie? Sure, but protein doesn't go down as well as sugar and caffeine does. At least that's what I told myself as I took a huge bite of my hard dough bread slice. My stomach churned uncomfortably as I felt the starchy, gluten goodness hit the base of my oesophagus but I ignored it. Hangover be damned – 7 a.m. workout should sort me right out. Today was going to be a good day!

After all, it had been a week of somewhat positive moves, with everything coming up Milhouse: I Very Nearly Had Sex (first base counts in my book), and potentially could Very Nearly

Have Sex again in the future; I'm on track to hopefully get a promotion at work by the end of this year; my little houseplant empire was slowly going from strength to strength; and I had recently started engaging with a handsome man from across the pond.

I was incisor-deep in my next bite of bread slice and in the middle of boarding the bus when I remembered that I hadn't responded to Ruben's latest Instagram message. I opened up my phone to his message after taking a seat and had a reread:

RubesCubes: Hey hey Aloe. Hope you've had/(are having?) a good day. I ordered the fertilisers you suggested, so hopefully they'll be able to revive my plant children, haha. I really enjoyed our chat the other day, by the way . . . x

I thought about how I would respond to it. The weird feeling I had when reading the message last night was still lingering inside me. For some reason I felt nervous about telling him any information about me, lest it ended up with him googling me, finding out what I looked like and promptly either ignoring or blocking me.

I've always been a confident person. My parents were a lot of things, but one thing they taught me from an early age was to develop pride and confidence in the body I was born in. At school, I would have the odd moments of self-doubt, low self-esteem and insecurities that all teenagers had at that age, but for the most part, I never allowed my body shape to dictate how I felt about myself in general, and grew up loving my curves and appreciating the softness of my rolls and bumps.

Then I started university as one of the few ethnic minorities and plus-sized people in my year, and as the terms rolled by, I started to feel my confidence being chipped away as my social circle consisted of upper-middle-class girls with perpetual eating disorders, with their constant discussions of diets, celebrity weight-loss treatments and surgery.

Every summer holiday over the next three years, I would go on extreme diets under the guise of 'smoothie detoxes' to see how much weight I could lose before the next term started. At first, I would do these detoxes as a challenge with my classmates just to see how much I could lose in six weeks (I always gave up after the eighth day, mind you). But then after a while, I noticed myself developing a slight obsession with doing it.

Thankfully, as soon as I graduated, sense returned to me. I concluded that constantly being around the negative-body-image-talk of the people at uni had probably contributed to my temporary lapse in confidence.

My self-esteem returned to normal, but as I started dating more regularly, I couldn't help but notice the ways in which men would either objectify and fetishise my fat body or avoid me altogether because of it. I would constantly hear things like 'I've never been with a big girl before', 'more cushion for the pushing!', 'I don't do fat girls, sorry', 'you're pretty for a fat girl!', 'why don't we workout together?', not to mention the famous 'I heard fat girls give the best head, is it true?'

Every now and again I'll give the fat fetishising guys a pass if I'm just after a meaningless, quick shag. At times, there can be something quite empowering about a guy saying seemingly nice things about your body in the throes of passion. Sometimes, I want to be worshipped, damnit.

But Ruben? He was different; for reasons I was keen to explore.

Outside of his looks, Ruben genuinely seemed like a nice guy, and the last thing I wanted to do was jeopardise this interaction by putting him off. In contrast to Anthony, who was just a bit of harmless fun, and whom I didn't wish to get to know on any kind of deeper level. Ruben was sweet, charming, funny and a great conversationalist (not to mention gorgeous to look at), and I low-key wanted him to genuinely like me. But I have an annoying habit of only falling for men who aren't into fat girls, and I was a bit worried that this may end up being the situation here with Ruben too.

Ruben was thousands of miles away in a completely different country, though. It wasn't as if anything could even happen between us – could it?

'If we wanna lose that belly, we gotta get those crunches in, I'm afraid!'

I've always loved fitness and working out. For me, it's been a form of self-care that allowed me to connect with my body and explore my inner physical strength, as well as let off some steam whenever I'd had a bad day at work. I almost see it as a sanctuary of sorts; a place where I can shut off the world and just work out to my favourite Beyoncé playlists and live my best life.

Recently I decided to seek the help of a personal trainer in order to guide me in the right direction as I took on heavier weight training. I'd made my instructions and desires clear from the off:

- I'm not here to lose weight
- I'm absolutely fine with my body and how I look

I'm here to build strength and tone my body *only*. Not too much to ask, right? You wouldn't think so. But this was my second session, and already my new trainer was back at it with the assumptions. After squinting at the ceiling for what felt like six hours, trying to determine whether I was moving closer to the floor or if the floor was moving closer to me, I completed my fifteenth crunch and responded.

'Yo, Yemi,' I panted as I sipped my water passive-aggressively. 'Remember the other day when I told you that my goal isn't to lose weight? I'm fine with my belly as is, actually. It's soft and comforting and brings me great joy, actually.'

Yemi – all six feet six inches of him – squatted down to meet my gaze. His quad muscles were ripe, bulging and glistening, making his thighs look like freshly glazed hams on a Christmas morning. Jesus.

'Yeah, I remember what you outlined in our previous session,' he said somewhat innocently, swiping the beads of sweat from his forehead. 'But I just think that if you push yourself a little harder, we could actually get in a bit of weight loss while you tone and build muscle – almost like doing two for the price of one, innit? You wanna be healthy, don't you?' As soon as I mastered and memorised these specific workouts that I needed in order to tone up, I was firing him. I didn't sign up for thinly veined fatphobic health assumptions.

He grinned wolfishly and stood back up. 'Now, on to the single leg deadlifts, let's go!'

The hard dough bread and coffee from earlier were trying to plan their exit strategy already, but I wasn't going to let this go.

It took me about six minutes to stand; by this point, my forehead was rattling against my skull while my intestines were doing an equal madness down below. My body was beginning to rebel against the torture I was putting it through.

'That's all well and good,' I replied, still catching my breath while clamping my butt-cheeks shut, 'but I just again wanted to make it clear that I'm not here for the weight-loss part of it. I know you're used to clients wanting to be shredded and paper-thin because they think that's how they need to look in order to feel pretty and worthy of attention or whatever, but that's not me; I'm just here to get strong and build my glutes so I can twerk, mmk? I want a fat ass.' As I twirled my arms in a circular motion around my bum and hip area. 'A. FAT. ASS. No BBL! Homegrown!'

Yemi looked back at me blankly, trying to suffocate a smile. I was sure this was probably his first time coming across a fat client who didn't make weight loss the main part of their goal.

'Oh forget it,' I huffed, half chuckling as I stretched.

'Aight – whatever you say boss lady. Let's work on those glutes then.'

'Umm. Could we probably work on something else? Matter of fact, could I have a little two-minute break? I've got a bit of a headache and everything is *so bright* in here.'

'We can take it easy if you like, but we still need you to maintain your current heart rate. We can't be having it dipping, babe.'

Fuck's sake. My body was fighting for its life. Coming here today was a mistake.

I followed him to the weights area, slouching slightly as I began feeling the effects of last night's alcohol and this morning's breakfast pressing against the walls of my intestine, begging to be let out. Suddenly, the caffeine kicked in and I realised that I wasn't going to make it. I needed to use the bathroom. I clenched my glutes and inched forwards slowly towards the weights, with Yemi watching me quizzically. *Deadlifts? Now?* I truly was the architect of my own misfortune, but like a true stubborn G, I decided to see it through.

I lasted approximately one-and-a-half-minutes before my vision started to blur.

'Yemi, I'm . . . so sorry.' I squirmed, doubling over in pain and crossing my legs.

'Are you OK, Temz? Do you need to sit down?" he asked.

'I . . . err . . . not feeling . . . that well. Look I need . . . I need to shit, I can't stay. Sorry!" I blurted out, before hightailing it to the bathroom to release my bowels.

All in all, it was the worst thirty minutes of my life – and it served me right.

After being in the bathroom for what felt like three to five business days, I stealthily made my way to the gym basement, out of Yemi's eyeline, found a treadmill that was separated from the rest of the main gym floor, and proceeded to walk for as long as I could. I needed to move my body to shake the alcohol off – shitting be damned.

Chapter 8

It had been about week or so since I'd started talking to Ruben and, in that time, we'd started to develop a bit of a routine. We'd message each other around 7 a.m. UK time – 11 p.m. Oakland time – and then again around 10 p.m. UK time, which was 2 p.m. Oakland time. It was pretty light-hearted chat at first, but every now and again we'd venture into semi-deeper-than-surface-level topics. It was a nice balance, especially as he seemed so open to talk about anything and everything. I decided to message him while on the treadmill; I needed something to distract me from the incessant feeling of my lungs burning as I climbed the incline.

SayAloeToMyLittleFriend: So how does your girlfriend feel about you getting all this love online from your female fans then?!

RubesCubes: Oh, you think you slick, huh?? I'm actually single. But that was smooth, I'll hand it to ya.

SayAloeToMyLittleFriend: Hehe, twas nothing more than an incorrect assumption, is all! I find it astonishing that a guy like you is single. Or by single do you mean you partake in situationships every now and again? X

RubesCubes: What's a guy like me? And no, I'm not a situationship kinda guy ... any more.

SayAloeToMyLittleFriend: You know – intelligent, creative, easy on the eye ... etc. One would have thought you'd be snapped up ages ago, so forgive me if I'm a little shocked!

RubesCubes: Oh, Aloe, you flatter me. Thanks! I've only ever been in one relationship that lasted around a year and a half, but that ended three years ago. I've had my fun here and there ever since, sure, but for the most part I've been concentrating on work and stuff.

SayAloeToMyLittleFriend: Ahh I see. May I ask why you guys broke up? And there's nothing wrong with being a single agent and having fun if that's where you currently are in life tbh.

RubesCubes: Um, well, to put it blankly, she cheated on me. When we broke up, I started having my fair share of frivolous dates and shit cuz it gets hard to trust someone again after a betrayal like that, you know? The no-strings stuff was fun for a while, but I've calmed down now. What about you?

SayAloeToMyLittleFriend: Oh, wow. Forgive my forwardness here, but what a dumb bitch to cheat on someone like you! I'm sorry you had to go through that bullshit, man. I hope you've been able to heal. As for me? I'm a single pringle too. Have been for a few years now!

RubesCubes: Thanks, ma, we'll see. You in any situationships, then?

SayAloeToMyLittleFriend: Of late? Not really. Although as much as I try not to get myself into a situationship, somehow I end up finding myself in the eye of the storm with a fuckboy every now and again!

RubesCubes: LOL. I would say come to the States, but truth is I think we have our share of fuckboys over here, too.

SayAloeToMyLittleFriend: To be honest, I'm always hearing that the States is where it's at. A few of my friends have divested and moved there for love and they seem to be doing well! I hear you guys are smooth and wear your heart on your sleeve. At least if I encounter a fuckboy over there, I'll be fucked over with a bit of rizz and finesse lol!

RubesCubes: Haha! You should maybe visit the States one day and I can show you that we aren't all terrible. I may drop the odd bit of charisma for real; can't be letting the side down!

SayAloeToMyLittleFriend: Listen, sir??? Don't threaten me with a good time now. O_O

I still hadn't followed Ruben from my personal Instagram account. In spite of my protestations about not going to the gym solely for weight loss, I upped my gym sessions from twice a week to four times a week. I'd promised myself that if I lost a stone in the next six weeks, I'd buy myself some new outfits, take some bomb ass photos and upload them to my account. Then and only then would I add Ruben, which when saying it out loud, I know sounded ridiculous. There was still a part of me that was petrified to reveal my true self to him, and I knew I needed to figure out the reason why that was. I didn't go through life being the amazing, confident Queen that I was, to be thwarted by a tall, dark-skinned, bald, attractive American man. So why the hesitancy?

I was at the gym yet again; on minute twenty-eight of a thirty-minute treadmill session when my message notification buzzed loudly in my AirPods, rudely interrupting the Beyoncé Megamix playlist I had going on. I took a quick look at my phone and saw that the message had come from Jean.

Jean: Babes, can I come over yours tonight for a catch up? I'll bring wine xx

Jean was typically the type to just show up at my flat with little to no warning – much to the annoyance of Natalie – so for him to ask ahead of time made me wonder whether something was up. I ended the session on the treadmill and quickly replied back:

Me: Is everything OK, hun? Of course you can x.

A few moments later, a response:

Jean: Mike broke up with me and I need to get hammered tbh

Oh, shit. And here was me thinking that this guy would actually last the distance with Jean. I replied back, informing him that my evening would be all his, complete with wine, snacks and a couple of pre-rolled blunts I'd randomly found at the bottom of one of my bags last week. I finished sending the message and made my way to the changing rooms to take a quick shower and to get ready for work. I normally detest washing in public places but my gym was a few minutes away from work and, most importantly, the membership came as an optional part of my job's package, so who was I to resist?

In the changing room, I took out my toiletry bag, Crocs and towel, and stripped down to the nude outside my locker. I was definitely one of the largest female members at this gym, a reminder I always got whenever it came time to take a shower. I noticed two blonde-haired, blue-eyed, waif-like women in their Lululemon sports gear and Nike Metcon trainers across the changing room, staring at my body. Their bodies were ripped and they looked like your typical upper-middle-class–Stay-at-

Home-Wife types you'd find loitering around any Whistles or LK Bennett store in Hampstead Heath. Or maybe Dulwich – they did have a 'you can't sit with us' vibe that only us South Londoners can perfect so easily. I'd become used to this, and had always found the dynamics of changing-room etiquette rather entertaining.

For some reason, I thought about what Ruben would have to say about this scenario, with me ass-out in the changing room. I still didn't even know what kind of woman he was into; he didn't strike me as a 'Lululemon Stay-At-Home-Wife' type of guy. After finding out about him being a homebody, he also didn't strike me as someone who was into people who were too extroverted either. I liked to think I fell nicely between the two types, perhaps.

As I was still talking to him as Aloe, I had yet to come up with a successful segue into talking about the specifics of his dating and relationship preferences from our general light-to-mid chitchat. Before putting my phone away in the locker, I opened Instagram to send Ruben a quick message wishing him a good night, with a little cheeky innuendo to boot.

> **SayAloeToMyLittleFriend:** Hey hey Ruben! I'm about to take a quick shower (don't go getting any ideas now . . .) so I'm signing off, but I hope you have a great evening!! Looking forward to chatting to you soon? Xx

I was turning into a fiend for this man and wasn't sure if it was a good or a bad thing.

I got into the shower and thought about him, imagining what his morning routine looked like. My mind logged through the different photos I had seen on his Instagram profile until I got to the image I was looking for: the one with him topless, cheesing at the camera. I began to imagine him showering with me, bear-hugging me from behind while slowly caressing my decolletage. It was like I could feel his breath tingling around my neck as my hands made their way down between my thighs. With my eyes closed, my hands remained there for a few moments, with my thoughts racing, thinking about how I wished those hands were Ruben's instead of mine . . .

I snapped my eyes open as my thought process took a turn I hadn't expected it to take: in order for Ruben's hand to even begin to caress that area, they'd have to make their journey across the gargantuan landscape that was my side fat, hips and Buddha belly.

Fantasy ruined. Had he been with a plus-size woman before? Was he all about the BBL-body-IG-model types? Going purely by how he looked, I guessed he would be into light-skinned 'Erykah Badu-esque' women. The kind of woman who wore her crochet locs in a permanent bun, wrapped in an Ankara-print cloth. Who only shopped at high-end, slow-fashion stores like Reformation and was into old-school R&B, matcha lattes and linen dungarees complete with Doc Martens. She'd be slim-thick, with an absolute SHELF for a butt, and she'd be into stuff like Sea Moss, Yoni facials and the complete works of Audre Lorde. Yeah. Sounds about right. I finished my shower and sat in the changing room moisturising my body, sighing as I did so, and thought about how many realistic gym sessions I could do within the next month in order to get my bum looking fat as hell. I was doing well with the interval treadmill running at a level seven incline, but this ass was not going to grow itself, oh no. I opened up my iPhone Notes app:

Note to self: Do a 3 x 15 deadlift set using a 20kg barbell. Also watch TikTok videos on Deadlift tutorials and 'Workouts for Fat Girls'.

I closed my app and finished getting ready for work. I then reopened the app to add:

Note to self: re-download TikTok and buy some Audre Lorde books off Amazon.

I spent the first fifteen minutes of my work day trying to upload an Instagram Reel of my new Chinese Money Plant onto my Aloe account that I'd shot last night at the request of one of my followers. If I wanted to take this seriously as a legitimate side hustle, I had to put the work in and I was not about to make a little thing like a full-time job get in the way of my dreams, damnit.

I was already being sent free products from plant brands on Instagram to review: soil fertilisers, plant feeds, hell, even free plants. If I wanted to make a go of this whole 'Plantfluencer' thing, I needed to take it seriously!

I was interrupted by an email from Stephen:

Good Morning, Artemis,
  I hope this email finds you well—

No, Stephen. Your email has in fact found me distracted and hungry. In any case, the opening sentence was super formal, which isn't like him, considering how hard he tries to try and be the 'relatable', 'cool' and 'down to earth' boss. In any case, his email actually found me hungry and now slightly (read: incredibly) anxious this morning, thanks, Stephen!

Can you let me know if you've got a quick ten minutes or so for us to catch up regarding Maranette Clothing? Let me know ASAP.
  Stephen

I read the email again, scanning for any nuances that may suggest anger or disappointment in his delivery. I started to panic. Did we not get the account? What could have possibly gone so wrong? The pitch went without a hitch and the clients seemed super engaged. They would be absolute fools to not want to work with us (read: me) and all the experience I would be able to bring, both as a marketing professional and a plus-size woman with a fashion addiction.

They would be lucky to have me, I thought to myself as I half considered creating an anonymous Instagram account to further troll and cancel the Maranette brand page in retaliation for rejecting my pitch.

I logged into my Slack account and messaged Stephen on there instead. I couldn't bear the waiting game, and would rather Stephen give the bad news to me straight with a *coup de grâce* instead of dragging it out over email.

> **Artemis [09:32]: Hey Stephen, just seen your email. I can pop into your office now if you're free?**

> **Stephen [09:35]: Sure thing, give me two minutes**

I tapped my fingers loudly on the desk, wondering what the hell was about to happen. I then pulled up Claudia's name on Slack:

> **Artemis [09:36]: Bitch, do you know what's going on with Maranette today? Stephen wants to see me in his office and I low-key want to shit myself.**

I heard a snigger behind me and looked up to see Claudia staring at her computer monitor, then at me, a huge grin on her face.

> **Claudia [09:38]: LOL. I would offer you some coffee for the nerves but I fear that may make the 'shitting' feeling even worse at this**

point. I wouldn't worry about it, babes. I'm sure Steve just wants to give you an update – I haven't heard anything on my end.

Artemis [09:39]: To be honest, I wouldn't mind a little flatulence accident right now to provide a distraction. I don't know why I'm so nervous. He was just so formal in his email. Maybe I'm reading too much into it?

Claudia [09:42]: Was he? Screenshot the email and lemme see?

I took a screenshot of Stephen's email and pasted it into the Slack channel. While doing so, I quickly glanced towards Stephen's door, only to see the CEO of Season Eight Digital – Priya Rai – strut quickly into Stephen's office. Claudia must have seen her at the same time, because we locked eyes in bewilderment. An appearance from Priya on our floor is as rare as snow on Christmas Day. It almost never happens unless . . .

Unless someone senior was getting the sack.

Oh, hi. It's me, the senior member of staff. I opened up Slack and typed furiously.

Artemis [09:45]: PRIYA?! Bitch, this is it. I'm getting the sack. Jesus, I didn't think the pitch went THAT badly, did it? D'you think that's the reason? D'you think they've been monitoring my internet usage on the computer? I always make sure to go on Incognito mode, so that can't be it? Oh Lord, Claudia, I'm gonna miss you so much sjkskjskjskj.

I could hear the clattering of Claudia's fingernails on her keyboard as she typed back equally as furiously:

Claudia [09:47]: FIRST of all, if you don't get the fuck out of here with the sacking BS pls. You're one of the best pitchers this company has ever seen. You've brought eight new clients to the agency this year alone. YOU did that. You aren't going anywhere anytime soon. However, I would suggest that if you have been watching porn or whatever on your computer, that you scrub that shit expeditiously. I don't want to be known as the friend of that girl who wanked off in the office. PS Did you clock Priya's suit? I need it! What do you think? Xx

I stifled a nervous chuckle as I read Claudia's Slack message. She was right: I'd been absolutely smashing the KPI targets left, right and centre this year and successfully onboarded some of our highest paying clients. Hell, one of my previous TV ad campaigns ended up being nominated for a Cannes Lions award last year. They'd be stupid to let me go now.

Stephen [09:52]: Hi Artemis. We're ready for you now if you'd like to pop in.

I glanced up at Claudia, who was already looking at me with an expression on her face that matched how I felt: anxious.

Artemis [09:54]: Right, I've been called in. If the worst happens, please know that I love you and secondly, grab your stuff and leave immediately because I'll be burning the whole place down post-haste!!

Claudia [09:55]: LMAO. Oh, babe, I love you too! I promise, everything will be fine. Breathe, bitch.

I took a deep breath, applied my favourite red matte lipstick from Fenty Beauty (because if I'm going to get in trouble or fired, I'm going to look amazing while it happens) and swiftly blotted my now-incredibly-oily face. After another deep breath, I made my way towards Stephen's office.

Chapter 9

'Thanks for coming in, Artemis. Hopefully this shouldn't take long.'

I looked from Stephen to Priya, and took a seat in the chair Priya pulled out for me. As much as I tried to maintain the appearance of calm, confidence and tranquillity, underneath the facade my heart was hammering a million miles per hour. *Just put me out of my misery already . . .*

'No problem at all, Stephen, and lovely to see you, Priya! I hope you've been keeping well?'

Claudia was right: our CEO looked absolutely impeccable in a mustard yellow co-ord suit. For some reason, this gave me pause. A person wouldn't wear yellow when firing someone, surely? Surely firing someone while wearing such a happy colour constitutes some kind of fashion violation? I'm sure I read about it on LinkedIn or something.

'I'm doing well, Artemis, thanks. I hear you've been having quite a busy couple of weeks in the office too, huh?' Priya sat on the edge of Stephen's desk, arms folded. It was at that point that I realised that both of them were smirking.

'Yes, it's been really good actually! The Maranette pitch went well and we're still waiting to hear back from them,' I rambled, trying to cite as many positive updates as possible. 'I'm currently

71

in talks to meet with an online banking brand who are looking to expand their consumer base to Europe and need help on the content and PR side. Oh, and we've also renewed retainer contracts for five of our biggest clients for the year, so yes, at the moment it seems like we're running on a good streak, which I'm so pleased about.'

I gave Priya and Stephen time to digest this while I readjusted myself in my seat. If there's one thing I'm good at, it's providing receipts. Let them try and tell me off after that. Priya glanced over at Stephen and smiled. Stephen peered at me for a while. His beady eyes somehow shone bright with an air of mischief. He looked . . . excited.

'So do you want the good news or the bad news first?' he said.

OK, so maybe not a firing. A demotion perhaps?

'The good news first,' I replied.

'Okey dokey. Well, as you know, Artemis, you delivered an incredible pitch with Maranette and the feedback I received from them this morning was very good. They were really impressed with your creativity and the range of ideas you brought to the meeting.'

Jesus is Lord! I was not new to winning clients, but with my current track record of success, the Maranette pitch was essentially my make-or-break chance to ask for either a pay rise or a promotion. I was super nervous about that pitch, but Lord knows, I deserved it.

'So, leading from that,' Stephen continued as he rose from his chair and walked around the desk to perch on the side next to where Priya was sitting, 'Maranette has confirmed that they'll be coming on board as our clients for our full retainer fee, starting in a month. In addition, they want *you* to be their account manager. This was all down to you and your incredible work, Artemis. Congratulations! Another one in the bag.'

My mouth formed a perfect 'O' as I took a couple of seconds to take in what Stephen had just said. *I won the account.* Deep down, I knew this would be the case as I'd put so much effort into it, but to hear it out loud made it all the more real.

'Congratulations, Artemis! You are an absolute star and an asset to this agency,' chipped in Priya, giving me a warm smile. In the midst of the celebration, I'd almost forgotten that there was bad news to come with it.

'Oh, but what was the bad news?' I asked, awkwardly shifting further into my seat.

Stephen and Priya glanced at each other quickly.

'Ah yes, that,' said Stephen, exhaling loudly. 'I've had to turn down their request for you to be the account lead, given your current role, as we think it requires someone in a more senior position.'

'Oh?' I replied, deflated.

They were gonna give it to one of the white male account execs, weren't they? That old chestnut.

Priya then took over.

'You see, Artemis, me and Stephen have been having a bit of a chat this morning about your role at the agency and we no longer think you are suited to the position of head of content.'

I waited with bated breath, urging them to continue. Surely they didn't drag me in here and build me up just to shoot me down?

'Taking into consideration your incredible efforts, creativity and continued dedication over these last few years,' continued Priya, 'we would instead love to offer you a *new* role – as the director of brand and reputation! If you're interested, of course. Stephen and I agree that you've definitely earned this.'

I gagged. Metaphorically.

Getting a promotion had always been in my five-year plan,

but I didn't think it would be coming as early as this. The ball of anxiety that had been in my stomach a few minutes before turned into a sphere of fluttering butterflies, spreading their warmth throughout every corner of my body. I felt elated. A WHOLE me? Director at thirty years old? A bitch was too stunned to speak.

'Artemis? Hey Artemis? What say you?'

I must have temporarily zoned out, as I looked up to see Priya and Stephen chuckling to themselves.

'I . . . I don't know what to say! I'd love to take this role, thank you!' I pause, suddenly curious. 'But can I also ask what happens to my current role?'

Stephen replied, 'We were actually thinking of putting Claudia there, as she's been creating some excellent work of late, too. No doubt due to hanging around and learning from you.'

Even better news. Not only was I being promoted to director, but my best work mate was being promoted to my old job! Oh, I was absolutely going to celebrate after work today.

'I'm so happy you've accepted, Artemis.' Priya smiled. 'You really are a credit to this agency and an excellent role model. I'll send you through a contract and description of the director role when I'm back at my laptop. Have a read through later and let me know your thoughts on it – we can be flexible on the terms, so hopefully it should all be fine!'

Priya and Stephen both beamed and gave me a hug. It was at that moment that I really wished I had a boyfriend to tell this news to. Interestingly, my mind briefly flitted to Ruben, wondering what he'd be doing right now. The eight-hour difference meant he'd probably be asleep. My subconscious was already obsessed with this man, and I didn't know whether to feel bashful or embarrassed about this new crush.

Jean and Aneni had to be first.

The Sisterhood of the Travelling Lace Fronts ♥
Aneni, Jean, You

Artemis: GUESS WHAT, BITCHES?
Jean: Bloop! Sounds like someone got the account! Come on, QUEEN.

Then my mum:

Artemis: Mum! Guess what happened at work today?
Mum: You got fired, didn't you? Kmt if you had just gone to law school like I suggested, you would probably be very successful!!!!!!!! I wasted all that money on your school fees for nothing. I always wanted you to attend that Greycoats girls' school but no ... your dad wanted you to go to Alleyn's School for a good education. Sixteen thousand pounds a year for what?? Down the drain. Don't you feel disgraced??
Artemis: ... Mum? pls.
Mum: Please what? We had to move to Dulwich to even be in the catchment area and I didn't have anywhere to buy my plantain and tilapia. You know that's why you didn't eat a lot of Ghanaian food growing up you know
Artemis: MUM
Mum: Ohh this child of mine ... absolute *Nkwasiasem*
Artemis: . . . . Lol I'll call you after work smh

Claudia was next:

Artemis: You're lucky. You and this office get to live to see another day. I won't be committing arson for now.
Claudia: Bitch, you were in there for a WHILE. What happened?!
Artemis: I'll share all the tea at lunch! Should we go to our usual spot?

75

Claudia: Omg YASSSSSS, OK, I'm down!

I opened up Instagram and logged into my Aloe account:

SayAloeToMyLittleFriend: Hey Ruben, I hope you're having a good day/night so far! Had something AMAZING happen to me at work so I'm absolutely buzzing right now. TTYL x

I was flying. Sailing across the stars right now. I spent the entirety of my lunch period filling Claudia in on the events of my meeting, with Claudia giggling and squealing like a little girl.

'Oh, Artemis, you brilliant, brilliant babe!' she screamed. 'I KNEW this was going to happen! No one deserves this more than you and, honestly, I cannot wait for what comes next for you!'

I smiled at her knowingly.

'Um. More news: you've got the head of content role now. But you have absolutely no idea of this, so act shocked when they tell you!'

'FUCK OFF, TEMZ!' Claudia exclaimed in a near scream as I gave her a long hug.

'No one deserves it more than you sis,' I said to her, wiping a tear from her eye. 'You've been so amazing to work with. I'm going to miss sitting near you, but that's what Slack and lunchtimes are for, right?!'

We hugged tightly again for a few moments, truly relishing in our wins from today. Is this what true joy felt like? Being two of only a few people of colour in the office made this accomplishment all the more poignant for the both of us. Creative! Corporate! Babes! Season Eight Digital were about to be exposed to some frankly fearless, plus-size corporate outfit looks from me. *They had better get ready.*

RubesCubes: Yo Aloe, I'm glad to hear you're having a great day, THAT'S what I like to wake up to! What happened?

I had taken a bathroom break as Ruben's message had come through, and instantly beamed.

I typed back, **SayAloeToMyLittleFriend:** Thank you so much, love! I won a new client account for my agency ANDDDD on top of that, I received a huge promotion. I'm absolutely over the moon!

I wanted to call him. To hear his voice or see his reaction of some sort. Every time I received a message from him, a heartstring snapped. A lump would appear in my throat and I would feel temporarily giddy. I hadn't felt this way in a very long time, and I wanted more of it.

So I erased my message and hit the voice-note button instead:

SayAloeToMyLittleFriend: 'Hey Ruben! I hope you don't mind me randomly sending you a voice note, just thought it would be faster to explain what happened out loud as opposed to text! Um, so remember that client at work I was telling you about recently? Well, we only went and won their account! And on top of that, I was also given a promotion! It's been such a great day so far, and um, yeah! I hope you're having a great day, too.'

The voice note length ran out just as I finished my goodbyes and I hit send. I really hoped I didn't sound too raspy. I'd tried to sound as light-hearted as possible. However, it still did nothing to calm my nerves when I noticed that the voice note icon turned from a pale-grey to blue, meaning that he had heard the message. A word appeared on the screen underneath it:

Typing . . .

And then moments later, a voice note!

I took a moment to mentally prepare myself to hear his voice. Over the last couple of weeks, I'd wondered what he would sound like – would it be a low, quiet soulful drawl? Or maybe quite eccentric and full of character? I closed my eyes, and pressed the 'play' button:

> **RubesCubes:** 'OK, so first of all, miss, your accent is so dang cute, thanks for blessing my morning with ya voice! That's really dope. Secondly, congratulations on your promotion! You must be hella excited and proud of yourself. What's the new role?'

I played the voice note back six times. Ruben's voice was everything I imagined it would be: super deep, slow and melodic. I also noticed that his accent had a slight Southern tinge to it, which sent me over the edge. Damn him for being so perfect!

Alongside my other work tasks, I spent the rest of my day being congratulated on my new role from the rest of my colleagues, and looking up one-bedroom apartments which I might finally be able to afford on Rightmove. I'd noticed this morning that Natalie had used the last of my curling hair gel again, despite me informing her several times that products meant for thick, Afro hair wouldn't work for her hair texture.

'But I've got naturally curly hair too, and the gel works wonders,' she whined as I fought the urge to not burst into laughter at the sticky, shiny, slicked-back mess that was her hair, which she'd attempted to control by encasing it into a high bun. Excess gel was sliding off the frayed strands of hair, making a mess on her shoulders.

The way I needed to leave that house was intense, and finally I may just have the chance to.

I had my Instagram open on my phone and spent a large chunk of the day sending voice notes back and forth with Ruben.

I asked him eventually, **SayAloeToMyLittleFriend:** 'So what's with your insomnia? Is it something you've had for a long time?

Not that it doesn't benefit me as I get to speak with you longer, haha, but I figure it must be annoying, right?'

> **RubesCubes:** 'Um, yeah, I've had it since I was a kid, really. I grew up in a super uh . . . loud household and so it always took me a while to get down. I guess it's just followed me into adulthood.'

Poor baby. I could definitely relate.

> **SayAloeToMyLittleFriend:** 'I'm so sorry to hear that, Ruben! I feel you; I've had issues with sleeping too. Did your family host a lot of parties or something? Mine did, and it would drive me crazy.'

Ruben voice-noted back, **RubesCubes:** 'Not quite. My parents just . . . shouted at each other, and at me a lot. So I'd just try and drown out the noise by listening to music in my room, but too many times I'd end up being wide awake at like 5 a.m. Anyway, lemme not bring the mood down. Tell me more about you! I feel like you've been interviewing me forever, haha! Tell me more about the UK. I've always wanted to visit. Do you have a personal IG account? It'll be nice to get to know the woman behind the plants!'

I appreciated his willingness to be so open about the difficulties and distractions in his childhood, especially as we'd only just started talking more frequently. It felt as if we could potentially have a lot in common, and I was interested in seeing where this could go – but there was just one problem.

He wanted to know whether I had a personal IG account, meaning . . . he probably wanted to know what I looked like.

The butterflies suddenly ceased their dance and dropped to the pit of my stomach, leaving me feeling cold and empty. He wanted to see who he had been talking to. A reasonable request, after all; if I had spent most of my time speaking to the Instagram account of a brand on non-professional matters, hell,

I would ask to see who I was talking to as well!

But I wasn't ready for him to see me, not just yet. My heart began to thump loudly as I thought of how to deal with his request. Suddenly, I was transported back to my years of university where the hatred of my body was at its peak. The old, insecure Artemis had wrangled her way back into my psyche, and was beginning to plant seeds of doubt and failure into my head. WHY was this happening? I needed to get to the bottom of why Ruben seemed to trigger my old self-esteem issues.

'What if he stops talking to you after you show him your Instagram account?'

Surely he wouldn't do that.

'But he's incredibly good-looking. What do you think he sees in you?'

I mean . . . I've pulled attractive men in my past, even recently with that Anthony guy. Why should Ruben be any different and, besides, he lives in America. This is all just a bit of harmless fun.

'Don't lie to yourself, Artemis. Your heart bursts into flames whenever you see a message from him. You're infatuated.'

Nope. I certainly am not. He's a cool online friend and we talk about plants, music and culture.

'Uhuh. Well. If I were you, I wouldn't show him a photo of yourself until you've lost about four or five stone, just to be on the safe side. Don't spoil something good!'

Don't spoil something good.

I was conflicted.

What happened next felt like an out-of-body experience. Staring at the open Instagram message box, I typed the following, not keen to say this out loud in case anyone overheard:

SayAloeToMyLittleFriend: First of all, thank you so much for sharing that and I apologise if I overstepped in asking you. That can't have been easy to go through growing up. As someone who had an annoying-arse mum who constantly shouted and criticised me, I can relate! It's also kind of the reason I got into looking after houseplants too, I guess. I see it as a form of escapism, from the critique of my mum and all my internal insecurities and shit. Being in a room full of living things that I look after, maintain and watch grow is so satisfying to me. It's almost like my therapy in a way.

Gosh, look at me rambling! Oh, yeah ... and nope, I don't have a personal page as of yet, but I may make one at some point.

Artemis, what are you doing?

A few moments later, Ruben typed back:

RubesCubes: Damn, that's dope, but also deep. Your love and passion for plants is so clear on your page too. I feel you on doing things that occupy the mind. I don't know many people our age who didn't have fucked up childhoods in one way, shape or form, to be honest, and we all just gotta try and find our ways to process the trauma and stuff. Me through music, you, through being a Plant Mom. I really hope it gives you the peace you need, Mama. Also? Wow . . . a Millennial without a personal Instagram account? The shock! My mind is kinda blown at the rarity of it all haha.

If only you knew, Ruben.

RubesCubes: Well, in that case, I'd love to see a photo of the delightful young lady I've been speaking with over the last few weeks, if that's OK, with you?

Shit.

The thunderous echo of my heartbeat could probably be heard across the office. I closed Instagram temporarily while I thought about what to do. What if I sent him a slightly edited photo of me where I looked a bit slimmer? Nah, I wasn't well enough versed in photo apps to attempt that. What if I were to just send him a clear photo of me with no make-up on, looking like shit, then abandon Instagram for a couple of days, giving him enough time to come to his senses and block my page? Maybe then the rejection wouldn't hurt that much.

What happened next was, admittedly, diabolical.

I opened up Facebook and started to look through my friends list. I didn't really know what I was doing or why, but I was powerless to resist as my fingers moved automatically. I looked and looked until I found the profile of one of my old classmates: Chantelle. Chantelle and I attended the same secondary school together, in the same classes. We were friendly with each other and hung out on occasion, but where I was bullied mercilessly by the boys in our year, she was one of the super popular ones due to having long, brown beautiful curls, light-blue eyes and light-caramel skin. All the boys wanted to sit next to her in class, and I remembered that even though she would occasionally acknowledge me, I'd secretly been a little envious of her, and would often dream about how badly I'd wanted to look like her, to get even a fraction of the attention she received on a daily basis. We'd kept in touch briefly after school ended before losing touch soon after, but I'd always see her content pop up on my Instagram explore feed.

In the years that followed school, it had seemed that she'd tried to become a bit of an influencer with what looked like middling-to-little success. She had 1,300 followers on Instagram, but had an average of ten to fifteen 'likes' on most of her photos, with the occasional post hitting over eight thousand comments, mostly written in other languages. She seemed to be the type of person to show up to the opening of an envelope.

Nevertheless, I felt bad for what I was about to do.

I scrolled through her recent photos and stopped when

I found the one I wanted. It was a photo of Chantelle on a beach somewhere and she was wearing a pair of high-waisted denim shorts and a neon orange bikini bra, covered by a beige crochet crop top. Her tanned face was adorned with freckles, and her long, curly hair was tied up in a loose bun. She beamed at the camera, showing off her incredibly perfect white teeth and dimples, and her body was an exaggerated hourglass shape. The perfect woman, according to a lot of guys these days.

Before my mind could compute my actions, I screenshotted the photo, went back to Instagram and pasted Chantelle's photo into Ruben's chatbox with the message:

SayAloeToMyLittleFriend: For the most part I don't tend to upload pics of myself online as I'm quite a private person, but seeing as you asked nicely, here you go! X

I closed the app, exhaled deeply, and stared blankly at my phone. What had I done?

Chapter 10

'So basically, Mike said that he needs to "find himself" and started going on and on about how he doesn't feel like he's the best version of himself for me and that he can't give one hundred per cent of himself until he's come into his own, or some shit like that.' Jean was splayed out on my bedroom floor, glass of Shiraz in hand, staring at the ceiling. Among all the drama that had happened today, I'd almost forgotten that he was supposed to be coming over to talk about his break-up. I'd quickly grabbed a bottle of wine and a few snacks on the way home as soon as he'd sent a text reminding me he was on his way.

The rest of the day had been a complete blur since sending Ruben that photo. I hadn't opened Instagram for the rest of the day, fearing what lay ahead. What if he recognised Chantelle's picture somehow? What if he'd done a reverse Google Image search and found out that I was a fraud? I had watched every episode of *Catfish* and thought through every possible way Ruben would be able to suss me out.

As much as I wanted to be there for Jean, I couldn't help but silently freak out about how this situation could potentially play out. It wasn't until I noticed a long period of eerie silence coming from the floor of my room that I snapped out of my train of thought to find Jean sitting cross-legged, staring at me.

'Oh. Hm, yeah I do think that's out of order, babes,' I quickly said, praying that the response was vague enough to cover whatever it is he had been saying.

'So, bitch – what should I do? Should I fight for this one? And you're not drinking your wine. Why are you not drinking your wine? I didn't come here to drink alone like a saddo.' Jean grabbed my glass from the floor and shoved it into my hand.

At that moment, a sudden flash in the corner of my bed caught my eye. It was my phone screen. I had thrown it off to the side in a bid to not be distracted, but now it was alerting me of a notification. My pulse started to race and I began to feel clammy.

'Jean, my love,' I began distractedly, before focusing on my friend, 'the thing is, there's nothing wrong with someone want-ing to find healing and wanderlust if that's what they think they need. People need to do what serves them. I know that you were great together but if that is how he feels, all you can do is respect it and allow him to move on, painful as it may be.'

Jean responded by taking a huge swig of Shiraz and looking at me up and down suspiciously. I tried to avoid looking over at my phone, instead concentrating on a tiny spider near Jean's foot, making its way under my bed.

Note to self: remember to get some eucalyptus leaves for the spiders.

'I mean that's great and all, but why can't he find himself with ME? Isn't the whole point of a relationship to grow and discover things with new people? I was low-key beginning to fall for him as well, fucksake.'

Jean put his glass on the carpet and stared at the floor morosely. In all the years I'd known him, I'd never seen him be this upset about a date or a partner before.

'Ohhh my love,' I cooed as I knelt onto the floor to give him a hug. 'I know it hurts, and you're allowed to feel sad about this. Mike was a good guy and you had great times, and if it was meant to be, you guys will see each other again if and when he comes back from – where is he travelling to again?'

'Las Vegas,' Jean muttered.

'I see,' I replied quietly, knowing damn well that Mike would probably be finding more than his own inner peace in Vegas, but I dared not mention this to Jean.

'Anyway,' Jean carried on, pouring himself some more wine. 'I've got other things on my mind. There's this exhibition taking place at the Tate around the end of the year that I'm tryna get involved in. It's been my dream to have my photos be shown in an actual art gallery – and a bitch needs to get paid.'

'Oh, Jean babes, that's WONDERFUL!' I spluttered, giving him another sideways hug. Jean was by far the most talented of us in our friendship group. As a photographer, he'd shot features for the likes of *British Vogue*, *Dazed* magazine and *Harper's Bazaar* and it was safe to say he was kind of a big deal.

Jean grinned dozily at me, blushing slightly. 'Thanks, babes. It's an exhibition celebrating Black photographers and I got an email from one of the curators asking if they could consider some of my work for exhibition. Not gonna lie? I was gagged, because – girl, what are you doing? Don't do this.' Jean gave me a side-eye as my eyes filled with happy tears for my friend.

'I'm sorry, babe – I'm just so proud of you! Why you're friends with an untalented corporate fogey like me, I'll never know. You should be living it up with the creative babes in Soho House and shit instead of slumming it with the little people, you know.'

Jean laughed as I took another sip from my glass. 'Yeah, well, I'm friends with you cause I need to be surrounded by the little people to help me keep it real, innit? Call me a man of the people.'

We both burst out laughing at this point, our drinks sloppily spilling onto the carpet.

'Anyway,' continued Jean, 'what's been going on with you and Mr San Francisco? Catch me up so I don't have to think about Mike.'

'First of all, Ruben's from Oakland, not San Francisco – apparently people in the Bay Area hate it when they get lumped in with San Fran.'

'Oooh, look at this one designating herself as Minister for Ruben Affairs. Aight then, sis! Have you told him you fancy him yet? When did you wanna take those pics for your profile?'

I jolted. I could see my phone on the bed lighting up, meaning more notifications. I pondered whether I should tell Jean what I'd done. But I couldn't be arsed about getting the third degree right now.

'Ha! I haven't told him I like him yet. There's no point, it's not like we're ever gonna meet,' I said hastily, wanting to move the conversation on from Ruben. 'But you know what, let's take some pics anyway, I could do with a bit of a boost after my little promotion today!'

'OH SHIT!' Jean shouted, slapping the palm of his hand to his forehead, eyes agog. 'I fucking forgot you got the big boss job today, didn't you?! I was so caught up on Mike that I flipping forgot to congratulate you – well, CONGRATULATIONS on securing that bag, sis! Tell me all about it, please!'

I sat cross-legged with my glass of wine in hand.

'OK, WELLLL, my new role is "director of brand and reputation", basically meaning that I oversee campaign strategy and look after the reputation of the agency. So I'll still be looking after Maranette Clothing, but now I'm looking after eight members of staff who all report to m—'

I was interrupted by Jean lightly touching my knee.

87

'Girl, I love you and I'ma let you finish, but we wanna know about that pay packet! Is the bag fully secured? I noticed how Aneni didn't respond in the chat too. Mmm.'

'Maybe she was busy at work or something, I dunno,' I replied, filled with too much excitement to think about Aneni's absence. 'So I'm being bumped up a little, which is great . . . for now.' I smirked widely. Jean gave me a knowing smile and raised his glass.

'Clink clink, bitch. Dinner's gonna be on you for the next six months, by the way.'

Jean's visit left me feeling energised and hopeful for the weeks ahead. Before he left, we managed to take a dozen or so cute-albeit-slightly-tipsy photos of each other that I reckoned would work for my Instagram profile. We took a few of me wearing boyfriend jeans, a white vest and a headwrap, barefaced and artsy with just the right amount of Afrofuturistic art in the background for Ruben (or whoever happened to see them) to think that I'm 'cultured' and 'deep'. On the off chance that Ruben ever saw my profile, I wanted him to know that Temz scrubbed up well.

We also took a few sexy pictures of me all made up wearing my favourite lilac Savage x Fenty BabyDoll lingerie, complete with matching peephole bra and undies. These weren't for the 'gram – just mere thirst traps for if and when the mood arose.

After Jean headed home, I quickly opened up my messages and saw that my Instagram had five notifications. I gulped slowly, my throat muscles painfully contracting together as I thought about what I'd done earlier with the picture to Ruben. Shitting hell. I needed some kind of distraction before I could face whatever was lurking on that app.

After taking a quick shower, I picked up my phone to text

Anthony. I wasn't interested in a date — I had no intention of getting to know the guy, I just wanted to bang.

> **Me: Hey Anthony, I doubt you remember me as it's been a while, but it's Artemis from the Prince of Peckham/your drunk sleeping pal haha. Sliding through just to say hey and to ask whether you fancied a drink at some point?**

I pressed 'send' and decided that I couldn't take the tension any more. I needed to rip the Band-Aid off and read my IG messages from Ruben. No use prolonging my sense of shame about it. By now, I'm sure Ruben had found out who the real person in the photo was and had either blocked me or was sending through a barrage of angry comments. In my direct messages tab, I saw one spam message, followed by four earlier messages from Ruben. I opened up his tab, squinting as I did so.

> **RubesCubes: Oh, wow**
>
> You're incredibly beautiful, Miss Lady. A pleasure to re-make your acquaintance.
>
> **RubesCubes: I know you said you're quite a private person and that's understandable, but having all that fineness locked away like that should surely be a crime!**
>
> **RubesCubes: Thanks for sharing, I hope you have a great rest of your day and I look forward to speaking with you later. ☺**

I gasped, only just becoming aware that I had been holding my breath while reading those messages. He hadn't cottoned on! A fucking close one, to be honest. Even though I did feel happy about getting away with using Chantelle's photo, and the prospect of him wanting to talk more, there was a part of me that felt kinda sad over his reaction.

Would he have reacted the same way if I'd sent him an actual photo of me? I couldn't recall the last time someone I'd been interested in actually found me 'beautiful', as opposed to just being desirable enough to fuck for an evening or two. Despite the fact that Ruben lived thousands of miles away with an eight-hour time difference, it felt like he was the first man who actually seemed to enjoy my personality and our conversations, which meant a lot. I wanted him to like ME, in all my fat, dark-skinned gorgeousness, but alas. Insecurity: 1, Artemis: 0.

I logged into Facebook again and spent the next twenty minutes scrolling through Chantelle's photos, guiltily screen-shotting her childhood and teenage pictures instead of saving them directly to my phone, and getting rid of the photo's source data that could potentially lead Ruben straight to the original photo (more women in STEM, I say). There was no way around it – the compliments Ruben had given earlier had given me a dopamine hit, and I needed more.

While scrolling her page, I came across a class photo in what looked to be an assembly hall. Chantelle was in the top left, grinning that grin that made all the boys in our year weak. Even back then, she was stunning. A wave of nostalgia hit me as I ran my eyes over all my old classmates, thinking about how much I hated school back in the day.

It wasn't that I was mercilessly bullied or anything like that; it was more so the neglect, isolation and extreme loneliness that cinched it for me. Outside of Aneni, I didn't really have a lot of friends, and would often spend my lunchtimes eating my sandwiches in the girls' bathroom cubicle to pass the time away from prying eyes. Being lonely I could sorta handle; having other students notice I was a loner was a different matter altogether.

I then stopped as I spotted the dark-skinned chubby girl on the bottom right hand of the picture, sitting down with her legs barely crossed, her round face displaying the faded echo of a smile and her hair in cornrows. The seams on her school uniform were on the brink of tearing, and her tights were laddered.

It was me.

I stared at the photo of a twelve-year-old me, overcome by waves of memories of school. I took a screenshot of the picture.

There were also a few photos featuring Chantelle on nights out, during what I presumed to be her uni days, looking fun and sociable. I screenshot those, too, alongside fifteen selfie photos she'd taken a few years ago, feeling like complete shit as I did so. I then hopped onto her Instagram page and made sure to screenshot some current photos of her, as well as screen recording any random videos she may have uploaded, on the off chance that Ruben would want to see 'me' in action. I felt over-whelming waves of guilt mixed with shame with every photo I screenshot, knowing deep down that this was all unnecessary; that I should have done the noble thing and just sent Ruben images of myself – his reaction be damned. But I just didn't have it in me to even begin to entertain the notion of being rejected right now. What I had going on with Ruben was too good, and I felt myself becoming addicted to it. Besides, now that I knew he liked the photos of Chantelle I'd sent, it had given me an indication of the type of girls he liked – which I was a huge departure from – and there was no way I could turn back now. After I was done mining Chantelle's page for content, I restricted her account from both the Aloe page and my personal page for good measure. I'd watched way too many *Catfish* episodes by that point to leave any traces or potential gaps in my . . . experiment.

A part of me still couldn't believe that I was embarking on this. I still had time to make things right – after all, I hadn't yet responded to Ruben's message after seeing the first picture. But at that point I was too nervous about his reaction to try and resolve the matter. It was all a bit of harmless fun.

I went back to my messages and replied to Ruben:

SayAloeToMyLittleFriend: Aww aren't you kind?! Thank you so much, and yeah I guess it's the Ghanaian in me that keeps me from showing my face everywhere ... Evil Eye and all that, yanno? I hope you're having a great morning/afternoon!

I inhaled and tried to swallow away the shame as I continued writing to him. 'It's only a game,' I repeated to myself, hoping that it would make me feel better, but also secretly wishing that I did in fact look like Chantelle so that it would make this whole process easier.

I looked down at the message. It had already been read, and Ruben was currently writing back. He normally never read my messages this quickly, and a part of me did wonder whether my little photo reveal may have been a reason why he was so keen on messaging back.

RubesCubes: Yeah, I feel you, it must be really frustrating and I know I've already said it, but again, you really are beautiful. You got a man? Lol?

My heart leapt at the 'beautiful' part. For a second, it felt like he was actually talking about me instead of the beautiful, curvy, light-skinned girl with dimples I'd shown him earlier. I spread out on my bed, sighed and decided to make an executive decision. I wanted to keep talking to this man, and he never needed to know what I actually looked like. It wasn't like we were ever going to meet. I sent Ruben a voice message:

SayAloeToMyLittleFriend: 'Hey Ruben! I hope you don't mind the voice note again, but I just wanted to say I really enjoy talking to you, and was hoping that maybe we could move to speaking on WhatsApp or something, if you were down with that? The one-minute time limit on Instagram audio gets annoying after a while ...'

I ended the voice note with the classic 'but no worries if not!' salutation, knowing that I would be plenty worried if he decided that he'd rather just speak over Instagram.

Ruben messaged me back a few moments later:

RubesCubes: Oh, for sure! Any excuse to hear your beautiful voice. We can change to WhatsApp, looking forward to it!

And after ten minutes of trying and failing to add the US number he sent through to my WhatsApp, I eventually sent him a quick 'hello' text to let him know I'd been successful.

Then several things happened at once.

Within four seconds of each other, I received messages from both Anthony and Aneni – and Ruben tried to WhatsApp call me. In my panic, I automatically declined the call, realising that my profile photo had the real photo of me instead of Chantelle.

I blocked Ruben's number temporarily while I rushed to find a new profile photo. I couldn't use a photo of Chantelle, otherwise my friends and family would be suspicious, so I chose a random photo of one of my plants that I had on my phone and replaced my photo with it. Just then, another message on Instagram came through:

RubesCubes: Heyyy Aloe, I ain't sure if I dialled the right number, but I think I tried to give you a call and it hung up? Let me know if I got it wrong?

No mention of my different profile picture at least, so I assumed I was in the clear. I hopped back into my WhatsApp to attend to the previous texts before I decided to call Ruben again. I wanted no distractions while I spoke to my future imaginary husband properly for the first time.

> Aneni: Hey babes, sorry I haven't been in touch recently. It's just been a bit busy at work but it'll be great to catch up next week or so, when you have time? Congrats on the job btw. Let's grab a drink soon!! Lemme know. Nenz xx

I'd found it interesting that she'd taken so long to get back to me about the promotion even though I saw that she'd read my message immediately after I'd typed it, but now wasn't the time to be petty. The time for that would be the next time we met up.

I typed back:

> Me: Not to worry, hun, work has been a bit chaotic for me too (as you probs know, haha) but yeah, let's meet up after work at some point, or this weekend if you're around? Xx

Aneni quickly responded:

> Aneni: Haha . . . ahh I can't do tomorrow I'm afraid, sis, and I'll have to check to see what I'm doing this Sunday. Saturdays are bad for me now as I'm with the Boy hehe, which I need to update you on actually! Are you OK to meet up maybe next Tuesday after work?

This girl was easier to read than a picture book. I had exciting news, so she's gotta one-up me with *more* exciting news. I took delight in responding back with the following:

> Me: Of course! C u next Tuesday ☺

After confirming things with Aneni, I quickly scanned over Anthony's reply.

Anthony: Well well well, if it isn't Artemis of Peckham, of course I remember you! It's not often I find myself waking up in the bed of a stranger I haven't fucked previously. How's your sexy self doing? I'd definitely be up for a drink, you free tomorrow night? Shall we head back to the scene of the crime? (The 'scene' meaning the pub, not your bedroom . . . unless the evening naturally takes us back there. 😃)

Fuck it, I had nothing better to do this weekend, and it could potentially be a distraction from the underlying guilt I felt about what I was doing to Ruben. I replied back to Anthony telling him I'd meet him at the pub tomorrow evening at 7 p.m. and made a note to myself to shave every inch of my body first thing tomorrow morning.

With Anthony and Aneni out of the way, I took a deep breath and tried to steady myself. I knew that I had to be super careful with any details I shared with Ruben, lest I muddle up a fact and blow my whole cover. I decided that I would be as truthful as possible when disclosing any information about myself, with the only lies being my appearance, my name, and where I work.

This was only a game. I kept repeating 'it's not like I'm ever going to meet him' to myself as I scrolled through WhatsApp, found his number and finally clicked 'call'.

Chapter 11

The phone rang for what felt like an eternity, which did little to hinder the insane levels of anxiety and tension I was feeling at that point. I needed the call to be perfect.

What if I forget how to say hello?

What if I accidentally use my real name?

What if Ruben is really boring and I suddenly get the ick?

What if that could potentially be a good thing, and in turn, could save all this hassle and deceit?

What if he thinks my voice doesn't match up to the photos I've been sending him?

Finally, he picked up and the most important call of my life played out as follows:

'Well, hello there, Miss Lady . . . um, how are you doing?'

'Oh, hey! I'm good, thanks, sir. Did I call at a bad time? I keep forgetting about the time difference.'

Miss Lady? It's giving 'Southern gentleman'. I love it.

'Not at all! It's like three-something over here and I'm just in a coffee shop doing some client work, drinking some coffee and speaking to a beautiful British lady over the phone. How are you?'

'Haha, aww you're really sweet, aren't you? I've heard about you Americans and your sweet talking. Well, let me tell you, you ain't fooling this one, OK? My eyes are wide open!'

'Says the lady who liked all my photos on IG in under ten minutes, OK, sure, lady.'

He got me there.

'Wow, really? Not you showing me up in 4K? OK, cool, I'll remember that little dig.'

'I'm just messing with ya. In all seriousness though, it's really great to hear your voice. I've really enjoyed our chats online recently, so I was kinda stoked when you suggested we talk on the phone. Dare I say, a little excited? But you didn't hear that from me.'

Did he just tell me he loved me? That's what I heard.

'You sweet, hilarious man. I'm glad you didn't think I was too forward with my approach, and by the way, in answer to your question, I don't have a man. I'm Single Betty over here.'

That's right, Temz, sow the seeds.

'Speaking of "Betty", it's really fucked up that I've just realised that I don't know what your real name is? That's so wild and I apologise profusely – I've just been calling you "Aloe" this whole time.'

Shit.

'Don't apologise! A clear testament to how awesome our chats are, to be honest. We dove straight into the convo, thus forgetting the fundamentals of the process.'

'Jeeze, OK, so two things: one, I love how British and poetic you are when you talk. You say everything in whole sentences and that pleases my ear for some weird reason, and two: I was the only one being deep with the convo! You've barely told me anything about yourself so today is where I'm gonna find out all about you, starting with your damn name!'

Think, Temz. THINK!

'. . . Hello? You still there?'

'Hey! Yep I'm still here, I'm sorry and you're right! We can talk about me. Um, my real name *is* actually Aloe. It's another reason why I feel so closely connected to plants and stuff. My . . . my parents are huge plant fanatics too and named me after the plant, I guess.'

I am positively the worst and most unimaginative liar of all time. It'll have to do for now.

'Damn, that's so dope. I LOVE that! Well, great to formally make your acquaintance again, Aloe. Beautiful name for a beautiful woman.'

Damn. If only he were talking about me instead of Chantelle.

'Hello? I'm sorry, I didn't mean to overste—'

OK, let's retreat for now before I accidentally say something I shouldn't.

'No, no, sorry I'm still here! I'm just low-key soaking in your compliments is all. Listen, sorry to cut this short but it's a bit late over here and I have some things to do tomorrow so I'm going to get some sleep, but it's been great talking with you!'

'Oh, um, of course, it's like eleven-thirty or something over there, right? Um, it's been great speaking to you too! I'd love to talk for longer when you're next free – if you want to?'

Absolutely gagged at him wanting to chat again. Well done, Temz!

'Yeah, yeah, I'd absolutely love to speak with you again! I'll let you know when I'm free tomorrow or Sunday and we can talk then. I hope you have a great rest of the day. Bye!'

I hung up the phone and stared at my array of plants littered on my windowsill and across my room. My four-year-old aloe vera basket hung majestically from the ceiling, its long tentacles casting a faint shadow on my wall in the moonlight. This was it. This was real. I couldn't turn back now.

I had to become Aloe, for real.

Chapter 12

The next day, internally I was shaking, crying and throwing up. Externally, I seem to have woken up with the world's biggest headache.

I was feeling super anxious about the conversation with Ruben from last night. I'd finally spoken to the man of my dreams (yes, I move fast!), and something that should have been fun, pure and cute just felt like pure agony to me. I couldn't pinpoint what it was. (A total lie. It was guilt; the feeling was guilt) but I felt on edge and uncomfortable the whole time I was talking to him. Underneath all the discomfort, though, were small pangs of glee.

He'd kept calling me beautiful.

Well, not me. *Her*.

Get it together, Temz. He doesn't like you. He doesn't know you. He knows Aloe. He likes speaking to Aloe.

I checked my phone to see that Ruben had sent me a text. It read:

Ruben: Hey Aloe, just wanted to say again how awesome it was talking with you! I'm looking forward to us talking again. I'm loving this little thing we got going on. You seem super dope!

Underneath the message, Ruben had sent through a selfie: he was in a coffee shop and was looking into the camera, faint laughter lines lightly illustrating the corner of his eyes as he smiled broadly, showing off his deep dimples. He had the most beautiful smile, almost giving off a mischievous energy as if he knew something no one else did. Why did I feel as if I was slowly falling for this man? I was down bad, and I didn't know what to do. Normally when placed in such moments of peril, I would fall back on my friends for advice, but I don't even think Jean would be able to handle the level of deceit I was currently getting up to. I couldn't tell him, and especially not Aneni. I felt trapped.

> **Me: I loved talking to you too, Ruben! I'm so glad you're digging the chat. Let me know when you're free and I'll hit you up again. Sleep well (and if you can't, try magnesium supplements. I swear they work!)**

Of course, I didn't inform him that the rest of my evening would be spent distracting myself from my guilt by potentially having my back blown out by a Jason Momoa lookalike I'd met some weeks before. I sent Ruben a selfie of Chantelle looking somewhat angelic yet staring seductively into the camera. She was wearing no make-up and her hair looked like it had just been washed. She was wrapped in a towel that just about covered her cleavage. A good mix of innocent, yet suggestive.

The photo was marked as 'seen' instantly, with Ruben responding:

> **Ruben: Damn, ma, had I known you were in a towel the whole time we were talking, I woulda switched it to video chat. Haha, iKid iKid. You look sensational. Look forward to talking soon ☺**

A wink emoji. I was moving up in the world. In Ruben's world. It was too late for me to talk to anybody about this, both figuratively and metaphorically. Aneni would never let me live it down as long as I lived, Jean would guilt-trip me until I confessed to Ruben, speaking to my mum was absolutely out of the question, and Claudia and her married self would probably never understand.

I let out a long, deep sigh of frustrated longing, and decided to take a nap until it was time for me to start getting ready for my date with Anthony later. I put my phone on silent and lay on my back, staring at the ceiling and thinking about how I could weasel out of the mess I had gotten myself into. This whole situation was messy, but admittedly, a part of me couldn't help but feel a bit of a thrill in what I was doing.

My mind once again settled on Ruben's face as I drifted off to sleep.

I awoke a few hours later, still feeling like utter crap. Thank God it was a Saturday otherwise I would have had to have pulled a sickie. My back and neck were aching due to the copious amounts of tossing and turning that I'd been doing throughout the night. Not surprising, due to the wild-ass dream I'd had that night that had quickly turned into the stuff of nightmares. In the dream, 'Aloe' (aka Chantelle) was in Ruben's apartment, and they (we??) were making out on the sofa. Pure hot and heavy stuff, and the shit was getting good, too. In the middle of it all, Ruben had gently pulled 'Aloe's' head back to get a better look before going in for another kiss, only to find that he wasn't making out with 'Aloe' at all, but with me. He stared at me in shock, and then went on to projectile vomit in my lap. I woke up clawing at my face halfway through the night, dripping with sweat.

Guilt is such a bitch.

But we move. I used that afternoon to beautify myself before my date with Anthony that evening, trying to not think about Ruben while doing so. I'd promised to call him before I left, but hadn't given him a specific time and, to be honest, I was low-key regretting the offer. I didn't want to be heading into this date feeling anxious and on edge having just spoken to him. Whenever I was in Dick Appointment mode, I would spend the day trying on several outfits, having several outfits rejected by local style guru Jean, and packing my Dick Appointment bag, which consisted of: a pack of condoms; spare underwear; deodorant; fanny wipes (I'd only recently found out that this was a *thing*); chewing gum; a couple of make-up brushes and some powder for touch-ups; lipstick; and my favourite orange and bergamot perfume.

And the Dick Appointment beauty regimen was my favourite regimen. I saw it as self-care. But while I waited for Natalie to finish using the bathroom, I opened my closet to try on tonight's date outfit options:

1. The black sequined jumpsuit from River Island with the tapered legs, batwing arms and deep V-neck. Cute. Flattering. But impractical. We wanted something that could be taken off quickly without faff.
2. The leopard-print midi dress with double slits down the left from Daily Paper. Generous on the cleavage enhancement. Shows a little bit of FUPA ('Fat Upper Pussy Area', for those uninitiated), but I'm not too worried about that. It could be a potential.
3. The green cropped jumper from ASOS Curve with a cut-out detail showing a bit of cleavage, teamed with my favourite pair of Levi's jeans that make my ass look perky.

Decisions, decisions!

I tried on each outfit, snapping a quick photo in each look to send to Jean for his final, trusted approval, and eventually made my way to the bathroom to begin The Process.

I turned on the shower and stared at my naked body in the mirror as I waited for the water to warm up. Then I slathered on my favourite face mask, hopped in the shower and took care of the fundamentals: shaving every inch of my body, followed by a thorough scrub down using my favourite coconut and shea butter body scrub, followed by an almond body wash. Anthony was going to be in for a treat and he didn't even know it.

I coated my body in my favourite cocoa butter lotion before adding a thin layer of coconut oil on top, a little trick I'd learned from my mum when it came to layering fragrances and having the scent last on the skin. I then spritzed on some perfume, went back into my bedroom and sat on the bed in my towel to let all the oils and juices marinate. There was nothing better than feeling like an absolute dolphin before a date. I could literally feel the feminism leaving my body as I lay in bed excited over the prospect of a man potentially enjoying me this evening, but I didn't care. It had been a stressful few weeks, and I needed to get laid.

I had a few hours before meeting up with Anthony, so as I lay back on my bed, phone in hand, I caved in and decided to give Ruben a call – but not before spying Jean's response to the photos I'd sent him earlier:

Jean: Ooh! The jumpsuit is CUTE but it's not the most appropriate for back-blowing hoetivities, babes. Too nitpicky. The jumper is nice too, but the boobs aren't really BOOBING like they should be, ya know? I vote for the leopard print – you look incredible and the girls are sitting pretty. Have fun getting your back cracked and I WILL

be calling you for a dick report tomorrow. You will tell me everything! Xxxx

I chuckled to myself and responded:

Me: Leopard print it is – I was leaning more to that anyway LOL. Thank you, babes, and I'll report back tomozzz, wish me luck!

I switched back to the main menu on WhatsApp, and saw that Ruben had changed his profile photo. Now it was a picture of him hugging another woman around our age while they both smiled brilliantly to camera. My heart jolted. Was she his girlfriend? During all of our conversations, he definitely mentioned being single, but maybe he'd lied? I guess he probably wouldn't want to divulge that information to a total stranger he'd just started speaking to. We'd also both been lightly flirtatious throughout, giving me the impression that he was a single man. Unless he had somewhat of a wandering eye?

Keep it together, Temz, I scolded myself internally, taking slow, deep breaths in an attempt to calm my heart rate. 'So what if he has someone else? You guys are just friends.'

Yeah, right. Friends don't fantasise about other friends while touching themselves in the shower. Friends don't have daydreams about wanting to be with their friends. Friends certainly do not catfish other friends. But here we are.

The woman in the photo was beautiful, and seemed to be the kind of girl I anticipated most men like Ruben would go for. She was light-brown-skinned, with a gorgeous lace front wig that must have come straight out of the vaults of Beyoncé herself, and the most beautiful straight white teeth. Oh, yeah, she was definitely his type.

Biting the bullet, I scrolled down to his name, pressed 'dial' and nervously picked at my nails until he eventually picked up on the seventh ring.

'Hey babygirl, I almost didn't think you'd call. How are you doin?'

Oh, my God. He must have just woken up. The levels of baritone his vocal cords were emitting made my eardrums vibrate with pleasure. And him calling me 'babygirl' in that accent? Jesus is Lord! His drawl was deep, and so incredibly sexy. I felt something stir between my legs.

'Oh, hey Ruben! I'm good, thanks. Sorry if I woke you up,' I replied nervously, my stomach vibrating at a million miles per hour with excitement.

'Not at all, I'm an early riser and was looking forward to your call.'

Not the virtual love of my life waking up early to wait for my call?! Whew! Before I could allow myself to get completely blown away by his charm, I knew I had to ask him about the woman in the photo. The last thing I wanted was to be wasting my time.

'Waking up for little old me?' I replied in a mock shocked tone. 'You're too sweet . . . your new girlfriend must love that about you!'

Nicely done, Temz. Nicely done. Smooth, even. I held my breath as I waited for confirmation.

'I . . . huh?' came his response.

'Your display photo, sir,' I replied. 'She truly is stunning!'

Ruben gave a small chuckle and scoffed loudly. Maybe I had gotten the wrong end of the stick. I hoped so, anyway, because the embarrassment of trying to call him out and failing would actually have me falling to my knees.

'First of all, ma'am, I already said I was single. And that's my cousin, Melissa. I'll pass on your compliments to her.'

I let out a great sigh of relief. We were still in the game.

'It's also really cute how you used that as a way to gauge

whether I was with someone though, even though I told you I was single before. You tryna catch me out, huh? You must want me baaaadly.'

The audacity of this man to tell the truth right now. I cackled as I responded: 'Want who? I have no clue what you're talking about, but give Melissa my best, all the same!'

'Yeah, yeah, whatever, sis. This is the second time now you've enquired about my relationship status. You want me. Admit it!'

'OK, Mr Ego, the sun must be shining too harshly on that bald head of yours because you're tripping.'

Ruben laughed, and I felt a part of my heart soften. 'Hearing you say "trippin" in a British accent is so cute and terrible, by the way.'

For the next twenty minutes or so, Ruben and I discussed a whole range of things – including serious pop culture topics.

'I'm not saying that Beyoncé ISN'T talented; I'm just saying she ain't no Whitney or Tina is all!'

'Oh, sir, you're absolutely delusional. She may not be Whitney or Tina, but she absolutely is deserving of all of her accolades and praise. Her work ethic is insane!'

Eventually talk turned to family and friends.

'So, are you an only child then?'

'Nah,' came Ruben's reply. 'I got a younger sister, Rochelle, who lives in Toronto. She moved up there for college and liked it so much that she decided to stay permanently. I go up to see her when I can. What about you?'

'I'm an only child, which kinda sucked growing up, but I also grew up with my best friend Aneni and she became sort of like my sister in a way, I guess, so that was OK?'

Ruben hummed in agreement. 'It's cool that you had some-one there, though. I low-key felt like I was alone growing up too. My sister was sick as a baby so she was always in and out of hospital. There was definitely a loneliness there, having no one to play with or speak to on a regular. I guess that's part of why I gravitated towards music. It was an escape for me.'

I just wanted to give him a hug. He'd suffered loneliness, like me.

'Well,' I replied, 'from one lonely misunderstood genius to another, for what it's worth if we had known each other as kids, I would have totally been your friend!'

'Pfft,' came his response as he chuckled. 'I woulda been too damn cool for you, peasant!'

Ruben also told me how he'd started his consultancy business with his best friend and business partner, Quincy (who I apparently 'must' speak to soon as he'd never heard a Black person with a British accent before), and most importantly, I got the courage to ask him a bit about his dating history, then waited intently for his response.

'Well, damn. Um, where to begin?' Ruben sighed. 'I'll try and tell a condensed version, I guess?'

'Please don't feel the need to open up about this if you don't want to!' I quickly interjected, realising I may be crossing some boundaries.

'Nah, it's cool,' Ruben said, then began to fake cry. 'I'm over the trauma now!' He chuckled a little as I let out a sly kissing of my teeth. 'So ... I was in a relationship with this girl I knew from college. We were together for about six months and it was sweet. I guess you could say she was my first love. I was head over heels for her and we moved into an apartment and everything four months into the relationship.'

I unintentionally gasped. 'Four months?! Whew, you move quick, sir!' I exclaimed without thinking.

'Ha! For sure. Like I said, I was a bit of a simp for her, actually. Anyway, we moved into this little duplex in Berkeley and everything was cool for a while, until I started noticing that she'd go out and come home later and later. Now I ain't one of those men who needs to have his woman home by a certain time or whatever, but you know? I did pick up on it and mentioned to her after a few weeks of it happening and she basically gaslit me into believing nothing was happening and shit.'

'Damn,' I muttered. I read somewhere that women are supposed to be the best cheaters; how'd she allow herself to get caught so easily? Not that what she did was right, of course.

'Yeah, so after that, things were cool for a while. I even went out and bought a ring like two months later—'

'A RING? After six months?' I interjected. *Ugh. A MAN!!*

'Haha, like I said! I was whipped, and we'd known each other for many years before getting together so it made more sense at the time! Anyway, I got back to the apartment earlier than she expected – I left work early to pick up the ring, and as I walked through the door, I caught her in our bed with some dude.'

My jaw dropped as a flood of emotions fell over me. Poor guy; that must have been horrible to witness.

'Oh, my God, Ruben. I'm so, so sorry. That is so fucking foul of her. Shit!' I replied. What woman would do that to such a lovely person?

'Yeah, I was . . . Well . . . I was heartbroken, Aloe,' Ruben replied weakly. 'I broke up with her there and then. I didn't want or need any details. I just wanted her to leave. It took me a smooth minute to get over that shit, to be honest. And then I did what Solange sang about and tried to sex it away, constantly, for about a year.'

'You became a fuckboy huh? Mm mm.' I snorted. 'Well, considering the origin story, I guess I can understand what led you to it.'

'Hey now,' Ruben interjected. 'I was an *ethical* fuckboy! I never slept with multiple women at the same time, I always used protection and I was always upfront with the women I dealt with – they all knew I wasn't looking for anything serious. After a while I just ended up feeling empty and sad, so I stopped. And it's been three years since I stopped sleeping around with women and stuff.'

'As in, you haven't had any sex? At all? In three years?' I asked, mouth agape.

'Yup. Hardest three years of my life and counting, haha!' he replied, laughing.

The most remarkable part of this story wasn't that he hadn't had sex for three years; how he'd been able to keep it in his pants without climbing the walls was beyond me.

'Damn. Well, thanks for telling me. I'm sorry that this happened to you. You seem like such a great guy and I really hope you find someone worthy of all you have to offer,' I said finally.

Ruben sighed. 'I hope so. I think I'm ready to go back into dating properly again. I got some trust issues, but I can't allow them to stop me from living my life . . . and potentially finding the right one and all that. What about you?'

I told him a bit about my dating fails (leaving out the whole fat fetishism, obviously), which led to a brief chat about Aneni and Jean, and soon I found myself telling him a bit about my childhood.

'I was a chubby girl,' I began cautiously, 'but I never really let that stop me from being confident, I guess. Like, I knew I was a little bigger than everyone else and it did make me a little weird at times, but I never considered myself "less than" for being bigger. For a while it was all good, but I guess my insecurities really kicked in around eighteen, when I started university. I used to hang around with a group of people who were super into their appearance and losing weight and stuff and I eventually fell into that scene for a few years. I guess the effects of that still sometimes linger from time to time. Ultimately though, I never let my insecurities stop me from grasping opportunities or taking part in stuff. Because I've always been a little introverted, I knew early on that the only person I could really depend on was myself, and I trusted myself to love myself loudly and unapologetically, because no one else would.' It felt good to tell him the truth.

Ruben remained quiet on the other end for a moment or two, before replying:

'That's great. I wish I could bottle up what you said and give it to my little sis, because she's always had issues with body confidence too. For what it's worth, you're beautiful now and I know you were beautiful as a child, too. Ain't nothing wrong with being a lil chubby! You've got such a gorgeous, positive soul. The type of soul that makes something beautiful out of negativity.'

I flushed, wanting the floor to open me up. I had tripped, fallen and was struggling to get up. The infatuation bug had sunk its teeth into me.

Ain't nothing wrong with being a lil chubby.

He's only telling me this NOW?

'I've always been a bit husky myself. I guess, as I got older, I learned to live with, and embrace it, I suppose,' Ruben said, and I thought back to a couple of his Instagram photos where he was kitted out in a white vest and cargo shorts, his wide, firm torso just *glistening* in the California sunshine. Whew. Lordy lordy.

I snapped back to reality as a sudden thought occurred to me.

'Sooo . . . Does the same thinking apply for the kinds of women you date? You like 'em thick, too?'

I'm not sure what possessed me to ask him, but on the off chance that he may have a penchant for plus-size babes, I could be in with a chance. 'Haha, I wouldn't say that I had a definite type physically, but in case you were wondering, you fall into what I like in a woman.' It was almost as if I could hear him winking through the phone.

I quietly sighed as I realised this meant that I would have to continue the charade for a little bit longer.

'Well, I'm happy to hear that. I'd definitely say that you fall into my type, too. It's a shame you live all the way over there though.' I breathed, more to myself than to him, but he'd heard me.

'Hopefully there'll be a situation that'll allow me to come out to London one day, or vice versa. Then we can have a proper first date!'

I grimaced at this suggestion, wanting to keep the text and phone conversations going as long as possible without having to think of us meeting. As gassed as I was to hear him talk about going on a date, he would still be expecting to meet Chantelle, not me.

'That would be amazing!' I lied, suddenly realising I was going to be late for my date with Anthony – a date which I suddenly felt weird about going to, given how much I was enjoying my current conversation with Ruben. 'Anyway, again I'm so sorry to cut the convo short but I'm heading out with a friend tonight, so we'll talk again soon. I hope you have a great day!'

I put the phone down and let out a deep moan of rage. Why was I falling for this guy, knowing nothing would ever happen?

Oh, Temz. You dickhead.

Chapter 13

Anthony: Hey babe. Just got to the bar and I've got us a booth. Looking forward to seeing ya. 😊

Me: I'm running a bit late, but should be there in about ten mins!

I quickly typed out my response to Anthony while speed walking down Denmark Hill to get my bus to the pub. I was running SUPER late. After getting off the phone with Ruben, I spent about twenty minutes daydreaming about what the sex would be like if we ever met and about what our kids would look like. I had it bad, but I had to keep him out of my head for now! It was twenty minutes I couldn't really afford, as I needed to dedicate time to lassoing my hair into place. It was due a wash and so I'd just been wrapping it up in a bun for the whole week. I quickly sprayed my head with some conditioner and water in an attempt to slick my hair down, but annoyingly it wasn't looking to cooperate and kept shooting off stray, straggly parts that wouldn't lie flat even when I applied the strongest of gels that near enough equated to Gorilla Glue.

'Fuck's sake!' I muttered under my breath, and, instead, ended up moulding my hair into an old-school fauxhawk situation, creating a tapering effect on the sides with some of the gel and puffing up the top-middle part of my hair. It came out somewhat decent. I put on the leopard print dress that had received the Jean star of approval and paired it with my favourite black Dr Martens boots and a black denim jacket. Jean was right; the titties really were s i t t i n g. After changing my bedsheets and giving my bedroom the quick once-over, I nipped over to the bathroom and quickly spritzed myself with the first bottle of perfume I could find on the counter; it was a heavy, thick and sweet scent and it reminded me of blueberries and leather. Seductive enough, I thought to myself as I added a couple more touches of perfume to my neck before heading off.

I arrived at the pub and gave myself one final inspection in the reflection of the pub window. I looked good! The shapewear I had on was really putting in work, keeping my FUPA locked down to a minimum while exaggerating my waist-to-hip ratio. My hair still looked great and my make-up was sitting matte and rock solid (thanks in part to the TikTok beauty gurus and their long-lasting-foundation hacks).

I could see Anthony through the window sitting in a little booth by the window, back hunched, looking at his phone in deep thought. There was no doubt about it; this man was hot, and by hook or by crook, he would be leaving with me.

But alas, my recent conversation with Ruben was still rattling around in my head:

Ain't nothing wrong with being a lil chubby.

If only he had led with this in the beginning; it would have probably saved all the trouble I had now gotten myself in. Did he really have no problem with chubbier women, or was he just saying that to be nice? I turned my thoughts from Ruben to Anthony as I faced the pub, trying to rationalise my thoughts. I needed the physical release of being with someone right now, and Anthony seemed like he would do.

I walked through the door and made a beeline for him. All eyes in the pub were on me as I strutted past various tables and squeezed my bum and hips in between occupied chairs. I looked good. I felt amazing, and this was going to go well in Jesus's name.

Anthony looked up at me as I approached, and I could feel his eyes drinking me in. He stared at my body from the floor up slowly, eyes agog. Once his eyes met mine, his face cracked into a brilliant smile and he stood up. I'd forgotten how huge he was; all six feet four inches of him taking a step towards me before enveloping me in a huge bear hug that swallowed me whole. Oh, this felt good. I was once again entangled in the wall of chest hair that peeked through his beige V-neck T-shirt. I quickly stepped back to assess him: along with the tee he was wearing some straight-legged jeans (thank the Lord he didn't opt for bootcuts or this date would have been over as quickly as it had begun) and had paired the outfit with some Nike low-top all-white Dunks. OK, taste!

'OK, OK, you pass the vibe check! Also a nice bit of nostalgia from our first meeting there with the chest hair. I see you.' I laughed as I tried to slide into the booth. Why the hell did he pick a seat where I couldn't move the table? I sucked my stomach in to make the final push as Anthony took his seat.

'Ha! I'm glad I passed. I can be a bit of a fashionista from time to time, don't you know?'

I slowly took my jacket off as I smiled at him. It would have been so much easier for me to get my seduction plans in motion if it weren't for the booth table gradually splitting me in two. I decided to just firm it for the evening and concentrate on the task at hand.

'Uhuh,' I replied, looking at him up and down. 'Sooo, are you going to be a gentleman and get a girl a drink or . . . ?'

He cocked his head to the side and gave me a wolfish grin.

'Wow. And here I was thinking I was going to be the one treated, seeing as I was the one who was asked out. What happened to feminism, huh?' He grinned, looking at the menu.

'First of all, I am all for women's rights but when it comes to first dates, you should know that I periodically allow the feminism to leave my body if it means getting a free drink. Let's just make that clear, OK?' I smiled at him again, and he responded by placing his hand on his chest and letting rip with a loud guffaw that made the folks sitting at the tables near us turn around in surprise.

'Oh! You're funny. I like you.' He smirked, again cocking his head to the side and hitting me with that devilish grin again, then asked me what I wanted to drink. I decided to pace myself and ordered sparkling water alongside a single rum and Coke to start. I also ordered some fries in a bid to soak up the alcohol. I wanted to be completely sober by the end of the night; I didn't need a repetition of last time we met.

As Anthony trailed off to the bar, I subtly rearranged myself in my seat in order to feel a bit more comfortable and opened up the Notes app on my phone:

Note to self: leave feedback for the pub to make booth seats wider. These are not plus-size-friendly at all.

Just then, I noticed two texts: one from Natalie – and the other from Ruben. I read Ruben's first; feeling a little awkward while doing so. In a perfect world, I'd be on this date with him instead of Anthony.

Ruben: Heyy Aloe, I hope you have a great night with your friend – looking forward to speaking with you again x

This guy was determined to get me to fall in love with him and, frankly, I did not appreciate that.

I opened up Natalie's message instead, and was faced with a wall of CAPS LOCK:

Natalie: DID YOU USE MY LE ROUGE OUDH PERFUME, ARTEMIS?! I can't find it in the bathroom cabinet. I bought that in Dubai for £300 cause it's got pure oudh oil in it, and I only use it for special occasions! I think we need to have a talk when you get back and perhaps go through some of the house rules again? I can't keep going back and forth with you over this. I think it's time we had a chat. Let me know when you're free xx

I read the text, sighed, then reread it. I needed to leave that flat, post-haste. I couldn't live like this any more.

I texted her back, inhaling deeply. *Keep it cute, Temz.*

Me: Nat. You left the perfume on the kitchen counter near the microwave. I saw it this morning. Have a wonderful evening xx

The message was immediately read and, as I expected, Natalie didn't respond. Typical.

I put my phone to the side as Anthony returned to the table with all three drinks balancing perfectly between his two hands. He sat down and proceeded to stare at me intently, that wicked grin of his making a comeback.

'What is this, some kind of flirtation technique you use to get women into bed? What's with the grinning?' I asked coyly, meeting his gaze while sipping my rum and Coke.

'I have no idea what you're talking about, lady,' Anthony replied, eye contact still intact while he took a sip of his beer. 'So,' he continued, his eyes darting from my face to my cleavage, then back up to my face again. This guy was not subtle at all. 'Seeing as we've already shared a bed together, I think we should probably continue getting all of the intimate, awkward things out of the way first, don't you think?'

'Sure,' I responded, giving him the ole 'Princess Diana-Doe-eyed-under-eyelash-stare'. That always seemed to work. *That's it, Temz. Reel him in.* Then I lightly swept my fingers over my collarbone drawing his eyesight to my cleavage, and looked over towards the bar with a flirty smile on my face. From the corner of my eye, I could see that he couldn't take his off me. *Yasss girl: he's falling for it!* Anthony seemed to shift uncomfortably in his seat. And we had lift off!

'So . . . how old are you? What do you do? Where are you from? What's your favourite colour? All in that order please.'

I turned to him and leaned back in my seat. Thinking about nothing, but wanting to rip his clothes off. I didn't necessarily *want* to go through the whole 'getting to know you' process. We both *knew* what we wanted, so why all the build-up? I decided to indulge him anyway.

'I'm thirty. I have a new role of director at the advertising agency I work at that starts next week. I'm from South-East London, and my favourite colour is yellow. I own a multitude of houseplants and have my own houseplant blog. Your turn!'

I knew exactly what he meant when he asked me where I was from, but seeing as he probably would never ask a white woman that same question, I decided to be aloof about it.

Anthony lightly bit his lip, something I found incredibly hot seeing as for a white guy he actually HAD a lip to bite, and ran his hands through his thick auburn hair.

'I'm thirty-five, I work in sales, I live in Clapham and my favourite colour is green. I have one houseplant, which died a year ago, but I haven't had the heart to throw it out yet.'

I raised my eyebrow at his answers. Suddenly it all made sense. Of course he lived in Clapham. Of course he worked in sales.

'Sales, huh?' I replied, stirring my drink slowly. 'I bet you're one of those Broadgate Circle wankers, right?'

Anthony let out another huge guffaw, his huge chest shaking up and down so rapidly that at one point I feared that he would end up launching into a full heart attack.

'What the entire fuck is a "Broadgate Circle wanker"? That's a new one!'

'Oh, please,' I replied. 'You know the type! White guy, normally sporting a greasy Patrick Bateman haircut. Ill-fitting suit from Moss Bros. Works in sales and notoriously always hangs out in packs with other "Sales Lads" around Broadgate Circle. Has a private members' club membership that they only use once every three months to take pics for social media to prove they're still actually a member. You strike me as that kind of guy.' I laughed.

With the palms of his hands cupping his chin, he gazed at me almost dreamily. My impact! This shit was hot, I couldn't lie. He gave me another smile.

'You're very cheeky, I see! And a very funny, beautiful lady, do you know that? It was an honour to have randomly woken up next to you.'

'Thank you kindly,' I replied. 'But who's to say that it can't happen again?' With that, I excused myself to go to the ladies, leaving him to ruminate on my parting words.

I made a big show of squeezing myself past other tables to get to the bathroom, knowing that he was watching me the whole time. The dress I had on highlighted every curve of my body, further sweetening the deal. By this point, I was absolutely ready to take him home, but I decided I'd indulge in a few more minutes of sexual tension and witty back-and-forths before making my move. For the most part I wasn't someone who was that keen on small talk, almost always getting the ick when the guy said something stupid/misogynistic/weird/insert-something-strange-here. Nothing dries up the vaginal canal faster – but this time, I figured I'd take the risk. I took a quick leak and checked my phone. No messages. After fixing my make-up and readjusting my SKIMS shapewear, I made my way back out to the bar.

Anthony and I spent the next ninety minutes talking about fun-but-surface-level stuff, everything ranging from the weak-ass *Game of Thrones* finale to our favourite documentaries and even our favourite sex positions. So far, I was liking the cut of his jib. However, it wouldn't have been a good ole interracial date without some potentially problematic and ignorant quips thrown in for good measure.

'I just don't feel like South London is all that gentrified, though,' Anthony told me, gesticulating enthusiastically. 'My family's been there for yonks, and it's *always* been relatively white – albeit working-class white, and—'

'Anthony, with all due respect, are you insane?' I interjected, letting out a guffaw loud enough to be heard from a couple of tables away. 'You're going to sit there, stare in my face and tell me – a whole Ghanaian woman – that neighbourhoods such as Brixton, Camberwell, Notting Hill and Peckham weren't overwhelmingly Black back in the day? Drop me out, man. You must be smoking fentanyl-laced crack.'

Anthony leaned in, trying to stifle his laughter. 'First of all, sweetheart, I'm not on the fentanyl tonight; my preference is a bit of blow every now and again. Secondly, it can be argued that no one demographic really "owns" an area. Demographics move from place to place. Before Black people settled in Brixton, I'm sure it was occupied by white people. People move. Way of life, innit?'

I squinted at him, debating my choices. Was potential good dick worth all this gaslighting? I was on the cusp of carnal greatness – but at what cost?

'Well, speaking of white people settling in Black spaces,' I quipped as I slowly started to put my jacket on, 'do you want to come back to mine? That is, if you wanted to join me . . .'

I was so smooth with it.

Anthony laughed and then gave me a faux-shocked face and replied, 'WOW, Artemis. Are you really trying to proposition me for sex right here and now? Right in front of my very delicious salad?' He picked up the bowl of half-eaten chicken Caesar he had ordered.

'That's *exactly* what I'm trying to do. So, are you game or nah?' I snorted back, giving him a teasing side-eye. Why this guy was trying to play so hard to get I had no idea – we both knew that this was what we wanted.

Anthony put his jacket on, went up to the bar to pay the tab, and from there he took my hand in his and led me out of the pub. This might even have been kind of romantic if my sole intent wasn't only to have my back broken by him.

We walked over to the number 12 bus stop on Peckham High Street in a total-yet-comfortable silence. As usual, I noticed the stares of passers-by as they clocked the seemingly strange-looking couple coming towards them: one very tall, very conventionally attractive white man, holding the hand of one tall-ish, very fat, very cute Black girl. You would have thought that living in one of the most ethnically diverse cities in the world would make people more used to seeing inter-racial pairings but, alas, the stares continued. Soon Anthony disentangled our hands and began to walk a few paces behind me, pretending to slow down while he checked something on his phone. Crimson flag.

When we arrived at the bus stop, Anthony turned to me and said, 'Was it just me, or was walking down that high street painfully awkward?'

'You've never been with a Black or a fat woman in public before, huh?' I laughed, looking at the confusion forming across his face. 'You'll get used to it, buddy.' I playfully slapped his back.

'Oh! No, it's not that, it's just I— I mean YES, I've been with a variety of different women of all races, and . . . girths . . .' he said, shifting uncomfortably on the spot. 'But I mean, like . . . I wasn't expecting so many obvious stares, you know? I'm sorry if it made you uncomfortable.'

'Oh, please!' I replied, shrugging him off. If I had a penny for every time I'd received a side-eye for being in the arms of a conventionally attractive man, I'd be living part-time at Soho Farmhouse by now. 'This isn't my first rodeo. It's cool. What *wasn't* cool was you distancing yourself from me when you clocked the stares, though. What was that about?'

Anthony continued to shift on the spot. I could tell that he wasn't really used to being confronted like this.

'Did I? Oh, I'm sorry, I just . . . Maybe I didn't want to make *you* uncomfortable being seen with a tall, geeky guy was all!' There went that wolfish grin again.

Uhuh. I looked at him up and down, assessing the damage. There was absolutely nothing 'geeky' about him. It was giving crimson flag, ladies and gentlemen, but I had gotten this far. I just needed to get the peen and never see him again.

I could see the bus approaching and held Anthony's hand once more. 'So anyway, you're coming back to mine, yes?'

'Yes,' he responded. Out of nowhere, he bent his head down slightly and gave me a kiss.

OK, I wasn't expecting that. At least not now. Maybe he wasn't *that* bad. The kiss was pretty great, that was for sure. His big, pillowy lips really came through, and I could taste the beer on his breath as he used his tongue to gently stroke mine. We kissed for what felt like fifteen minutes but was in actuality maybe about ten seconds. I came up for air almost a little discombobulated, but recovered just in time to flag down the bus as it approached.

Time to get this show on the road. We hopped onto the bus and while Anthony was on his phone, I stared out of the window the entire way back home, forcing myself to keep thoughts of Ruben out of my mind.

Chapter 14

'Here we are. This is where the magic happens and all that!' I said as I ushered Anthony into my bedroom. 'I'm assuming you've already seen the rest of the flat from last time.' Anthony smiled and looked around as he took off his jacket and sat timidly on the edge of my bed. The remnant scent of the Fig and Cedarwood candle I'd lit a few hours ago still lingered in the air, which gave the room a slightly musky, sweet aura that worked with the overall 'seduction lair' aesthetic I had been trying to set up in my room earlier that day: fresh sheets; all embarrassing photos, souvenirs and sex toys hidden away in my drawers, etc.

'Nice,' Anthony said, turning his head to look at the artwork on the walls. 'You have an eclectic taste in art.'

I raised an eyebrow. Since when did only having African-inspired artwork constitute having an eclectic taste? I decided not to question him on that. I'd come way too far to suddenly get the ick.

'Thanks. It's mostly by Ghanaian artists. I haven't been back to Ghana in such a long time, so the artwork is a way to make me feel connected to the Motherland and all that.'

'That's cool, so you're Ghanaian then?'

Time for me to cut this small talk off at the root. I took off my jacket and sat next to him, admiring his rings.

'I am Ghanaian, yep. Would you like a drink or anything?' Going to the kitchen would serve as a good opportunity to have a quick look and see whether Natalie was still lurking around. On the weekends, she normally went home to her parents' house in Westbubbafuckshire or wherever she's from, but her text about wanting a chat the following day made me wonder whether she was still in the flat.

'D'you know what? I'd absolutely kill for some ice-cold water.'

I grinned and took my phone as I got up. 'An ice-cold water, I can do. Coming right up.'

On my way to the kitchen, I gently knocked on Natalie's door, hoping that she had packed up and fucked off somewhere else for the night. There was no answer, but I knocked again just to be sure. I opened her door just a crack to confirm that she wasn't there, and made my way to the kitchen.

I decided to quickly check my phone while cracking out the ice cubes for the water and saw a message from Jean sent twenty-three minutes ago:

Jean: Y'all fucked yet? I need deets, I'm bored man.

Me: Lmao hopefully it'll happen soon, we just got back to mine!

I typed back, chuckling to myself.

I completed another flat search just to triple-check that Natalie was nowhere to be seen, locked the front door and headed back to my room. Anthony had now taken off his shoes and was in the middle of inspecting a shelf where I kept all my awards from work. I sauntered up to him as seductively as I could and handed him the glass of water.

'You're quite an accomplished young lady, aren't you? Look at all these awards!' He gently stroked a golden circular sculpture that had the head and torso of a lion popping out in the centre. 'What does this one mean?'

'Ahh, this?' I picked up the award statue and mockingly held it against my bosom lovingly. 'This is my Cannes Lion Award. It's one of the most prestigious awards in the marketing and PR space. I won it for heading up a huge TV campaign that ran a couple of years ago.'

Anthony whistled, and I could see his eyes sparkling against the soft rays of my lamp's filtered light.

'So . . . you're used to being in charge, huh? One of those strong, aggressive types then. You're the big boss around town. Should I be nervous?'

Strong? Aggressive? CRIMSON FLAG #2.

I gave him a side-eye, with a dollop of raised eyebrow for good measure.

Anthony didn't seem to notice. He turned to face me, took a long sip of his water and then took the award out of my hands. With his eyes still on me, he enclosed my hands in his, and moved closer towards me. So close that I could feel his breath on my lips. I could feel him circling my palms slowly with his index fingers, which for some reason, was a huge turn-on. My eyebrow lowered with the quickness. I couldn't believe I was selling myself out for dick like this, but it might be worth it.

'Why would . . . you need to be nervous . . . ?' I stuttered, now staring at his lips hungrily. When it came to one-night stands, I *was* sometimes pretty dominant. There wasn't usually any of this build-up and anticipation, though? This was hot.

Anthony moved his hands to my waist, slowly reaching around the circumference until he'd clasped both hands around my back and interlaced his fingers.

'I'm just saying,' Anthony continued, his lips barely moving as he lowered his face towards me even more while slowly walking me back towards the bed, 'a strong and independent, feisty, curvy girl like yourself could make any man feel weak under the weight of your achievements, that's all.'

I slightly winced at his response; he was ploughing through all the Black women stereotypes this evening, wasn't he? I couldn't be bothered to acknowledge it at this point.

His hands slowly moved towards my bum then moved up the small of my back. Anthony definitely knew what he was doing, leaving me hungry for more. In my underwear I could feel how badly I wanted this to happen. I moved my face slowly towards his, and kissed him. Deeply. Passionately. I wasn't even feeling him like that, but there was something about this encounter that made me feel . . . I don't know . . . more desired than I had ever been before, which was annoying because his personality definitely gave me the ick. I knew Anthony found me attractive and I knew he wanted to sleep with me, and those were the only two important things I cared about right now.

Our tongues continued to explore each other hungrily as Anthony slowly rolled my dress up over my thighs and waist as I climbed onto the bed. I clumsily peeled my SKIMS bodysuit from my body and kicked it to the other side of the room before he had a chance to get involved. The thought of him trying to unroll my body out of the tightly packed Lycra was more than I could bear. Very unsexy.

Standing by the bed, Anthony took off his T-shirt, revealing the dense thicket of chest hair I'd accidentally fallen into the first time we met. It formed a slight love heart shape, with a landing strip leading down towards his pubic hair.

'Nicely rocking the seventies shag there I see.' I laughed, attempting to break the sexual tension. Anthony chuckled in response.

'I'm glad you appreciate the fuzz. I've always been a fan of hair on girls, too. I don't believe in the whole notion of women having to wax their pubes or whatever.' He shimmied out of his jeans and climbed onto the bed, hovering over me.

'Ah, well tonight you're getting the bald eagle special, I'm afraid,' I replied, pulling him closer for another kiss. The build-up was driving me wild – all I wanted right now was for him to be inside of me.

Anthony laughed at my response, sounding uncomfortable, but I decided not to question it further. We continued kissing, and I wrapped my legs around his torso as he unhooked my bra and started fondling my boobs with his hands and mouth.

'Jesus,' he mouthed intermittently, 'you are so fucking beautiful. I want you so badly.'

I could barely pay attention to a word he was saying. All my concerns went by the wayside, because Anthony seemed to know exactly where on my body to touch and lick and stroke. I was too deep in the throes of pleasure to reply. All I could do was moan to let him know I was enjoying what he was doing. I could feel him getting hard as he slowly made his way towards my belly, hands beginning to slip my panties off.

'Stunning,' he muttered again under his breath as I opened my legs slowly for him. He gently stroked my vulva while I used my hands to direct his head to where I wanted him. Anthony suddenly stopped and looked up at me, concerned.

'Um, I don't . . . I don't do that, by the way.' He looked at me apologetically as he made his way up towards me to kiss my mouth again.

Fucking come again?!

'Huh?' I replied, dumbfounded.

'I don't, err, I don't really like going down on women, to be honest. Oral sex has just never been my thing.'

I stared at him, perplexed, for a few moments. In the twenty-first century of our Lord and Saviour, we are still encountering men who don't enjoy giving oral sex? Jesus Christ. *CRIMSON FLAG #3!*

'What do you mean "never been your thing"? As in, you don't like to do it to someone you've just met for the first time? Or you only like doing it if you're in a relationship, kinda thing?'

Anthony went back to kissing in between my boobs, which annoyingly was a hotspot for me. I flopped back down on the bed and allowed him to continue, all the while processing this disturbing information.

'I've never really enjoyed it, it feels like a lot of work for no return,' Anthony replied in all his gall. I couldn't believe what I was hearing. I was all for bodily autonomy and freedom of choice when it comes to sex, but men who didn't give head were a waste of time as far as I was concerned, especially as I loved returning the favour. Men who brazenly admitted to purposely not wanting to please their women always gave me the supreme ICK, and I couldn't be convinced otherwise! How can someone even admit so openly to not doing it in this day and age? Did he not see what happened to DJ Khaled?

However, right there and then was not the time for debate, and I decided to ignore it, counting myself lucky to be getting any at all.

'Mmm. Well, OK, no worries,' I replied, filled with nothing but worries and agitation. From that moment on, my attitude had been activated, and I assumed that my pleasure would be capped at 40 per cent that night. That, however, did not turn out to be the case. After slipping on the condom, Anthony entered me slowly and proceeded to grind into me, matching my speed. I hated to admit it, but the man had rhythm, I can't lie. As much as I wanted to hate it, the intensity of his thrusts were telling me a different tale.

'God, you feel amazing, Artemis, wow.'

I know that's right.

He then rolled over so that he was on his back, taking me with him. OK, that shit was smooth. He didn't even strain as he propped me on top of him. I stared down at his face, instinctively cupping my breasts to keep him from seeing how saggy they were, but he slowly broke into a grin as he took my hands away.

'You don't have to hide them, babe, they're perfect.'

I blushed. He guided my hands down to his hips as he moved inside me again, and each thrust felt, frankly, incredible.

I started getting into the swing of things, matching his energy by steadily rocking back and forth as he watched me hungrily.

I closed my eyes as I continued; these thighs were getting a workout, for sure! I started thinking about Ruben and what he was probably up to. I couldn't believe how quickly things had progressed between us, even if it was just a friendship. (Though who was I kidding?) I missed talking to him already, and thought about giving him a text after I was done. God, I was such a slag. But needs were needs and I craved having a physical connection – so Anthony would have to do for now.

I thought about how good Ruben looked in his last couple of Instagram photos, bulging biceps strained and against a brilliant white V-neck tee, grey sweatpants (oh, he knew what he was doing!!) sagging semi-loosely against his legs, with me being able to trace the unmistakable outline of his peen-print because I was a perve looking for anything to get me going at that point. As Anthony thrust deeper and deeper, the images of Ruben became more visible in my mind's eye. I imagined that it was him inside of me instead of Anthony, and with that,

I grabbed Anthony's back, pulling him further into me as I could feel myself approaching climax. The dick at this point was lightly caressing my lungs. I moved my pelvis up slightly as I rocked in rhythm, wrapping my legs around him like a praying mantis to drive him into me even more. I continued picturing Ruben's face as my breathing quickened.

Dear reader: the dick was sensational.

And then it happened.

'Oh, shit, Ruben, I'm coming!' I yelled at the top of my lungs.

I heard an imaginary record scratch rip across my room. Anthony froze mid-thrust and looked down at me, confused.

'Who's Ruben?'

Temz, you absolute whore!

He lifted me off him and moved to sit on the edge of my bed, a thin yet awkward smile spread across his face. I traced his back, trying to come up with a feasible enough lie. A lone bead of sweat travelled down his spine from his neck, before landing in a splash on my bed sheet. A wave of guilt and panic spread over me as I thought about how to respond.

'Um, Ruben . . . Ruben Studdard. He's an old R&B singer from the early Naughts who sang sexy slow jams, and, um, I always imagine his music playing in the background whenever I'm getting intimate I guess, haha.'

Oh, Artemis, you absolute spin artist. I glanced up at Anthony, trying to gauge his response. I then quickly grabbed my phone, opened up Spotify and played one of Ruben Studdard's songs to solidify and validate the lie.

'See?' I muttered quickly, the shame vibrating through me in waves. 'He's a real singer! With real slow jams!'

Anthony continued surveying me, and then my phone. Finally, after what seemed like ten agonising minutes, he smiled but started putting his clothes back on.

'I must say, beautiful, that really did throw me a bit. I was wondering whether you said another dude's name in retaliation for me not going down on you or something.' He threw on his T-shirt and looked at me curiously, head cocked to the side. 'I'm sorry I couldn't finish, but, um, considering . . . you know.'

I covered my naked body with my bedsheets, feeling a wave of guilt and a sense of grim dissatisfaction. As much as I low-key wanted him to stay, a huge part of me also wanted him to leave so I could speak to Ruben.

'I'm so sorry; that's never really happened before and I'm not really sure why it happened then,' I lied. I wasn't sorry. 'Are you sure you don't wanna stay for a parting drink at least?'

By this point, Anthony had finished lacing up his shoes and was sitting on the edge of my bed again, looking at me in what felt almost like . . . pity? The imbalance of power in this moment was beginning to get to me. I didn't want him thinking I was some poor, pathetic woman who was struggling to get over an ex or some shit. I didn't want him to feel sorry for me when there was nothing to be sorry about. Anthony wrinkled up his nose and shook his head.

'Oh, Artemis. You're an interesting little sprite, aren't you?'

And with that, he CLIPPED MY NOSE like I was some kind of Victorian child chimney sweep who'd been caught stealing bread from the servants' quarters. I blinked, not knowing whether to laugh or start cussing.

'Yeah, erm. Sure? But don't do *that* again, it's incredibly patronising.'

'Oh, it's not like that – I think you're reading it wrong,' Anthony replied slickly, wolfish grin intact. 'Sorry if you took it that way though.'

The disgust on my face must have been super apparent, because he then continued:

'I think you're a fascinating woman, and up until that last part, I was having a great time with you. I would definitely like to see you again, but I'm going to need to get going now. Got stuff to do in the a.m.' With that, he picked up his phone and wallet, and gave me a short salute. 'I'll see myself out and, once again, it's been a pleasure.'

And with that, he disappeared. That was that, I supposed.

I decided to distract myself from my shame with Anthony by scrolling through Instagram for a while before going to bed. Aneni had uploaded a new IG Reel featuring her unboxing a brand new Chanel bag. No doubt one of the latest gifts from whichever Sugar Daddy she had been seeing that week. The hashtags included: #ChanelBag #BossBabe #PresentsfromBae #LondonStyle. This girl wanted to be an influencer by any means necessary. I 'liked' the Reel and continued scrolling and engaging in content of some of my favourite plant and horticulture brands, making mental notes to purchase some new seedlings and plants next week. I had a backlog of sponsored posts that I needed to write on my blog, as well as some video content, and was deciding on whether to start writing them that evening. My houseplants always found a way to soothe me, whether it was tending to them or writing about them. It was just something about being able to pour myself into something that would eventually grow and become beautiful that made tending to houseplants so therapeutic. Seeing as my maternal arse wasn't quite ready for a baby yet, houseplants were the next best thing. I walked over to my Fiddle Leaf Fig (Tamara) to tend to her leaves. Tamara was definitely a needy, messy plant that was all about the drama, and would shed her leaves at the drop of a hat. Too warm? Shed leaves. Too cool? Shed leaves. Too dry? Shed leaves. Too moist? Those leaves were gonna shed!

I sprayed a light mist of water on her stem, careful not to douse her in too much water as I softly wiped the debris and dust off the delicate leaves, an old Erykah Badu song on the tip of my tongue. I needed the world's biggest distraction right about now, and an evening of self-care, plant life and self-soothing sounded like just the thing.

But that's when I saw it.

Ruben had posted a photo that had been up for all of eighteen minutes. It was a simple picture. Nothing out of the ordinary or special from a layman's point of view – but I stared at the photo all the same, shock coming over me in waves. The image was of an aloe vera plant, seemingly placed in his kitchen. It was an absolute unit of a plant too, with its healthy, plump spear-headed leaves reaching up towards the heavens. Some rays of the filtered sunlight were bouncing off it, leaving a beautiful kaleidoscope of intricate shadows on the table. It was a gorgeous photo. The caption underneath simply read:

RubesCubes: Thinking about my Aloe.

Complete with one plant emoji and one green love heart emoji. In that moment, I could have sworn I felt my womb quicken. Before I could even digest the enormity of the photo, I stared at one of the names of the people who had liked the picture.

Liked by AneniLdn and 94 others

Aneni.
Et tu, Aneni??

Chapter 15

Six Years Earlier

'Look, Temz, I just don't see it happening, OK? We've already gone through this. It's over, man.'

'Amari, please,' I responded in annoyance. I gathered the bed-sheet under my arms to hide my nakedness. We'd been naked in front of each other many times, but there was something about post-break-up sex that ignited an extra bit of shame in my nudity. 'I'm not saying we should get back together, so hold your horses. I'm just saying, maybe we could talk things through and, like . . . I dunno, work on being friends again? Despite everything, we were always great friends first, and I don't wanna lose that.'

Amari quickly slid his boxers back on, his attention no longer on our conversation – a move he always pulled after sex that used to infuriate me. He wasn't the 'cuddle-after-making-love-until-we-both-fall-asleep' type, which was one of the reasons why we'd broken up a couple of months ago. That, and the fact that we both realised we were better as friends than lovers.

'I just think that now ain't really the right time to be talking about it, Temz,' Amari continued, his back turned to me as he continued tying his shoes. 'It's been over for a while now, and yeah . . . Maybe this shouldn't have happened, but can't we just chalk this up as having one last session for the road?'

Ew. The last thing I wanted was for this man to assume I wanted him back romantically. Don't get me wrong, the relationship was fine and all, but I was as happy about it ending as he was. We'd been together for a couple of years, and sometimes I wonder if our relationship was born out of boredom and loneliness more than anything else. Amari was lonely and in a low place at the time and so was I. It just seemed natural to go from friends to more at that point in time. Our relationship had since run its course, and we mutually agreed that it should end with no hard feelings.

Amari continued getting dressed as I reached for my bra. 'I mean, sure that's fine. Like I said, I'm not asking to get back together. I just don't want us to lose the friendship is all. This was just a one-off and maybe after a couple weeks or whatever after we've both had time to chill, we can be friends properly again.'

Amari looked down at me, his hands busy attempting to fluff out his teeny-weeny Afro that he'd been trying to grow out for years. I'd kept telling him to just shave it off, as it was a weird length and it made his head look tiny.

'Aight, I hear you,' Amari concluded after a moment. I breathed a shallow sigh of relief. Things didn't need to be more complicated than they had to be.

'We probably shouldn't do this again. But it was fun though, innit? Can you pass me my phone? It's behind you on the pillow.'

He turned around to finish fixing his hair in the mirror, and I reached for the phone behind me. On his screen I noticed a message sent to him thirteen minutes ago.

It was from Aneni.

The little blurb of text read:

Aneni: Hey hun, are you still at your dad's house? Let me know when you're free and I'll give you a call. Miss you already! xx

What the fucking fuck?! I reread the text again, making sure it was actually Aneni's number and not another chick called Aneni. I stared at the back of Amari's head as he smiled and glanced in my direction in the reflection of the mirror.

'Why the hell is Aneni texting you?' I said, taking deep breaths as I tried to control my temper. Amari turned around instantly and snatched his phone out of my hand.

'Why does she think you're at your dad's? Why does she "miss you"??'

In my head, I knew the answer, but I wanted to hear confirmation from him before going nuclear. *Aneni. My oldest friend.* My mind couldn't comprehend what I was seeing.

I got out of the bed and threw my clothes on, waiting for an answer. After swiftly putting the phone in his pocket, he held up his hands defensively.

'You guys have been sleeping together, haven't you? While we were together? Answer me!' I tried as much as possible to keep my voice from shaking.

'No . . . no! I swear! Look, Temz I swear down, we— it was just— look, I'm sorry you had to see that. I really fucking am. It was nothing, I promise you.'

It wasn't until I suddenly gulped that I realised that I had been holding my breath.

'I mean . . . it's clearly something if she's saying how much she misses you though, isn't it? We've only been broken up for two months, bro. Are you moving on to her now? Is she the one you secretly wanted all along then?'

'NO, Temz, look . . . be real. Two months is kind of a long time, innit? We both need to move on. She messaged me last week to ask me about some work stuff and we just . . . started talkin. I swear, it was just a one-time thing, a mistake. I shouldn't have entertained it.'

It was almost as if I could hear my heartbeat in the middle of my brain; every heartbeat became louder and louder until it was all I could hear.

Granted, I wasn't falling over in tears when I told her that me and Amari had broken up, but that didn't mean that it didn't still hurt. I would never have done this with one of *her* exes.

'When did you see her?' I finally replied.

'Umm, like two days ago,' Amari replied.

TWO DAYS?!

'OK,' I replied coolly. I drew in a breath. 'And did you guys sleep together?'

Amari shifted on the spot uncomfortably.

'Um . . . Yeah.'

Wow. This one moved on quickly.

'You are such a fucking lizard, Amari. Two days? TWO DAYS? Sleeping with my best friend, and then me again? I want you to leave now. Like . . . do you not even feel embarrassed? Just go, man.'

I didn't care to hear his excuses at that point, I just needed him to exit my atmosphere post-haste. I needed to think. I was angry, but not necessarily because he had slept with someone else so much as because it was with my *best friend*, one of the people who's supposed to know me better than anyone. Had she been plotting this the whole time? Had I offended her in some way? What would possess her to even cross that line?

I needed answers.

A few hours passed as I seethed.

I looked at my phone, trying to decide how I would confront Aneni. I didn't particularly want to speak to her or meet up with her in person. She'd just use her smooth talking and gift of the gab to reel me in, and I couldn't have that. Texting would have to do for now.

I opened up my messages and typed Aneni's name.

> **Me:** Aneni. Are you actually sick? Do you have some hidden beef with me that I know nothing about? I know about you and A. Don't try to deny it either, Amari's already confessed.

Minutes later, a response:

> **Aneni:** Umm. Do you think this is a discussion we should be having over text, hun? I'll call you and we can talk this out! Xx

Seconds later, my phone started to ring, but I rejected the call.

> **Me:** I don't wanna talk on the phone. Just tell me why, Aneni? Why would you do this to me? Do you hate me? Have I wronged you? I don't wanna hear you try and talk your way out of this like you talk your way out of everything else.

I could see Aneni beginning to type in the text box, with frequent pauses in between. As far as I was concerned, I was done. In my head I was preparing to construct a friendship break-up text of epic proportions when her response eventually came through:

> **Aneni:** Fair enough, I can sense you're upset. I promise you, babe, it wasn't anything malicious AT ALL. I was just asking him about a work referral thing he said he'd do for me, and he invited me round his. I swear down for most of the evening we were just talking about you and how amazing you are! Then we'd both had a bit to drink and we were a little tipsy, and I guess one thing led to another. I promise you, Temz, I was in no way trying to hurt you, and I was going to tell you this week because I've felt awful and—

I stopped scrolling at this point because I'd read all I needed to read. She felt 'awful'?!

I typed:

Me: Not awful enough not to still be texting him and telling him that you missed him, though? You're hilarious. I can't talk to you right now.

I lasted two weeks without speaking to her before Aneni sent me a bouquet of flowers, bought me a pair of £300 Axel Arigato Marathon trainers I'd had my eye on for over a year, and a twelve-minute video apology.

I eventually caved. Aneni always knew how to rope me back in.

Chapter 16

Present

'Bitch, CALM DOWN and start from the top! Lidl Momoa didn't want to lick Aneni's what??'

I exhaled sharply as I paced up and down my kitchen. It had just gone midnight and I was wearing nothing but that evening's underwear and an oversized Mr Blobby motif T-shirt, trying to control my sheer rage and low-key terror. Aneni was *not* going to be the cause of my downfall. Not today. I took a deep inhale and retold the story to Jean over the phone once again. As annoyed as I was with the situation, I could always make time for piping hot TEA.

'Jean, STAY WITH ME, OK?? Also, first of all, "Lidl Momoa"? Hilarious. Basically, Anthony and I slept together but he said he doesn't go down on women, which in this day and age is like . . . Who doesn't do that? My vagina started to shrivel up like a raisin in the sun after that, *but* then he really got into it in other ways, and . . . The stroke game turned out to be magnificent, honestly.'

Jean sighed.

'OK, so after he refused to go down on you – hold on, I hope YOU didn't go down on him, by the way??' Jean replied.

'Absolutely not! I'm not a dickhead,' I scoffed, aching to get to the new Aneni development with Ruben.

'OK, OK,' Jean said. 'So, y'all were fucking and then you accidentally screamed out Ruben's name? Oh, Artemis, you're an absolute whore of Babylon and I NEED you to acknowledge this – and I'm not judging by the way. I'm *living* for you doing that!'

I half-smiled at his comment. As good as it was, whether I saw Anthony again or not wasn't as much of a concern to me; I'd sampled what I'd needed to sample, and outside of the 'me-shouting-out-Ruben's-name-and-lying-about-who-it-was' thing, the sex was pretty mind-blowing. But it couldn't happen again. Right? We move.

'Haha, I knew you would like that part,' I replied. 'But anyway, so after Anthony left, I went on Ruben's IG page and saw his latest post. Mate – he's uploaded a picture of an aloe vera plant with the caption "thinking about my Aloe"!!'

There was a brief silence from Jean as I waited to hear this reaction.

'And I'm supposed to be excited about this because . . . ?'

My best friend was being very useless here.

'Nah, Jean, don't par me off, please?' I barked, annoyed at having to drip-feed the revelation to him. 'What's my plant IG username? Where did me and Ruben start chatting?' I said, begging him to connect the dots.

'OHHHHH! SAY ALOE TO MY LITTLE FRIEND!! Oh, shit! Well, that means . . . I mean he's talking about you, right? You guys have been hitting it off lately, moving to WhatsApp and all that? Whew!'

He was right – we have been hitting it off. I was pretty much ready to believe that Ruben may also like me, too. Maybe I was fully leaning into my delusional girl era with open arms, but it could be true.

'I mean, I *think* he's referring to me, but who knows? Anyway, that's not the biggest gag! The gaggery of it all is that fucking *Nenz* has started following him and started liking his posts. Like, what the fuck is she doing, Jean?'

In my head, all I could think about was Aneni potentially sliding into Ruben's DMs. How on earth did she even find him? Have *they* spoken, too? How would I confront her about it? And most importantly – has she told Ruben anything about me?

After seeing Aneni's 'like' on Ruben's post, I went through about twenty of Ruben's latest photos, only to find that Aneni had liked and commented on them all. The suppressed rage I thought I'd managed to lay to rest regarding Aneni and her proclivity for inserting herself in my situations had risen to the surface almost instantly. I had had half a mind to call or text her and drag her for filth, but thought better of it and so I'd called Jean instead for a rant. Would this be the event that finally ended my friendship with her? Only time would tell . . .

'Sis, I've been trying to tell you about her,' Jean replied softly, albeit matter-of-factly. To his credit, he *had* been trying to tell me about her raggedy ways for a while now – ever since he found out about the incident between her and my ex. I was the stupid one for constantly trying to give her the benefit of the doubt, and now it was coming back to bite me in the butt.

'I know, I know. I'm seeing her next week, so I'm going to wait and bring it up with her then. I think it's better face-to-face. I just don't understand why she does these things? I have nothing for her to be jealous or territorial about. Throughout our friendship I've ALWAYS been considered the "ugly" one. Why can she not just let me be ugly in peace??'

'Artemis, if I slap you across your fucking face, you'll know I'm doing it with love,' Jean snapped immediately. I knew he hated it when I spoke down about myself. 'You're a bombshell and we all know it. In fact, I low-key think that part of the reason why Aneni hates me is because I've slept with you and haven't shown any interest in her whatsoever. Now that we're able to speak frankly? She can choke for all I care. I think you should definitely ask her about it, and also tell her how you feel about Ruben, too. And while you're at it, tell *Ruben* that you like him already. I'm confused as to why you haven't made that move yet.' He pauses. 'Well, I mean, I can think of one reason – can we talk about the fact that this man lives thousands of miles away? Like, have you made any plans to see each other at some point, or talked about how this situation could work?'

I couldn't tell my best friend that the reason I hadn't made my move on Ruben or discussed visiting plans was because I was catfishing him. I knew Jean's concerns were valid, and in an alternative universe I would be thinking about the logistical prospects of a long-distance relationship, but I couldn't think about all that now; it wasn't relevant to the current situation. I had to get to Aneni first before I quizzed Ruben about anything. I couldn't risk her accidentally (or purposely, if I'm being honest) revealing the truth about me to him.

I also didn't really feel like talking to Jean about my little indiscretion right now. The humiliation of it all would be enough to tip me over the edge and, if I was being real with myself, I quite liked the fact that I had my own little semi-secret that I could keep all to myself. A little bubble where I could imagine myself as the heroine of my own story, looking the way I thought I was supposed to look and having the man of my dreams.

As kids in secondary school, me, Aneni and the other girls would always fantasise about having American boyfriends who resembled guys like Morris Chestnut, Lil' Romeo and – God forbid – Raz-B from B2K, and even though they were just the childish fantasies of thirteen-year-olds who didn't know any better; with Ruben it felt like it could actually become a possibility – albeit virtually.

I wasn't prepared to allow Aneni to ruin this for me.

After my call with Jean, I spent the rest of the super eventful night scrolling through Aneni's Instagram, looking to see whether Ruben had engaged in any of her photos. He'd 'liked' four of them. No comments though. *Fuck.*

It was currently a little bit after 4 p.m. in Oakland right now. Should I call Ruben out of the blue? What if Aneni had started messaging him and somehow mentioned me? What if he went to scroll through Aneni's friend list, spotted the Aloe page and started asking Aneni questions about me? Could he potentially put two and two together?

It could also be the case that I was severely overthinking the situation. I sometimes have a tendency for flights of fancy; something I owned and accepted fully. A true #DelusionalBabe.

Halfway through my Instagram stalking, a message from Anthony (although I now preferred his alternative moniker of 'Lidl Momoa') came through:

> **Anthony: Beautiful Artemis. I had a great time with you earlier, and despite the little hiccup towards the end lol, you were amazing. ☺ If you're ever free in the coming couple of weeks, I'd love to hang out again. Night night, Tony xx**
>
> **PS: I looked up that Ruben Studdard fella's music too. Did you know he was on *American Idol*? I didn't even know that show was still a thing! He has a smooth voice, I can see why you'd shout his name while in the throes of ecstasy. You strange little one. ☺**

I scratched my head in confusion. Any other guy would have run for the hills, but for some reason Anthony was still super keen. He was either very whipped, very desperate or very strange.

As much as I felt grateful that Anthony had allowed me a bit of grace for what happened earlier, I still wasn't sure at this point whether he was someone I envisioned myself seeing again. I mean, the dick was sensational, let me not lie, but . . . eh.

I'd been having a Lonely Girl Summer for the last two years now, intermittently getting laid every now and again, and it had been fun – but something was always missing. Although it had been difficult to acknowledge for a while, deep down I knew that I was ready to be in a relationship again. It just had to be the right one.

I replied to Anthony's message:

Me: I appreciate you for looking past the whole Ruben Studdard thing; it won't happen again haha! I'll let you know when I'm free; it would be great to hang out again. Maybe it'll give me the opportunity to give a better second impression. ☺ Until we meet again, have a great rest of your weekend x

I shamefully bowed my head and scratched the nape of my neck as I hit 'send'.

Hey. Dick is still dick, right? My diaphragm is still trying to recover.

Chapter 17

I should have been excited about starting a new week in my brand-new role of director. It was going to take a few days to transition into the position with the admin changes and all that jazz, but really all I could think about was Ruben and Aneni. I'd spent most of Sunday cosplaying as an investigative journalist, flitting between Ruben and Aneni's Instagram pages looking for clues while being consoled by Jean, who made it a point to keep telling me that nothing was going on between the two of them, but what did he know? He wasn't the one at risk of having his lies thrown back in his face.

After I'd replied to Anthony the other day, I sent Ruben a quick text to see how he was doing to gauge his mood. He'd seen the message three minutes later, but left me on 'read'. I didn't sleep that whole night because I was convinced that Aneni had probably let slip that she knew the real me, or worse, was flirting with him. As of this morning, Ruben still hadn't replied, and I was shitting an absolute brick. What a mess.

Ever the one to clutch at straws, however, I'd seen that his 'Aloe' IG post was still live on his page. Surely if someone had just found out that the person they'd been talking to was catfishing them, they'd delete any reference made to them online, right?

This morning, I'd texted Aneni.

Me: Looking forward to seeing you tomorrow. Shall we meet at Sheila's Cafe in Vauxhall?

I'd decided that I was going to use our catch-up drinks as a way to low-key mine her for information regarding Ruben.

My new role meant that I'd had to move to a different floor, leaving my beloved Claudia and all my other colleagues. This floor had a fancy little kitchenette complete with hot drink-making facilities, and even little free snacks (but they were all healthy, so I wasn't really interested in all that). I was at the coffee-maker absent-mindedly brewing a cappuccino while looking into the distance when I got a reply from Aneni:

Aneni: Sounds good to me. See you tomoz hun x

Tomorrow couldn't come soon enough.

I went back to my desk and spent the morning answering emails, meeting a few other C-suite staff members and preparing my brainstorming session for Maranette Clothing, whose account I would now be in charge of with some support from Stephen at first. It would be my first meeting as one of the big bosses, and I was keen to impress. I'd opted for a mustard-yellow suit: tapered cigarette pants with a white sleeveless tee, complete with the matching oversized boxy blazer thrown over my shoulders. To keep things slightly more casual, I paired the look with my favourite white polka-dot high-top Converse trainers.

At 10.45 a.m., I picked up my laptop and made my way towards Boardroom B to set up and have a last-minute run-through with Stephen before the rest of the team and the client came in for 11 a.m.

'How are you feeling about the meeting then, Artemis?' Stephen asked as I loaded up the presentation on the projector.

'I actually feel OK, to be honest,' I replied, trying to sound as confident as possible even though deep down I felt like crying and throwing up. 'I think the guys downstairs have done a brilliant job with the creative, and I'm looking forward to seeing what Maranette thinks.'

Stephen nodded, face beaming like a proud parent watching their kid's first day at school. 'Wonderful! That's what I like to hear. Remember I'm only here for emotional support. I'll be in the corner if you need me, but I think you're going to absolutely smash it.'

'Thank you so much, Stephen, I appreciate you!' I said, beaming back at him. Despite all his little quirks and annoyances, I was grateful to Stephen for always championing me, and for being quick to hear my ideas and letting me voice my thoughts on projects. He was one of the few seniors who worked here that actually liked to hear the thoughts of others as opposed to loving the sound of his own voice. It was refreshing to have that kind of support every now and again.

Minutes later, Claudia and the rest of my team, alongside Maranette Clothing, began to file into the boardroom. I internally went through my opening speech. I could feel the water I'd drunk earlier now fighting for its freedom within the pits of my bladder, but I had to hold it together until after the meeting was over. I was in control. I had this. I was confident. I was smart! I was in control. *Control it, Temz.* I knew the client inside and out, and I was going to fucking smash it.

'Welcome, everyone! I hope you've all had awesome weekends, and thank you so much for coming in today,' I started. So far, so good. 'For those who don't know, I was recently made director, so moving forward you'll be in direct comms with me, which I'm really excited about.' This last sentence was met with applause around the room, to my surprise. Oh, I could get used to this.

'So, I thought we could pick up where we left off last week regarding our reputation overhaul for Maranette. As we discussed via email, we'll be combating this with a multi-level strategy to ensure maximum impact. This includes fresh new content that is not only interactive and visually appealing, but is also informative and can speak to the individual consumer in a way that is more . . . socially aware.'

'So basically, you want the brand to be more woke?' a voice from the back of the room piped up, interrupting my flow. I looked up to see one of the members of the Maranette team I hadn't met before. A short, balding man who was probably twice my age and twice as pissed off that he had a thirty-year-old telling him what to do. *There's always one.*

'Um, no, I wouldn't use the term "woke" per se? More . . . socially aware. Sensitive, fair and democratic towards certain social issues that may come up within general online and in-person discourse. We don't want a repeat of the mass cancellation of the brand online again, do we?' I retorted, keen to get back to where I was. This wasn't the fucking Q&A part of the meeting, Darren, or whatever the male version of a 'Karen' was.

'As I was saying,' I continued, looking straight at Darren-RealNamePending, daring him to pipe up again, 'we want to hit this campaign with a multi-pronged approach, and that will include working with the content teams to create better press releases and social media copy for both the traditional media and digital platforms, upping our spend on paid media and SEO for the next four seasonal collections that come out, and also putting aside some of the budget in order to work with influencers on social media campaigns – we can utilise their social media followers to create more awareness of new-and-improved Maranette, as well as collaborate with plus-size influencers and designers specifically to create a small collection.'

'Uhh, we don't work with influencers. It's not a part of our business model, and I'd like to think that we've been quite successful as a brand so far without it,' DarrenTheKaren piped up again without raising his hand or indicating that he'd like to speak. The whole room looked at him and then back to me to see whether I would reply. It was turning into some weird game of tennis, with this bloke determined to undermine my suggestions at every turn.

'With all due respect, and as I mentioned in the pitch meeting previously, one of the main criticisms of the brand has included not being as diverse as they could be when it comes to offering more inclusive sizing within the collections,' I replied, fighting every urge in my body to start cussing him out in front of everybody. 'If we want to show the customers that we care about their style, their perspectives, their thoughts and how they express themselves through fashion, we have to go above and beyond and actually talk the talk. Show them that *all* bodies are worthy of being included when it comes to style. Show them that we want to do more than just apologise for our previous indiscretions. The actions you take with the brand moving forward will be pivotal, and they have to mean something outside of being performative, because guess what? Consumers can smell dishonesty from a mile away. These days, you can't get away with an IG apology post and not expect to act on your words. Working with influencers isn't just a huge way to promote awareness of the brand, but it's also proven to be much cheaper than traditional PR campaigns. I definitely think it's worth a shot.'

With that, I pulled up my various graphs and charts and continued my presentation, every now and again purposely standing in front of the Darren guy just to annoy him. A brief look around the room told me that everyone – especially the clients – seemed impressed with what I was serving.

'Thank you so much, everyone, I'm now going to pass it to Claudia, our new head of content, to fill you in on our digital outreach strategies for the first quarter of next year, alongside a robust content plan.' I winked at Claudia as I went to sit down next to Stephen at the back of the room.

'Stephen, who is that guy that kept interrupting me?' I whispered softly.

'Yeah, I'm sorry about that. That's Kevin – one of the content leads for Maranette. He's been working there for twenty years, almost a part of the furniture. Resistant to change,' Stephen replied, sounding almost as exasperated as I felt. 'I'll have a word with him after the meeting about that.'

Kevin. Mm. I should have guessed he'd have an old-ass name like that. If I was going to prove myself in this new role, I knew that I needed to confront him myself instead of having Stephen fight my battles for me.

'Actually, thanks, but I think I'll have a chat with him myself, actually. I want him to know who he's dealing with,' I whispered back, chuckling at the end to let him think I was speaking in jest. I absolutely wasn't.

After the presentations, my team, Stephen and the Maranette team had a couple of minutes to debrief and take in some refreshments. Claudia caught my eye and walked briskly over. I could already sense what she was thinking before she uttered a word.

'What the fuck was that?' she mouthed silently, directing a slight nod in Kevin's direction. I rolled my eyes in response.

'Girl, I know. I'm gonna have a chat with him. I don't care how long he's been with the company, or how old he is. He's gonna learn how to put some respect on my name. You were also magnificent with your presentation, by the way – well done! I knew you'd smash it!' I said the latter part a little louder so it didn't look to others like we were just cooped up in the corner throwing shade, which is what me and Clauds did most times we got together.

A few moments later, after spying Kevin sitting on his own near the alcove in the meeting room, I gave Claudia a quick hug and made my way towards him. He was perched on a couch nursing his drink and reading a copy of *Campaign* magazine, looking a bit pissed off. He had big, round glasses to match his round face, complete with a cul-de-sac hairline and a physique that reminded me of the Penguin from the *Batman Returns* movie.

'I hope you don't mind me sliding in here,' I said as I shimmied my way onto the couch next to him. Kevin didn't raise his head or react in any way. Bastard. 'Actually, I wanted to have a word with you, if that's OK? About my presentation?' At this, Kevin proceeded to make a grand gesture of folding his magazine in half, puffing his chest, removing his glasses and peering over at me.

'What about it?'

OK! The sass was strong in this one. If he wanted to get froggy, all he had to do was leap and I would do the same. I wanted to match his energy, put the stereotype of the 'Angry Black Woman' to good use. #MakeRacismWorkForYou! However, I knew that I had to tread carefully and apply some tact here. Given that Kevin was a senior member of the Maranette team, I didn't want to risk upsetting the brand or risking our retainer.

'Well, I appreciate you letting me know your concerns about the project. I wanted to let you know that I have every intention of creating the perfect campaign for the brand, and to make you all proud. I have proven experience of working with influencers on campaigns and, at present, ten of the twelve advertising campaigns I've directed have gone viral, not only online, but within the traditional press as well. I'm absolutely open to collaborative ideas and for hearing your views on what you think could work for this project, too, though!' I smiled sweetly as Kevin stared at me blankly, no doubt contemplating how he was going to respond. The air around us grew awkward as I waited.

'I'm aware of your previous work and accolades,' he responded coldly. 'And I appreciate some of your ideas. I am just keen to make sure that we keep some of the traditional PR themes running within the campaign, as they are tried, tested and proven. I've been doing this job at Maranette for fifteen years now and they haven't failed me once. I'll send you a previous deck of mine when I get back to the office so you can see how we do things.'

'Great!' What an arrogant prick. 'Well . . . thanks,' I muttered politely, trying as much as possible to eradicate all irritation from my face. 'I'll be sure to try and take on board feedback where I can.' It took everything in me to not add '*CAPEESH?*' at the end for dramatic effect. Jean would have been so proud of me.

*Note to self: relay entire conversation to Jean, adding in the '*capeesh*' part. Also relay conversation to Ruben, adding in the 'I looked sexy and authoritative, yet calm as hell' part.*

With that, I got up and sauntered out of the room, giving it my best strut. I caught the eyes of Stephen, who gave me a discreet nod and smile, and Claudia, who gave me a look as if to say, 'Bitch we are gonna talk about this later on Slack.'

Filled with newfound confidence after holding my first-ever strategy meeting as a director, I went back to my shiny new office to catch up on work for the rest of the day. I'd taken to this new role like a duck to water, and even though I was still in my first week, I could already feel myself smashing it. Funnily enough, taking more of a supervisory and business development role meant that I had a bit more free time than normal. This time, thanks to said shiny new *private* office, I could browse the internet and IG in peace without having to worry about people watching over my shoulder. It was bliss!

After I'd finished all of the important work essentials, I decided to take my lunch break in the office to catch up on my own personal housekeeping:

- Upload new plant content to the IG page
- Start looking at new one-bedroom flats
- Buy more suits!!
- Browse furniture for new home!!

Excitingly, I'd also received an email from a huge plantcare company requesting a collaboration with my Aloe Instagram account; they wanted me to film a one-minute 'Repot My Monstera with Me' video featuring their soil mix, and would pay me a *grand*. I couldn't believe that the hard work and dedication I'd been putting into my plants and the content on my IG was finally beginning to pay off. I was stepping into the realm of being a 'proper' micro-influencer, getting paid for doing what I loved. It felt amazing. This is what Aneni felt like on an everyday basis.

I was being ambitious, but the growth of my side hustle alongside this new role with a nice little pay increase had lit a fire up my butt to get my shit together. I needed to concentrate on making moves elsewhere in my life to distract from the chaos that my *love* life had recently become. I needed to start manifesting shit. I had a 'Moving Out' savings fund I'd started a couple of years ago, the week after I'd moved in with Natalie. I now had enough money in it to keep me going rent-wise for at least six months in a new place, so my plan was to book a few flat viewings, give my notice to Natalie and get the ball rolling. I had thirty-two flat rental tabs open to browse through, and in the next few months or so my broad plan was to be living my best bachelorette life in some gorgeous one-bedroom apartment overlooking the Thames with a balcony and an island in the kitchen. I was excited.

Ugh, Artemis, you absolute boss!

Ten minutes into browsing for flats, my WhatsApp notification sound went off. I briefly glanced at my phone and read the message preview.

And in an instant, my blood ran cold and I was frozen to the spot.

Ruben: Hey Aloe, sorry for not getting back earlier. We need to talk.

'We need to talk'?

Oh, Aneni. What have you done?

Chapter 18

The rest of the day was a blur. I switched to auto mode as I wrapped up meetings and finished research for various prospective clients. Physically I was present; mentally, my mind had been spending most of the morning trying to construct a story (read: justification/~~lie~~?) to tell Ruben. I didn't want him to know that I'd read his message, so I'd kept my phone on 'Do Not Disturb' for most of the day. When someone sends a message saying, 'We need to talk,' you know it's going to be bad.

Fucking hell.

I zoned out during the journey back home, fretting about the upcoming conversation that needed to be had. I listened to one of my all-time favourite songs, 'Stormy Weather' by Etta James, as I stared morosely out of the overground train window, my mind grasping at straws. Part of me knew that I was overthinking things, but the other, more neurotic part of me had already taken over.

As soon as I arrived home, I grabbed a bottle of water from the fridge and went straight to my room, locking the door for extra privacy in case Natalie tried to barge in. I changed out of my work clothes, then decided to try and distract myself by creating the video content for the plant brand. I lunged to pick up the huge Monstera whose repotting was way past due and set it down opposite my window where it would get the best lighting. After carefully positioning my phone camera on its tripod to frame the scene, I clicked 'record' and I made sure to keep the framing tight, only concentrating on the plant and wearing long gardening gloves in case Ruben happened to see the video and wondered why Aloe had all of a sudden developed a deep tan.

As I started the process of carefully digging around the sides of the soil to loosen the plant from its pot, there was silence as the dry soil fell into the plastic bag I'd laid on the floor. After some gentle nudging, the plant and its roots were free. I laid the Monstera on the bag, picked up the new bag of soil and showed it to the camera, ripping open its contents and allowing my hands to gently cascade through the thick, rich earth. I gently poured the soil into a new, bigger pot, and added some shop-bought worm castings to fertilise the soil.

Then I picked up the Monstera, trimming off some of its longest roots to stop it from growing any bigger, and gently laid the plant into the soil. I finished off by adding some more soil on top to stabilise the plant, and then gave it a thorough watering. Taking my gloves off, I picked up my camera and took several close-up shots of the soil, the leaves, and the full frame of the plant, feeling proud of my work. I would add a voiceover to the content later on before sending it through to the client.

There was something so calming and enriching about being one with earth. Growing and moulding new life had always felt so grounding for me, and at that moment, being one with my plant was exactly what I'd needed to calm myself down to prepare for this damn phone call.

I quickly washed my hands and changed into an old tracksuit. If I was about to get exposed, I wanted to feel comfortable while it was happening. *Breathe, Artemis.* I quickly checked the time to see whether it was appropriate for me to call: 10.45 a.m, Ruben's time. I figured that would be OK. I went into my WhatsApp, found his name and pressed 'call' before I could chicken out.

It rang for what felt like hours, but truthfully only probably around twenty-five seconds or so. With each ring, I contemplated just hanging up, blocking him and pretending like this whole affair hadn't happened in the first place. Just as I was about to put the phone down, Ruben picked up on the 234th ring.

'Good morning, babygirl.'

If I weren't feeling so tense about the upcoming conversation at hand, I would have creamed myself right then and there. It sounded like he'd just woken up, so his voice was all deep and croaky and sexy-like. This man had definitely talked himself into some knickers before, my goodness. I let the ghosts of his last words penetrate my eardrums for a couple of seconds before I responded.

'Hey! I'm sorry if I woke you – I've just seen your message so I thought I'd give you a call instead of us texting it out. Is everything OK? What happened?'

Not me pretending like I don't know what was going on. Where the hell was my Academy Award?

'Nah, not at all, you called at the right time anyway. I needed to get my ass up for a meeting I got in a couple hours. Um, thanks for calling. It's great to hear your voice again.' *It's great to hear your voice again?* Hmm. That's not something a man who'd just found out he'd been catfished would normally say. I gripped the phone harder, but felt my anxiety decrease a little bit. Maybe I wasn't in trouble after all.

'Why thank you! It's always great to hear your voice too. I know you said you've been busy lately. I've missed our little daily chats.' The tension was killing me, but I knew I had to keep level-headed and sound as calm as possible. I hated not being in control of a situation.

'I've missed you too, but I'm sure you already knew that with the aloe vera plant I posted the other day, huh?'

So it WAS about me. We had confirmation! My heart began to pound harder, and the butterflies that had been lying dormant in my stomach began to slowly stir again. Is this what it felt like to have someone think about and miss you? But I knew I wasn't out of the woods yet.

'Oh, Ruben, you are such a sweetheart! I did see it, but I didn't wanna assume anything, you know?' I gushed, still trying to sound in control but failing fast.

'I mean, it kinda surprised me too, I guess,' he replied. 'I was at the garden store the other day and saw it, and it just reminded me of you so I picked it up.'

My heart was thudding at a million beats a minute; is this what American men were capable of? I briefly thought of the old adage: 'If a man wanted to, he would,' and smiled to myself. I had missed this feeling.

'Um, so . . .' he continued, 'apologies if my message came off a bit serious, I was half asleep when I sent it. Um . . . I mean I'm not really sure how to say it, so I'ma just say it.'

This guy was talking in riddles. Was he going to expose me or nah? This felt like it was taking a completely different turn.

'I mean, take your time ba—'

'I like you. A lot,' Ruben interjected. There was silence for about fifteen seconds, but all I could hear through the phone was a heavenly gospel choir singing in the background as I began to spiritually ascend. I had been dreaming about someone like Ruben saying those magic words to me my whole life. All those daydreams I would have as a teenager, fantasising about having an ideal Morris Chestnut-looking man was coming to fruition.

While in my almost catatonic state, I hadn't noticed that Ruben was talking again.

'. . . know we've been talking for a while, and even though we haven't met yet I can't stop thinking about you. There's something that's super mysterious about you that I really wanna get to find out about, you know? I haven't liked someone in so long so when I realised that I was slowly getting a lil crush, it threw me off a bit. It feels . . . nice?'

I snapped out of my bubble and returned to the call – because there was still the minor glitch of me pretending to be someone else. As much as I wanted to fully embrace this moment, I knew that deep down I couldn't. I'd gone too far, and now he'd caught feelings for someone who wasn't really me.

Yet the only thing I could do in this moment was to continue the lie.

'Ruben . . . I don't know what to say! This was definitely the last thing I expected to hear, but I do really like you, too. I think you're awesome, and I love how easy it is to talk to ya and um . . . yeah!' I clearly didn't have much practice navigating these conversations. 'Have you ever liked someone you met online before?' I asked, attempting to deflect from how fucking awkward I was being.

'I can't say I have, no. It's weird, I know, but I'm happy to roll with it if you are? I'd love to come to the UK one day and take you out or something.'

If we lived in an ideal world where I hadn't resorted to catfishing, I would have liked that for me too, Ruben . . .

We then spent the next hour on the phone talking, debating and sending each other photos. At this point, I'd kept a full stack of freshly updated photos and screen recording-videos of Chantelle in a folder on my phone, just in case. After a while I started to relax into our back-and-forth, remembering how much I liked him.

Me: 'So when did you realise you liked me then? Enquiring minds would like to know.'

Ruben: 'Hmm. Maybe like a couple weeks ago when you tried to do an American accent and failed miserably? Although I'm still tryna decide if it's what made me like you, or pity you.'

Me: 'Oh, whatever. We both know I was brilliant! I guess I haven't really been the best at hiding the fact that I like you. Subtlety is not my speciality.'

Ruben: 'Well, duh, Ms "I bet your *girlfriend* would be so proud of you!".'

Me: 'I said what I said!'

Ruben: 'You got an aloe vera plant too, right? I think I saw it on your page?'

Me: 'Sure do! Her name's Ama. I've had her for about five years or so. They are so easy to look after, love her!'

Ruben: '"Ama"? That's such a pretty name. What does it mean?'

Me: 'It's a name given to a girl who was born on a Saturday. In Ghana, we have traditional names that we get given depending on what day we're born. So my Ghanaian name is "Abena", meaning "girl born on a Tuesday".'

Ruben: 'Oh, that's lit! I love that, and I've always wanted to go to Ghana, too! I ended up doing a 23andMe DNA test and found out I'm 35 per cent Ghanaian Ashanti, so it would be hella cool to visit the Motherland. What would my Ghanaian name be? I was born on Friday.'

Me: 'You're Ghanaian too?! Oh, wow, well this just keeps getting better and better, doesn't it? You're essentially family at this point!'

Ruben: 'Uh, let's hold our horses now. I don't wanna be having lustful thoughts about any "family" members and shit!'

Me: 'Ha! True, true. OK, so your Ghanaian name would be "Kofi", seeing as you're a Friday born.'

Ruben: 'Kofi. So you pronounced it like "coffee", right? I love that.'

Me: 'Kinda! You need to add more emphasis on the "fi" part. So it's kinda pronounced "Koh-fi" phonetically.'

Ruben: '"Koh-fi". I love it. Here's hoping you can teach me more of our shared heritage, Abena.'

Me: *dies inside*

Me: 'Something I wanted to ask a few weeks ago actually: why tech? You're so talented and you have such a gorgeous voice, why did you go down the tech route?'

Ruben: 'Aww thank you, ma! To put it plain and simply? For money, haha. A guy needs something stable to fund his creative hobbies, after all. But um, I've always loved computers and coding and I was a lot of a nerd as a kid, so it seemed natural for me to go into it. Didn't like the thought of being an employee, so I set up my own freelance thing and it's been going well so far.'

Me: 'That's so inspiring! Wait, hacking isn't one of your specialities, is it? Do I need to be on high alert?' *only half-joking*

Ruben: 'Nah, I don't do the hacking shit. I consult with companies and brands mostly, and then I do a little website coding on the side. It's a good gig. I enjoy what I do, and I make a decent living.'

Me: 'How decent we talking?'

Ruben: 'What's it to you, gold-digger?'

Me: 'Um, because if this relationship is going to work, we both need to be bringing in the bacon, babes.'

Ruben: 'I mean I do aight. It's a nice six-figure situation.'

Me: 'I see. Excuse me while I book a ticket to Oakland. We're officially together now.'

Ruben: 'HAHAHA you fucking gold-digging hussy.'

Me: 'Please. I'm just a girl!'

Ruben: 'So . . . Aloe. How would you describe your ideal man?'

Me: 'HA. Why'd you have to ask that like some sleazy dating chat show host? And besides . . . I'm talking to my ideal man right now . . .'

Ruben: 'Oh, you're slick with it! That's another thing I really like about you. You have this confidence and sass that's so . . . alluring. I love confident women who know what they want, and you strike me as someone who's exactly like that. It's sexy.'

Me: 'That's me! Look up "sexy" in the dictionary and you'll find a photo of me looking sexy as hell, just emanating pure sex appeal. Yup.'

Ruben. 'Yeah . . . you're also awkward as hell. I love it.'

Me: 'I'm not awkward. I'm sexy.'

Ruben: 'Uhhuh. Speaking of, I'd love to see more of you – wait, not in a nudes kinda way, just more of your face. I wanna build a picture of you in my head.'

Me: 'Umm . . . Yeah, sure! Give me a couple mins and I'll send you a few pics of me.'

I must have sent Ruben about eight or nine photos of 'me' by that point. I was also hoping that the quip he made about coming to the UK was just a joke and nothing more, as for now, I was happy to stay in this bubble with him. We talked about his new plants, my new venture into becoming a 'Plantfluencer' (I made that up. Catchy, innit?) and my new position at work (being careful not to divulge *where* I worked). I think it was safe to assume that although Aneni and Ruben had started following each other, she hadn't contacted him yet. And that was how it was going to stay if I had anything to do with it.

Time seemed to stand still whenever I was the phone with him. Suddenly, sleep didn't matter. Nothing else mattered in those moments but me and him. I knew how incredibly wild it was to be in a situation where I'd fallen for someone who lived in another country, but shit! Life was short, and I wanted to grab these opportunities by the balls when they presented themselves to me. It's what I deserved!

Eventually, as our call moved into the second hour, the subject turned to living arrangements. He sent me an old Instagram video of himself giving a tour of his apartment, and it was just as I had imagined. He lived in a fancy new-build loft apartment with exposed brickwork and an open-plan living room/kitchen area. His whole apartment was filled to the brim with artwork and plants, and he had a little studio space in the spare bedroom for his photography. I could also see that he had a keen eye for design, with his West Elm and Hay furniture. Oh, he was FANCY fancy. The video he'd sent concluded with him jumping onto his extra-king-size bed and giggling like a small child in a candy shop. 'And this,' he stated in the video, 'is where none of the magic happens, but who knows? That may change in future, ha.'

If it was this man's aim to get me to fall in love with him, he was succeeding, because I was falling fast.

'How do you find living on your own so far? I feel like the San Francisco area is hella expensive to rent, no?' I asked, trying to distract myself from the intrusive thoughts that featured me and him in his bed.

'Hella? Well, look at you getting into the Bay Area slang already! We've been talking for too long, that's what that is. Next thing you know I'ma start saying shit like "Pip pip, cheerio!" and all that.'

'First of all, you need to stop watching British period dramas and assuming we all talk like the Royal family because we absolutely do NOT, and secondly, you know you're in love with this British accent, so quit playing.'

Ruben let out a deep laugh that made my heart melt.

'You're right, I do love it. And I love living alone, I'm a little introverted so being in my own company is the best.'

Then – without any warning whatsoever – he sent a request to change over from an audio call to a video call. I heard the notification beeps on my phone, and my stomach dropped.

In a panic, I ended the call. I turned my phone off and waited ten minutes while I tried to think of an adequate lie to tell Ruben for hanging up. I could blame it on the Wi-Fi signal maybe? Or just say I hadn't done any phone updates for a while? Eventually, I decided to go for the classic excuse. I tentatively turned the phone back on and sent Ruben the following message:

> **Me: I'm sooo sorry about that! Just realised I hadn't been charging my phone and it died on me. Gonna get a bit of sleep now as I'm a little tired but as always, it was great catching up with you and I hope you have an amazing day! Xx**

Immediately, I received a response.

> **Ruben: . . . Ohh OK. I hope your phone is aight now. Anyway, you catch up on your beauty sleep, babygirl, and we'll talk tomorrow. Sweet dreams till Sunbeams find you xx**

I melted, but the adrenaline rushing through my veins at the thought of him prospectively seeing my actual face was still too much for me to bear. He *needed* to keep believing I was Chantelle. That near-miss told me something for sure: that my feelings for Ruben were increasing day by day. At this point, I

1

1

didn't feel the need to try and talk to anyone else as my every thought was occupied by him. As far as I was concerned, the last thing I needed was any other impending distractions. I swiped my phone screen, looking for the folder entitled 'DATING BITS'. Inside were all the apps that had entrenched themselves within the fabric of my life over the last couple of years. First up was Bumble. I pressed 'DELETE'.

Tinder. DELETE.

Hinge. DELETE.

Raya. DELETE.

Happn. DELETE.

BBW Lovers. DELETE.

I then took a deep breath, and composed a text message.

Me: Hey Anthony. I hope you're doing well. Sorry for the radio silence over the last few days, but I just wanted to let you know that even though it's been fun with you (it really has!), I've kinda met someone else now, and am looking to see where it goes. No hard feelings? Artemis xxx

A few moments later, I received a response from Anthony:

Anthony: Ah. That's a shame, but thanks for letting me know all the same. And here I was, starting to really like you. Well. I'll be here if you ever get bored of your current situation. ☺

I cocked an eyebrow and closed the message.

But I decided to hang on to his number. Just in case.

Chapter 19

'This is the budding love story that the streets – aka me – have been waiting for!' Jean screamed down the phone as I updated him on my phone call with Ruben yesterday. It was lunchtime at work, and I had locked myself away in my office with a tuna niçoise salad and a croissant from Pret, not wanting to be disturbed by any of my colleagues while I relayed this VERY IMPORTANT INFORMATION to my best friend.

Obviously I didn't give him the full story: how I had been sending Ruben photos of a conventionally pretty, light-skinned former classmate of mine instead of photos of me for weeks now.

Over the last few days I had been trying to come up with a battle plan to make the best of the complicated situation that I'd put myself in. My current idea was to slowly up my engagement with Ruben's profile using my personal account by randomly liking and commenting on his content. If he added me and reciprocated, then I would try and strike up a conversation with him as myself. If I felt like he was engaging positively, then I'd lessen the amount of time talking to him as Aloe, until I eventually blocked him. Hopefully by then, he would be so enamoured with talking to the *real* me that he'd forget all about Aloe. Was this still delusional? Very. But right now it was all I had, and I desperately needed someone to bounce my ideas off so they could advise me whether I was doing the right thing or not. Could that person be Jean? I wasn't sure yet . . .

'Wait,' continued Jean hurriedly. I could hear him practically panting through the phone. 'What did you say back to him? How did it end? What did his apartment look like? Have you guys gone on cam yet? When is he flying out here to claim you? Answer me, answer me now!'

I began to feel a knot the size of a walnut slowly creep up my throat. Suddenly everything began to move in slow motion, and my skin started to feel super clammy.

I took a sip of water and unmuted myself. 'Babes, we'll have to do a full debrief at some point this week, but I did say I liked him back! I don't know if we'll ever see each other, but we're keeping it cute for now, innit?'

'Well, you're gonna have to debrief me next week. I'm off to Peru in a couple days for a photo shoot with *Elle* magazine so update me when I get back, yeah?'

'Oh, look at this one doing up "Mr Worldwide" huh?' I teased. 'Must be nice!'

Sometimes I wished I could exchange my life with Jean's. He had a fun job travelling around the world for free, taking pictures of beautiful people. His life was literally a movie at times, but he'd worked hard to get there and deserved every accolade.

'Says the bitch that's getting loved up on by a Morris Chestnut lookalike from California, yeah aight.' He would have a point if my situation weren't covered in lies, falsehoods, fallacies and untruths. I sighed, bid him *adieu* and ended the call. I had the conversation with Aneni to think about at the end of the day, and I needed to plan how I would approach this mess . . .

I ploughed head-first back into my work emails, and then

onto my plant Instagram page to answer a couple of the fresh batch of queries I'd received.

> **@TashaBreezy:** Hi Aloe! I hope you're good! I loved your latest post on the different types of snake plants available. I wanted some advice on my peace lily. The flowers have died and there's like . . . a weird stick inside the stem? I'm not sure what to do! Xx

I cracked my knuckles and got to work.

> **SayAloeToMyLittleFriend:** Hey my love! Thanks for getting in touch. OK, so basically once a peace lily flowers and eventually dies, that stalk will never reflower again, so the best thing to do is the cut the stalk off to encourage new growth. Hope this helps! X

> **@MikeOnThePod:** Hi Aloe! My cactus seems to be wilting away unexpectedly and I'm not sure what to do about it. I've been watering it three times a week – am I doing something wrong? Thanks!

'Ooh girl . . . no,' I mumbled beneath my breath as I typed my response back. Cactus care was one of my frequently requested subjects, which always baffled me as they are the easiest plants to ever take care of. I replied:

> **SayAloeToMyLittleFriend:** Hey babe! OK, PUT DOWN THE WATERING CAN! Most cacti are succulents, meaning they store a lot of water in their trunks. You should be watering it once a month at the very most, as overwatering can kill it. They thrive off neglect! X

After answering a few more queries, I closed the app and just as I did a notification popped up on my phone.

Ruben: Happy Tuesday, babygirl, read the text. Immediately, my eyes glazed over and my heart began to beat a little louder

169

than normal. I was officially someone who received 'good morning' texts, and I felt elite.

> Ruben: I hope you slept well last night. I was thinking about you before I went to sleep *and* when I woke up so I wanted to say hi lol. I enjoyed our talk yesterday, looking forward to speaking later X

This was such new territory for me. Being thought about? Being prioritised? Being desired (kinda)? It took me a few minutes to gather my thoughts and reply.

Me: Good morning, babe, I replied, surprised that I was even calling anyone my 'babe'. Me! Temz! HA. **Me: I hope you're getting some decent enough sleep, it's still super early out there for you, isn't it? I've been thinking about you too. I hope you have an awesome day.**

Ruben read the text immediately and had replied with a selfie of him lying in bed, topless, complete with . . . a cream durag on top of his head? My man was bald, y'all.

> Me: Sir? We can all see that you look incredibly sexy in the morning, but riddle me this! Why are you wearing a durag when you're bald? I look forward to hearing your response ASAP xxx

A few minutes later and I get a response:

> Ruben: HA! Damn, you're gonna do me like that? First of all, a thousand thank yous, Oh Kind One, for your compliments – it means a lot. Second of all, fuck you! My bald head gets cold at night, OK? It needs the warmth xxxxx
> Anyway, babygirl, I don't wanna get in the way of your work and I gotta make my way uptown for a couple of meetings and stuff, so I'll see if I can call you later . . . maybe around 10 or 11 your time? I don't wanna keep you up too late . . .

I was floating on Cloud Nine at this point. Nobody could tell me nothing.

> **Me: You could never get in the way of my work, babe. But I also don't wanna get in the way of yours, so I hope you have a great day! 10 or 11 is perfect. Speak soon and I hope your meetings go well xx**

> **Ruben: Aight cool. Maybe we can have a proper video chat this evening? I wanna see those cute dimples in 3D! Xx**

It took me a minute to register what he'd said as the last time I remembered, I didn't have any dimples?

But Chantelle did.

Fuck. FuckFuckFuckFuckFuck. I knew this was bound to happen. You couldn't live in the era of *Catfish: The TV Show* and not want to see what someone looked like on video these days. What on earth was I going to do? How the fucking FUCK was I going to explain my way out of this one?

I thought through several possible scenarios:

- I come clean THIS EVENING to Ruben about what I had done. It was still early enough for him to hopefully forgive me.
- I take the video call under cover of darkness and tell him that we're in the middle of a blackout.
- I pull a Cyrano de Bergerac by messaging Chantelle, coming clean to *her* about what I'd done and then ask her if she'd be willing to chat to Ruben for a few minutes while I feed in messages telling her what to say.
- I could block Ruben and start talking to him from my actual private account.
- I risk losing the love of my life anyway.

I was deep in thought contemplating the above scenarios when I was suddenly interrupted by a knock at the door and the floating head of Stephen peering through. *Now isn't the time, Stephen!*

'Hey, Artemis! Sorry to disturb you, I know you're super busy at the moment,' Stephen started. Little did he know. 'I just wanted to see how you were getting on?'

Couldn't this have been an email? Or a Slack message at least?

'Hey Stephen!' I muttered back, with as much enthusiasm as I could muster in that moment. 'Yeah, uh, yeah I'm doing great so far, thanks. Did you want to book a time for a meeting or ...?'

'Oh, sure we can do,' Stephen replied. 'But I was just passing through and quickly wanted to see how you were doing, is all! I hope things are going more smoothly with Kevin on the Maranette account.'

Why's he mentioning that? I raised an eyebrow. Had Kevin gone all Karen on me after all and snitched about our little chat after the presentation?

'Why? Did he mention something about it?'

'Oh, no, not at all! I did notice he looked a bit peeved after your chat, but he's been at the company for a long time and he's old-school. I'm sure he'll come around to some of the newer ideas you'll throw at him. You know what people our age are like, haha. But we need to keep him a little bit sweet for the time being!'

Phew. On top of all the catfishing charges I was trying to beat, I didn't want to have to think about being perceived as the Angry Black Woman at work too.

'Oh, definitely. I don't doubt that we'll be able to come out with solutions that suit us both,' I responded, adding a little giggle at the end so he knew I was all good. 'I let him know that he could contact me regarding any further suggestions he had and he seemed to be cool with it. Honestly, I've been all good. I'm enjoying the role so much, and I'm excited to get this campaign with Maranette up and running with the rest of the team!'

At that, Stephen smiled, nodded and bowed out of the room.

I was alone to contemplate my romantic fate once more.

I decided to take a casual scroll of my Instagram feed in a bid to put my mind at ease and think of something else. My video content for the soil company had been a success, racking up over 75,000 views in a day. The company was super impressed and had agreed to work with me on a monthly retainer basis as one of their ambassadors, which was great.

I distracted myself by answering some more queries and responding to some of the follower comments under the post. But then I got an alert for a newly uploaded Instagram story – Ruben had uploaded something, and being the complete Ruben-fiend that I was, hastened to take a look.

My jaw hit the floor as my vision suddenly turned blurry. I exited out of the story, and then I returned to it, took a quick screenshot, and opened the picture up on my phone so that I could properly examine it. I glared at it, feeling hot tears beginning to prickle behind my eyes.

Ruben's Instagram slide contained a repost of one from Aneni's. In Aneni's post, she had added a photo of Ruben with the following text:

@AneniLdn: @RubesCubes is my #MCM y'all! Whew . . . He is so fine!! It's been so awesome getting to know you recently, would love to meet you one of these days! He's also an amazing singer too, so check out his SoundCloud link in his bio! xx

On Ruben's repost he'd written: **RubesCubes:** Haha right back at you, ma! Thanks for the love. If you ever come to Oakland, hit me up!

In a split second, my anxieties and fears about the two of them talking had turned into pure, unwavering rage.

Getting to know him *recently*?

How recently? Since when? Why didn't she tell me?

He said 'right back at ya!' Right back at whom?!

You mean to tell me that while I've been sitting here doing nish, Aneni has been out here making moves? On *my* man?

Oh.

This bitch was going down.

Chapter 20

It was 6.45 p.m. and I was making my way through Central London to meet Aneni at Sheila's Cafe. She was already there, having texted me moments earlier saying that she'd saved a seat for us, so I was doing my best to pick up speed to get there on time. I hated being late; it gave me less time to compose my thoughts and shit.

It was raining heavily, and I'd forgotten to grab an umbrella when I'd left home that morning, so I was currently fighting for my life as I left the warmth and dryness of Vauxhall tube station to face the battling winds and monsoon-type rain outside, but I didn't care. All I could think about were those Instagram Stories I'd seen earlier. My mind envisioned them having late-night conversations via FaceTime, and perhaps even speaking on the phone like we had. Why had Aneni done that, KNOWING I would see it? I was angry at Ruben for entertaining her. I was angry at Aneni for being Aneni. I was furious that yet again, she seemed to be trying to rob me of my small joys. The current wind and rain had nothing on the Red Mist that was building up inside my chest right now.

It was only a three-minute walk to the cafe, but by the time I arrived I had the appearance of a drowned rat: my hair was plastered down the sides of my face and I could feel the now-liquified gel running down my neck. My white shirt had turned semi-see-through, revealing my very pink Curvy Kate bra. My shoes were soaking wet and squelched when I walked. This was not the first impression I'd wanted to give Aneni when I walked into the cafe. I'd wanted her to see a composed, amazingly dressed boss bitch who had her life together and who was here to talk real business and set the record straight. Not a pathetic, drenched whale. But we move. I saw Aneni perched at the back of the cafe, looking stunning as usual. She hadn't seen me yet, so I used that as an opportunity to dash to the bathroom and try and fix myself up a bit.

That was where I was able to see my true form.

I looked in the mirror and, to my dismay, noticed that in addition to everything else my mascara had run something terrible. My foundation had also begun to streak heavily in the rain, meaning I'd been walking around Vauxhall looking like even more of an absolute train wreck than I thought. I quickly grabbed some tissue and dabbed at my eyes until they looked halfway decent. If Aneni enquired, I'd say it was a new eyeliner. I applied a fresh lip and did what I could with the remnants of the foundation left on my face. After doing a reasonable job at air-drying my shirt, and reapplying a generous spray of my favourite citrus perfume, I felt somewhat ready. I took one final glance in the mirror. I wasn't casket sharp, but I was reasonably presentable, all things considered.

You can do this, Artemis.

She's trying to take your man.

Fuck years of 'friendship'! Has she ever been a true friend?

After psyching myself up in the mirror, I left the bathroom and made my way towards the back of the cafe. Aneni just *had* to be a vision every time. She had on a new 26-inch wig with light-brown ombre tips. The lace of the wig was nowhere to be seen, of course. Her Van Cleef & Arpels earring-and-bracelet set were in full view (whether it was genuine Van Cleef or the counterfeit set we'd both bought together while on holiday in Egypt a year ago still remained to be seen).

This bitch had also somehow finessed her way into the MaxMara showroom and was wearing a white pinstripe double-breasted striped blazer with matching palazzo trousers. The suit alone I knew cost over six grand. She'd paired the outfit with a pair of black satin Yigit platform pumps by Amina Muaddi that I knew cost at least a smooth grand. She finished the look with her black calfskin Chanel 2:55 bag. She looked absolutely sensational. I felt sick.

She glanced up at me and beamed, showing all thirty-two teeth.

'Temz, my babes! About time, how the fuck are you?'

Aneni stood up and gave me a lingering hug, and I could instantly smell her Penhaligon's perfume radiating from her pores.

'I'm good, thanks. You look great,' I replied coolly, already feeling a little deflated but remembering to keep my eye on the prize. 'How on earth did you get this MaxMara suit, by the way? I swear it's literally fresh off the runway?'

Aneni looked down at her outfit and smiled knowingly.

'Oh, babe, do you want me to hook you up? I know the PR people and they gave me a good price! I'll have to see whether they do larger plus-sizes though, but leave it with me! What are you? Like a size twenty-eight or thirty?' With that, she started writing something in her Notes app, smirking as she did so.

There was absolutely nothing wrong with being a size 28 or 30, but that brief, sly smirk that made its way across Aneni's face told me everything I needed to know. She was trying to be spiteful.

'Um, no I'm good, thanks babe, and I'm a size twenty-six. My new pay packet is great but it's not that great yet,' I responded feebly. *Get your head back in the game, Temz.*

After I ordered us both a coffee and something to eat, Aneni launched into her monologue of updates: how she was dating a *new* guy she'd found on sugardaddies.net, her upcoming trips to the Maldives and Saint Lucia, how she'd been contacted by several brands via Instagram asking to work with her on an influencer basis, the results of her recent Botox appointment, and how annoying she was finding work.

'I think I may just go into influencer stuff full-time, you know,' Aneni continued as she looked down at her nails and sighed softly. 'It just feels so much easier than this nine-to-five shit. Do you know how much MONEY the content creator girls are getting these days for just posting one photo to Instagram? Shit, I need to get on that.'

I DID in fact know how much the content creators were getting paid, seeing as I was one myself, kinda. Also having experienced working with some of the creators from a professional point of view, I've been privy to the rates some of these people command. I can absolutely understand why Aneni would want to move into that sector – some of these creators were making upwards of 40k a MONTH. To be honest, I also think she'd be great at it. But again, not why I'm here.

Focus, Temz.

Aneni finished playing with her nails and looked up at me, matching my eyeline.

'What do you think about me doing it?' she asked.

'I think you'd be great at it, sis,' I replied, seeing as that's what she really wanted to hear.

But it was fast approaching the time where I wanted to hear some things from Aneni, too. We caught up over small talk while we waited for our food to arrive, and when it eventually came

I decided to use that small sliver of silence as an opportunity to launch into what I was really here to talk about.

'So,' I started, between mouthfuls, 'I saw the other day that you started following my man on Instagram, and today you guys are reposting each other on your Stories. Um . . . what's that all about?' I tried to keep my tone light, but Aneni looked up at me and froze. Then after an awkwardly long time, her lips cracked into a wide smile and she started laughing performatively in between mouthfuls of lasagne.

'Wait, sorry? *Your* man? You and Ruben? When did this happen? You've been keeping me in the dark, girl! You better spill!'

I narrowed my eyes. Why was she avoiding my initial question?

'I haven't been keeping you in the dark. But umm . . . yeah so . . . how did you find his profile again in the first place? Were you trying to do research on him, or check him out for me in advance or something?' Part of me wanted that to be the reason.

Aneni would always do this super annoying thing where she would gurn her mouth whenever she tried to avoid questions. She was pulling those same silly faces now, I guess in a bid to distract me, but all it did was make me more inquisitive as to her intentions with Ruben.

Aneni's face stiffened as she looked at me dead on, eyes squinting at me as she tried to figure out my angle. 'Babe . . . no offence but you guys haven't even met yet! It's not that deep, really. I followed him when you showed us his profile at the pub for the first time. I just wanted to see what all of the fuss was about. I ain't gonna take him from you or anything, don't worry. Our chat has mostly been about influencer and singing shit really. Besides, from his follow list it already looks like he has a certain . . . type.'

My blood had become hot enough to fry raw plantain.

The nerve. The audacity of her to already assume that Ruben wouldn't be interested in me. Aneni, the golden girl who had always received everything she ever wanted in life and had, over the years, turned our friendship into that of main character and sidekick, had once again succeeded in making me feel like absolute shit.

At that moment all I wanted to do was shout at her, but I didn't want to make a scene, so I tried to keep it as cute as possible.

'And what type would that be? Considering he's already told me he likes me?'

'Well, as far as I know, you guys haven't seen each other in real life, right? So I'm assuming he's just going off your personality . . . I mean – you know what I mean, Temz.' She quickly tried to backtrack her words as my frozen reaction turned into one of rage.

'Aneni? Either try rephrasing that,' I responded, taking low, deep breaths, 'or tell me how you really feel.'

If we were going to finally have it out after years of being seemingly cordial and pretending like her sleeping with my ex never happened, I wanted to just have it out here and now.

Aneni looked down at her nails again and took a deep breath.

'I'm not saying that Ruben wouldn't find you attractive,' she began carefully, 'but obviously until you meet in real life, it's just going to be a little online thing, isn't it? Like, you're not taking it seriously, are you? You're still dating other guys outside of this online stuff, right?'

'I actually happen to like him a lot. What I have a problem with is you all of a sudden following him out of the blue and chatting to him like you guys are friends.' I decided to throw down the gauntlet. 'Remember – we both know what you can be like.'

Our voices were very much lowered so as not to draw a scene, but you could cut the tension in the air with a knife. Aneni stared at me for what seemed like hours before answering.

'Oh. So that's what this is all about, huh? The fact that men tend to go for me rather than you? You're still hung up over that kind of stuff? You're still holding Amari over my head even though you told me you'd forgiven me? Have you even spoken to Ruben on the phone or video chatted with him yet? You just need to grow up, Artemis.'

She only called me by my full name when she was mad or upset, so at that point I knew that I had gotten under her skin. I didn't care; I was feeling froggy and thus I leapt.

'Aneni, every time I get into a situation with a guy – whether serious or casual – you find some way to insert yourself, and frankly I'm sick of the fact that you can't seem to be happy for me. I'm sick of you always putting me down. I'm sick of you flirting with people I show interest in. I should never have shown you Ruben's profile!'

I exhaled. The elephant in the room that had been hanging over our friendship for years was finally coming out. I was tired of being the LeFou to her Gaston. And I wasn't done yet.

'You always ask me why Jean seems to dislike you, and it's for this reason! We've been friends a long time and I love you like a sister, but you've always thought yourself better than me, both in your looks and how you live, and you seem to go into these quiet, weird moods anytime something good happens for me! I'm the one that always has to reach out and call you or arrange something with you, and frankly I'm actually fucking tired of this one-sided friendship. It's not fair on me, Aneni. Not at all,' I continued, reaching for the final crescendo. 'And leave Ruben alone – he's not interested.'

I uttered the last sentence a little louder than the rest, causing a few of the patrons sitting next to us to turn around in concern. *Go back to eating your shepherd's pie, Sheryl!*

Aneni opened her mouth wide in shock, showing her recently Invisaligned teeth. Then she stood up and started to put her coat on, uttering, 'You're a real bitch, you know that, Artemis?'

As she picked up her bag, she added, 'It's not my fault that he prefers flirting with me, by the way. Maybe if you fixed yourself up a little, you could get on my level instead of having your little victim mentality. And maybe – just maybe – stop going for men who are way above your station. Then maybe you wouldn't be disappointed all the time when they show interest in me instead.'

I was planted in my seat, shocked. I had told her to tell me how she really felt, and here it was in living colour. Everything I suspected had been true. But now all I could think about was trying to stop her from speaking to Ruben and telling him the truth about me . . .

'I honestly don't give a fuck about what you think about me any more, k?' I replied, glaring at her with all the venom I could muster. 'If this friendship dies, so be it. It's probably been heading this way for a while, if we're being honest. I've tolerated you for this long because I was lonely! I always wanted a sister, and you just happened to be there.' I took a deep breath. 'I want you to leave Ruben alone. That is the least you could do. I don't want you to talk to him, I don't want you to mention me, I don't want you liking or commenting on his stuff, none of it. I've never asked you for anything in this friendship, so as a parting gift, I would like you to at least do that for me.'

Aneni straightened out her suit and held her head up high, seemingly trying to fight back tears. I was surprised to feel absolutely nothing.

'You're petty. You've been projecting your insecurities on to me since we were kids. I don't need this any more.'

Without meeting my gaze, she turned and walked out.

As Aneni walked out of the door (incidentally, leaving me with the bill), I called out after her, 'MAKE SURE YOU UNFOLLOW HIM TOO, YEAH? CHEERS, HUN!'

Aneni gave me one final, scathing look and strode off in dramatic fashion.

I smiled to myself as I tried to continue eating my food. Was I slightly unhinged? Probably. Petty? For sure. But low-key it was kinda vindicating to get all of that off my chest.

Aneni and I grew up together, our mothers were best friends, we attended the same primary and secondary schools – she was always just there, so from the jump it felt somewhat like a friendship of convenience. She was a very beautiful, lonely, only child who wanted a friend she could feel superior to, and I was a somewhat insecure, lonely, only child who wanted to feel popular and desired by people, even if only by association. Maybe it was a friendship doomed to fail from the start, but we did care for each other deep down. I could always understand the parts of Aneni that were rooted in loneliness and just wanted to be seen. In the same way I grew up feeling dehumanised and hypersexualised because of my appearance, it was the same for her; we shared a common woe, ironically. I suppose I stayed friends with her because in a way, she needed me.

But I'm not her mammy figure, or anyone else's, for that matter.

And as for Ruben and his interactions with her? The more I thought about it, the angrier I was with him, too. But it is well. I planned to deal with him later.

With fire still burning through my veins, I took out my phone and sent a message:

Me: Hey Anthony. You free this evening? Let's hang. Temz x

I immediately received a message back.

Anthony: That didn't take long! I can be free this evening. Yours? Around 8 p.m.?

I'd entered my villain era.

Chapter 21

In the few days since my confrontation with Aneni, I'd flitted between considering if I should message her to apologise for my outburst, or blocking her outright for the hurtful things she'd said in response. Even though I had no regrets about speaking my mind at the time, doubt had slowly begun to creep in. But I knew I had to stay strong and stick to my gut. I was clearly in the right. Aneni had been a shit friend, and that was all there was to it.

Also, in a random turn of events, I'd noticed that Ruben had requested to follow my personal account back on Instagram.

Ruben. Sent a follow request. To my personal profile.

Calm down, Artemis. Was this not a part of my overall plan? As I sat at the train platform with my cappuccino trying to play it cool, my brain was processing a thousand times a minute. I had cooled things off with him for the last couple of days by saying I was too tired to chat, but this was definitely a surprise. I didn't think this turn of events was Aneni's doing – if she was going to hurt me in some way, she would have contacted Ruben the minute she'd left the cafe, so he would have mentioned it before now, especially as it sounds as if they'd been having little chit-chats here and there. Sometimes I was still pissed about that.

I'd already had a close fucking call last night. Ruben had posted my plant page alongside a photo of the woman he thought to be me/Aloe but was actually Chantelle, with a cute caption: (So much beauty in one pic; the plants are cute too!) By the time I'd seen it, it had been up for seven hours. My fingers couldn't move fast enough as I caved in and called to get him to delete it, citing that I 'valued the anonymity of my profile' and 'wanted my page to be professional' or some bullshit like that. In actuality, I just didn't want Aneni to see it, otherwise my cover would have been blown.

I stared at Ruben's follow request on my phone for what seemed like hours. What the fuck was I going to do? My master plan of revealing my true self to him gradually was initially meant to start taking place down the line when I felt ready (and was three stone lighter). Maybe I was too quick with 'liking' every single bit of content he uploaded onto Instagram, and he probably wondered who this obsessive girl was. Did he know something was up? If so, why was he pretending like we were cool? Was this an attempt to stage some kind of grand exposure in the long run?

As my train slowly pulled into the station, I contemplated my available options for this random turn of events:

1. Come clean and tell Ruben, despite that meaning he may never talk to me again, thus breaking my heart.
2. Accept his follow request, do nothing else, and just see how it goes.
3. Accept his follow request, strike up a conversation with him, seduce him and hope that he'll fall in love with me and forget about 'Aloe'.
4. Have a panic attack, call Jean and confess my crimes.

Option 4 was looking more and more like the appropriate action to take right now. I felt my heart rate increasing minute by minute as I struggled to find a seat on the packed train. After traipsing through several of the train cars, I eventually found a seat at the back near the toilets and put on one of my favourite weekly topical podcasts to try and calm myself down.

After a while, I went into my Aloe account, opened up Ruben's Instagram page and liked a few of his Instagram Stories to try and balance things out. He'd posted some videos of him at what looked like an art gallery. Ruben was panning the camera towards several different art pieces and sculptures, commenting in the background about things such as 'Cityscapes' and 'movement of the light' and other artistic lingo that I had no clue about. Jeeze, he was so cultured and intelligent. My heart softened once more as I watched through all his Stories. The last video was of him in bed wearing a pair of Simpsons pyjama bottoms, looking sexy and adorable.

'*This train is now calling at London Victoria*,' came the announcement over the tannoy on the train. I snapped out of my Ruben bubble, disembarked and made my way out of the station and onwards to work.

On the way there, I received a text from Anthony. He generally seemed to be just fine with our informal Friends with Benefits arrangement. I felt a bit guilty about having seen him the other day, but now that this situation with Ruben was getting even more complicated, I decided I needed to slowly cut things back with Anthony. Trouble was, he didn't really seem to want to take the hint.

Anthony: Hey there, sexy. You up to anything this week? I've been having fun with your body of late and I've been aching to see your hot bubbly rolls again! Let me know, Tony x

Hot bubbly rolls? This man may be unhinged, I fear.
He'd started to refer to me via my body rather than me, the

person, whenever we met up. Don't get me wrong, the sex had continued to be incredible, and he definitely had a knack of making me feel confident in my body. But it was starting to low-key give fat fetishism now, and that was wearing thin on me, because:

a) The objectification of my body was icky
b) He isn't Ruben, and

Well, not sure I needed more reasons. But there was still the issue of the 'no oral sex' situation, too, which was frankly, blasphemous. I couldn't do it any more. I texted back:

> **Me: Hey Tony, I'm actually super busy this week but I can let you know about next week in a few days or so. Temz.**

Short and sweet. I wasn't about to lambast him over the politics of fat fetishism and objectification because, frankly, I didn't like him enough to do all that. I decided to park Anthony for now and concentrate on bigger matters at hand.

The Sisterhood of the Travelling Lace Fronts ♥
Jean, You

Aneni has left the group

Jean: Finally.
Jean: Lmaooo
Artemis: Took her enough time to leave tbh. She barely messaged in here anyway.
Jean: Honestly, it's for the best.
Artemis: I'm sure she'll come crawling back eventually.
Jean: I mean, you dragged her for filth, and rightly so may I add. You didn't finish the whole story of what happened – you kinda left me hanging!

Artemis: I mean, you've been sunning it up in Cuba or wherever, so I haven't had the chance to tell you!

The truth was actually that for me to tell Jean the full story about my fight with Aneni would mean that I'd have to spill the beans about my little situation with 'Aloe' and Ruben. I'd been avoiding Jean since he'd come back from his work trip but it was becoming clearer to me that I had to confess what had happened to *someone*. I needed to clear my conscience, and Jean — as chaotic as he was as a general human being — was the pillar of morality in our friendship threesome (twosome?).

I absolutely knew that I would be in for a pretty exhaustive drag session, but he would do it with empathy and understanding (at least I hoped so), and that was what I really needed right now.

Jean: First of all bitch, I was in PERU – close, but no cigar. And secondly, you know when it comes to drama and shade, nothing but death can keep me from it. I love mess!

Artemis: LMAO. OK, well, I actually need to talk to you about something related to the argument anyway. Let me know when you're free and we can hang.

Jean: Uh, OK. Are you OK?

Artemis: Yes and no? But I think talking about it will make me feel better.

Jean: I'm always here for you, babe. Lemme check my schedule and get back to you ♥

Work turned out to be the perfect distraction for me, what with the flurry of emails, multiple meetings, content strategy briefs and supervisory work I had to do. There was no time to think about my Instagram-fuelled problem.

I was in the cafeteria enjoying a quick lunch break with Claudia when I saw Stephen hot-tailing it towards me, balancing a salad bowl and two coffees.

'Oop. Someone's in his tractor beam,' Claudia said between bites, of her ham and cheese panini.

'Oh, Lord,' I replied in mock exasperation. 'Is lunch not even sacred any more? I was really just looking forward to us having this cheesecake in peace!' Again, Stephen's lovely, but since my promotion he had become a lot more involved in my work affairs than normal. At first I assumed it was just him trying to mentor me in this new role, and then I thought maybe he was just one of those micromanaging types, but lately it had become a flurry of Slack and chain emails which I kept getting CC'd into, but also screenshots of Twitter memes and random messages asking 'how I'm doing' and to 'shout if I needed any extra assistance'. I wanted to give Stephen the benefit of the doubt seeing as he was instrumental in me getting this promotion, but the smothering was starting to become a problem.

'I still call it, Temz,' Claudia said as she munched. 'I still think that good old Steve has a little thing for you. It's sooo obvious.'

I stared at her in mock concern and scoffed loudly.

'Obvious to WHOMTH?' Then I paused. 'Wait, do other people think this too? I don't think he *likes me* likes me. I think he probably *is* trying to micromanage me, just in a way that comes across as passive maybe? Thing is, I feel like I've been doing a good job in this role so far, don't you?'

'Of course you have! You're a fucking breath of fresh air, mate. You could probably run this whole place with your eyes closed!' Claudia replied, patting me gently on the back. 'And to answer your question, yeah – a couple of us have a sneaking suspicion that Steve may wanna board the Artemis train.'

'First of all, I don't want or need that kind of imagery of Stephen in my life right now! Secondly, you're my favourite sycophant, you know that?' I chuckled.

'I know. Remember that when you get your next promotion,

yeah?' Claudia replied quietly as Stephen arrived, accessorised with a beaming smile.

'Hey guys!' he said happily, placing his salad and hot drinks on the table as if we'd invited him to sit down. The caucasity really knew no bounds in the advertising industry, even during lunchtime. He was dressed head to toe in monogrammed(!!) Helly Hansen – a brand that for some reason seemed to have the majority of white, upper-middle-class men in a chokehold.

'Hey Stephen, how's tricks?' I made some room for him to sit down and briefly caught Claudia's eye, before rolling my own in mock annoyance.

'Nothing much, Artemis! Oh, hey Claudia.' Stephen briefly nodded dismissively at her. She took this as a sign to make herself scarce.

'Hey Stephen. I'm gonna pop to the off-licence to pick up some snacks . . . enjoy your lunch guys!' She winked at me as she made her getaway. That woman was a menace.

I was left alone with Stephen, who looked like he was struggling to open his salad bowl.

Jesus be a pair of earphones.

'So!' began Stephen after a couple of minutes of silence. 'How is work coming along? Are our clients happy still?'

I wouldn't have minded this question if it weren't for the fact that I'd sent him a full brief containing updates of all our clients this morning. He was clearly just trying to make small talk.

'Since this morning? Why yes, I believe everyone is still happy,' I replied, tucking in to my jollof rice so I had something to do with my mouth instead of talk.

'Ah yes, of course, of course, my bad,' replied Stephen, mirroring my movements with his salad.

We continued eating in silence for a couple of minutes, during which time I managed to send a cute message to Ruben.

I took a quick photo of my food (jollof rice with two pieces of chicken) – making sure that I didn't include my hands or any other part of my body – and sent it to him, alongside one of the cheesiest messages I managed to conjure up from my arsenal:

> **Me: Eating these snacks for lunch but thinking about having a whole meal** 😊

I mock-gagged as I typed it out, but I knew Ruben would be all over it. He was a sucker for cheesiness, and a few moments later came his response:

> **Ruben: LOL. You're so cute. You're the only meal I wanna be eating right now too.** 😊 **Hope you're having a great day at work, beautiful.**

The little elastic bands that had been gripped around my heart were slowly becoming loose. Ruben had quickly sprung up to be the highlight of my days, with my face breaking into a beaming smile whenever I received a text alert from him. However, when I remembered that I had yet to also respond to his follow request from my *personal* account, my smile faded and the previous fluttering in my tummy turned suddenly into stones of despair.

It wasn't until Stephen had called my name for the fourth time that I snapped back into reality.

'I wanted to run something past you regarding a potential upcoming,' he was saying. 'Basically, we've been in talks with One Nation Athletics – they do gymwear and trainers and all of that, and we've been trying to get on their books for literally years in a bid to expand our portfolio into the American market. We've finally managed to get a meeting with them over in the States.' Stephen ran his hands through his brown curly hair at the mention of what seemed to be a stressful operation. 'Unfortunately, I can't go to the meeting any more due to some personal stuff I have to take care of that week. So, seeing as you've been absolutely smashing it over the last couple of months, I wanted to ask whether you could take my place? After you're fully briefed on the client, that is.'

Stephen was offering me the opportunity to visit America *on the company's dime*, yet the way he asked me felt like he was asking to have sex with my dad or something. Of *course* I was going to say yes! Being given such a huge responsibility so early on in my new tenure must mean that they have faith in me. *Bad Bitch mode reactivated!* A slow grin spread across my face.

'Stephen! That's a huge fucking deal! First of all, well done for securing the meeting! But also, are you sure you want me to handle it? I'm super honoured, of course – this is incredible!'

'I'm so glad you're on board with this!' Stephen exclaimed, smiling broadly. 'I was a bit nervous that you'd have a lot on your plate with other work projects and the fact that the meeting's taking place over in the US, but I'm excited to chat this through with you and get the ball rolling!'

I nodded. 'With regards to logistics, where and when exactly would I be going?' I asked, thinking more about my wardrobe than the actual work at hand.

'So we've booked the meeting for the fifteenth of next month at their offices in California. One Nation has already made arrangements for us regarding the hotel stay, and apparently they're hiring out a really swanky suite in some posh hotel with a private car and everything! They're really pushing the boat out for this meeting, so we'd want you out there for a few days. Feel free to add a couple of days to your trip though, if you want to sightsee or chill. I know how intense these corporate visits can be.'

This sounded amazing. A brand-new, fresh environment and the opportunity to prove my skills to a new client? Inject that shit into my veins!

'Thank you again for entrusting me with this opportunity, Stephen,' I repeat. 'I'm not gonna let you or the agency down.'

'Oh, I know you won't, Artemis,' Stephen replied. 'You're an integral member of the team, and you're gonna smash it!'

I smiled to myself as I finished off the rest of my lunch.

'Their office is based in San Francisco. Beautiful city, if you've not been.'

I stopped mid-chew.

San Francisco?

'San Francisco . . . ?' I coughed, trying to remain as relaxed as possible. This was not a part of the plan. The One Nation headquarters were meant to be located in Orange County!

'Yup,' replied Stephen, completely unaware of the chorus of alarm sirens currently making a ruckus inside my head. 'They've recently relocated offices; something about the rent in Southern California being too high on their office space or something. It's not a problem for you is it?' Stephen smiled at me nervously.

As in the San Francisco BAY AREA? The same San Francisco that is located fifteen minutes away from Oakland, where the future love of my life was located San Francisco?

Oh.

But. I couldn't let Stephen down. Not now; I had something to prove.

I gulped down the rest of my food and gave Stephen a strained smile.

'No problem at all! It's gonna be fun, I've never been to San Francisco before!'

The season finale of the shambolic reality show that was my life was reaching its climax.

Chapter 22

The glimmers of anxiety and doubt I'd had before were nothing compared to how I was feeling after being told I'd be travelling to San Francisco in under a month's time.

On the way home after work, I received a text from Jean:

Jean: I can come over to yours in a couple of hours if you're free hun? Xx

Mentally, I was hanging off a cliff, but maybe all of this was a sign for me to just come clean and tell Ruben everything. It was scary to think about, but maybe it would be a great opportunity to start off with a clean slate.

Perhaps the universe had had enough of my shenanigans and conspired with unforeseen forces to disrupt my life once and for all. Whatever it was, I knew that I had to tell Jean what was going on.

I texted back:

Me: Oh, that would be brilliant. Bring some kind of alcoholic beverage cuz it's gonna be a long one ☹

The message was read instantly, and Jean responded:

Jean: Oh, honey ☹ I'm here for you. I'ma be non-judgemental (as much as I can be lmao) and try and help as much as I can. I love you boo xx

A couple of hours later, Jean rolled through with an arsenal of a bottle of Wray and Nephew rum, a packet of gummy bears and some popcorn. He went to the kitchen to grab glasses and poured out a couple of shots for us both while I tried to work up the courage to tell him everything. I figured that not only was it good for me to confess, but I felt like I owed it to him at least. Over the last couple of weeks, Jean had been constantly asking for updates on what had been going on with Ruben and me, but the more he asked, the vaguer I was. Eventually, he just stopped. He probably already assumed that something was up and now, he was going to find out just how much.

Jean handed me my glass and sat cross-legged on the corner of my bed. I let out one last exhale, then turned to face him.

'OK, so,' I began.

'So,' he repeated. Jean had this super calming way about him that always managed to make me feel at ease. I was praying that this would go well. I needed all the allies I could get.

'Aight, so boom. Basically, there's like . . . three things I need to update you on so bear with me, OK?' I said, taking a huge gulp of my rum afterwards to steady my nerves. Jean nodded in response, taking a sip of his own.

Just rip the plaster off, Temz. He's your mate.

'OK, so regarding the whole situation with Ruben – when we started talking, we were chatting from my Aloe account, right? And, well, eventually it came to the point where he kept asking to see what I looked like because I keep the Aloe page anonymous for the most part, and—'

I glimpsed quickly at Jean and noticed that his face had darkened. I think he knew where I was going with this.

'Um, so in a panic, I just . . . You know how we took those photos of me beforehand right? But I still just wasn't feeling that up to scratch, and so when he asked to see a picture of me, I kinda just . . .'

'Sent him a picture of someone else?' Jean finished.

I looked up at him, feeling ashamed.

'Yeah . . . I didn't mean to! I guess I just wanted to gauge his reaction, but then it got out of hand. I sent some photos of this girl I used to go to school with and, well, he literally just fell in love with her face as soon as I sent it to him, so then I felt compelled to just keep sending *more* photos, and he keeps asking me to get on FaceTime and I keep saying no and I'm scared that he's gonna clock what's happened because it's been weeks now, and then fucking Aneni had to go and add him as a friend so now I'm scared she's either gonna try and continue flirting with him and take him away from me or I dunno what . . . And then I started following him on my private account to kinda keep tabs and he sent me a follow request but it's just sitting in my inbox cause I'm too scared to accept it, and now at work I've just been told that I gotta go to San Francisco for a work meeting for a few days, and obviously San Francisco is literally next door to where he lives in Oakland and I wanna see or stalk him, but 'cause he's added me on Instagram he may already know what I look like and so what if he sees me? What if he clocks? What if I've just ruined it? I just feel so bad, and—'

It wasn't until Jean grabbed a hold of my hand that I'd realised that I had been sobbing uncontrollably throughout my rambling monologue that had turned into a soliloquy of inner thoughts spoken aloud. It felt like finally squeezing a blackhead that had been developing and growing in pressure. I felt the huge weight release itself from my chest as I calmed myself down and took another sip of rum, looking up at Jean to determine the scale to which he probably now hated me.

Jean took a big sip of his own drink, thought for a moment,

and eventually said, 'You know, no shade at all, Temz, but I did kinda wonder if this was the case a couple of weeks ago. You were being so vague about Ruben, and I was confused as to why. I thought maybe you guys had either stopped talking or that . . . I don't know, SOMETHING weird was happening. I just didn't wanna confront you in case it was kinda sensitive.'

I stared at him, mouth agape. It's almost like Jean knew me better than I knew myself. I suddenly felt an overwhelming sense of shame. All this time I had been pretending like everything had been hunky-dory with me and Ruben, when underneath it all my best friend had suspected that there was fuckery afoot. Fuckery most foul.

'I'm glad you told me eventually, sis,' Jean continued, caressing my hands. Then we both heard the slam of the front door, indicating that Natalie had come home.

'I'm sorry I kept this from you. I've been wanting to tell you for AGES but it's . . . pathetic you know?' The corners of my eyes began to sting as more tears trickled down my cheeks. Upon seeing this, Jean put down his glass of rum and crept over to give me a hug. I allowed myself to be buried within his embrace, eventually letting go for a full-blown cry. As stupid as I felt in that moment, I was glad to be sharing it with Jean.

After our little bonding moment, he took me by the shoulders and stared at me again.

'Girl . . . OK! So now that THAT'S come out, I'ma need you to run through everything you just said again and we'll break it down bit by bit, OK?'

I nodded my head in between muffled sobs. 'OK,' I replied.

I ran through the different incidents again, making sure to be as thorough as possible.

'. . . So, you used photos from this girl you went to school with. She doesn't know?' said Jean eventually.

'Correct. I blocked her, and sometimes I'll unblock her every now and again to screenshot more up-to-date pictures and stuff . . .' I responded sheepishly.

'Rah. It's giving commitment. But anyway . . .' Jean moved swiftly on, noticing my scowl. 'So Ruben follows you on your plant account *and* he's requested you on your personals.'

'Right.'

'And Aneni started following Ruben recently?'

'Yep. I confronted her about it after work the other day, and she ended up taking the fucking piss. She basically insinuated I was too ugly for Ruben to talk to, and made it sound as if I'm jealous of her because of how she looks, which totally isn't the case!'

'Oh, no that bitch didn't.' Jean growled, grabbing his glass once again and pouring more rum into his glass. 'Let's take a pitstop at Aneni for a minute and sort this one out. First of all, you've always known how I've felt about that girl. Bad vibes. Cheap weaves, and – oh, my bad, only the weaves you guys didn't buy together,' Jean quickly backtracked upon seeing my cocked eyebrow at that last dig. Forty-inch bust down wigs were anything but cheap.

'You get what I mean though, right? I know you guys have been friends since you lot were young but, babes,' Jean grabbed my shoulders and stared directly into my eyes again, all humour gone from his face, 'she is fucking toxic, and never been the type to wish you well. When has she ever seriously been there for you? Who do you call first when you're feeling low or having a great day? I know it's not her, is it? Your friendship with her is contingent on her always looking or being better than you in some way, and it's not on, considering how much of an absolute diamond you are, babe.'

I knew Jean was right. I knew that cutting her off would

hurt, but nonetheless I think I've always known that it would come down to this.

'Man. I know, I know,' I sighed, pouring myself another shot of Wray and Nephew. This was going to be a long night.

'Aight, so let's park you and Aneni's shit friendship for now. When you're in the mood to, we can unpack and process your feelings about all that. In the meantime, seeing as Ruben sent actual-YOU a follow request, that speaks volumes, babes. Have you even considered that?'

I hadn't, funnily enough.

'No,' I responded, feeling myself getting more and more tipsy as the minutes rolled by.

'Well, chile, you need to. Maybe you didn't need to use a fake picture after all. But we'll cross that bridge when we get to it.'

Me and Jean spent the next couple of hours covering all my bases, getting through three-quarters of the bottle of rum. By the time it came for Jean to book his Uber home, we'd come up with a list of action points which we ran through again while he was putting on his shoes.

'OK, so! Point one. Cali . . . California!' Jean slurred lazily. 'You are *definitely* going to California. You are . . . definitely having that meeting for work and you will definitely *not* take a day trip to Oakland to find that damn man, OK?'

'Yes! Yes, got you, no stalking,' I confirmed, a little bit waved from the drinks myself. 'I'm gonna stay in San Francisco and not cross that damn bridge, and I'm gonna do my meeting and it's gonna be awesome because I'm a fucking awesome babe!'

'YES QUEEN!' Jean shouted. 'But also . . . I've lost my boot somewhere in your room . . .' He hiccupped while I knelt down laughing, looking for Jean's other Doc Marten boot under my bed.

'And, and, point TWO!' I exclaimed, locating his boot and holding it in the air like a trophy. 'I'm gonna follow Ruben *back* on Instagram and slowly start chatting to him as myself and slowly stop talking to him from my Aloe account. Let's see where that shit goes!' I threw Jean's boot at him, which he failed to dodge in his drunken state. The boot hit him in the chest.

'You've got a strong arm, man,' Jean said, laughing while struggling to put the boot on. 'I think you should still talk to him as you have been for a bit as Aloe, though, in case he gets suspicious. ALSO, I think you, as you, should let him know you're coming to California! He may wanna meet, for all you know?'

I grabbed the bottle and swigged a bit more. 'I ammm gonna have to face Aneni at some point and tell her that the friendship is fully done, but I'll do that after the whole Ruben situation is sorted!' I punctuated this with a loud burp.

'*Wunderbar!*' shouted Jean, checking the status of his Uber driver.

'Do you even know what *wunderbar* means?'

'I do, actually. You're not the only one who's watched *The Sound of Music*, you know. I'm cultured, too!' We both burst into fits of laughter.

'OK, OK, in all seriousness though,' continued Jean, 'I'm gonna fucking hold you accountable for all this, OK? We can fix all this shit if you stick to the fucking plan.'

'I WILL I WILL, I PROMISE,' I shouted, perhaps a bit louder than necessary.

Out of nowhere, came three sharp thuds on my wall: Natalie's attempt at trying to get us to shut up. Jean looked at the wall, then at me.

'Sorry about her,' I muttered.

'Oh, please,' Jean replied, grinning mischievously. 'She's just mad cause she's dull, innit? How can you be pregnant for nine months and go through days of agonising labour just to look at a newborn and name them *Natalie*? And she's as boring as she sounds.'

I gulped and laughed loudly. I just knew Natalie was going to let me have it tomorrow morning. I shouted from the top of my lungs, 'SORRY, NAT!', and burst into fits of laughter.

'You need your own space, man,' Jean said sleepily, checking the app again. 'I honestly couldn't deal.'

'Yeah, she's always passive-aggressive. Gets right on my tits,' I replied. 'In fact . . .' I reached over for my phone, opened up Instagram and started typing in my Instagram Stories:

SayAloeToMyLittleFriend: Excited AF to be moving out soon and seeing the back of my neurotic, Taylor Swift-stanning, oat-milk-drinking, Peloton-owning, passive-aggressive super Karen of a flatmate LOL

I threw my phone back onto the bed, closed my eyes and exhaled. It felt good to release some of that frustration.

'And you know what?' I slurred. 'I'm gonna accept Ruben's follow request because it's only polite, and it's not – hic – nice to ignore people!'

'Yes the fuck you are! That, and viewing one-bed flats ASAP so you can get out of this fucking apartment.'

I groggily hugged Jean goodbye as his cab arrived, and the door had barely shut before I'd fallen straight into a drunken sleep.

Chapter 23

Except for the raging hangover, I woke up the next day brand new. I had a little pep in my step, a game plan, and physically I felt so much lighter. I'd definitely made the right choice confessing all to Jean, and as I strolled in to work fifteen minutes late, cappuccino in hand, wearing a pair of bright-yellow Loewe sunglasses that violently clashed against my lime-green J Crew suit, I felt untouchable. Almost like a little piece of me was back.

It had been hard to admit to myself before, but speaking to Ruben while keeping this massive secret had been slowly taking its toll on me, both physically and mentally. Every morning I'd wake up anxious, not knowing if today would be the day that Ruben found out about my lies. Not to mention the extreme guilt I'd been carrying about the fact that I'd been consistently lying by omission while falling deeper and deeper for him.

Am I currently still lying? Absolutely.

But the key here is that progress has been made on finding a way out, and while it's a small step, it's still something.

I arrived at my office and instantly jumped online to order a mini chocolate cake with the words 'Edelweiss' inscribed on top to send to Jean, hoping Jean would get the *Sound of Music* reference. After dealing with a plethora of email responses, press quotes and potential client briefs, I uploaded a couple of plant posts on Aloe's account. This week, it was a simple photo of my new Swiss cheese plant with the caption underneath:

> **SayAloeToMyLittleFriend:** Hey guys! Meet my new plant of the week and the newest addition to Chez Aloe – his name's Ruben! Isn't he a handsome one?

I was being super cutesy, I suppose, but it felt nice. Was this what it felt like to do normal, couple shit? The post got over 1000 'likes' within the next hour, including a few love-heart emojis from Ruben, and a WhatsApp message:

> **Ruben:** You're so damn cute, haha. I'm so honoured to have my own plant – an Aloe Special! Ugh. Wish I could give you a hug right now. Have a beautiful day, babygirl ☺

I replied:

> **Me:** It's what you deserve, babe! Sleep well, I look forward to speaking tomorrow xx'

Ruben instantly responded:

> **Ruben:** Hopefully on video or somethin? X

This damn video request. I really wish he would let that go.

A few days later, I decided to complete one of my action tasks set by Jean and finally accept Ruben's follow request on my private account. After all, what's the worst that could happen? He might just lazily look at the profile of a random British woman, find out she ain't really worth looking at and then exit out of my profile and never look at it again . . . I mean, sure, that would be heartbreaking, but I didn't want to think about that right now. I took a deep breath and clicked on 'accept', and then I followed him back. It was done.

Then I stared at his Instagram page, waiting for . . . What? I had no idea. Maybe a direct message from him? Maybe a subsequent unfollow after realising the terrible mistake he'd made? From my personal account, I made sure to 'like' his latest photos so I'd stay fresh in his mind once he eventually checked his account.

Minutes passed, and still nothing.

Fuck it.

I opened up my messages and got to typing.

Me: Hey! Thanks for adding me on here, and apologies for the excess spamming. I'm really loving your plant collection, and your music clips, too! Have a great day x

I stared at it. Sounded plausible enough? I didn't think I was coming on too strong or anything. I could feel the nerves beginning to boil within the pits of my belly as I pressed 'send'. I waited with bated breath for the dreaded 'read' receipt. Still nothing came, so I closed the app and decided to try and distract myself by doing some more online flat hunting.

After arranging dates and times to view six flats over the following week, I shut my laptop off and tried to go to sleep, but my brain was too fixated on the thought of Ruben checking out the real me. This web of lies was starting to get entangled, and I needed to get my head straight if I was going to play this correctly.

'Do you think you're ready for San Fran?' Jean asked as we walked along the Embankment after work.

'Yeah, I think I'm ready you know,' I replied, interlocking my fingers with Jean's. 'I've had a few back-to-back calls with the brand and have gone over the presentation I did with Stephen a while ago, so I think I should be all set. I'd be lying if I said I wasn't nervous about pitching for my first international brand, but I think – *I think* – I'll be able to nail it. I just need to keep the confidence up, I suppose!'

Jean gave me a look as if to say 'poor baby' and eventually replied: 'I mean, that's cool and all, sis, but I was actually talking about the whole Ruben thing. Remember we decided that whatever happened, you were NOT going to go around stalking or hiding in the bushes or some shit tryna get a look at him from afar, right? You're there to work, and work you shall. If you do *have* to see him, you have to come out with the truth.'

I felt my smile slightly fade as we approached the restaurant. Jean was right, but hearing him saying it out loud still didn't feel that great. How would I be so close, but yet so far from seeing him? Ruben and I had been talking for ages and what with him being a creature of habit, he'd often visit the same workspaces, coffee shops or office buildings during the day, with him turning on his camera occasionally so I would watch him work every now and again. I had a feeling I could find him without needing to try too hard . . .

It was tempting, but I told myself that the risk would be too great. Although, I guess it wouldn't hurt to let him know that I would be visiting as myself? That way, I could still get my fix and see him, and he'd be none the wiser that I was the person he's been talking to for weeks?

Shit. Is liking someone supposed to be this hard?

'You're right yet again, my friend,' I replied to Jean, grabbing a seat in the outside area of the seafood restaurant while the waitress brought our menus.

'Speaking of possible surprises, Temz – guess what?'

'What?' I replied, grateful for the subject change.

Jean reached into his bag and pulled out an issue of *Marie*

Claire magazine. Gracing the cover was Lupita Nyong'o in a denim co-ord suit, looking absolutely incredible. She was lying down in a field of sunflowers, looking pensively yet elegantly at the camera. Jean opened up the magazine to the editor's page and tapped his fingers at the credits.

'Photographer . . . Jean Morel . . .' I looked up at him. 'Oh, my God. OH MY GOD! So THIS is the secret shoot you were working on? Jesus, Jean!' I exclaimed, disturbing the patrons who were sitting near us. I glanced at the cover again, beaming with pride and joy at my best friend getting his first international fashion magazine cover.

'Babes, I can barely believe it myself. Do you know how hard it was to keep this shit a secret?' Jean beamed, his face breaking into his beautiful signature grin. 'The whole process of getting to this point was fucking chaotic, but we did it, babes, we did it! Hopefully the Tate exhibition is next!'

I leaned across the table to give him a hug. It made me feel good knowing that both of us were at great places in our lives and that we had each other through it all. I leaned into the hug even more, feeling the weight of my anxiety slowly leave my body.

In another lifetime, I'm sure that Jean and I would have made the perfect couple, but I also loved the state of our current relationship: a paradox of chaos and stability. That – in and of itself – is what made us incredibly tight-knit.

This was a lot of deep shit to be thinking about on a Wednesday, however. After I'd finished my dinner with Jean, I high-tailed my way through rush-hour traffic to get to my flat-viewing appointment in Streatham Hill.

Since I began my quest for the perfect flat some time ago, I'd probably seen about twelve flats, with none being to my liking. But I'd found this quaint little Art Deco place on Rightmove at around 3 o'clock in the morning a day ago during a long chat with Ruben.

> Me: . . . Yeah, but my thing is, if you don't have anything nice to say, then fuck the fuck off, innit?
>
> Ruben: Every day I'm learning new British things and I love it babe, haha. 'Fuck the fuck off'? I'm keeping that.
>
> Me: But it's true though! I hate online trolls so much, and you've done nothing to warrant those stupid comments on your YouTube video – you literally sound like an angel.
>
> Ruben: It's all good! It comes with the territory when you put yourself out there online, but I love the fact that you're willing to go to war to defend me, you're adorable!
>
> Me: Hehe. Anything to protect— hold on. I think I've found a fla— an apartment I like the look of!
>
> Ruben: Oh, yeah? What's it like? Does it fit your criteria?
>
> Me: Mmmmmm yeahhh but give me two secs, I'm gonna email the estate agent so they see my message as soon as they get into the office later on in the morning. This flat is gorgeous!
>
> Ruben: You go girl, I hope you're able to get a viewing!

It was a modern, fifth floor, two-bedroom, two-bathroom flat situated on the corner of Streatham High Road and Leigham Court Road, complete with a modern kitchen and bathroom, and loads of natural light – something I'd insisted on due to the number of plants I owned. And while the rent was eye-watering, I reckoned that I would be able to just about manage it. I was a big woman now. Doing Big! Woman! Things!! It felt good to be back in the driver's seat.

When I eventually arrived at the flat in Streatham Hill, I was greeted by the hugely enthusiastic estate agent, who looked about fifteen. After taking the lift up to the fifth floor, we entered the flat and the first thing that blew me away was the amount of natural light – I was literally bathed in the glow of the sunset, with the heat feeling incredible on my face. The flat was spacious, with a huge open-plan reception area shared with the modern kitchen space. The electric stove was centred on its own island with storage space on either side, and wide windows took up the entire width of the wall. It was incredible.

'The tenants moved out a few days ago, so we will be repainting the walls just to go over the artwork scuff marks, of course,' the estate agent grinned as he walked me through the flat. Some light paintwork was definitely needed, but outside of that I was already sold. I took photos of both of the small bedrooms – my idea was to use the second bedroom as a guest bedroom, with some added wardrobe space for me as well – and the main bathroom was gorgeous. It featured a waterfall walk-in shower with gold hardware, underfloor heating and a huge bathtub that could easily fit two people.

I was in love with the place. It was simple, neutral, modern and flooded with light. The view wasn't bad either, with a south-west-facing view of both the Streatham and Brixton Hill skylines. There was a calmness about this flat that just seemed to vibe with my energy. I could be happy here.

'Honestly? This place is absolutely stunning,' I gushed to the estate agent. 'How many viewings has it had so far?'

'You're the second,' he replied. 'I have another two viewings after you in a couple of hours; we think it may prove to be a popular place. You're right near the station, and you've got several buses going directly to Brixton, Clapham, Croydon and Crystal Palace, so from a public transport perspective, it's a fantastic location.'

I couldn't agree more. I let the agent know that I wanted to make an offer immediately, throwing in a cheeky eighteen-month break clause arrangement to sweeten the deal.

'Oh, fabulous!' he exclaimed, clasping his hands together. 'Well, if that's the case, if you can fill out the offer form and provide the holding deposit this evening, we can get things moving and hold this place for you, as well as cancel tonight's viewings!'

'Sounds great to me, thanks!'

This was it! Was it all moving a little too fast? Maybe, but I was going with the flow. This place felt right. The beginning of a whole new chapter.

Later on that evening, by grim circumstance, I received yet another message from Anthony:

Anthony: Hey hey, when are you going to let me taste your chocolate again? Can't wait to see you. 😊

Why wouldn't this guy leave me alone? I let out a sigh and deleted his message. An Instagram notification from my phone diverted my attention. It was an update from Aneni's account, but sent to my Aloe account. I'd forgotten to unfollow her from that one, but unable to help myself, I abandoned my 'life list' and checked to see the latest in Aneni's oh-so-glamorous life. As long as she didn't notice that I was still following from that account, I decided that I'd keep following her from it, just to spy on her from time to time.

I scrolled past a few of her most recent posts, which were typically all the same: selfies of her surrounded by expensive products, wearing expensive things. *Groundbreaking*. Her recent IG Stories consisted of her dancing at what looked like some random industry party, surrounded by C-list rappers and bottles of what looked like expensive champagne. *Meh*. I wasn't missing out on much, then. As I scoffed to myself, my phone (which felt like Clapham Junction Station with the amount of traffic

I'd been receiving today) pinged again, delivering a notification from my personal account:

You have received a message from RubesCubes.

Oh, shit! We were in the endgame now.

Chapter 24

I called Jean immediately.

'Jean, what do I do? I'm scared to read it. What if it's bad? I don't know what I was thinking messaging him from my personal account.'

I had been pacing up and down in the kitchen in a frenzied panic, mug of tea in hand as I fretted down the phone to Jean. In the grand scheme of things, it was only a fucking response to my message, but it didn't stop my mind from catastrophising.

Note to self: find a fucking therapist.

'Bitch, I need you to calm down,' Jean replied. 'It's just a message and, besides, what's the worst that could happen? Think of it this way: if he wasn't interested in your profile or anything you had to say in that message, why would he have bothered to hit you back?'

Jean had a point.

'I dunno. He's a nice guy and maybe he took pity on me or something and replied to be nice, like he sees me as a fan or something,' I replied, taking a large gulp of my tea in an effort to calm my nerves. I was an expert at always going straight to the worst-case scenario.

I heard Jean chuckle to himself on the other end. 'I mean, sis . . . you *are* kind of a fan of his, innit? But I digress,' he quickly followed as I bellowed out an exasperated sigh. 'Just give it a chance and stop expecting the worst, Temz. You're gonna be fine. Do you wanna stay on the phone with me while you read it?'

On hearing that, I suddenly felt an overwhelming pang of shame in the pit of my stomach. I wasn't seven years old, and I didn't need an adult to hold my hand. I was one of the senior directors in one of the biggest advertising agencies in Europe, and here I was too terrified to open a little message. I sighed.

'Nah. I'm just freaking out, I'm sorry,' I replied. 'I'm all good, babe. I'll open it in a bit and let you know what he's saying. Sorry for calling you so late.'

I ended the call and stared at my phone. Another gulp of tea later, I opened up Instagram to face the message head-on. Whatever happened, I was still an awesome bitch. As I scrolled through to my DM page and opened the message, I felt goose-bumps raise on my skin in reaction to the slight draught in the kitchen air – or at least I thought that's what it was.

RubesCubes: Hey Artemis, thanks for the msg (and for adding me!). You have a gorgeous name, it's so regal and powerful. Don't worry about the spamming, haha. It's all good and you're super kind. I'm glad you like the music and I hope everything is going well across the pond 😄

The world didn't end, and the stars didn't fall to the earth. I reread the message several times, a massive beaming smile spreading across my lips.

He was probably so used to women messaging him being thirsty, in all fairness, *but he liked my name*! Shoutout to my parents for naming me such excellence!

'Girl, all that drama for nothing. I TOLD you it was going to be OK!' Jean yelled as I immediately called him back to debrief.

Now that I'd made successful contact with Ruben, I knew that I needed to start enacting Step Two of my plan.

'OK, so now my plan is just keep trying to have conversations with him, and slowwwwly stop talking to him from my Aloe account,' I said, simultaneously writing down my points in bullet form. 'I was thinking about straight blocking him on WhatsApp and IG once it feels right, just to make a clean break. But that's cruel, innit? I don't want to hurt him.'

Jean snorted. 'Ha! Oh, girl, you think you're me! Yeah, don't do that. You have way too much empathy to be a savage. We are a strong people; a proud people,' he replied as we both chuckled.

'He's already liked about five of the photos on my personal account, so he must think I'm at least a *little* cute? Jean, I can picture it in my head already; he'll begin getting more and more distant from Aloe, we'll get closer and then *he'll* block Aloe altogether and declare his love for me at some point. It's perfect, right?'

Silence, on the other end of the phone.

I carried on. 'I'm gonna have to see if I can finesse a work phone so that when I give him my number, it won't be the same as Aloe's. Fuck, I'm gonna need to start upping those gym sessions. I want him to be OBSESSED with me.'

The silence continued.

Eventually, Jean's voice broke through the emptiness.

'Artemis Owusu. You are my girl, and you know I love you down – but you truly are one of the most unhinged people I know. This is cool and all, but remember how amazing you are; you don't need to be doing all this for a man. You're amazing as is. And anyway, you don't need to get a new phone, just use one of those Google Voice app things that gives you a fake number.'

He was right. I needed to pull it back, just a little.

'You always know just what to say, Jean. Love you – and thank you for low-key enabling me!'

'Girl, bye.'

One of the perks of my new role was that I could work from home as and when I wanted on the days where I didn't have any meetings or business development tasks. Today was one such day, and so I had a lie-in, waking up at 8.30 a.m. and sighing groggily underneath my sheets as my body tried to hang on to the last bits of warmth before being pulled out of bed. The events of last night and Ruben's friendly message back were still fresh on my mind, and a broad grin spread across my face as I hopped out of bed.

Ruben replied to me! And it was nice! And he was making genuine conversation, showing interest in my things!

I cracked open my laptop with a bottle of Supermalt in hand, telling myself that today would be spent on finalising my pitch presentation for One Nation Athletics, but I was still a little distracted. *Ruben had added me and was liking my real-life, full-bodied photos.* The dopamine hit was intense.

He'd 'liked' a photo of me at my birthday party after my face had been slammed into my birthday cake. Bits of cake were strung throughout my hair, face and bosom, and I was wearing a very tight purple bodycon boob tube dress that showed every curve of my body. He'd even taken the time to scroll all the way back down my feed and 'like' a photo of me on my first day of work, looking like a super awkward newbie in an ill-fitting blazer suit and a goofy, lopsided smile.

He'd scrolled through my entire feed. He actually wanted to see more of me.

The guilt I had been trying in vain to compartmentalise again reared its ugly head; this could have been so much easier if I had just led with the real me. Damn it.

215

He commented on my most recent photo, featuring me and a beautiful white Pomeranian dog we'd met in Clapham Common, writing 'This is hella adorable!' Whether he'd meant the dog or me I wasn't sure, but a win was a win. The fact remained that he was currently enjoying ME and the content that I was putting out. Maybe I could pull off my plan of having him fall in love with the real me after all? A girl could dream!

Testing out my new-found confidence, I sent Ruben a message.

Me: Everything goes well this side of the pond, my friend (notwithstanding the weather, of course). How long have you been singing? I loved the cover you did of Tyrese's 'Shame'. Your tone is so gorgeous. Do you have an EP out or anything?

Easing myself into his good graces via the age-old 'potential buyer' scam seemed like the best way forward for now.

Eventually, I wrestled myself away from my phone and turned to my laptop to get going with work. Halfway through finalising my presentation, I heard Natalie knocking about in the kitchen, banging pots and pans and generally being louder than normal, to the point where I wasn't sure whether she was doing it intentionally to annoy me or not.

'One Nation Athletics have established themselves as one of the pioneers of the athleisure trends in the United States,' I mumbled out loud to myself, trying to concentrate as I read through my presentation notes.

Bang! Clink! Crash! came sounds from the kitchen. I reached over for my earphones to drown out the racket, and continued rehearsing:

'. . . cementing themselves as a heritage brand, whose legacy has included creating the first pair of breathable, compression leggings—'

Slam! Bang! Smash!

I shut my laptop in frustration. Didn't Natalie know that I was preparing for one of the most important pitches in my career? I took my earbuds out as I had a quick thought: I should use this opportunity to tell Natalie I was moving out. Something in hindsight I should have told her a couple of weeks ago, but meh, we're here now.

I put on a pair of slippers and made my way to the kitchen to make a cup of tea. May as well try and take the sting out of what would perhaps gear up to be an awkward situation. I pulled out a chair to sit down at the table to wait for the kettle to boil. Natalie was near the sink, aggressively piling crockery into the dishwasher as if the appliance had wronged her in some way.

'Umm, Natalie d'you want a cup?' I asked her.

'No.'

'Are you OK? Look, I'm not sure what you have going on for the rest of the day, but I was wondering if you would be down for a quick chat?'

Natalie responded by slamming the dishwasher door shut, sighing and standing upright to face me.

'What, pray tell, would you want to chat with me about, Artemis?'

Que??

'Um, I'm not sure what's gotten your goat today, babe, but where's the attitude coming from? What's going on with you? Did you get broken up with again or something?'

OK, that was uncalled for, I'm such a villain. But her projecting her nonsense onto me was also not called for!

Natalie squinted at me and scoffed. 'No, Artemis. I'm absolutely fine, but let's chat, seeing as you have something you need to get off your chest.' She made a grand display of pulling out one of the chairs to sit down at the table.

She was so bloody pathetic. I had originally intended to break the news to her sensitively, but fuck that. 'Uhhh. OK, cool. Well. I was planning to move out soon. I was hoping to give you notice after I got back from my work trip, if that's OK? To give me time to pack and sort my stuff out?'

Natalie's face did not change or react in any way. Instead, she continued staring at me, with a weird, sly grin spreading across her face.

'Do you have any response to that . . . ? What's going on with you?'

The silence and the staring continued. Just as I was about to return to the sanctuary of my bedroom, Natalie finally spoke.

'So. It took you that long to finally let me know, huh?'

'Let you know what? About me leaving?'

'Well, what else would I be talking about?' Natalie spat, her face slowly turning a deep shade of puce. 'Weren't you the one who said you were, AND I QUOTE . . .' She reached into her pocket to get her phone, scrolling to whatever it was she was trying to find. I was still completely baffled.

'OK, here we go. Did you or did you not claim to be "Excited AF to be moving out soon and seeing the back of my neurotic, Taylor Swift-stanning, oat-milk-drinking, Peloton-owning, passive-aggressive super Karen of a flatmate LOL"?'

Oh, shit. She'd seen it.

My drunken IG story from the other night. I'd forgotten I'd actually posted it. More importantly, I'd forgotten that Natalie followed me on my Aloe account, so of course she must have seen it! The memory of me writing that a week or so ago was vaguely coming back to me now – she must have screenshot it. No wonder why Natalie had been super quiet with me lately. I'd just assumed that she was going through yet another break-up and wanted to be alone.

Ugh. There's absolutely no way I could lie myself out of this one. The facts were there in black and white. I just had to take the L.

'I apologise, but I was angry, Natalie. You'd kept banging on my wall when Jean was over to chill because I was super upset that day. I wrote it out of anger, and I'm sorry. You just haven't been the easiest person to live with . . . it's been tough!'

Natalie's mouth formed a perfect 'O' before quickly returning to a thin slit, as did her eyes. For a few seconds there, she reminded me of Voldemort in the face.

'Well, it hasn't been a day at the park for me either you know,' she finally replied, hands on her hips, sweat beads forming on her forehead. I could anticipate the beginnings of a full-blown rant, and considering I hadn't told her about my plans to move, oh, and the whole social media post thing, I guess I deserved it this time. I sat down and braced myself for impact.

'I would have thought you'd be grateful for the room, but since you've been here, it's been nothing but thirty-minute showers, weird-smelling, disgusting food in the fridge, your wild hair clogging up the shower drains all the time and you bringing random guys home at all hours of the day and night. Have I ever complained though? No!'

I stared at her as I tried to process this information. Did she just call me a—?

I should be *grateful*?

Weird-smelling, disgusting food?

'Wild' hair?

'You didn't exactly pluck me from poverty, Natalie. I saw the room because you posted it on the flatshare site. YOU were the one desperate for a roommate. And by "weird-smelling, disgusting food", you're talking about my Ghanaian stews that I cook and seal tightly in a Tupperware box in the fridge?'

Natalie's gaze lowered at this. I wasn't sure whether she knew she'd crossed the line, but she was still on a roll.

'Whatever it is, it stinks. I just wish you would cook normal food! And yes, you should be grateful that I gave you discounted rent. I picked you for a reason, and after everything your people had been through, I would have thought that you'd—'

'Hang on,' I interrupted, trying to piece the bits of information together. I could feel a rage deep inside me beginning to cook as I realised what Natalie may have been alluding to. I just needed her to say it, confirming my belief before I reacted.

'Why did you choose me to live with you? And what the entire fuck do you mean by "your people"?'

At that, Natalie's expression instantly transformed into one of sheer panic. Her eyes darted to and fro as she tried to clear up her rant.

'I mean . . . given what happened that summer with the Black Lives Matter movement and everything . . .' she started, stuttering over her words. 'I was actually trying to be a decent human being, and I did my part. I chose you out of all the other people that I'd met with who seemed loads more . . . more compatible. I discounted your rent because I wanted to actually be an ally! I—'

Natalie immediately stopped speaking as she studied the shift in my face. I stared at her, silently daring her to continue. Finally, I stood and turned to face her directly, trying as hard as possible to remain calm.

'So,' I huffed, pacing myself. Turning into an 'Angry Black Woman' right now would only reinforce the stereotypes that Natalie clearly already held of me. 'Firstly, that comment about "normal" food? Unnecessary, disrespectful and pretty fucking racist.' Natalie took one step back, grabbing the countertops. Was she – cowering? *Was she being for real right now?!*

'Secondly, are you saying that you only accepted my application to move in because I'm Black and you wanted to be "down for the cause"? Are you fucking for real right now? And why do you keep stepping back? You think I'm gonna hit you or something?'

Natalie's breathing was getting shallower and shallower. I couldn't tell if she was gearing up for another shouting match or whether she was going to pass out, and frankly I couldn't give a shit. This stupid, racist, performative bitch had gotten on my last nerve.

'I don't understand why you're getting upset over that!' Natalie retorted, her hair falling into her eyes. 'I thought it would be good to help someone out who was in more of a financial bind than me!'

I'd always known that she had bad vibes, but the levels of fuckery right now were incredibly spectacular.

'Less fortunate? I graduated from Cambridge University at the top of my class, and when I came to view this flat I could absolutely pay my way, so what the fuck do you mean by "less fortunate"? Do you hear yourself?'

Natalie had stopped quivering. Instead, she just stared at me. I stared at her, the two of us — after months of living together in a thick cloud of tension — now knowing where each other stood.

'Whatever,' Natalie replied. 'The damage has been done now. Maybe it's for the best anyway. When did you say you were gonna leave again?'

I pursed my lips. 'I wanted to put in my notice after my trip, like I said.'

'Maybe you should leave sooner than that.'

Was she taking the piss? I knew that things had become tense, but I would be flying out to San Francisco in just over a week. How could she expect me to pack up all my shit and move while I still had this pitch to complete?

'You know that I'm going to the States, I'll be away soon. You have to allow me to stay until I come back and can sort everything. I'll hardly be here anyway, so we can just stay out of each other's way!'

Natalie paused, then turned around to face me, arms crossed. 'Whatever. When you're in the States, I'll start showing your room for viewings, then.'

'Great.'

And with that, I hastily finished making my cup of chai tea and made a beeline to my bedroom, my mind buzzing after that confrontation. I always knew I was living with a Karen, but I didn't know how deep the levels went.

I couldn't leave fast enough.

Chapter 25

A week later, making sure that Natalie was nowhere in the flat to be found, I belted out the lyrics of one of my favourite Beyoncé songs, wading through the absolute cesspit that was my bedroom. I had been packing for the better part of the day and I'd just had a bottle of my beloved Supermalt along with some homemade jollof rice to fuel my second wind. In the corner of my room lay a suitcase half packed for San Francisco, while strewn across the breadth of the floor and bed were piles and piles of clothes, bags and accessories that I had started packing into boxes, ready for my exciting big move into the new flat I'd just signed a lease for. I'd lucked into it just after my argument with Natalie, and it would be baby's first solo apartment. I was so gassed to be moving into it in just a few weeks. Natalie hadn't spoken to me since our little confrontation, which, to be perfectly honest, was fine with me.

In the middle of my perfectly executed choreography of 'Crazy in Love', yet another message came through from Anthony. Over the last week, he'd been sending increasingly gross messages that were starting to creep me out, though I hadn't blocked him yet – I just kept them all on 'read'. I couldn't bring myself to cut the cord just yet. What if I needed one last hurrah on a bad day?

Anthony: Hey hey sexy lady . . . can't stop thinking about you and your chocolate self. U up? Tx

Anthony: Hey Miss Chocolate, don't know if you saw my message above, you up? Xx

Anthony: You have no business being this gorgeous, hun. I can't believe you don't miss me too! Was this about the oral thing? I can change for you, haha.

Whew. I was unaware I'd made this much of an impact. It felt good, in all honesty.

Jean was coming over to help me dissemble and move around some of the bigger furniture bits, like my mirror, the bedside table and my chest of drawers. Despite the current chaos around me, I was in a good-ass mood.

Why?

Because my random daily check-ins with Ruben on my own account seemed to be proving fruitful; positive, even. Even though they were rarely more than a few sentences long, and we'd mostly talk about nothing, I felt like I was falling for him all over again now I was able to be my more authentic self.

RubesCubes: Hey Artemis! Thanks for the compliment on my photo; I work in tech but music is my main passion. I haven't had time to do an EP yet, but it's definitely something that's on the list – that would be the dream!

ItsArtemis_O: Please, call me Temz for short. 😊 That's so cool! The world needs to hear your gorgeous voice. I hope you're having a great day xx

RubesCubes: Thanks beautiful, appreciate your support. 😊

ItsArtemis_O: ♥

RubesCubes: Have you ever been to the States before?

ItsArtemis_O: I have! I've been to New York a few times with friends, and Vermont randomly, but that was coz I went on the Ben and Jerry's factory tour. Ahhhh ... good times.

RubesCubes: LMAO. I ...

ItsArtemis_O: Hey now ... not too much on Ben and Jerry's. It's a supreme brand of ice cream and I'll defend it to the death!

RubesCubes: First of all, I agree. BJ's are good. They are my favourite too. Secondly, I find it hilarious and charming that you only visited that boring-ass state for the ice cream tour, and THIRDLY, you need to get your ass over to the West Coast if you've never been. Best part of the States by far. 😃

ItsArtemis_O: I'm going to assume you meant to add an ampersand between the B and J? Not that I'm complaining; I also think BJ's are good, depending on your interpretation of said acronym ...

RubesCubes: HA. You're a weird, funny lady. I like that. I will neither confirm nor deny your implication ma'am. 😃 #LongLiveBJs #&&&&&

ItsArtemis_O: I constantly have this discussion with my friends, though! It feels like from the outside, American guys seem a lot more emotionally intelligent and romantic than UK guys. We are THIRSTY for attention out here!

RubesCubes: Haha! You would think so but I'm not too sure on that! I can't speak for all the men out here, but we do have our own share of fuckery here as well. I like to think I'm a decent guy though – at least I try, haha.

ItsArtemis_O: Uhuh, I'm sure you more than try! An attractive man who can sing? Babes you're taking it. This is purely based on my assumptions, of course ... 😊

RubesCubes: LOL! High praise coming from a pretty lady such as yourself. Thank you, ma! You're too kind.

Every time he called me 'beautiful' or complimented my appearance, I felt a pang of guilt in the pit of my stomach; maybe I should just come clean as myself instead of carrying on the Aloe ruse. Our conversations weren't as long as the ones I had with Ruben as Aloe, but even though I knew that male validation over my appearance was totally unnecessary, somehow it still made me feel really good about myself. He saw me for who I was, and seemed to like me anyway. I wasn't used to men like Ruben talking to women like me, and I was hooked. The attention he gave me was addictive. I had to stay on guard every time we spoke, however – there had already been a couple of occasions where I'd gotten confused and almost accidentally messaged him from my Aloe account instead of my real account and vice versa:

SayAloeToMyLittleFriend: Hey babe ♥ not you uploading thirst traps for the whole world to see?? Wowowow this relationship is ...

Oh, shit! Delete, delete, delete!

Another time, I accidentally sent him a photo of one of my Aloe plants from my personal account, but once again the time distance Gods were on my side and I was able to quickly delete the message before Ruben had the opportunity to see it. Chile! I was skating on thin ice.

I smiled to myself as I packed my cleavage-enhancing black midi dress into one of the black bags. Ruben had liked a pic of me in that dress, and I made a mental note to wear it out more often.

My Beyoncé sing-a-thon was interrupted by a call coming through on my phone. It was Ruben. *Shit.* Mere weeks ago, seeing his name come up on my phone would incite feelings of excitement, but these days, with the pressure of realising what I had done combined with the newfound connection I'd been able to spark with Ruben as myself, I felt nothing but dread. I needed to cut the head off this snake, and it looked like merely ignoring him for large periods of time wasn't doing the trick.

Around the ninth ring, I picked up.

'Hey you.'

'Hey babygirl. How are you doing? Long time no hear.'

'I'm good, thanks, how are you?'

This was already feeling awkward as fuck.

'I'm good. I've missed you.'

What was that I heard? The sound of my heart breaking in two? *Oh, Temz, you absolute bitch.*

'Aww, I've missed you too!'

That's right, Temz. Keep it short and sweet.

'Huh. You sure about that? I've been trying to call you a few times lately but you always seem to be busy, which is absolutely fine if you have shit going on and stuff. I just wanted to make sure my favourite Brit was OK.'

Ugh, he makes it so hard to avoid being drawn to him.

'Haha! Well, I wouldn't want you to worry. She's doing just fine. I've been really overwhelmed with work at the moment, sorry I haven't caught up with you for a while. How have you been?'

Every fibre in my being wanted to tell him right there and then that I was Artemis, and to just come clean about everything. Leading this double life was affecting my mental health. There was no doubt in my mind that I wanted this man, but in a perfect world, I wanted to have this man as me, Artemis. Not

227

as some conventionally pretty, mixed-race slim woman. This was all such a mess.

I was too balls-deep in my own self-loathing, however, to hear the next words that came out of his mouth.

'Huh? What did you say?' I asked quietly.

'I said, you don't happen to know of a chick called Artemis, do you? I added her on Instagram a while ago and I saw that she follows you, too, so I was only wondering. As a matter of fact, I've been getting hella interest from the UK ladies recently, haha. Don't get jealous now!'

In today's episode of 'When Hearts Attack . . .'

I went numb for all of 2.5 seconds before I responded:

'Err, no, I don't think I know anyone by that name. What's her username?'

Viola Davis could NEVER!!

I had to sit there squirming, listening to Ruben spell out my own username to me. Despite me wanting nothing more than to rid myself of this guilt, I couldn't bring myself to confess yet. The words weighed heavy in my throat, ready to reveal all, but the confidence that I had been slowly building up had transformed into fear.

'Hmm. No, I don't know her. Maybe she's a fan of the plants! You added her, though, eh? You're not . . . CHEAT-ING on me, already are you?' I replied, trying to sound as humorous as possible. Americans were never good at picking up sarcasm.

'Haha! Nah, not at all, my bad for thinking y'all all know each other over there. She musta seen one of my comments on your photos and added me or some shit. And besides, I'm an Instagram whore. I just end up following people who follow me. It's polite.'

'Uhuh. I got my eye on you!'

'Believe that. My attention is fully occupied with you. How have you been?'

'I've been OK. It's really good to hear your voice. Sorry if I've been a little distant, there's erm . . . a lot going on and stuff.'

'You don't have to explain anything to me. I understand what work can be like, ma.'

Ugh. He was the biggest sweetheart.

'Ugh. You're the biggest sweetheart.'

'Anyway, I don't wanna take up too much of your time. I've been thinking about you a lot over the last few weeks and about this connection we've been able to form. I really hope it's something you feel, too. I don't want you to think my feelings for you have, like, subsided in any way or nothing like that.'

Feelings? Que??

At this last comment, I sat upright, ears pricked. We'd always said we liked each other and how much we wanted to see each other in person one day, but this was the first time I was hearing anything about *feelings*. Was he about to declare his love for me? Was I truly 'that girl'? Well, I didn't need to have to wait to find out what happened next on Dragon Ball Z, because Ruben then followed up with:

'Um, so like . . . I really care about you, Aloe. Like . . . I really like you.' In the background of the conversation I could hear my heart hammering at 300mph. *Isn't this what you wanted, Temz?* I said to myself. *Wasn't this outcome the whole fucking point of talking to him in the first place?*

I paused for a while after he'd finished speaking, allowing myself to internalise his words. Words I genuinely thought I would never hear from someone like him. I didn't want anyone else but him.

'I really like you too, Ruben. Talking to you has quickly become the highlight of my day.'

Sis. Why would you say that?? You are trying to DE-TACH.

I regretted it as soon as I said it. This is something I wanted to declare as me, Artemis, not as Aloe the fraud.

'I wish I could see you right now, baby. I can't wait until we're able to meet. I've been wanting to see the person I've been getting to know. It sucks that your phone camera still ain't fixed. You got insurance on that thing?' Ruben chuckled softly.

He was killing me. I knew this wasn't fair on him, but I couldn't stop now.

'I know we haven't spoken much lately, but if you're ever feeling down or need someone to talk to when things are rough, I hope you realise that you're able to talk to me about anything,' he added.

I was dying inside. Why did he have to be so perfect?

'I . . . wow, um. Thank you so much. You're always so sweet to me, and hopefully we will be able to see each other someday soon. I can't wait!' I was smiling through my silent tears.

The fact is, I was in too deep. It had been a good amount of weeks since we first started talking every day. Despite the plans I'd made with Jean to sort the situation out and come clean once and for all, too many feelings had been invested on both sides for me to rip his heart out now. I didn't think I would be able to take the rejection and disappointment if he somehow found out what I'd done. It would destroy me.

In order to keep my anxiety under control, I decided that I would just cross that bridge when I got there. No use in causing trouble and ruining a great thing, especially now when he's been so incredibly open and wholesome about his feelings for me – or for Aloe, I suppose. It's not as if this was all a *complete* fabrication; he knew nearly everything about me except for how I look and what I did for work (I'd vaguely told him that

I worked in public relations, which was kinda-sorta true?). My feelings about him weren't fabricated, and neither were our deep conversations, which sometimes lasted hours.

I had been so lost in thought about my part to play in all this that I'd completely tuned out of what Ruben was saying on the other end of the line. He had seemingly moved on from the cutesy, wholesome chat, and now was talking about something to do with LA. I snapped out of my internal monologue and entered back into the chat.

'Huh? You're in LA right now, did you say?'

Ruben paused and laughed. 'You ain't listening, huh?'

'I did. I am! I just need you to repeat that one thing, there was a dog barking outside.'

Nice save.

'I said that I'ma be heading to LA for a few days soon. I managed to get a spot to perform at Boomtown Brewery club. I'ma go down there and do a little set real quick. I'm super psyched for it.'

'Oh? Oh, yes, a gig!' I said, trying to make it sound like I was listening to him talk the whole time. 'That's wonderful news, baby! How long are you going to be there for?'

'Thanks. Like two days.'

'Awesome! I bet you're super excited about it,' I said, feeling a bit disjointed. 'Erm, I hope it goes well. I'm really glad we were able to catch up, and hopefully we can speak again before you go? I do have to go, unfortunately, as I'm working, but I'll call you a bit later?'

Was I being too abrupt? I knew that doing a gig was a big deal for him.

'Oh, wow, aight cool. Well, yeah. I'll speak to you later, I hope you have an incredible rest of the evening. Hey . . . I miss you.'

'Thank you so much, babe. I miss you too. Have a great day!'

As if by perfect coincidence, Jean rang the buzzer as soon as I hung up.

I waded through the endless boxes in my room to go and open the front door. Jean stood there looking somewhat mysterious and cunning, then slithered past me, went straight into my bedroom and sat cross-legged on the bed, regarding me knowingly.

I closed the door and walked into my bedroom, confused.

'What's happened? Why are you looking like that?'

Jean continued smiling while he got out his phone. Finally, he said, 'So. Have you heard from Aneni yet?'

'No, haven't been following her since that whole thing in the cafe, why?'

'She messaged me on WhatsApp trying to drag you,' Jean said, seeing my face change. 'She kept talking about finally understanding why you were being so protective over Ruben, and why you didn't want her to talk to him. I fucking let her have it, OK? I know you've known her longer and shit like that, but I dragged her for filth and let her know what a horrible friend she's been to you, and then I blocked her. Frankly I wasn't here for any kind of explanation from her. I hope you don't mind that,' Jean finished, while taking off his coat and rolling up his sleeves.

I stood rooted to the spot. 'What did she mean by "she finally understood why I was so protective of Ruben"?'

'Sis, I have no idea,' Jean said. 'Before I went in on her, I tried to ask her what she meant by it. I dunno if it means they've been talking or whether she said it to piss you off, but she's got a dark spirit, that one.' Jean squinted and kissed his teeth loudly.

'Maybe she knows about the whole catfishing thing?'

'Nah, how could she know, Temz? I'm sure you were covering your tracks.'

'Yeah, but like . . . Maybe she means I was protective because of the whole "her sleeping with my ex" thing again? I don't know, it could be anything.'

Jean leaned in to give me a side hug. 'Well, babes,' he replied, 'whenever you're ready, just give me the signal and I'll drag her again! From scalp to toe!'

'As much as I appreciate you, babes—' I laughed '—let's hope it doesn't come to that!'

'Haha, OK, OK! Anyway, tell me where you're at with all this packing so I can get to work while you update me about this trip and how you're absolutely *not* going out there to secretly stalk your online lover.'

Sometimes, I really hated having friends with morals.

⋆Note to self: moving forward, try and befriend more debaucherous individuals. Maybe visit Shoreditch after dark. Or Ipswich.⋆

Chapter 26

This was it. The plane was descending, and I was about to enter Ruben's domain. On the one hand, I was super excited; I kinda digged the romantic adventure of it all and often daydreamed about the moment we might finally, coincidentally meet; how our eyes would lock and we would run towards each other in slow motion like some God-awful couple on some Channel 5 made-for-daytime-TV movie. I would get butterflies whenever the thought hit me. But then those butterflies would metamorphosise into demonic, dusty moths as soon as I remembered all the lies I'd told. How chaotic.

'*Ladies and gentlemen, British Airways welcomes you to San Francisco. For your safety and the safety of those around you, please remain seated with your seatbelt fastened, and keep the aisles clear until we have arrived at the correct gate. Thank you, once again . . .*'

As a child, I remember my first dream job being that of a flight attendant. The thought of spending most of my time in other countries, living in and out of suitcases and meeting hundreds of new people every day while wearing pretty little hats really appealed to me. That was until I found out that there was a certain weight limit and make-up code, and I swiftly said, 'Aht aht!' and changed career direction.

I stifled a yawn on the plane (where I was also flying business class for the first time – check me the fuck out) as I looked out of the window. Soon I'd be breathing the same(ish) air as my Ruben.

Throughout the eleven-hour plane journey, I had been battling my intrusive thoughts, and I was low-key scared that they were winning . . .

Surely it wouldn't cause any harm if I were to just . . . pass by his neighbourhood?

What's the worst that could happen?

Yeah! What's the big deal anyway? He probably wouldn't recognise me – he only just followed my personal page. I could be anyone to him.

Good point: you know he finds you attractive, and you have good banter; I'm sure he'd be glad to see you even if he did recognise you!?

As long as I kept distancing Aloe from him, hopefully he could phase her out and I could take her place, just like I've been planning.

I mean, yeah? That still sounds viable. I'll have to plan my steps carefully though . . .

You know you want to see him. You have to; this trip is more than a coincidence. You have to tell him, then you have to meet him!

I sounded delusional, even in my own mind. For all I knew, this plan could blow up in my face. But then again, it could potentially go excellently . . . I'll cross that bridge when I get to it, after my presentation. Pun hopefully not intended.

After we landed, I turned on my phone and switched my roaming data on to let work know I'd arrived safe. I received a sweet text from my mum.

Mum: Hello my dear, it's Mummy here. I'm trusting you are well and that you have arrived in the US safely BY THE GRACE OF GOD. Please can you buy these things for me: Aunt Jemima pancake mix, Shea Moisture hair conditioner, bagel seasoning from Trader Bill's, 4 pairs of jeans from

**Levi's in a size M, dry salted grits and strawberry Kool-Aid?
Also try and visit your Auntie Rosemary if you can, OK?
You know she's not well and you never call her. xxx**

I sniggered. If there's one thing African parents will do when
they find out their child is travelling, it's give them a list of shit
to buy and mule back for them. I responded quickly.

**Me: Hey Mum! Yep, just touched down, thanks for checking
in! 1) You can buy Levi's and Shea Moisture in London –
why do you want the US ones? 2) It's Trader Joe's 3) Auntie
Rosemary lives eight hours away in Baltimore. I don't think
I'll have the time, I'm afraid. I'll see what I can do about
the rest, love you! xxx**

I also WhatsApped Jean. We hadn't spoken since he'd told me
about the conversation he'd had with Aneni where he'd eventually blocked her. Since then, all I could think about was her
saying she 'understood why I didn't want Ruben to talk to her'.
She was never this understanding when it came to other guys
she'd taken from me. Why now?

I breezed through the airport uncommonly quickly and
headed towards the car that had been booked for me. I felt
like Naomi Campbell in my neon orange co-ord suit, neon
orange Crocs, oversized Loewe sunglasses and my brand-new
26-inch straight Brazilian lace front wig. I always wore wigs
when flying, due to the cabin pressure and lack of humidity
constantly fucking up my natural hair. I looked like a VIP, and
heads turned towards me as I slipped into the black BMW car.
This was the life I deserved!

We hit the freeway towards my hotel (the Four Seasons hotel,
btw, get into it) and I allowed the fresh coastal air to bathe my
face as I gazed at the terrific skyscraper skyline of San Francisco.
I had to nail this pitch by any means necessary, and I believed I

could, because frankly I was awesome at what I did. Especially given I'd been piecing it all together during my various personal meltdowns and transatlantic dilemmas.

'And right across the Bay over there,' my driver said, breaking me out of my deep thought, 'you can see the City of Oakland. And wayyyy across in the distance back there – you see all those hills?' He rolled down his window and outstretched his arm, directing me to the distant mountainous landscape that stretched back as far as the eyes could see. 'That there is Richmond, my hometown, which is another city in the Bay Area.'

I looked across the Bay to Oakland and sighed. Ruben was literally there, right now. Probably at a coffee shop working from his laptop, or at a meeting in Berkeley. I was so close, yet so far away. I'd promised Jean that I wouldn't do anything stupid, so I had to behave myself.

'Do you prefer Oakland or Richmond to San Francisco?' I asked my driver.

'Oh, absolutely!' he replied, the enthusiasm pouring from his lips. 'We're so much more laid-back in the Oak than in Frisco – people are friendlier, the food is better, the music slaps way harder too . . .'

I listened to my driver go on about the perks of living in Oakland while I closed my eyes and imagined seeing Ruben at his favourite hotspot. How would he react if I *were* to randomly bump into him? I spent the best part of the eleven-hour plane ride wondering if I should just let him know I was here and see what happened, but I couldn't. I had to tie things up with Aloe first. Ruben had thrown a spanner in the works by declaring his 'like' for me as her. If I turned up and explained things to him in person, surely he would commend me for being honest?

I arrived at the hotel twenty minutes later and immediately unpacked my things. My pitch meeting with the athletics brand was in two days' time, meaning I had a couple of days of time-zone adjustments and sightseeing to do before then. As soon as I put away my suitcase, I noticed a missed call notification on WhatsApp from Ruben. Without thinking, I called him straight back.

'Hey baby, sorry I missed your call, what's up?' I said brightly.

'Oh! Uh, I'm sorry I called you, babygirl, it was accidental. Um,, what are you still doing awake?'

Oh, shit. The time difference. It was 6 p.m. local time, meaning it was 2 a.m. back in the UK. I should be 'asleep' by now.

'Oh! I was just packing the rest of my clothes and room bits with Jean. I guess time got away from us, that's all. He left not too long ago so I literally just hopped into bed. Um, how are you?'

I was desperate to move the conversation on quickly to allow myself time to come up with new lies. *That was a close one, Temz. Must be more vigilant next time.*

'Oh, OK. I hope you were able to get a lot of stuff done. I'm aight, I'm in LA for that gig, remember? I'll be back home tomorrow.'

Damn. I'd forgotten that he was going to be in LA.

'Yes, of course. I hope you're having an amazing time. If you get any videos of your show, please send them through. Gimme something to brag about to my mates. They all need to know I'm associated with a sexy-as fuck SUPERSTAR! Get back to Oakland safe,' I replied, faking a yawn.

'Ha! You glory chaser. I will, babygirl. I'll tell you all about it when I get back,' Ruben replied, and I imagined lying in the crook of his arm in bed while he told me all about his time at the festival. Me just stroking his arm softly while he spoke gently into my ear . . .

Temz, calm down.

'I'm happy I was able to hear your voice before going to bed, babe,' I replied, itching to get off the phone so I could continue my fantasy in the shower. 'Love yo—'

I froze.

From the sounds of it, Ruben was also speechless. Seconds passed as we both processed the magnitude of what I'd accidentally spat out.

Ruben eventually replied, voice slightly trembling.

'You . . . Huh?'

I gulped several times and panicked. *What the fuck, Temz?* Did I really just use the L-word with Ruben? Surely it was accidental. I tell my friends I love them all the time. Ruben was a friend? I'm sure that's how I meant it . . .

However, instead of communicating this to Ruben like an adult, I ended up saying: 'I . . . I said "olive juice". I need to remember to buy olive juice for a recipe tomorrow. OK, bye!' and with that, I mashed the 'end call' button and went to go and hyperventilate underneath the fresh hotel bed covers.

Why was I such an enemy of progress?

'Artemis Owusu! You told that man WHAT?'

I was still splayed out on the bed under the bed covers, trying to recover from the events of a few moments earlier. Ruben had sent me a text soon after we hung up, but I refused to open it. *Was* I in love? Regardless of whether I was or not, I had always been of the mindset that I would rather eat a denim jacket than tell a man that I loved him first. Just . . . yuck!

'I accidentally told him I loved him, Jean,' I repeated. 'I feel like such a fucking mug. What have I done?'

I could practically hear Jean's scoffs on the other end of the phone. I was down bad, but now was definitely not the time to have him judging me.

'Well, sis. I think if that's how you really feel, then that's absolutely fine and it's cute and everything,' Jean replied. 'I do think that the moment would have been a lot more special if you'd told him as yourself instead of Aloe. What happened to you pulling back on your convos with him?'

I grimaced. 'I was supposed to! But I don't know, I guess I'm still a bit scared of how he'd react if I told him. I will get around to it, I just need to do it in my own time, when I'm ready.'

'Ain't no time like the present, sis. You're literally there! In his hometown! I understand you're scared, Temz. But you also need to remember that the longer you continue with this, the deeper you're going to hurt him when he finds out the truth. I'm sure you don't want to break his heart, but if you keep this up, you may end up doing just that.'

Jean was right, and I was incredibly grateful that I was able to open up to him.

'You're absolutely right, babe, I WILL tell him soon. I'll tell him on this trip. I just, you know, need to toughen up and shit.'

Jean kissed his teeth on the other end of the phone.

'You're so annoying by the way. Bye, girl!'

I lay in bed in silence for a while after the call ended, jetlagged, hungry and full to the brim with anxiety, but otherwise excited. After soaking in the world's biggest bathtub for a while, I decided to be a productive member of society and try my hand at a bit of sightseeing, with the aim of picking up some food on the way.

It was warm 29-degree July weather, so I decided to wear my favourite Diane Von Furstenberg orange wrap dress that showed the perfect amount of cleavage, and teamed it with some brown espadrilles. I looked in the mirror and admired myself. I scrubbed up pretty well. If only Ruben could see me now. The fantasist in me would hope that he would absolutely gag with delight.

I left the hotel and walked up Market Street, taking in all the sights and smells of San Francisco, and came upon the Museum of the African Diaspora and the Museum of Modern Art, making a mental note to visit both later on in the week when I had time. After about fifteen minutes of walking, I started to regret wearing the wedge espadrilles. These steep San Francisco streets were no joke! I was contemplating booking an Uber for a three-minute drive up the road when I saw a Cheesecake Factory restaurant in the distance in Union Square, which motivated me to power-walk the rest of the way.

I got a table overlooking the square and ordered a light lunch, followed by an absolute unit of a cheesecake slice. If it's one thing America does well, it's food, although I didn't need to see how many calories were in each serving on the menu, to be quite honest; what happened to being able to eat 3,000 calories in one sitting, guilt-free? 'This used to be a proper country,' I muttered to myself as I dived into my dessert, laughing at my own joke like a loser.

At my table, I turned to my phone, uploading some pre-written captions for my Aloe Instagram posts as well as going through some work emails, making sure I hadn't missed any big news or updates from the team. Despite this being such a huge opportunity, and having wanted to visit California for so long, I noticed myself already beginning to suffer from slight FOMO. I missed the guys at work, and Jean.

Deciding I needed to stop moping and make the most of this trip, after lunch I took a stroll down a few backstreets, silently reciting the notes for my presentation in my head. All I wanted was to nail this meeting and then for it to be over so I could concentrate on how I was going to confess all to Ruben. After accidentally dropping the 'L' word, I had to sort this shit out fast. The guilt that had been eating me up for months had finally reached its apex, and I needed to try and put things right before they devoured me whole.

A buzz from my phone interrupted my thoughts. It was Instagram notifying my personal account that Ruben had commented on my Story. It was one from a few hours ago on the plane, showing me living it up with a glass of champagne in Business Class with the caption 'VIRGO ENERGY'. Ruben's message read:

> **RubesCubes:** Haha you better live your best life girl! Where are ya headed? Safe flight 😄

He'd left another comment underneath a bare-faced selfie on the next Story slide:

> You're so beautiful. 😍

HEART EYES EMOJI?

I found a couple of seats parked outside a closed coffee shop and took a seat; my heart hammering a thousand times a minute while I stared at my phone. As much as I didn't want to go down the rabbit hole to try and read between the lines of these messages, I couldn't help but wonder if there was a part of him that maybe, kinda liked me too? My lip quivered at the thought. I *could* feel myself falling in love with him, and it was scary, yet exciting.

Of course, there was also a part of me raising a huge side-eye over the fact that he seemed to be flirting with who he *thought* was another woman while allegedly having 'feelings' for 'Aloe'. I felt . . . conflicted. Imagine him cheating on me with . . . me?

My life was an absolute joke at this point.

But if he was talking in this way with the 'real' me, could he be talking like this with other women? *Save that worry for another day, Temz. He's showing interest!*

In that moment, with the rush of adrenaline running through me, I felt the urge to see him. I wanted to thank him for being so sweet to me. I also wanted to tell him how I felt. I really was falling for Ruben.

I replied to his comments under my selfie:

ItsArtemis_O: Aww thank you so much! Coming from someone who is equally as beautiful, I take it as a huge compliment ...

What emoji should I end on? The 'heart eyes' one feels lazy, like I'd simply copied his. The winking eye emoji? Nah, too suggestive. A simple smiley face? Boring. I needed an emoji that showed gratitude, but also let him know that I was digging him too. In the end, I settled on the blushing emoji combined with the blowing-a-kiss emoji. *Yeah. That oughta do it.*

I then went back to the last story frame he commented on. This newfound adrenaline and my need to see him had me on a roll. I took a deep breath, and started typing.

ItsArtemis_O: I touched down safely, thanks! I'm in the Bay area by the way – you're gonna have to send me a list of your recommended places x

I exhaled deeply, my hands slightly shaking with nervous energy. Not wanting to waste it, I switched to WhatsApp and scrolled down to Ruben's name.

I was going to tell him how I felt before I chickened out, even if it wasn't as 'me'.

I was sitting in a random back alley in San Francisco, about to tell a man I loved that I loved him via text, all the while deceiving him into thinking I was this thick-bodied, light-skinned babe. You really couldn't make this shit up.

**Me: Hey Ruben, I know this is going to seem really random, and I can't call as I'm a bit tied up right now, but I can't hold it in any longer so I'm just going to come out and say it: that wasn't a mistake before. I do think I love you, and I think you're amazing. You make me feel things I haven't felt about others or myself in a long time, and I'm super grateful for you. Have an amazing day, my love!

I read the message out loud, making sure it sounded cute and somewhat sane before sending. I felt the shame of what I was doing flood my body, feeling empty and sad that I didn't have the courage to admit my feelings about him as myself. I was close to unsending the message before noticing that he was already coming up with a response.

I sat up straight in the chair with bated breath. What if he sees my message as me and asks to meet up while I'm here? What if he thought I, as Aloe, was a weirdo for falling in love with him so deeply, so quickly? I stared at my screen, in a slight daze with my heart pumping about 8,000 beats a minute as his voice note came through:

Ruben: I think I love you too, Aloe. It sucks as I kinda wanted to say it first, but um, yeah. I know it's super weird and shit but ... I can't deny how my heart feels. It sucks that we can't be in the same room right now. All I've been thinking about doing since I started talking to you is hanging out with you, kissing you, you know? You're intelligent, compassionate, kind, down to earth, funny – *sometimes* haha – and I feel like I can talk to you about anything. I can't wait to talk to you again soon xx

I wanted to call Jean, to call my mum – anyone really – and just sob. The man of my dreams just confessed his love to me, a whole dark-skinned, fat babe like me, and I wanted to shout it from the rooftops.

Did this mean I had a . . . boyfriend?

A 'boyfriend' who thought I was someone else, though. This was bittersweet to say the least.

I texted back:

> **Me: You are incredible, I need you to know that, babe. Whatever happens. I need you to know how much you mean to me.**

Ruben then texted his response immediately.

> **Ruben: You've come to mean a lot to me too ... damn this is crazy, haha. Umm, also, my bad that I keep bugging you about it but it's just annoying that your phone camera has been playing up for so long – I mean, I can see if I can send you some cash towards a new phone or something if that helps? I just want to see that beautiful face of yours.**

Damn it. He just had to have all the solutions, didn't he?

> **Me: You're so kind, but honestly you don't have to do that. You'll see my face soon enough, I promise. I'll sort something out, it's been long enough.**

Ominous, perhaps, but I was determined – now more than ever – to somehow get a chance to see him on this trip, despite what I'd promised Jean. I couldn't keep this up any longer, not now that proper feelings were involved.

Ruben typed back:

> **Ruben: I really hope so, babe. I'm even happier now that my – uh – girlfriend (I guess?) has just *officially* confessed her love for me!**

I clutched my imaginary pearls. Girlfriend. Whew! Before I had time to process, Ruben signed off with,

Love you. Talk to you soon. Oh. Looks like I'm gonna be back home from LA early, tomorrow afternoon – got a work project I need to do, but I'll catch you up on how the show goes when I get back!

I typed that I loved him back, and then put my phone back in my bag, feeling bewildered. So much had happened in such a short amount of time. Ruben had said he loved me.

He also said he'd be coming back to Oakland *tomorrow afternoon*.

I was left sitting in that random street in San Francisco, feeling like the best and worst person in the world.

Chapter 27

A day had passed since the 'I love you' event, with me and Ruben talking intermittently during the last twelve hours, both as Aloe – and as myself.

RubesCubes: Say whutttt? You're in the Bay? That's dope, ma, welcome to my city! I can hook you up with some hot spots to hang out at. How long are you over here for?

ItsArtemis_O: Aww thank you so much, pal! I'm excited to be here. I'm only here for a few days for work, so I wanna try and see as much as I can.

RubesCubes: Ahh that's dope. I think you'll love it. I'm making my way back to Oakland in a couple hours actually. I'm at the airport. Hey, I don't know if you're into poetry and open mics, but I'm going to a lil poetry slam night up in San Francisco this evening. If you want a real Bay Area experience, you should come check it out – I'll be doing a lil performance, too!

ItsArtemis_O: Oh, you doll! Thank you so much. I am partial to a bit of spoken word ... Send me the address and I'll see if I can swing by if I have time. It would be great to see you!

RubesCubes: I gotchu! 3036 24th Street, 94110. 😊

And I actually *was* thinking of attending – albeit incog*negro*. I wasn't sure if I could stand talking to him in the flesh when he was in love with 'Aloe'. Still, who was I to deny the temptation to be in the same room as Ruben when the opportunity wandered so willingly into my midst??

All of this back and forth was really beginning to tire me out, though; constantly having to remember that when I was talking to Ruben as Aloe, I had to maintain the ruse of having an eight-hour time difference even though we were in the same time zone. It was beginning to get exhausting.

'Hey babe, have you landed yet?' I said the last time we spoke on the phone, faux yawning to give the illusion that it was the late evening and I was in the UK.

'Not yet, sweetheart, I'm at the boarding gate though. They should start boarding in a few minutes I reckon,' Ruben replied, emulating my yawn. 'Guess what, though?'

'What?' I was stretched out in the middle of my king-size bed, staring at my suitcase and wondering about what to wear for my one-sided date with Ruben that evening. I hadn't even decided fully if I would actually go; it was a dangerous gig with too many things that could potentially go disastrously wrong, but it didn't stop the delusional babe in me from trying to analyse and rationalise the different scenarios. I grabbed the bedside table notepad and stared at the list I'd penned earlier on:

- I show up as me. Make sure to deepen my voice a bit so I sound a little different. We hang out and get on well. He starts to like me (as me!). I then actually execute the plan to start withdrawing from him as Aloe and start talking to him more as me, and then I can be the one to mop up the pieces of his broken heart when I eventually 'break it off with him' as Aloe . . .

- I show up, but don't go up to him. I watch him from afar and take the opportunity to properly drink him in. Stay at the slam for a little while and then come back to the hotel. *It's giving 'stalker' though . . .*
- ~~I make an excuse to not go, and continue talking to him as both me and Aloe online (finding this v v stressful though tbh)~~
- ~~I make an excuse not to go, and continue talking to him as Aloe until ???~~
- ~~I go. Hang out with him for a bit, then come clean about who I am. He shouts at me and never talks to me again. I come back to the UK feeling like a dick~~

My mind was in turmoil. I wanted to see him, but at what cost?

'So,' Ruben had said, 'that Artemis lady I was telling you about? She's in San Francisco right now, which is crazy.'

My ears perked up as I sat upright on the bed. 'Oh?' was all I could muster as I grabbed a bottle of water from the side table. My mouth had gone bone dry. Where was this going?

'Uhuh. She said she was over here for work. I invited her to an open mic night I'm hitting up tonight.'

On the one hand, I appreciated his transparency here. Me and Ruben had been getting on well on my personal account – not that I was saying he fancied the real me or anything – but I appreciated Ruben being upfront with 'Aloe' about it, in any case. We love an honest King. In stark comparison to myself – a dishonest Queen. Believe me, I could appreciate the irony in that moment.

I could feel my heart thumping heavily as I fantasised about us meeting up at the open mic night and somehow hitting it off.

We'd flirt and stare into each other's eyes as the sexual chemistry grew stronger. I'd then take him aside, telling him that I needed to

249

confess what I had done. After telling him, he'd stare into my eyes lovingly, telling me that everything was going to be all right, and that he'd preferred me anyway. He'd hold me in his arms as we both caressed each other under the blue strobe lights of the open mic event space while a Miguel song suddenly plays in the backgr—

My delusions were reaching fever point. *Get it together, Temz!* I snapped back into our conversation:

'Already going on dates with other British girls, huh? Developed a bit of a fetish, one might say?' I sniggered, trying to cover my underlying anxiety. *Be careful, Temz. Stay calm.*

'Ha! Nahh, not at all! I just thought it would appeal to your interests, with you being a fellow Brit and all, you know? She's really cool, I think you'd like her.'

We're more alike than you know, babes. The love I had for Ruben as Aloe was real, but felt capped at 50 per cent. I didn't feel like I could love him with my whole chest — a hole was burning through it because I couldn't love him unashamedly and unapologetically in the way I wanted to.

I had to dissociate from the whole Ruben saga, however, as my Big Meeting was happening tomorrow. I spent the majority of the day in the hotel suite in last-minute chats with Stephen and my team, making sure I had all the key action points and key demographic slideshows in place. Ruben and his prospective arrival in town today had taken up too much real estate in my brain, and I needed to get my head back in the game.

It helped that I also received a really cute email from Stephen that afternoon:

Hi Artemis,

Apologies for sending this so late. Just want to make sure you receive this in the morning, your time.

Just popping through an email to let you know how proud the team and myself are of you with this One Nation Athletics deal. We all know that you're going to make the agency proud, and you're going to absolutely smash the meeting! You're a huge credit and asset to our team as always, and we are all wishing you the best of luck.

Stephen

I loved my job.

I went through my notes again, picked my outfit for the meeting (a white silk shirt from Reformation, a killer co-ord suit I bought at a steal from eBay consisting of an oversized magenta blazer with a matching tapered pant, and my lucky Christian Louboutin 'So Kate' 120mm pumps that I always brought out for special occasions) and decided to do a little dress rehearsal. I balanced my phone by the table lamp as I dialled my mum's number for a video call. If anyone was good at critique, it was her.

She picked up as I was halfway through tucking my shirt into my pants.

'Abena,' my mum answered groggily, wiping sleep from her eyes. I'd again forgotten the time difference – *yikes*. 'It seems like sense has chased you your entire life, but you are faster. Can you not see what time it is?'

★Note to self: write that insult down to use for later. No one can form an insult like Africans can. But also? It was actually only 8 p.m. there.★

'Soz, Mum,' I responded. 'I don't wanna keep you long, I just wanted to quickly practise my presentation so you could let me know your thoughts on—'

'And you couldn't call me in the daytime because . . . ?' my mum questioned, cutting me off. 'Abena, I'm old you know.

I need all the sleep I can get. I can give you ten minutes and then I'm going back to sleep. Begin.'

'I— it's not that late, is it? Well, OK . . .' I mumbled, fumbling through my notes. A direct babe. We loved to see it. I exhaled. 'OK. Hi everyone, and thank you so much for joining—'

'Wait. Is that what you're wearing?'

I looked over at myself in the mirror. I looked pretty dapper if I did say so myself. The outfit was serving 'executive CEO' vibes.

'Yeah, why?'

'Mm,' my mum scoffed. 'You don't have any skirts or any-thing? The pink is very loud, sha.'

'Nah, I look good, Mum,' I responded. 'You've probably got sleep in your eye and it's restricting you from seeing the true fabulous-ity and bad bitch-ery of the ensemble.'

My mum laughed in the background while I twirled around jokingly.

I rushed through as much of the presentation as ten minutes would allow before taking an over-the-top bow at the end. I thought I'd done pretty well, and looked at Mum hopefully, awaiting her response.

'It was good, Artemis,' she finally replied, which I took to mean 'exceptional', seeing as she only called me by my actual first name when I was in her good books. 'It's very professional. I have no idea what you're talking about, and you could have slowed the pace a bit, but overall, very good. Well done.'

'Gee, thanks, Mum. I mean, you only gave me ten minutes so I had to rush through—'

'OK, OK, great! Good luck on the meeting and let me know when you get home. Bye! Oh, wait – don't forget to pick up my list of things from Trader Jack's. OK, bye, bye, bye . . . !'

And with that, she ended the call. At least I got a seal of

approval of sorts. Job well done! I took off my outfit and laid it carefully on the sofa, taking care not to crease it. After getting a bite to eat, I decided to go for a bit of a wander around the area to clear my head. I changed into some light sweatpants and a crop top, wrapped my hair in a scarf and made my way out of the hotel in the direction of Union Square. As I arrived at the Square, I noticed the nearby Powell Street BART Station, heading in the direction of Oakland. I stared at the underground station, debating my options. Dare I take a sneaky trip? After all, Ruben was likely back already, and if I didn't end up going to the show, then at least I'd have taken a peek. The adrenaline started to sour in my veins as I thought about intruding into Ruben's space, though. That really was stalker shit. Besides, I probably *would* be seeing him anyway this evening at the open mic . . . But what would be wrong with me having a little preview? During our chats, Ruben had told me about a plethora of places in Oakland that meant the world to him – including the address of his apartment. Surely there wouldn't be any trouble in me just taking a harmless stroll through the neighbourhood? If only to just get a sense of his environment? I made a note to try and be back by 4 p.m. so I could start getting ready for the open mic. It wasn't enough that I was already a delusional liar. I had to add 'stalker' to my résumé too. A mess!

Chapter 28

I couldn't believe I was doing this, and the day before my Big Meeting. But a little chaos and the odd adrenaline rush here and there never hurt anyone!! I descended into the BART station and looked for the signs going towards Oakland. I had no idea what I was doing, but the excitement filled every inch of me as I boarded a train headed in the direction of Antioch. Sitting in a vacant seat, I opened up my Notes App to find the list of places in Oakland Ruben had mentioned.

'*We are now approaching Embarcadero Station*,' came the announcement as we approached the next stop. At that moment, Ruben sent through a text to Aloe:

> **Ruben: Just got home! Exhausted, can't wait to talk to you later when you wake up. I hope you're having an awesome evening. Love you x**

I gulped, suddenly feeling like Lara Croft in *Tomb Raider*. He was back, and I was already on my way into Oakland, meaning I had to be *super* incognito during this excursion. I was nervous, but also low-key filled with excitement too; I was so close, yet so far from the love of my life! Besides, it would be great to see all the places Ruben had told me about. Visiting some of the places that meant a lot to him would make me feel closer to him, too.

I gazed down at my list of places Ruben had previously told me about.

- Jack London Square
- Lake Merritt (to chill and take a walk. Ruben lives in an apartment overlooking the lake, posh bastard)
- The Starry Plough Pub (Berkeley Poetry Slam Nights)
- Oakland Athletics Coliseum (Baseball? Meh)
- MUA and Hopscotch restaurants (dinner date options)

As it was early afternoon, I decided to opt for just a couple of the places, and decided that I'd get off when we reached the stop nearest to Jack London Square. After loading up Google Maps, I put my earphones in and took in the scenes of Oakland from the window, picturing Ruben working and running his errands in this city that he loved. From a distance, the skyline of the city reminded me of London, but hotter. There were skyscrapers galore mixed in with the local, tree-lined streets filled with pretty, Victorian houses.

'*Next stop: Twelfth Street and Oakland City Center,*' came the next announcement as the train crossed the Bay into the hustle and bustle of the city. I put my earphones away and prepared myself to get off. As I did so, a deep, booming voice suddenly pierced through the relative quiet of the train car:

'Hey babygirl, you looking thick as hell in those pants! You sexy as fuck!'

I turned my head in horror as I felt my skin go cold. The voice sounded exactly like Ruben's. But I quickly remembered where I was and that there would probably be plenty of dudes who sounded like Ruben around here.

Calm down, Temz. You got this! Keep your head down and blend in.

I left the 12th Street train station to skyscraper views of

Downtown Oakland. I searched for Jack London Square and took off down Broadway, drinking in all the sights and sounds. The vibrancy of the area could not be matched. On every corner there were vivid, illuminating graffiti artworks depicting the history and culture of the different neighbourhoods. There was an intricate spraying of ink and paints depicting the members of the Black Panther Party — which originated in Oakland — lighting up Broadway in all its magnificence, and the many hole-in-the-wall cafes and restaurants exuding the aroma of bacon and pancakes caused my belly to rumble with longing.

I passed the historic Regal Theater that showed all the old-school Blaxploitation movies Ruben had talked to me about at length, snapped a quick photo of the venue and kept on walking, past the infamous Yoshi's Jazz Club where Ruben had reminisced about many a night where he'd witnessed some of the finest soul and jazz live acts he'd ever seen, until the smell of barbequed meat and freshly baked bread tantalised my nostrils and I followed it until I reached a restaurant called Everett and Jones — another Black-owned restaurant by the marina that Ruben had also waxed lyrical about. I peered through the glass, looking at the several spits of rotating rotisserie chicken. Freshly baked cornbread had been placed on the counter and in the back I could see the chef removing what looked like ribs from the grill. It smelled like heaven.

After about thirty minutes of roaming around and taking in the sights, I finally decided to take the plunge and visit Lake Merritt — which was where Ruben lived. I knew he was at home. This was my moment to catch a glimpse of the man I'd fallen so quickly for . . .

As long as you're in his area, if you see him you should just tell him. Maybe you could say hello to him? He'd be none the wiser. Lake

Merritt is a popular attraction; he may see you bumping into him as a pure coincidence.

Maybe he wouldn't be that upset if you surprised him?

Best-case scenario, he'll declare his love for you. Or at least hear you out.

Worst-case scenario, he's upset but he still ends up liking you as a person?

I sighed, knowing I was kidding myself with that 'worst-case scenario'. It could potentially go a lot worse than that. But positive vibes and all that.

Being willingly delusional hadn't steered me wrong yet, so I decided to go with that feeling.

After figuring out the route to Lake Merritt, I took a short seven-minute Uber ride, and as I stepped out of the car I was faced with a vast green common filled with joggers, people walking their dogs and couples taking casual strolls. In the middle of the common was the gargantuan lake, filled with a plethora of different kinds of ducks and other pondlife. The sun was high in the sky, its reflection illuminating on the surface of the still, calm water. On the other side of the lake stood a building that resembled some kind of spaceship, and an instant memory flooded in of Ruben telling me that his apartment overlooked a cathedral that looked like 'something out of *Star Trek*'. I walked away from the cathedral, only to be met with a swanky new-build apartment block that was around seven floors high. I stepped back a little, taking in the building in front of me.

Here it was. Ruben's apartment. I was sure this was the one. From the video tours he had shown me in the past of his home and the view from his living room, the surroundings looked familiar. My eyes wandered towards the top floor, trying to imagine which of the penthouse apartments belonged to him.

From the outside, the building was beautiful and modern, and even had its own reception. I took my phone out and snapped a photo of it, wanting to treasure this moment. I could almost picture us as a couple, walking back to his place from the nearby grocery store, hand-in-hand as we laughed at some lame joke I made. We'd stop outside the building and look towards the lake, watching the sun slowly set across the glass cathedral. His hands would be entwined in mine as we looked towards each other, taking each other in, and then time would stop as we slowly embraced each other . . . And then we'd share a tender kiss as he tells me he loves me . . .

I sighed, turning around and walking over to a lone tree in the middle of the park. Man, Ruben really had the greatest view. Multiple patches of grass were filled by dandelions, daisies and bluebell flowers. There were bright-pink tulips, bushes of fragrant lavender and even a few clusters of white hydrangeas. *Hydrangeas?* In this economy?

Oh, this area was bougie as hell, I thought to myself as I sat on the grass, my trainers digging into the soil as I breathed in the warm, fragrant Bay Area air. All I needed in this moment was him.

As I peered up at the apartment building, I noticed several people going in and out the front door. I wondered which of them were his neighbours, and whether they were nice people. From the corner of my eye, I spotted a tall, dark-skinned, broad-backed bald guy in a white tank top and black sweatpants walking towards the building, grocery bag in hand, biceps just glistening in the sun.

I lowered my sunglasses and stared without blinking to make sure I was really seeing what I saw.

It was him. It was Ruben.

In the flesh. With groceries, going home.

And I was about ninety yards away from him.

I quickly tipped my shades back on, making sure not to make any sudden movements. I didn't want him to notice me. Or did I?

No. No!

He was taking his key fob out of his pocket. He was nearly there. *Just try and turn around slowly, facing the tree. Nice and easy . . .*

With my head still tilted down and looking through my eyelashes, I slowly began to rotate my body while he seemed to take an age getting his key fob from his pocket. I quickly turned my phone camera on 'selfie mode' so I could catch a glimpse of him from over my shoulder. I could hear the blood rushing around my head and I was hot with fear, excitement, longing and nerves as he finally found his keys.

As he opened the door, Ruben turned around, looking directly at me. He stared a moment, took out his phone, and appeared to take a picture of the landscape around me – the very sunset I'd just been fantasising about had obviously caught his attention.

SHIT!

Hopefully from his point of view, it would look as if I was someone just taking a casual selfie, but as I stared into my camera, zooming in on his figure, I couldn't help but wonder if he noticed it was me. At that thought, my heart may as well have formed wings and taken off for flight with the way it was thundering around my chest. All of this happened in what felt like hours but was probably no more than twenty seconds. Still, it was twenty seconds too long. Ruben *finally* disappeared into the apartment building, and I sighed a huge breath of relief, almost dizzy from the nerves. *Wasn't seeing him what you wanted?* It was, but when the time came, all I could do was panic.

The little I saw of him was beautiful, as if he were carved

from the Elgin Marbles. After floundering for a few moments more, I decided to make my way back to the hotel. I'd seen enough. But the real question was, what had *he* seen? Did he have any inkling it was me under that tree? If so, surely he would have said something, or at least walked up to me to confront me, right?

On the train back to San Francisco, I opened up my Notes app and wrote down some of my preliminary thoughts of Oakland to help with my pitch for work, trying as much as possible to distract myself from the shenanigans that had occurred earlier at Lake Merritt.

At work we hadn't yet broached the idea of representing tourism boards, but there was something so immediately inspiring about seeing Oakland during my walk that I thought it would be a good shout to at least approach the topic with Stephen once I returned to the UK. I made a note to research both the Oakland and California tourism boards to see whether they had any representation. Then, unable to resist, I quickly checked Ruben's Instagram for any new updates or Instagram Stories; I envisioned opening up his page to see a new post featuring a zoomed-in image of me sitting under the tree looking like a complete stalker with the caption: 'SHE WAS A CATFISH THIS WHOLE TIME Y'ALL', but was relieved to find no new content on his page as of yet. I exhaled deeply as I continued the journey back to San Francisco, adrenaline on 1000 and in full 'daydream' mode. I daydreamed about an alternative universe where I somehow was able to represent the Oakland tourism board for work and could fly to and from here every month, staying at Ruben's swanky penthouse apartment on the days I would fly in. Doing my boss girl shit at work and having date nights and subsequent squirt sessions with my American boyfriend throughout the night. I closed my eyes briefly as I imagined this perfect scenario; however, my daydream was interrupted by a notification buzz on my phone: Ruben had uploaded new Instagram Stories. I froze. Here it was. I was about to be exposed.

Lord.

I sat upright in my seat as I opened the app to see what he had posted. It was the photo he'd taken of the park earlier. It featured the hydrangeas I had walked past, a couple of benches, and in the far left of the photo – almost out of frame – the large tree with me sitting underneath it, facing the tree and appearing as if I'm taking a selfie. My heart stuck in my throat – but underneath his caption just read: **RubesCubes: Glad to be back home, with some of the best views in the Bay Area!**

I didn't know whether to laugh or cry. He didn't recognise me. I had managed to pull off the closest of shaves, and my nerves were all over the place. Frequently being on the cusp of having a heart attack was no way to exist!

My heart began to race as I zoomed into the image of me in the corner. If you squinted and cocked your head to the side, I guess you could kinda-sorta-potentially make me out, if you were familiar with my frame from the back? Can't lie though; my silhouette was really silhouetting in this shot. I was giving BAWDY and I wasn't mad.

I quickly sent Ruben a message on Instagram as Aloe:

SayAloeToMyLittleFriend: Hey baby, just saw your IG story. I'm glad you got back to Oakland safely! How was your gig at Boomtown Brewery? Can't wait for you to tell me all about it. Love you xx

I hit 'send' and stared at the message, waiting for some kind of response. After a few moments, the status of my message changed to 'Read', but no reply followed, so after a while I swiped my phone shut and closed my eyes.

'*The next stop will be . . . Montgomery Street*' came the train announcement, and I prepared to get off. Ruben had still left my message on 'read'. I figured that he was probably tired after a long day's travel and not really looking at his phone, or maybe he was in a late work meeting or something. I decided to just put all the stuff with him aside for the moment and spend the rest of the evening going over my notes for the big meeting tomorrow.

It was early evening by the time I got back to the hotel, and now that the dust had settled I was feeling oddly exhilarated with the day's events. Even if things were severely confusing and awkward, at least I'd finally seen Ruben in the flesh!

And I decided – I had to see him once more.

I took a quick shower, lathered myself in the fanciest body oils the hotel had at its disposal, and changed into a simple black midi dress that had cinching around the waist, exaggerating my hips. You couldn't go wrong with a Little Black Dress. I put my hair in a high bun, slapped a bit of make-up on and ended the look with a bright-red lip for a bit of extra razzle dazzle. I could do this. I still needed to decide if I wanted to meet him or just stick to watching him from afar (I was never going to beat the stalker allegations at this point).

Ultimately, he only knew me as Temz, so I would be safe in that instance, but I was more concerned about blabbing something wrong. If I did meet him, I would need to be incredibly careful about the details I shared, lest he connect them to Aloe. I knew I had a habit of yapping away when anxious, and at this point, could I trust my mouth not to get me in trouble?

I went through the plan again in my head as I awaited an Uber. I'd scoped out the poetry slam venue on Google Images to see how big the event space was. It was pretty huge; the perfect place for someone to mingle among the crowd without being easily spotted. My plan was to watch the slam from a distance, and then eventually work up the courage to say hi to Ruben. I packed my sunglasses into my bag for that extra bit of security, and made my way downstairs to meet my driver.

Twenty minutes later, I was standing outside the Medicine for Nightmares bookstore, located within the Mission district of San Francisco. It seemed to be the super hip, artsy part of the city, with many intricate, vibrant murals decorating the sides of buildings and locals dancing on the street corners while cars blasted out old-school hip hop. The smell of enchiladas and melted cheese filled the air as I realised that I hadn't eaten all day. The poetry slam wasn't due to start for another twenty minutes, and I didn't want to risk drawing any attention to myself if I showed up early, so I took a quick detour to a nearby taco joint, bought some tortilla chips and guacamole dip and sat in the corner scrolling through the One Nation Athletics 'About the Company' page for some last-minute revision, and to also take my mind off the events that were to unfold this evening. I was filled with excitement, nerves and fear at the idea of actually talking to Ruben. I knew what I was doing could potentially turn into a huge nightmare if I said the wrong thing, but my state of delusion had taken me this far; why not push the boat out even further? All I needed to do was think before I spoke, and speak slowly, making sure I didn't say anything that could be linked to Aloe in any way.

Just then, I received a new notification that Ruben had posted a story, and quickly clicked in to the app. He'd posted a photo of the outside of the Medicine for Nightmares bookstore with the caption: **RubesCubes: Back in my safe space for the evening – needing that positive energy tonight, man.**

Ruben was next door. We were sharing the same airspace, yet again. My heart began to pound at 1000mph once more as I tried to steady my breathing. Every bone in my body wanted to order a cab and just go back to the hotel, but I was here now. I felt like I owed myself the opportunity to see it through. We may end up actually having fun – as ourselves. I finished my tortilla chips and put my sunglasses on, then went back to the story and liked it from my personal page.

With the knowledge that he was in the building, I decided to hang back just a little bit longer, maybe wait until the slam actually began, so as to use the distraction of the performers on stage to slip into the bookstore and watch from a distance while I got my courage up. After a further fifteen minutes (complete with concerned stares from other patrons at the taco joint who probably thought I'd been stood up), I retouched my lipstick and made my way towards the bookstore. Taking a deep breath, I entered and made my way to the second floor, with my legs feeling as if they were about to buckle under me. *You got this, Temz.*

As I reached the second-floor concourse, I could hear the blaring of the microphone as the host announced the next act, which was met with a huge round of applause.

'That'll be ten dollars, sis,' said a lady with the most gorgeous dreadlocks I'd ever seen as I approached the ticket stand. I paid the entry fee, and she cheerfully said, 'Have a great night!' as I scanned the hall. There were rows upon rows of seats, and the audience was packed to the brim. This is what I had counted on.

'Thank you, sis!' I replied in the worst American accent I had ever done, but I didn't want to draw attention to myself just yet.

I placed my sunglasses loosely on my face as I stood at the back of the room, taking everything in. There was a poet currently on stage performing a piece about the cost of living crisis in San Francisco, with the audience going wild, clicking in unison, and whooping and hollering at every witty point he made in his verse. The atmosphere was electric, and I became sucked into the camaraderie of it all. Everyone in the audience looked amazing: style on point, freshly moisturised and beautiful. I became so engrossed in the atmosphere that I almost forgot why I was there in the first place.

I was knocked back down to earth by a tall, bald man rising from his seat near the front and lightly jogging past me, broad smile plastered across his face, as he headed towards the nearby bathroom. He was wearing a chocolate-brown co-ord sweatsuit, complete with dark-brown-and-white low-top Nike Dunks. On his head was a chocolate-brown skull cap, and his dimples, visible on his freshly trimmed face, were on full display.

Ruben. *My man my man my man!!*

It was as if time had stopped in that moment. He looked even more beautiful up close. Every inch of me was drawn to him. I could positively feel my ovaries convulsing at an alarmingly rapid rate. He was so *tall*. So *stylish*. So . . . *big*. He reminded me of all the leading men in the Black romcoms I'd grown up watching over the years. Phew. America sure did know how to make them.

I slowly exhaled as I watched him make his way into the bathroom. I had to keep my composure; he hadn't seen me, which was good. I wanted to be in control of us meeting. I stared at the men's room door until he exited a few minutes later, adjusting his sweater while staring at the stage and breaking into applause as the next poet took to the mic. I was drunk in lust with this man, and didn't want to take my eyes off him. After the poet on stage ended his set, the MC took the mic to announce the next performer.

'And now, coming up next, ladies and gentlemen, we've got a treat for you! One of our very own local talents who just got back from performing a sold-out show in LA, with a voice as smooth as his shiny-ass head . . .' The audience started to laugh as Ruben stood up to move to the side of the stage, Cheshire Cat-grinning from ear to ear. 'We got the Town's own *Ruben Alexander!*'

I watched Ruben jog onto the stage to rapturous applause, with the majority of the applause coming from a row of excited women in the front row, no doubt his local fans.

Or groupies . . .?

Don't start thinking like that, Temz. Ruben's a good-looking guy who can sing; of course he'll have fans. He chose you. Well, Aloe at least. And what if meeting him as you goes well too? It will. It must.

Ruben looked so beautiful on stage, his chocolate skin bathed in the warm glow of the spotlight, making him appear almost ethereal. He looked out towards the crowd and as he did so, I dipped my head down low to avoid any accidental eye contact. I felt a burst of excitement as he approached the microphone. Even though a part of me felt voyeuristic, I couldn't tear my eyes away from him. The butterflies in my belly had taken flight, and I was hypnotised.

'Hey y'all!' Ruben said into the microphone, his voice sounding all deep and sexy like Billy Dee Williams in *Lady Sings the Blues* (but without the villainy). 'I'm so glad to be here tonight with y'all. It's been such a great show thus far, and we gonna keep this thing movin'. I got a couple new songs that I've been writing over the last few months but they ain't ready yet, so instead I'ma sing one of my favourite songs from one of my favourite artists, Musiq Soulchild. It's called "Love".'

Ruben bowed his head and stepped closer into the mic. My eyes were fixed on him as if I were in a trance and, as his lips parted to sing the first verse, I felt a tear slowly roll down my cheek. As he sang, he looked out into the audience, seemingly staring at nothing in particular. He looked distant, and dare I say, somewhat sad.

He'd sung to me over the phone a few times, but to hear him live and in the flesh was a different experience altogether. His voice was like molasses to my ears, with each riff and run he sang cascading beautifully in tune as he approached the crescendo of the song. I kept my head down as I wiped my tears, wishing more than anything that I could look up at him, and him at me. He was perfect. Everything about him was perfect.

And I felt terrible.

Every part of me wanted to go to him now and introduce myself. To hug him and gaze into his big doe eyes. But in that moment I realised one thing: if I wanted to have any kind of communication or relationship with this man, I had to be honest with him. I had to tell him the truth. This had gone on for long enough. Did I want my first memories of him being me stalking him behind bookcases and trees? It was frankly psychotic. Upon that mini-epiphany, I took one final glance at him before he finished the song, walked swiftly into the lobby and touched up my face, adding another layer of lipstick. It was all or nothing.

I was going to talk to Ruben.

Chapter 29

I went back into the room, trying hard to stop my knees from buckling under me. Everything seemed to be moving in slow motion, my rapid heartbeat thundering hard against my ears being the only thing I could hear clearly on top of the muted tones of the room.

Ruben was now about eight feet in front of me, surrounded by people congratulating him on his stellar performance. His bright, piercing eyes, which were creased into a squint, could only be matched by his charismatic, broad smile as he gave a hug to a man standing on the right side of him.

Exhaling slowly, I meekly walked up to him, praying for the lone bead of sweat currently making its way down my face to absorb itself back into my temple. *You've got this, Temz. Deep breath in. Hold for three seconds. Exhale. Don't throw up. Don't ramble. Don't stare at him like a weirdo.* He was now engrossed in conversation with the audience member to his left. *Just treat this like a business meeting, Temz. You're smart. You're interesting! You look great tonight too!*

Another step further as my heart continued to thump violently. I kept walking as my internal dialogue droned on. *What if I say the wrong thing? What if he takes one look at me and laughs in my face? Have I put on enough perfume? What if he asks for my*

WhatsApp and sees it's the same number as Aloe's? What if—

'ARRGH!' I shrieked, as my face suddenly collided with something solid.

'Ayy, you aight, ma? Oh! Um, Artemis? You're here!'

I took a step back and looked up in horror as I realised what had happened.

I had been so lost in thought that I didn't notice myself walking straight into Ruben's chest – accidentally biting my lip as I did so? Honestly, what was it about me and walking into men's chests??

I was absolutely mortified and, in that moment, wanted the ground to swallow me up. As I sucked on my bruised lip, I gazed up at Ruben, taking in his megawatt smile – and somehow in that moment, everything just felt . . . right. My heartbeat slowly returned to normal as I took in his face and realised that his arm was around my waist, steadying me from the recoil of my collision. I wanted to close my eyes, to savour this moment of Ruben – *my Ruben* – having his arm around me like we were the only two people in the room, but quickly had to snap back to reality when I realised I had been staring at him like a nutter for way more than was comfortable.

Say something, damnit.

'Um . . . Yeah! It's me! I've always been one to make an entrance, haha. I'm so sorry!' I took a step back and peered up at him from under my eyelashes the way Princess Diana used to, all flirty and doe-like. Ruben looked down at me, chuckling softly. His dark-brown eyes, surrounded by long lashes, pierced mine unflinchingly, catching me off-guard. He had soft laughter lines that illustrated the sides of his face, and dimples so deep one could swim in them. Ruben flashed me a smile as I continued to drink him in. All thirty-two teeth were intact, straight and white, we thank God! I couldn't believe I had done it. Here I was! With my dream man! IN REAL LIFE. And it doesn't seem weird! For the first time in my life, I was absolutely speechless; to be honest, I was happy to just admire him. All of his six feet and four inches.

'How have you been?! Thank you so much for stopping by. Did you enjoy the show?' Ruben asked, staring directly at me, his gaze never moving from mine. His eye contact was absolutely crazy and so alluringly sexy; I wanted to melt.

Suddenly remembering that he had never heard me speak before, I coughed subtly and deepened my voice a little.

'I'm good, thanks. The jetlag is kicking my arse but otherwise I'm all groovy. You were amazing, by the way!'

'Groovy'? When have I ever used that in a sentence?

As the other audience members scattered towards the exit, Ruben gestured towards the door.

'Thank you so much, I appreciate you! Hey, there's a coffee shop downstairs that closes in an hour – you wanna grab a coffee?'

My brain was well aware that this was an innocent request to chill with a friend he'd made online, but the delusional part of me read this as our first official date. Ruben was asking ME for a coffee. A whole me. He actually wanted to hang out with me, and in-between feelings of pure ecstasy and delight, the feelings of guilt were also beginning to rear their ugly head. Knowing that I could have avoided all of this unnecessary stress and deception by just being myself made me feel awful because I knew I had to tell him the truth eventually. But all I wanted to do in this moment was cherish this experience and cement it in my memory forever. I smiled at him.

'Coffee? You're speaking my language. I'm down!'

Ever the gentleman, Ruben opened the door for me and kept close behind me as we walked downstairs towards the little independent coffee shop on the ground floor. He was so close behind me that I could feel his breath on the nape of my neck and, in that moment, I suddenly felt an overwhelming case of shyness. This is what I had been dreaming of for weeks now, so why was I suddenly bashful?

Ruben broke my train of thought as we took our seats in a booth. 'What would you like?' he asked in that sexy deep voice of his. I traced his mouth with my eyes dreamily as I replied. 'I think I'll have a decaf cappuccino please – that's so kind of you!'

As he went to the counter to place our orders, a moment of clarity hit me. I quickly took out my phone and switched it off in case Ruben suddenly decided to text Aloe while we were together. I couldn't risk any distractions at this point. I quickly looked in the camera mirror and used a napkin to pat the remnants of my lipstick down to a matte finish and wipe the beads of sweat from my forehead. I still looked cute, and that was good enough for me. I continued to slowly exhale under my breath as he returned with my cappuccino and an Americano for him.

He sat across from me and stared at me; almost as if he was studying my face with his laser-like eye contact. It was a little intimidating, and I could feel myself blushing fiercely as I took a sip of my cappuccino.

'Thanks for the coffee!' I said, adding a bit of gravel to my voice. 'Your voice is absolutely out of this world, I have to say. When you mentioned me coming to an open mic night, I envisioned a small smoky room full of incense, scented oils, dudes in dashikis with ankh jewellery and mixed-race poets performing pieces about not fitting in with their white or black communities.'

At this, Ruben let out a guffaw. God, I loved it when he laughed. I took another sip of my coffee. So far, so good.

'So because it's an open mic and based in the Bay Area, we automatically gotta be Hoteps? I can't stand you, haha!'

'I'm just saying! I did my research before flying out here. I even brought a faux loc lace front wig with me, just in case.'

He grinned at me as he sipped his coffee all sexily. I was rooted to the spot. I still couldn't believe that I was here.

'Aight, Sista Souljah. Well, if it's all the same to you, I prefer you with the Afro puff. It suits you!'

He liked my hair. I screamed internally.

'Well, thank you,' I replied, slightly biting my lip in a bid to somehow come across as alluring.

His eyes briefly glanced over my lips as I did this, and I swore I saw the faintest echo of a smirk appear on his face before it suddenly disappeared. A self-satisfied grin reached my lips as I took another sip of coffee. I was enjoying this, and deep down, a wave of relief washed over me as we continued to banter back and forth. We spent the next thirty minutes talking about our jobs (with me nearly slipping up by asking how his gig in LA went), our favourite movies and our respective neighbourhoods, before he eventually said the thing that shook me to my core.

'You're from South London too? My girl's from there, and she was talkin' about the divide between South and North London like it's some gang-type shit. I didn't know y'all were beefing like that!'

Tread carefully, Temz.

On one hand, I felt happy and slightly proud that he brought up Aloe in this situation. It showed me that even though it looked like there may have been some light flirting earlier (mostly by me, let me not lie), he made it a point to let it be known he was taken. I loved that. On the other hand, it also cemented to me that I absolutely had to tell him the truth. Things had gone far enough.

'Haha yeah . . . us South Londoners are super patriotic about our turf,' I replied, my voice faltering a little. I needed to keep my composure, but I could feel the nerves shooting up my spine.

'It means a lot that you took the time out to come and see my little show,' Ruben continued after finishing the dregs of his coffee. 'I know you must have a super busy schedule, so I appreciate it! If you're ever out here for longer and you want some suggestions on places to chill out, please hit me up and I can show you some spots!'

If only he knew that I had already beaten him to the punch. In that moment, everything in my body wanted to admit the truth to him. This wasn't fair, on him and on me to a degree. We clearly had some kind of chemistry, and he didn't recoil in horror after seeing me, so why not just admit it and get it all over with? But I couldn't do it. I needed to plan how I would execute my confession. I needed more time.

'I appreciate that, Ruben,' I responded, being drawn into his magnetic stare yet again. 'I'd love that! I should probably get going so I can adjust my sleep to this damn time zone.'

With that, we both stood up. As he opened his arms to hug me, I inhaled deeply, wanting my senses to remember this moment: the way he looked, his scent, how his breath felt on my skin and the rich, deep tones of his voice. I didn't want the embrace to end. But it had to.

Ruben spoke softly as he released me. 'It was great meeting you, Artemis. Have fun over here, aight? Hopefully I'll see you around.'

Hopefully you will. And hopefully you can forgive me when you do.

Chapter 30

It had been a DAY, and I was absolutely shattered. The thrill of meeting Ruben, hanging with him, hugging him and doing it all while undetected had powered me with enough energy to light up half of San Francisco. I had met the man of my dreams and it was everything I hoped it would be – but it also left me with a huge task to do. I loved him, and hurting him was the last thing I wanted to do, but I had to tell him the truth. Who knew lying would be so exhausting?

Seeing as everything was on work's dime and I was in dire need of some dinner, I went all out on the room service, ordering a starter, main and dessert, complete with one of those mini bottles of rosé, because why not? I had planned to get my *Home Alone 2* on during my whole stay and besides, I felt like I deserved it. Today especially, considering I'd interacted with Ruben; I needed to take the edge off. I had an abundance of energy, and needed something to occupy my mind for a while. In the corner of my hotel room, I noticed the most beautiful fiddle-leaf fig plant that stood around five feet in height, perched next to the full-length mirror. I hadn't posted much plant content from Aloe's account lately, so I took a few photos of the plant and created a post on Aloe's Instagram, complete with a few fun facts about the fig.

Later, I ran the world's biggest bubble bath, sipping my rosé. I could absolutely get used to this lifestyle. I looked at my Instagram messages as I slipped into the warm, aromatic bathtub, wine glass in my other hand as I went over the day's events. One thing that was bothering me: it had been at least a couple of hours since I had returned back to the hotel, and Ruben had still left me-as-Aloe on read. I wasn't *too* concerned, seeing as he did spent the evening not only performing, but also hanging out with yours truly. I was a true double act! Still, it was a bit unlike him.

It was risky, but as Aloe, I wanted to hear from him. I opened up WhatsApp and decided to give him a call – but the phone rang through until it automatically disconnected. That was . . . new. I felt my heart skip a beat. What was going on?

I checked his Instagram. No new posts, but he had uploaded a new Instagram story about thirty-five minutes earlier. It was a pitch-black screen with one word in white font in the middle:

RubesCubes: WOOOOOW.

My heart began to race. I had no clue what was going on, but at that moment I decided I had to put it aside for now. I couldn't afford to investigate what had happened – or maybe I was scared to, due to how well today had gone. I couldn't bear the thought of him suddenly realising I was Aloe the whole time. Besides, I had been careful; there's no way he could have found out, could he?

I had to focus and get my head in the game for tomorrow – the last thing I wanted to do was mess work up, too. Maybe the 'wow' was in relation to the amazing poetry from this evening? In spite of myself, I resolved to send him one last WhatsApp message as Aloe before I logged off for the night:

Me: Hey babe! Apologies for the late response. You OK? Was your trip good? Call me when you see this xxx

I tossed my phone onto the bathmat and sank further into the bubbles, allowing the hot water to sooth my aching, tired bones and thumping chest. As much as I wanted to know what this big development was with Ruben, I couldn't let myself spiral. Tomorrow was my Big Day and I had to focus all my energies on smashing it.

For the rest of tonight, Ruben would have to be on the back burner.

Chapter 31

It was 9.30 a.m. and I was in an Uber heading to the private members' club where the meeting was going to be taking place. I'd made sure to wake up super early that morning to go through last-minute checks:

- Outfit re-steamed? Check.
- Notes all typed and semi-rehearsed? Check.
- Hair washed and styled? Double check

I looked great, if I did say so myself. Hours of intense preparation had led to this point.

'Temz, babes! You're going to absolutely kill this presentation, but you already know that,' Jean had screamed down the phone during our FaceTime convo as I was getting ready earlier. I'd decided that he didn't need to know about my little detour into Oakland yesterday, or that I'd met Ruben – I needed for my whole head to be in the game today, and a headache from Jean would only complicate things further. I still hadn't heard anything back from Ruben since my last message and was now officially A Bit Worried, but I'd have to deal with that after the presentation.

'Thank you so much, my love!' I replied. 'Honestly I'm

shitting a brick – I wish you were here, man.'

'Babe, you're gonna be fine. But even if I could come over there, I'd probably take a rain check right now. Umm, there have been some . . . *developments* since you've been away.'

I paused halfway through putting on my pumps.

'What developments? What's happened? Are you OK?'

'Oh, I'm fine, sis! It's just . . . well, Michael got back in touch recently and we're . . . I guess reconnecting,' Jean said coyly, a wicked grin spreading across his face.

I gave an exaggerated gasp. 'Whaaaa? Y'all are back together now? Since when? Honey, you need to spill the tea as soon as this meeting is over. I NEED to hear it!'

'Aight, aight, calm down,' Jean said, chuckling. 'You've been in the States all of ten minutes and already here you are turning into Wendy Williams. We're not, like, back *together* together, we're just, you know . . . trying to talk through things and sort our issues out.'

I squinted at him.

'While fucking on the side, huh?'

'While fucking on the side. Yes.'

We both fell into fits of laughter. Jean was always the worst at giving me advice he could never take himself. When he first announced that he and Michael were over, I empathised, but always knew they would end up reuniting again. Jean was never the best at being alone for long.

'Oh, babes,' I replied, wiping tears from my eyes. 'Just be careful, OK? Protect your heart and don't do anything I wouldn't do, OK?'

'Oh, you mean like catfish him? I ain't you, sis.'

'That's harsh.'

'Harsh but true. Speaking of doing things you wouldn't do, what have you been getting up to out there? I hope you haven't been stalking the guy or anything like that. Have you been keeping your promise?'

As he said that, I quickly swiped over to Instagram and checked my Stories, making sure I hadn't accidentally uploaded any photos or videos of Oakland onto my accounts.

'No! I haven't done anything of the sort,' I lied, chucking on my coat. 'Although he's being a bit funny with me today. Equally, it could all be in my head.'

Jean put down the cup of tea he was sipping, looking concerned.

'What do you mean? Is he saying weird things? D'you think . . . d'you think he knows something's up?'

'I don't know. He's started ignoring me. When I sent him a message welcoming him back from his trip to LA and asking how it went, he read it but ignored me. I sent him a follow-up message on WhatsApp, too, and he's just left me on "read".'

Jean looked pensive. 'Hmm. That's weird. Maybe he's super busy or something and can't talk. Give him a call later and see what's up.'

'Yeah . . .' I replied, trying my hardest not to get caught up in it all right now. I took a deep breath. 'Anyway, wish me luck! Lemme go and smash this meeting real quick so I can get back and gist with you more about Michael. I need to know what kind of hat I need to buy for your wedding!'

Jean rolled his eyes at me. 'You're such a bitch. Have a great meeting, my love, you're gonna smash it, as usual!'

I arrived at the private members' club dead-on 10 a.m., giving me just enough time before the 10.30 a.m. meeting to go through last-minute prep in the meeting room we'd booked for the morning, make sure I looked good, have a quick bite to eat . . . and it also meant I could text Ruben.

I know, I know . . . But I couldn't resist. I ordered a double espresso and started setting up the presentation in the meeting room, then when everything was done, I sent Ruben a quick text on Aloe's account to see how he was getting on. Up until this point, he'd been ignoring my messages on both platforms.

SayAloeToMyLittleFriend: Hey baby, I hope you're doing OK? I'm just checking in as I didn't hear from you yesterday. Let me know if you're OK. Love u, Aloe.

To cover my bases, I waited a few minutes then sent him a message from my personal account, too:

ItsArtemis_O: Hey friend! It was so good to see you last night, and thank you so much for the invite (and my coffee) once again! I hope you're having an amazing morning. ☺ !

I hit 'send'. He had to respond to at least one of my messages. *OK, enough of that for now.* I had to get my game face on. Putting my phone down, I started pacing up and down, trying to remember my notes for the meeting. I looked great. I felt confident, and I was self-assured in the data, research and convincing points I wanted to drive home to One Nation Athletics. This could potentially end up being one of the biggest client acquisitions in my agency's history, and while I wanted to do them proud, I also knew that I needed to do this for myself as well. My ambition had no limit, and I knew that to clinch this deal could go on to mean big things for me at the company.

After rechecking the projector and making sure everything was good, I went to put my phone on silent – and saw that Ruben had replied to my – Aloe's – WhatsApp:

Ruben: I'm kl.

OK, something was wrong. I quickly checked my personal Instagram – he'd read the message I'd sent, but not replied. Before I had time to respond to his WhatsApp, the door to the meeting room opened and the receptionist told me that the One Nation Athletics clients were here. I gulped loudly, took a final swig of my espresso and turned my phone off. I would have to deal with Ruben later.

Moments later, the clients arrived. The head of marketing for One Nation – a Mr Nathan Fielding – was tall, solid-looking and seemed to be in his mid- to late fifties, with a head of grey hair. He was wearing what I guessed to be a current-season Ozwald Boateng three-piece navy suit complete with a gold watch that I'm absolutely sure cost a couple of hundred thousand. He had dark, squinty eyes but overall looked to have a kind, jolly demeanour. He looked like someone I would have no problem trying to convince.

His colleague Annabelle followed in behind him; Annabelle Parker was the VP of One Nation and already from what she was wearing I could tell she was RICH-rich. Not new-money 'monogrammed designer labels everywhere' rich, but quiet luxury, 'wearing a basic white T-shirt that cost $500'-type rich. She was beautiful in a way, with her thick 4B curls braided back into intricate cornrows, showing off her solid gold Louis Vuitton hooped earrings. She had on a plain white Loewe-stamped ribbed tank top teamed with last season's Thom Browne beige utility trousers that I knew cost at least £1,500. She'd finished her look with a pair of Christian Louboutin stilettos. My girl had taste. From her outfit, I could also tell that she had an intricate eye for detail and was probably someone who could see through facades very easily. I smiled my award-winning smile and greeted them both with a handshake as they arrived and took their seats.

'Thank you so much for meeting with us today, and for coming all this way!' Annabelle exclaimed in a thick Southern accent. 'We also have William joining us. He'll be here in a moment; he just has to use the restroom.'

'No worries whatsoever!' I piped up, trying to match Annabelle's super chirpy tone. 'I'm so happy that we've finally been able to meet. I know Stephen was heartbroken that he's been unable to come, but he's left everything in my very capable hands, so hopefully I can do a great job impressing you today!'

A tad overconfident? Maybe, but my response was met with beaming smiles, which I hoped were genuine as opposed to smiles of pity. Moments later, William, who I was told was one of the advertising executives on the brand account, entered the room seemingly a little dishevelled but also dressed up to the nines in a smart, if crumpled, suit. His face looked a bit clammy and pale, and for a moment he didn't seem to know where he was. A quick glance at his nostrils, though, told me everything I needed to know. My guy was high out of his mind on coke. I could see the remnants of powder trickling out of his nostril, into his moustache. These business people really had no shame whatsoever.

I smiled and allowed him a few seconds to gather himself.

'Hey uh, I'm so sorry I'm late, guys,' he said, walking towards his chair while trying to subtly brush the powder from his nose. I glanced towards Annabelle and Nathan and saw brief glimpses of disgust and embarrassment on their faces. This was awkward.

'No problem,' I responded quickly, shaking his hand as I tried to fill the uncomfortable silence. 'We're happy you could be here. Would any of you like tea, or some coffee?' I asked, looking directly at William, who was struggling to sit down in his seat. He looked like someone who could have probably done with a chamomile tea or something that could calm him the fuck down.

Out of nowhere, my heart started to beat a million miles a minute. It didn't feel like your typical, run-of-the-mill nerves either. *Don't let this get away from you, Temz!* I used my hand to steady myself as the team made their niceties and took their seats. After a quick swig of water, I cleared my throat and re-adjusted my Award-Winning Smile. I was going to clinch this deal, irregular heartbeat and possible impending anxiety attack be damned.

After they'd all made their drink orders with the receptionist, the presentation began.

'I just want to start off by thanking you all for coming today,' I began, slowly pacing around the room, making sure to offer each client eye contact. 'I believe this meeting has been in the works for at least a couple of years now, and I'm so glad we've been able to make it happen! I appreciate One Nation Athletics for kindly hosting us, and I'm excited to get into the ways in which I think One Nation and Section – I mean, *Season* Eight Digital can collaborate.'

Christ. Knocked it out of the park there, Temz.

As I turned towards my laptop to move to the first slide, I caught a quick glimpse of William, who was staring past me at the whiteboard, looking seemingly bored. As I smiled awkwardly at him, he hit me with a very subtle wink, and rubbed his nose again. I averted my gaze and started with the presentation. Suffice it to say, I was bright, articulate, well versed in the brand's ethos and history, and engaging. You would have thought those attributes would have made for a great presenta-tion, right? Wrong – *ish*. Alongside the positive skills I tried so hard to demonstrate throughout the presentation, I was also clumsy, distracted, irritated, worried and anxious. All traits that ultimately could potentially cost us the brand deal.

I was constantly distracted by William's nose-sniffing and

general jitters, which made me super nervous. Not only did I end up blanking out on the numbers for an important piece of data *twice*, but twenty-five minutes into the presentation I had already mistakenly called Nathan 'Ruben' three times, and knocked my glass of water over the boardroom table. Complete chaos.

Internally, my mind was filled with anxiety over not hearing from Ruben. He had seemed in such good spirits when I met him. *Why was he ignoring Aloe now?* I needed to call him, to message him. I needed to know what was wrong. I didn't know if something had happened to him or if he had been purposefully ignoring me, but either way, I knew I had to wrap this up and just see him again in person to confess all. As the presentation came to a close, I had been internally trying to sort out the logistics of how to make a meeting with Ruben happen when I heard Nathan's voice in the distance.

'Artemis? Artemis? Haha, hey!'

I subtly snapped back into the room, attempting to mask my blank expression.

'Nathan, hey! Did you have a question?' I replied a little too enthusiastically. *Get your head back in the game, Temz.*

'Yeah – I wanted to ask whether you saw influencer marketing as a big part of the brand strategy for the next year? Admittedly, it's a new area for us, so any insight would be greatly appreciated.'

As I answered Nathan's question, I could feel William's eyes all over me, looking me up and down. Almost as if he was judging me. I began to sweat, and my heart was thumping loud as fuck. All I wanted was for this meeting to be over.

I stared at William, whose eyes were zoned in on my cleavage at this point. As if this couldn't get any worse!

'Um, do you use much influencer marketing right now?'

I asked as I managed to finish answering Nathan's question, turning to William as I spoke. 'It would be good to see where you're all at with it so I can add on with suggestions that I think could work if you took us on!'

Heh. That was smooth.

'Sure, we can do that,' William answered, smoothing his tie.

I smiled and suggested a five-minute break, subtly bending down as I passed Annabelle to ask for a quick word with her outside of the boardroom.

'Annabelle, first of all, I'd like to apologise for the clumsiness I displayed earlier on in the presentation, I think I'm just a tad nervous,' I said.

'Oh, honey, don't worry at all! We were all in your position once, and frankly, you're doing a great job!' Annabelle responded enthusiastically.

Well, that was good to hear at least.

'Thanks! I also just wanted to ask whether William is OK? He seems a little . . . distracted.' I smiled apologetically as Annabelle's face stiffened, then fell – the expression of a boss who had dealt with his shenanigans before.

'Oh, darlin',' she replied sympathetically, 'he's probably had a long night. I apologise on his behalf! I'm so sorry. His behaviour, of course, does not reflect the ethos of One Nation as a whole. I'll talk to him.'

We thank God.

The rest of the presentation took place without incident, but it was a little awkward, to say the least. I couldn't help feeling a little defeated, like I'd let myself down – and all because of the mess I'd got myself in with Ruben.

Le sigh.

Chapter 32

By 5.30 p.m. that afternoon, I was back at the hotel on the sofa, mindlessly watching an infomercial selling pain relief medicine where the side effects of the medicine sounded a lot worse than the actual illness itself. It had been a long day with One Nation Athletics, and all I needed in that moment was to chill out with a glass of something cold and refreshing before confronting it all. I really hoped that my anxiety and clumsiness throughout the meeting hadn't ruined any chances of us getting the account. The whole Ruben situation had completely thrown me off my game, and despite our positive meeting the other day, I couldn't shake the feeling that somehow, something weird had happened with him and Aloe.

I sent an email update to Stephen to tell him how it went, conveniently missing out the part where a member of the client's team was high on coke, and my awkward performance at the presentation, of course. My email was met with his usual response of Absolutely brilliant news! We all knew you could do it and I'm so proud. We're due to hear their decision by the end of next week at the very latest!, followed by a plethora of smiley-faced emojis. Then I texted Claudia and informed her of the real tea:

Artemis: Claudia, all the guy did in the meeting was stare at my tits for like forty-five mins. He was SOARING through

the clouds, high on that stuff! Also, I think I did really shit.
I called one of the directors the wrong name three times
and I kept zoning out. Ffs, man.

Clauds: God, Temz, that's fucking gross about that guy . . . but
if it means we get the account, I too, salute your breasts,
as problematic as that sounds. And also, I'm sure you did
fucking amazingly, please don't doubt yourself. We all zone
out every now and again!

Artemis: That's very fucking problematic, and I absolutely
agree. I guess the presentation was OK, I just hope we
can clinch it based on that alone, but if we end up getting
it due to corporate guilt, I'm also not mad at that xx

Jean seemed less than enthused when I messaged him about
it, though.

Jean: I hope he fucking gets fired. What a knobhead!? That
is NOT OK.

Artemis: Yeah. But overall, I was just clumsy and all over the
place. That's what I'm really worried about, man. Today is
so shit, ugh. But here's hoping it all comes through in the
end. #WeMove

Jean: . . . .

Jean: Girl, I guess. I'm happy that the presentation went OK,
despite that guy being unprofessional AF, and I'm sure you
absolutely smashed it regardless, but the Artemis I know
wouldn't be allowing guys to rattle her like this. The Artemis
I know wouldn't have made a lot of the decisions you're
currently making, tbh.

And he didn't know the half!

I splayed out on the cream white sofa with a glass of some
random kombucha-type drink from the minibar, growing
sleepier by the second as I replayed the events of the day. Jean

was disappointed in how I handled the meeting, which I kind of understand, but all the other stuff about other decisions I'd been making kinda had me a bit lost. Did he really think I had changed? I was still the same Artemis he'd always known, just with 30 per cent more chaotic energy, I guess. In some ways, I was in total control: new flat; new job position. Getting flown out on the company dime. Everything was kinda–sorta coming up Milhouse and it was all due to my doing. I deserved at least some kind of congratulations, at the very least? But when it came to the romance department, I was admittedly a bit of a shambles.

A few moments later, my phone started to ring. By this point I was mentally exhausted and really didn't feel like entertaining any conversations – but after seeing it was Ruben calling, I sat straight up. My anxiety had been all over the place since he'd been ignoring me; I needed to see what was up as my nerves couldn't handle it any longer. This would be an opportunity to figure out what was wrong with him. I pressed 'accept' and answered.

'Hey! Nice of you to call, I was worried,' I said, slurring a little as I tried to sound as nonchalant as possible.

There was silence at the end of the phone for a moment.

'Are you drunk, Aloe?'

'Huh? Nah, I'm just tired. It's been a long day is all. How are you? Why didn't you get back to me earlier when I texted you?'

Silence yet again. Damn. I could have done with a coffee right about now. I needed my mind to be sharp.

'Um. I was just tired too, I guess,' he said. 'So, what have you been up to? Catch me up.'

Hmm. Something was afoot. But I decided to play the long game before asking what was wrong.

'It's been meh, I guess,' I replied, sitting up. I needed to get my stories straight. 'I had a long day of meetings and fighting fires at work; pretty sure I smashed the presentation I was telling you about before, though.' Silence on the other end of the phone. I continued. 'Erm, I came back to the hotel not too long ago, so now I'm just chilling, and—'

Hotel? Why did I mention that??? Temz, you dickhead.

'Oh . . . You're at a hotel? What hotel you at?' Ruben cut in. No 'congratulations', no 'I knew my baby could do it!' Nothing. Normally he was so affectionate. Was he on to me?

'Um? Huh? What do you mean? Why?' I muttered quickly, wanting to move past this convo as soon as possible.

'I wanted to know so I could send you some flowers, was all,' Ruben responded curtly. I could suddenly feel a warm, slow pulsating of panic coursing through my veins as I processed this change in tone. He knew something. He must know.

I replied anxiously, 'What's the matter? You've been weird with me all day and I don't understand why. If there's something up, please talk to me. Have . . . have I done something wrong?'

Girl. You've done everything wrong.

Ruben responded by chuckling softly down the phone in that husky tone that he knew turned me on. Bastard.

'Ay yo, I thought your voice was deeper? Or is this your normal voice?' He sounded weird himself.

'Huh? What are you talking about? I've always sounded like this!' I lied.

He definitely knows. This was it. This was game-time.

I tried a last-minute attempt to change the subject as I could feel my voice wobbling. I wasn't ready . . . I couldn't do this now. *Please no . . .*

'I may sound a bit groggy as it's been such a long few days! I'm celebrating a big win with a client today and there are just a load of apartment admin things I need to do. That has been stressing me out a little, to be honest. I completely forgot how long the process of moving takes these days but I may get my friend from work to help me mo—'

I was suddenly interrupted by Ruben. 'Ummm, yeah, that sounds great, *Aloe*. Happy for you.'

I was about to respond when something caught me. The way he said Aloe's name. Why did he put so much stress on it like that?

'I, um . . .' I spluttered, completely getting caught off-guard. 'I'm sorry. Have I done something to offend you? I'm not sure why you've been so off with me.'

'I'm fine, Aloe. I've just had a really long week. Now, can I have the name of the hotel you're at? Is it South London? That's where you're at, right?'

My Spidey senses were going haywire. I quickly googled the name of a hotel near my workplace as a cover. The flowers will probably be dead by the time I get them, but if it means getting Ruben off my back, then so be it.

'Um, yeah I'm in London, I'm staying at The Ned,' I replied softly.

'Aight. I'll google it. Catch me up to what you've been up to. Actually, why don't you give me a tour of your hotel room, I wanna see what a London hotel looks like.'

With that, my phone started to vibrate, which indicated the dreaded 'Ruben would like you to switch to video' request notification – my eternal foe in this dance of deceit with him.

'Babe, what are you doing?' I shouted a little louder than necessary. Ever since we'd had a conversation about how awkward and shy Aloe felt in front of the camera, Ruben had promised not to try and coax me to show myself on a video call. Why now?

'What? You can turn the camera around, I just wanna see what the room is like. I know it's, uhh . . . *late* over there or whatever, but I thought you wouldn't mind showing your boyfriend how your company's putting you up. Or is your camera still *broken?*'

Again with the emphasis, now on the word 'late' and, now that I think about it, the way he said 'broken' with regards to my phone's camera.

I caught my breath.

'Um, Ruben, babes, I'm not in the best headspace right now. Can I just call you later?' Then I put the phone down without waiting for his response. Moments later, he sent a WhatsApp message:

> **Ruben: Uh ... OK? You didn't need to put the phone down like that.**
>
> **Ruben: It's damn frustrating to be in a relationship with someone you care about and never see them, though.**
>
> **Ruben: Don't you feel the same? Ain't this frustrating for you too? Like ... what are you hiding from me? Is there anything you wanna tell me?**

My brain felt as if it was about to implode.

Did he know what had been going on? It felt like I was on the cusp of losing him, and I wondered whether this would have been a lot easier if I hadn't meet him at the open mic. What if he had figured it out? But if that were the case, surely he would have hit me up on my personal account? It was so difficult to tell where his head was at. The more I lied, the worse it had become. I could never forgive myself if he were to end up hating me. I had no idea where to go from here and all I could think of was the fact that I may lose him. I wanted to throw up. *Deep breaths, Temz. Just take deep breaths.* I texted back:

> **Me: Babe I know this is super frustrating for you. It is for me too! I thought all the photos and videos I'd been sending**

you would be enough. My camera is still down, and it kills me that I can't do anything about it for the moment!

Ruben immediately clapped back with:

Ruben: Use a friend's phone then. Or get on your laptop and we can Zoom. You have options, sis.

'Sis'. Oh, my man was getting sassy. He got me there with the Zoom trap. *Shit.* I considered my options: broken MacBook charger? Laptop robbed on the bus? Malware? As I thought about my next move, an Instagram notification came up on my *private* account, from Ruben:

RubesCubes: Having fun in San Francisco, Artemis? It was great seeing you at the open mic. If you're still here, it'll be great to meet up again and I can show you around more of the city, if you're not busy of course?

I stared at the screen, transfixed. Either he knew something was going on, or he was attempting to cheat on me . . . with me.

Maybe this was my sign to come clean once and for all. I'd been saying this the whole trip, yet not following up on it. How many more signs did I need? I was allowing my lies to continue in the hopes that I could find the right time to tell him when I was ready, in a setting of my choosing and when I felt less anxious, but this was beginning to unravel faster than I could have comprehended.

What in the Jerry Springer had I landed myself in? This was all getting sticky, and I couldn't even talk to Jean about it right now since as he seemed to be in some kind of funk with me about this whole situation. I'd told him that I would handle it, but now it was spiralling even more out of control.

I hopped onto my personal Instagram and quickly clicked through a couple of the Stories I'd uploaded earlier of me posing outside the Golden Gate Bridge, me at the Disney Museum, a corny picture of me outside the *Mrs Doubtfire* house, and a photo of the outside of the open mic venue. I clicked to see the list of people who had viewed each story and just as I had suspected, Ruben's profile was at the very top of each one. Not only had Ruben seen the open mic image story, he'd also 'liked' it, approximately forty minutes ago. But it's Aloe he seemed to currently have an attitude with, not me. Not Artemis.

I could potentially turn this around.

I went back to the messages and saw that Ruben was online. How could I possibly spin this? Seeing as I was flying back to the UK soon, I thought about my options. I could:

a) Chance it, and take up his offer of meeting up again. Once linked up, I'd explain everything. The worst-case scenario the encounter ending up super awkward, he could end up being a massive prick, or I just turn into a hermit and refuse to speak. The best-case scenario would be him forgiving me, us having an amazing time, him eventually telling me he'd fallen for me as *me* and that he could sense the sexual chemistry between us at the open mic night, we'd end up getting together, he moves to the UK to be with me in my lavish new apartment and we both live happily ever after, forgetting entirely about the whole Aloe situation.

b) Tell him I was tying up some work loose ends and that I wouldn't have the time to meet up right now. Maybe throw in the fact that I would be flying back to the UK in the morning, for that extra razzle dazzle.

I started to type, with absolutely no idea of what to say. I decided to just let whatever I really felt inside flow through me and appear in the message box; the double life was tiring, and my anxiety was beginning to reach its peak. The wild part was that I could have easily just told Ruben the truth then blocked him and pretended that he no longer existed. Then I wouldn't have to face any real repercussions for it. But my feelings for him had become intertwined in this whole saga. I didn't have it in me to hurt him like that, and we'd become really close. I couldn't face losing this relationship. I truly loved him and didn't want to let him go.

> **ItsArtemis_O:** Hey Ruben! Yeah, was so good to meet you! I enjoyed our coffee and I wished we could have hung out for longer. And I've been good so far; it's mostly been back-to-back meetings otherwise. I forgot to tell you, I'm flying back first thing tomorrow so I don't think I'll have the time to meet, annoyingly! Let me get back to you though – I'll let you know if I can make time before I go! Hope you're having a wonderful day xx

Was that the coward's response? Maybe.

It was instantly read by him, followed by a simple reply:
RubesCubes: K. Cool.

My stomach sank. Something was definitely off here, too, and I was at that awkward, fear-inducing intersection of not knowing what the problem was, but also not wanting to investigate in case it led to him finding out the truth.

So I just turned off my phone and headed to bed.

I stayed in bed for the next day at the hotel, not eating or venturing outside at all. What an absolute shitshow. As much as I wanted to tell Ruben the truth in an ideal world, I was petrified that I would end up losing him for good. I was scared of his probable rejection of me. Scared of losing a friend and potential partner, scared of going back to how life was back home; the insignificant, meaningless dates with fuckboys who only wanted me for my body, and most of all, scared of losing out on the potential future I could have had with Ruben.

My phone stayed off as I continued to soak my pillows with tears that seemed determined not to stop. I'd go from relentlessly and dramatically sobbing and shaking, to quietly lamenting under the sheets. I'd made such a mess of everything, and I couldn't even confront any of it because I was still so afraid of Ruben's reaction. Jean told me this would happen. But, to be honest, when did I ever listen to sense?

The thought of heading back to London without at least even seeing and explaining everything to Ruben was driving me up the wall. Maybe it was fate that I was here? I mean, what were the chances of the HQ of a potential client being located in the very same place my somewhat-quasi-boyfriend lived? Maybe it was a sign for me to finally sort my romantic life out.

Yep. I was gonna do it. I needed to, for the sake of my mental health at this point. I was relieved to have finally made the decision, and managed to get some sleep at last.

The next morning, I typed out the plan for the day on my Notes app:

- Take super long shower
- Go for long walk round the block
- Write apology script – rehearse out loud
- Order lunch (does a cheesecake count as lunch?)
- Rehearse apology again
- Meditate???
- Make room for any last-minute freakouts etc.
- Call Ruben and confess

I stretched and groggily made my way to the hotel room window as I contemplated the plan. The sun had barely risen over the San Francisco skyline, with the clouds illuminating the sky with an almost menacing magenta glow, as if we were entering the apocalypse. *The irony.*

A couple of hours later, after my walk, I was back at the hotel on the sofa, going over my lines.

'Ruben. There's something I need to talk to you about, but before I talk, I need you to promise me that you won't get mad, OK?'

Mm. Not quite. He'll have every right to get angry.

'Hey baby, there's something I need to confess, and I don't really know how to start so I'm just gonna say it: I'm not Aloe. I'm Artemis.'

Eh. Too abrupt for my liking.

'Haha, oh babe, you'll never guess what?? I've been lying to you since May and I'm not actually the woman in the pic. We've actually already met and you didn't suspect a thing, haha! Funny, huh? HUH?'

Too unhinged.

'Hey Ruben, I think we should talk. There's something I've been keeping from you, and due to how I feel about you, I don't think it's fair to continue lying to you.'

Yeah. Something along those lines sounded about right.

I wasn't a bad person, I just did a bad thing. As long as he could feel how sorry I was and that, despite the fake photos, everything about me and how I felt about him was real, I was sure he'd take some pity on me – perhaps even continue to feel the same. Our meeting already established that we had some kind of chemistry; I was praying that it was enough to hold our relationship – or friendship – together at this point. I decided to take the plunge, opened up Instagram and sent a message:

SayAloeToMyLittleFriend: Hey Ruben, I hope you're good. I've just realised that I've got some free time this evening or maybe tomorrow. I don't know if you're free, but I'd love to hang out with you again and possibly have a chat? Let me know if you're down. X

I put my phone down and exhaled. If he accepted, then I'd be confessing all potentially today or tomorrow.

I put on a guided meditation podcast that dealt with anxiety, and proceeded to sit on the floor, cross-legged as the lady with the sleepy voice spoke out the instructions.

You can do this, Temz.

'Close your eyes, and start to breathe. Take deep breaths in through your nose and out through your mouth. In for the count of four, and out for the count of four . . .'

Everything is gonna be fine. He may not even be that mad.

'Bring your focus to your breath, and really pay attention to how your lungs expand and contract when you inhale and exhale . . .'

You're a strong, confident woman, and you're going to be clear, honest, confident and calm when you talk to him.

'Notice your jaw, and if you feel any tension here, just notice it, don't try to change anything . . .'

I unclenched my jaw and took several deep breaths in and out.

In . . .

Ring! Ring!

And out . . .

Ring! Ring! Ring!

Whoever was trying to call me needed to scram – I was trying to get into ZEN mode here. My phone stopped, then started ringing again. I exhaled, opened my eyes and glanced at the screen.

It was Ruben. How odd. He never normally called Aloe around this time. He was supposed to know the time difference.

I wasn't sure what he wanted, but I wanted to save all my energy for tomorrow's conversation. *Just hurry him off the phone and tell him that 'you'll' to speak to him later.*

I picked up.

'Hey Ruben! How are—'

'What's going on, bro?'

Ruben's voice sounded strained. And very, very quiet down the phone.

'Ruben . . . ?'

'Who are you, Aloe?'

At that moment, every blood cell in my body turned to ice.

'I . . . I don't know what you mean?'

He took a deep breath before he continued.

'I knew it. I knew something was up and I didn't want to believe it.'

'What?' My throat felt tight.

'Remember that girl from England that follows me that I asked if you knew? Artemis? She just asked me to meet up later. Here, in Oakland. But her message was sent from *Aloe's* account. What the fuck is going on?'

I put Ruben on loudspeaker as I silently scrolled into Aloe's account messages, only to see my message to him, there in black and white.

SayAloeToMyLittleFriend: Hey Ruben, I hope you're good. I've just realised that I've got some free time this evening or maybe tomorrow. I don't know if you're free, but I'd love to hang out with you again and possibly have a chat? Let me know if you're down. X

I'd sent it from the wrong account.

Fuck.

No time like the present, I guess.

Chapter 33

'Shit. Um, oh God, Ruben . . . I'm so sorry. I'm so, so sorry.'

I could feel the burning of tears as they began to trickle down my cheeks. It wasn't supposed to happen this way. I wasn't supposed to be caught unaware in this moment, neither did I ever want him to find out so abruptly like this.

There was silence on the other end once more. I could hear my heartbeat thumping loudly more than ever before. I decided to break it.

'Ruben . . . are you OK?'

'How could I be OK, Aloe? Or, sorry, should I say *Artemis*?'

He said my name with such poison that it almost caught me off-guard. I needed a way to guide the conversation to a more honest and open place without him getting too mad, and to do that meant being as honest as possible. If there was any way that this relationship could be salvaged, I wanted to make sure I could at least try and facilitate that. With my heart full of adrenaline, I took the plunge.

'I'm going to video call you, is that OK?' I asked.

'Whatever.'

I had a quick look at myself in the mirror but, to be honest, I had reached my worst possible moment. There was no point in trying to tart myself up for someone I'd just spent the last few months lying to. I had remnants of old mascara running down my face, my eyes were blotchy and a bit damp from the onslaught of silent tears, and my hair was running ragged, but shit, this was me, and this was what he was going to get, moving forward.

The camera turned on and there he was again, this beautiful, sad-looking man whose eyes looked puffy with what looked like tears looking up at me. I was expecting at least a grimace, or some kind of registration of disgust on his face but there was none. Just sadness as he stared at me.

It took everything in my spirit to not burst into tears or shut the camera off, with the feeling of shame invading my whole body like an aggressive parasite; but instead, we just gazed at each other for what felt like hours, each of us taking the other in for the first time. After a few moments, Ruben spoke.

'There you are.' He looked at me, not once taking his eyes off me. 'Live and in the flesh once again. I shoulda clocked on earlier. Fuck, man . . .'

I looked down and sighed, feeling the overwhelming pressure of shame mounted upon my shoulders. I wanted to cry. To beg. To shout. To mourn. But I knew I had to keep my composure. Ruben's feelings were the priority here, not mine. I had to give him the answers he needed and deserved.

A few moments of silence once more before he dropped a bombshell.

'Your lil friend also confirmed you as a liar, by the way.'

I stared at him, the shock clearly registered on my face. Ruben scoffed.

'Which friend?' I replied, breathing in slowly. I could feel my heart drumming against my chest even though deep down I already knew which friend it was. It could only be one. Aneni.

'It doesn't matter right now. That ain't important,' he almost snarled. Oh, man. He was furious.

All I wanted in that moment was to console him; to hug him, apologise and tell him everything was going to be OK. Neither of us spoke for a while. Instead, Ruben just continued to glare at me, expressionless. I couldn't read him at all, and this made me nervous.

'Please. Say something, Ruben,' I said eventually.

Finally, he spoke.

'You're still in San Fran, right?'

I didn't like where this was going.

'Um. Yeah. Why?'

'I don't wanna do this over the phone. Let's meet, and you can explain to me why you did this. I deserve that at least.'

The panic must have shown on my face, because the next thing I knew, Ruben let out a scoff.

'Oh, what? You can't even do that now? You seemed to be down to meet up tomorrow, though? I wanna look you in the eye as you confess. You owe me that.'

He was right. Of course he was, and, to be honest, it had been leading towards this point anyway. Easier to rip the plaster off instead of prolonging the pain.

'Of course. I'm— I'm sorry. Um, I'm actually free this evening, if you wanted to chat,' I muttered, my voice barely rising past a whisper.

Ruben then switched his camera off, prompting me to do the same. I didn't want him to look at me any more. I was a pathetic mess.

'Aight,' he continued. 'Meet me at the waterfront at Jack London Square – near this jazz club called Yoshi's. Around nine-thirty.'

Little did he know I'd already visited that part of town. I tapped the name of the club into my phone as I replied, 'OK, I'll find it. I'll be there. And Ruben? I just wanna say—'

Click

And he was gone.

I've normally always been good at compartmentalising my feelings in order to focus on the situation at hand, but at this point I was at rock bottom.

An hour or two later, I gave myself a final rundown in the mirror before leaving to go and meet Ruben, hoping that I'd somehow managed to nail the Wholesome Girl aesthetic. I didn't want to look as if I were trying too hard in case he assumed I wasn't taking the situation seriously. I needed to be modest, yet cute:

- Beige linen midi dress that hugs me in just enough places (with added v-neck for allure) – check.
- White hi-top Converse trainers (comfort over style today) – check
- My Ghanaian gold 'Gye Nyame' necklace (for protection) – check
- Hair in a fluffed out Afro (for peak cuteness) – check
- Make-up: minimal foundation, no eyeshadow but loads of mascara for that 'doll eye' effect, a touch of highlighter and a sheer pink lipgloss – check

Even in the midst of a nervous breakdown, I'd still managed to pull off a fierce look.

I looked at myself in the mirror. I looked great, but who was I trying to kid at this point? This wasn't a job interview or a first date. I wasn't heading out to try and entice him in any way; maybe I didn't need to wear the form-fitting dress. I wanted to feel comfortable for what was about to happen. I took off the dress and swapped it for a pair of denim shorts and my old and very worn-in 'Sister Sister' logo T-shirt, which I tucked into the shorts.

'There we go,' I said out loud, giving myself the once-over. Ruben was going to get the real me, once and for all. Worn-out T-shirt and everything.

Grabbing my bag and keys, I ordered an Uber to the location to save me looking a hot ass mess by the time I got there.

I did some last-minute breathing exercises to calm my nerves.

You got this, Temz.

He's a nice guy, he won't be mean to you.

Lead with honesty. It'll all be fine.

What's the worst that could happen?

Famous last words. Heh.

I arrived at 9.15 p.m. with the intention of getting there a few minutes early to settle my nerves, but to my dismay Ruben was already there, sitting on a bench overlooking the docks. His back was hunched, as if in deep prayer. Under the bench, I could see his legs bouncing away anxiously.

As if sensing he was being watched, Ruben slowly turned his head to look towards me, and I felt a shiver go down my spine. In that moment, the beautifully shaped almond eyes I'd come to know and love were ice-cold as he stared at me for what seemed like forever.

I suddenly began to feel self-conscious, dropping his eye contact and looking to the floor. I couldn't do this. The shame that had been hiding deep inside me for so many months seemed to have reached its crescendo, and I felt about two seconds away from bursting into tears right there and then.

Hold it together, Artemis. You can do this. You're strong.

But the silence was deafening. I lifted my head up again and slowly walked forward, eyes meeting his again.

He was still so beautiful up close. One of the most beautiful men I'd ever come across. His skin, a rich mahogany, was glowing in the diffused rays of the setting sun, highlighting his high cheekbones and full lips. He was tall, and incredibly broad, like he could bench press ten of me with no problems.

As I reached him, I spoke. 'Hi, Ruben.'

The icy glare in his eyes quickly faded and was replaced with a mournful look. I could see how much I had hurt him. He stared at me for a moment, his sad eyes piercing my soul. Shame overtook my body once more.

'We meet again, I guess. Umm. Aight so, let's sit and you can start from the beginning.'

The location was beautiful; the boardwalk overlooked the Bay, with its gigantic white cranes illustrating the background, which reminded me of something out of *Star Wars*. This would have been somewhat romantic if the current situation wasn't so mortifying.

I sat down on the bench, facing straight ahead while he also did the same. I couldn't bear to meet his gaze.

Before I could start, he spoke again. 'You know you fucked up, right?'

'I know.'

'Why would you do this?'

My eyes winced as his voice broke on the word 'why'. Why indeed. After months of refusing to face the truth, it finally hit me why I went down this path of destruction. I had been lying to myself the whole time and it was time to finally admit it to both myself and Ruben.

I turned to face him. He was looking straight ahead, crestfallen.

'Ruben, I— first off I wanna say how sorry I am that you had to find out this way. I have been wanting to tell you for months, and I guess that's why I ended up following you on my private account. I was planning to tell you, but—'

'But what?' Ruben interrupted, his eyes now alive with annoyance as he turned to face me. 'You thought it would be dope to lead me on a bit more? Make me out to look like some gullible loser? Which was it? You had the nerve to even come to the open mic to see me and you couldn't even tell me then? Do you know how stupid that makes me feel? Do you?'

'No! Not at all! You're not the stupid one here, I am!' I retorted desperately. 'It wasn't like that at all. I'd fallen in love with you, and I was scared of how you would react if I told you the truth, OK? It seemed easier to keep playing along.'

Ruben stared at me, waiting for me to continue. I decided to spill.

'I *do* have a huge love of houseplants. That part is true! I've had the plant IG page for a while, and I've always separated it from my private page because the influencer stuff is a lot more public-facing. I never really saw the need to show my face as it was always meant to be about the plants, you know?'

Ruben grunted in response. I couldn't tell if he was being sarcastic or if he was actually following what I was trying to say, but I decided to continue anyway.

'When we started talking, I felt like . . . I felt myself fall for you instantly. We developed such a connection over such a short period of time, and it seemed a little too good to be true. When you asked me for a pic, I panicked because I thought you wouldn't like the way I looked. There was a part of me that wanted to just stay in this bubble. I saw the kind of girls you followed on Instagram and just . . . I don't know. I guess I was a little intimidated.'

At that point, Ruben glanced at me directly and let out a pointed chuckle while scratching his ear. Even when he was angry, he was sexy. Fucking hell.

'Uhuh.'

You could cut the tension with a knife. I took his ongoing silence as my cue to continue my verbal diarrhoea.

'Everything I felt – everything I *feel* about you – is real, Ruben,' I pleaded, edging closer to him. 'Only the pictures I sent you weren't me. Everything else was. Lying to you about that is something I'm going to regret forever. I shouldn't have done it. I should have acted like a fucking adult and just sent you a pic of *me*, regardless of the outcome. I wanted to feel like someone liked me and I just . . . acted like a dick. My whole life I've been fooling myself into thinking that I'm this super confident woman who didn't care what people thought, but the truth is . . . I guess I still have some old insecurities that I still haven't healed from. I'm so ashamed of myself.'

He still didn't respond. I could feel the blood rushing through my veins. I wanted nothing more than for the floor to devour me whole. This shit was PAINFUL.

'Ruben, from the bottom of my heart, I am so sorry that I lied to you. It wasn't to intentionally play you, or make you come across like a loser. It was me. It was all me and my fucked-up issues. I wanted to tell you when we met, but I didn't have the courage to.'

At that, Ruben raised his head and stared at me. 'So you going out of your way to con me was basically because of your low fucking self-esteem and control-freak issues, huh?'

Well, that was unexpected.

'My . . . huh?'

'And now you're tryna place the cause of your actions on me and what you thought I'd go for in a woman. You're tryna shift the blame, ain't it?'

'I . . . I don't know what you're talking about. I am not a control freak, I was just saying that it was my insecurities that—'

'Yeah, your insecurities that made you turn into a damn *control freak*! Trying to control the situation, assuming that you knew the type of woman I liked, and manipulating me so things go in your favour with me none the wiser. And like a clown, I went for it. And you made a fool of me by coming to my show. I fell for it, like a dumbass. This is so fucked UP!'

He stood up and walked to the railing of the pier. After a couple of seconds, he walked back to the bench and sat down, breathing slowly. I knew that I deserved this dragging. All I wanted to do was throw myself into the Bay.

'Look,' I said, trying to control the hurt I felt at his accusations, 'I didn't deliberately manipulate you. I just had a moment of panic, and in that moment, I guess I wanted to fit in. You were so kind and interesting when we were talking, and when we met, you were so lovely and it felt as if the chemistry was there and I wanted you to like me and—'

'Did you not think I would like you as you are?' Ruben was full-on shouting now. 'Why couldn't you let me decide how to feel about the real you? Did I walk away when you came up to me? Did I call you ugly? You're such a gorgeous woman as it is. I just don't get it.'

I gulped and choked back tears. Ruben thought I was beautiful. This whole time. *Fuck's sake, Temz*. This makes it all even worse.

'Ruben, I'm so sorry.'

'Was any of it even real? You should have told me that night at the slam. You should have just . . . TOLD me from the beginning. You didn't even give me a chance to get to know you or fall in love with you as "you". You took that choice away from me, and the wild part is that I was hella enjoying talking to the real you. I loved our little date the other day. You seemed like a really fun, cool person. But this . . . nah, this is . . . I can't deal with it, man. I got trust issues as it is.'

What else could I possibly say outside of 'sorry'? I continued listening to him as he ranted at me, feeling the tears roll down my face and slide down my neck. I wanted to console him, to hold him and tell him how much I cared about him, but I was the cause of his pain, and I couldn't do anything about it at this moment aside from listen.

'And the women I follow,' he continued. 'I've worked with a lotta them professionally in the music industry, and some of them are just fans. I always wanna respond and be nice to them in return for their support. It don't mean I'm fucking them. I don't *have* a preference!'

'But you didn't have to outrightly tell me your preference!' I barked back in an attempt to defend myself. I'd seen a couple of the comments he would leave under some of those girls' photos, which looking back, may have been harmless in retrospect, but . . . 'I remember the conversation we had where you were talking about your exes. When you thought I looked different, you said they all looked like me but not as beautiful. I saw you leave comments complimenting these *fans* on how good they looked. You clearly have a type, Ruben, and at that moment I didn't feel confident to present my real self to you. Can you blame me for trying to live up to all that?'

Ruben stared at me as if to speak, but suddenly stopped himself and continued looking out towards the Bay. Finally, he said, 'So what are you trying to say? That it's my fault you lied to me? You've clearly been monitoring my Instagram activities super hard. That doesn't seem weird to you?'

'Of course it's weird! I know it is, and it was a stupid thing for me to do! Those women on Instagram are the kinds of women I've been told are the golden standard all my life. My worth has never been contingent on my looks, but when it comes to dating and shit, it's fucking frustrating to always either be fetishised or passed over in favour of women shaped like wisdom teeth.'

I briefly looked up at Ruben and . . . was that a smile I just caught? The sides of his mouth briefly turned up at my last little quip, before settling back down into a frown. 'I still love you,' I continued. 'I'm not blaming you, I'm just trying to provide more context to why I didn't feel one hundred per cent confident in showing you my real self. I like to think I'm a confident person, and I wouldn't necessarily say I grew up having self-inflicted issues about my body. Every negative thought I've had about it stems from outside sources. From how I've been made to feel by men. By society. I could love myself as much as I want, but that love isn't going to stop someone from calling me a fat bitch, or hinting that my size isn't "girlfriend material". It doesn't stop family members from commenting on my health and suggesting my weight is the reason why I'm single. Me loving myself fully means nothing if fatphobia keeps weaving its destruction all around me. And yeah, sometimes it can have an impact on my self-esteem. It can hurt, as much as I try not to let it. And in this case, I let that doubt and fear and anxiety over my looks affect my relationship with you.' I sighed. 'Everything I *said* was real, though. I don't expect you to believe or forgive me, but I believe in the connection we have . . . or had. I know I've hurt you, and I feel like shit. You deserve to be mad.'

Ruben turned to face me head on. He looked me up and down before eventually meeting my gaze.

'By the way, I found out about the girl whose photos you stole. The Chantelle chick.'

OK, this one got me. I stared, stunned.

'Huh?'

'Yeah. I scrolled through your friends list. I bet you didn't think about that, did you? I found her, another influencer type. I'm assuming she was in on the lil scam too, huh?' He let out a sarcastic chuckle.

I continued staring slightly open-mouthed at him. 'Umm – no, no, she wasn't. She doesn't know that I— I mean she isn't aware that I used her photos . . . Did you speak to her?'

My sweat ran cold as I waited for him to answer, which took longer than necessary. If this was his attempt at fucking with me, he was succeeding.

Finally, Ruben responded. 'I thought about it. But frankly I wanted to hear it all from you.'

I let out a brief sigh of relief.

'You know you gotta tell her what you did, right?'

'I know . . . I know,' I responded heavily, the guilt weighing on my conscience over what I'd done to Chantelle. She was as much a victim in this as Ruben was, and I hadn't given her so much of a second thought.

Silence once more, as I waded in my guilt. Ruben stared out to the Bay, looking crestfallen. My heart had shattered into a million more pieces.

'This is a lot to take in, man,' he said eventually. 'Um, I can't talk to you right now. I need time.'

And with that, Ruben got up, gave me one final glance, and then walked away down the boardwalk, leaving me on the bench, my lap wet with tears of shame.

Chapter 34

'*Ladies and gentlemen, we welcome you to London Heathrow. The local time is six-thirty p.m. For your safety and the safety of those around you, please remain seated with your seat belt fastened and keep the aisles clear until we are parked at the gate . . .*'

I stepped off the plane both relieved and annoyed to be back in the UK. I still had my phone off, not wanting to face the pending realities of what had happened in California. I passed through the arrivals gate in something of a catatonic haze, barely aware of what was happening around me. Whether it was depression or the fact that I'd been unable to sleep during the whole flight, I didn't know, but all I needed at that point was the warmth of my bed, and ice cream – lots of it.

I was halfway down the stairs to get the train from the airport when the reality of what had happened on this trip slammed me. *Ruben. The confrontation. His anger. Our shared heartbreak. My shame.*

I made it to the bottom, dropped my bags in the middle of the train platform and burst into tears. I couldn't hold it in any more; I was giving Viola Davis in the movie *Doubt*, with a thin veil of snot slowly running down my nose. I swiped at it, and my eyes. I was exhausted and stressed, and for one minute wished that I could just check out of life for just half an hour or so to rest my mind and body. As I continued to silently cry while wondering how many bottles of wine I would need to consume to make me sufficiently catatonic for the evening, I felt a tap on my shoulder.

I turned around to see a middle-aged lady with a fabulous trolley staring up at me with a smile. 'Are you OK, my dear? Would you like a tissue?'

I stared at her, filled with gratitude and slight embarrassment. There was nothing more horrifying to me than crying in front of someone. I hated it with all my heart.

I sniffed a little. 'Oh, um, yes please – that's very kind of you, thank you so much!'

I took the tissue from her, and as I blew my nose, I heard her say, 'Whoever it is that hurt you, they're a cunt. Remember that.' With that, she walked away.

If only she knew who the real cunt was in this scenario.

After loading all my luggage on the train, I finally decided to turn on my phone and face whatever music I had coming to me, whether it was Ruben, or Jean's Jiminy Cricket-ass and his constant need to hold me accountable for my actions, or the anxiety of not knowing if we clinched the deal with One Nation Athletics yet or not.

As soon as I turned on my phone, a plethora of notifications pinged onto the screen in a flurry of app updates, news updates and food delivery app menu changes. I also saw a message from Natalie.

Natalie: Got a new tenant for your room. They're gonna be moving in officially in three days. Make sure you have the room professionally cleaned. Nat x

Was she kidding me? I couldn't move into my new flat for another *four* days. This was the absolute last thing I needed to

Focus on an object to distract yourself, Temz. Breathe out slowly. Then back in.

'So . . . you essentially told him who I was, then.' If I could breathe fire, I would.

Aneni scoffed on the other end. 'He asked me who owned the Aloe account and I simply confirmed it was you, that's all. All this mess is down to you and your inability to tell the truth, babe.'

The train passed through Heathrow Central Station as it started to spit down with rain. I watched as the train passed the gloomy retail parks and desolate estates that had now been turned into some kind of shanty town overrun with foxes. The sunshine and glitz of San Francisco was great, but boy did it feel good to be home, bleakness and all.

It was pointless for me to enter into a back and forth with her. I'm sure she was already loving the fact that I'd picked up the phone in the first place. I needed to make this short and sweet.

'Bye, Aneni,' I replied calmly.

And with that, I ended the call.

A lady sitting opposite me looked up at me, winked and said, 'Good on yer, sweetheart. Men are trash!'

I grinned sadly and continued to stare out the window. I'd deal with the rest of my mess tomorrow.

Chapter 35

The Sisterhood of the Travelling Lace Fronts 🖤
Jean, You

Jean: Baby girl, you good?

Artemis: I've been better. Aneni called me yesterday though.

Jean: That skank really doesn't give up, does she?

Artemis: Jean!! LMAO

Jean: WHAT?? You guys aren't friends any more, I don't have to pretend to be civil.

Artemis: Chile, I guess.

Jean: When are we meeting up? I need all the goss!

Artemis: I'm free this eve if you are. I'm packing though. Natalie wants me out by Friday, you know.

Jean: Fucking hell. I can come and help you finish up, don't worry.

Artemis: Thanks, babes. We need to talk about Ruben too.

I still hadn't heard a word from Ruben, but I wasn't sure I should be surprised given how we'd left things.

I'd spent the day at work replaying the events in my head over and over. Wondering what I could have done better. I felt empty, yet somehow was still able to somewhat function – barely. This didn't go unnoticed by Claudia, who kept pressuring me to tell her what was up. In a bid to get her off my back, I told her that me and Ruben had 'broken up'.

'Mm. Maybe it was for the best,' she replied nonchalantly as she bit into her four-cheese sandwich. 'You don't have to go into details, but you could do so much better. His head was too bald for my liking anyway.'

'Clauds!!' I shouted, chuckling. She always knew how to make me laugh.

After Claudia went back to her desk, I opened up Instagram and perpetuated more emotional harm to myself by deciding to creep on Ruben's Instagram for any new bits of content. I hadn't been on the app since yesterday, and I wanted to see whether he had moved on.

Only to find that he had blocked both of my accounts.

The pain in my chest intensified.

'OK . . .' I said to myself, trying not to cry. After all, he had every right to block me after what I did to him. Nevertheless, the knot in my chest became tighter still. Tears started to slowly roll down my face as I began to hyperventilate. I jogged over to close my office door and then stared out of the window, trying to find something to focus on while I attempted to regulate my breathing and counted down from five to one.

Five . . . I could hear my phone ringing yet again in the background, its shrill ringtone piercing through my eardrums.

Four . . . I needed to apologise to Chantelle. She was a victim in this too.

Three . . . I looked out towards a hoarding advertising a pair of trainers that I'd recently seen going viral on TikTok. My breathing began to slow as I pondered whether I needed a pair of those trainers. When was the last time I'd been to the gym? Could I even lift any more, bro?

Note to self: schedule in some gym time.

Two . . . I turned around and walked towards my desk, balancing myself by sitting on the edge of it. I looked down towards my phone, praying to see a missed text or call from Ruben.

Girl, give it up. You're never hearing from him again.

One . . . I slowly exhaled for the last time and sat down, grabbing a bottle of water from the edge of my desk.

After two hours of serious work (which included updating my houseplant website and Instagram account – a flurry of new growth shoots from some of my older plants), I received an email from Priya and Stephen.

It was about the One Nation Athletics meeting.

In the flurry of recent chaos that had been the flat move stuff, the whole Ruben situation and my fight with Aneni, I had completely forgotten about the huge, potentially life-changing, chaotic presentation I'd recently spearheaded. It looked like their decision had been made, and the fact that Priya had emailed me and CC'd in Stephen gave me slight hope that we'd potentially clinched the account. Lord knows I needed a distraction.

Before I could open the email, Claudia bounded into my office, slamming the door behind her as she hopped from leg to leg, a wide grin on her face.

'Did you get the email from Priya, Temz?' she said, her grin widening with every word. Claudia's reaction was all the confirmation I needed.

'Not yet no, but from your Cheshire Cat-looking smile I sense that it's good news?' I replied, hurriedly clicking on the message and scanning its contents. Claudia laughed and came to join me around my desk as we read it together.

Dear Content Team,

Myself and Stephen are incredibly happy to announce the

onboarding of the Californian-based One Nation Athletics team
to Season Eight Digital! This merger has been an incredibly long
time coming, and we couldn't have done it without the impeccable and tireless work of Artemis Owusu. We will be sending
through the marketing materials for One Nation this week,
and our first official brainstorming will be in the next couple of
weeks!

Thank you all so much for all the hard work you've put in for
this. Go team!

Best,

Priya

'I . . . oh, wow. Well, damn!' I exclaimed, a little louder than I
perhaps wanted to. 'We did it! We fucking did it!' I stood up
and bear-hugged Claudia for what seemed like an eternity. It
wasn't until we touched that I realised how much I actually
really needed a hug.

'No – YOU did it, Temz. You did this! I overheard Stephen on
the phone with them earlier on; the One Nation team apparently were super impressed with your professionalism and the
amount of research and effort you put into the pitch,' Claudia
replied, grinning. 'But between me and you, I think the whole
"coke-fiend-ad exec staring at you rudely" thing also helped.'

'How dare you imply that I didn't get this on my own merits,
ma'am?!' I mocked back. 'When Stephen came round to congratulate me on my pitch earlier, I did think about telling him but
I think that's something we can just keep between us for now!'

She could have a point though. I honestly thought it would
be touch and go for a minute, but hey, for me a win was a win.

Later on that evening, Jean came round as I packed up the
last couple of boxes in my room and as I filled him in on the

details of my trip – complete with fresh tears. Jean spent the rest of the evening consoling and hugging me as we completed the last box.

'I think what you did was really brave, sis, and I'm so proud of you,' said Jean, taping up a cardboard box containing my make-up products. 'I know it couldn't have been easy, but you did the right thing, and even though you completely ignored me telling you not to meet him—' he stuck his tongue out at me at saying this '—it's good that you were able to get things sorted.'

I sighed as I stacked a suitcase near the door.

'Thanks, love. He's blocked me and I've ruined everything, though. He's probably dating someone else and my heart hurts, and I should be excited about moving but all I can think about is how terrible I am.'

Jean came in for yet another hug, tissue in hand to wipe away my tears.

'You're not a terrible person, sis. You just panicked and did something out of character. You've rectified it now, and I know it hurts, but maybe once he has time to process everything, he'll get in touch for closure or something maybe?'

'Maybe,' I replied, dejected. But deep down, I knew it would probably be the last time I heard from him.

Friday eventually came around, with my new landlord very kindly allowing me to start my tenancy a day early. I had officially moved into my new, gorgeous flat and, in true Artemis fashion, had already unpacked 80 per cent of my boxes on the first day; now it was just a case of waiting for some furniture deliveries. On the way home on Sunday, I stopped by the supermarket to pick up a bottle of Captain Morgan rum to celebrate and christen the new flat.

After arriving home and putting the rum on the kitchen

counter, I checked my phone, which I'd put on silent mode earlier. My plan was to write an apology and send it to Chantelle, but I wanted to feel completely settled and at home first. I stretched out on the new three-seater, bottle green velvet modular sofa that had been delivered (and sloppily left in the corridor outside my flat door) yesterday. I'd already had a semi-detailed plan of how I wanted the flat to look. I wanted it to be a sanctuary filled with interiors that appealed to all my senses; I was going for neutral, clean, earthy tones and super minimalistic spaces. In anticipation, I'd started watching loads of interior design shows on Netflix in a bid to get my Marie Kondo on and only have things in the flat that would inspire joy and all that shit.

Right now, though, everything was still pure chaos, but the arrival of the sofa marked the beginnings of a fun transitional period for me in this space. I went to the kitchen to make myself a rum and Coke, then returned to the living room and lay spread-eagled on the sofa, drink in hand as I put on an episode of *The Simpsons* in the background and mindlessly scrolled Instagram while I worked up the courage to message Chantelle.

Remembering that I was blocked, I signed out of both of my accounts and typed in Ruben's IG handle into my phone's web browser in order to access his page. He'd uploaded more video clips of him singing, which sounded, of course, beautiful, but then I took a gander at his Instagram Stories. He'd uploaded a story thirteen hours ago featuring a photo of him looking delectable in a white, tight vest and cargo pants with the caption: **RubesCubes: Figuring out what to wear for date night.**

I immediately screenshot the story, my stomach dropping.

So he was already dating? Just like that, I'd been forgotten. He had every reason to, of course, but I just didn't expect for him to move on so soon, while I lay here in a pit of despair, pining for him. *Damn.*

My chest felt as if I'd swallowed a stone that had become lodged in my chest. I could feel the beginnings of teardrops forming in my eyes again as I dialled my mum's number.

'Ayeee Abena, my daughter. When was the last time you called me? I could be lying here dead and you wouldn't even—'

My mum suddenly paused as I sniffled down the phone.

'Artemis! Why are you crying? What's wrong?'

'Mum,' I cried, trying to steady my breathing between sobs, 'I just . . . I just miss you, is all.'

'Why? What's happened? Is it work? Abena, if you had gone into law like I wanted you to instead of doing up "creative babe", you wouldn't be sitting here cry—'

'Mum . . . no. Please,' I interjected. For once, I just needed her to listen.

'OK, OK.'

I let out a deep sigh. It was hard enough telling my best friend what I'd done, let alone thinking about how to explain catfishing a man you fell in love with online to a middle-aged traditional Ghanaian woman.

'I . . . I broke up with someone I cared for deeply and I'm just in a lot of pain right now. I don't really know how to deal with it. It hurts, everything hurts right now.'

And then my mum did something I didn't expect. There were no scoffs. No 'I told you so's', no 'why weren't you a better girlfriend?' remarks. Instead, she started to softly hum the melody to Sade's 'By Your Side'.

It was our favourite song. She used to hum it to me as a child anytime I'd hurt myself or was feeling upset. My eyes filled with tears as I lay back and listened, my hands clutching the phone for dear life.

After about a minute, my mum spoke. 'My dear, I feel for you. I really do. I know we don't really discuss things like love and, you know . . . the things you've had to deal with as a woman. But I want you to know that I am so proud of you, mmm? We'll have another conversation about why you didn't tell me you were courting someone in the first place, but I can hear the pain in your voice. I wish I could be there to give you a hug. You are strong, OK? So incredibly strong; you take after me, sha! You will get through this. Allow yourself to feel these feelings. Heartbreak — as horrible as it is — is necessary in building character, and ultimately you will come through this feeling stronger and more prepared for whatever comes your way next.'

This was the first semi-serious conversation I'd had with my mum for a while, and it felt good. I suddenly found myself wishing that we'd had more conversations like this growing up, that I'd had a safe space with her to be vulnerable, instead of compartmentalising and feigning that I could do it all on my own. It felt good to be vulnerable in this moment.

'Thank you, Mum . . . I love you so much,' I replied between sniffs.

'I love you, too, Abena,' she responded softly. 'Remember I told you, you'll be OK, in the end. Men are also very mad, with no one to tell them. I'm even sure this one will come running back like an idiot after a few weeks. You'll see!'

Of course she had to end on a one-liner. Good old Mum. I chuckled. 'Cheers, Mum, I'll talk to you later. Love you.'

I hung up and wiped my tears.

Jean called me in a flurry while I unpacked some more boxes the next day. I'd taken annual leave in order to sort the flat out and see to any admin bits.

'Girl. You have some explaining to do,' he snapped.

'Huh? What's happened?'

'You didn't give me the full tea over what happened with you and Aneni, that's what.'

Oh, snap. In the midst of everything that had gone on, I'd forgotten to relay Aneni's part to play in the Ruben saga. Not that she was that important to the story anyway.

'How'd you find out?'

'She randomly messaged me on Instagram, ranting about you ignoring her! I ignored her, too. I know she's seething.'

'Yeah,' I responded dully. 'She confirmed my Aloe account with Ruben, but, to be honest, I'm over her. I don't even want to bring her up any more – she's in the past now.'

'Agreed,' Jean said, sighing. 'She's bitter. Always has been, I think. Her grassing you up to Ruben was foul – she literally could have ignored him or claimed ignorance or whatever. The bitch.'

'Yeah . . . I guess,' I replied. I could feel my eyes prickling with tears. Aneni had reached the peak of her villain era, but ultimately, I was the one who was accountable for all of this; it was all my fault at the end of the day.

'Babes,' Jean piped up a few moments later, a tenderness in his voice that filled me with tears once more, 'I love you, you know that? You are an incredible woman, you'll move past this, and I'll be with you every step of the way.'

The tears continued to fall.

'My little Jiminy Cricket,' I sighed in response. 'Jean, I need you to know that I love you so much, and I wanna thank you for being my rock through this, even though I know you disapproved of my shenanigans.'

'I love you too, sis. Always and forever, and remember, you GOT this! Regardless of the outcome, I'm proud of you for stepping up, and don't worry about Ruben too much. Give him some time to process what's happened, because you also need to process this too. You're strong, and I have no doubt that you're gonna come out stronger for this. Love you.'

'I love you too, babes,' I replied, sighing. Jean was right.

I ended the call, ruminating on the conversation.

Chapter 36

ItsArtemis_O: Hey Chantelle,

I hope you've been doing well, and congratulations on recently being signed by that talent agency! You absolutely deserve it.

Look, I wasn't really sure how to go about doing this, but decided that a message would be best as it'll allow me to get everything out coherently.

I need to apologise to you. Wholeheartedly and unreservedly. I did something very bad, and I am incredibly ashamed of my behaviour. I'll cut right to the chase.

In May, I was talking to this guy I liked on Instagram on my plant account. After some time, he asked to see a picture of me, and for some reason in that second, I sent him a picture of you. I don't know what possessed me to do it – maybe a random moment of low self-esteem, perhaps? But I did it, and I continued doing it the whole time we were in correspondence.

I don't want to spend the majority of this message talking about my feelings, because I can acknowledge that, as you read this, you probably don't care about all that. I'm not expecting you to ever talk to me or reach out again, but I thought it was important to let you know that this had happened, and for you to know how truly and deeply sorry I am that I violated your privacy in such a horrible way. I've always thought you were absolutely stunning, even back at school, and when the guy asked me what I looked like, you were the first person that came to mind as an ideal. I realise that I have my own self-esteem issues to work on, and I am working on getting therapy to address this.

Again, I'm so incredibly sorry. I have deleted your photos, and have also told the truth to the person I gave the photos to. What I did was incredibly selfish, and you should have in no way been a part of that. I'm happy to talk if you have any questions, and completely understand the anger that you must feel right now. Sorry this was quite long!

Take care of yourself,

Love, Artemis

The message was read immediately. As someone who seemed chronically online, I wouldn't have expected anything less from Chantelle. I could relate . . . My first thought was that she would probably block me. People tend to block others for lesser crimes, and it would be totally within her right to do so.

The minutes crept by as I waited. After twenty-five minutes, a new reply hit my message box. Chantelle had responded.

@BlueberriesandSprinkles: Helloooooooooo!

Errrm . . . ! OK? This is really wild, Artemis. Really wild. Really disappointing. But shoutout to you for owning up to it and telling me the truth, I guess. I actually get people catfishing my photos all the time so this is nothing new, but to hear it from someone you know is a bit startling tbh.

Anyhoo, as long as you don't do it again, thanks for letting me know, I suppose?

PS Can I screenshot your message above to use in an upcoming episode of my 'Chantelle Shares' Podcast? I won't mention you by name, but I think it would be interesting for me to explore the concept of catfishing online for my engaged audience, and I wanna talk about my experiences with it. Lemme know if you're up for having a short pre-recorded convo with me and I'll loop my manager in. I'll send you a PDF of the podcast format etc. too! You can check out some of my previous eps on this link here. Lemme know!

Stay blessed x

I read that response eight times to fully process what I was seeing. I clicked on the link that took me to her podcast. Seven subscribers. Bless her heart. I knew I shouldn't have sent that damn message in the first place. Influencers! Jesus. I declared that part of my apology tour done and dusted.

Hours later, I was at Natalie's collecting a stack of books I'd left behind. I ventured into my old room, which had now been taken over by her new flatmate, some guy named Eric who was currently away on business. Natalie watched from the doorway as I hurriedly tried to stuff the books in my bag.

'It didn't have to end like this you know,' Natalie suddenly said, sighing.

'Sure . . . I guess,' I mumbled, wanting to get this awkward exchange over and done with as soon as possible. I wasn't really in the mood for small talk.

'Look,' Natalie continued, oblivious to my clear discomfort, 'I know that at times I could be a bit annoying, and the things I said during our last chat were bang out of order, but I've always thought you were cool. And you didn't exactly make it easy, you know?'

This piqued my interest. What else did she have to get off her chest?

'Oh? What do you mean by that?' I made my way out of my old room and headed to the kitchen with Natalie trailing behind me. I sat down by the dining table, looking up at her calmly. The last thing I wanted was to be dragged into another argument.

'You're really reserved, Artemis. It's like . . . you don't allow people to get close to you, and it can come across as a bit standoffish. You have this passive-aggressive streak where it's like . . . I dunno . . . You never really confront things face-to-face, and instead you get super dismissive and closed off. That's why I always kept a distance.'

I stayed silent for a moment, pondering this revelation. I knew that I've always been a little introverted at times, sometimes even aloof, but passive-aggressive? That was a new one.

'I . . . I never intentionally tried to make you feel bad or anything, Nat. I just tend to keep myself to myself. I'm sorry for not noticing that and for hurting your feelings in the process.'

Natalie hastily moved forward towards the dining table and sat down opposite me, trying to meet my gaze. She looked on the brink of tears as she began to speak.

'Thanks, Artemis.'

'It takes me a while to warm up to people,' I added. 'And you haven't been the easiest to live with either. You've said things in the past that came across super dodgy and racist, and they weren't appreciated either.'

Natalie sank further into her seat, her cheeks glowing a bright fuchsia and her eyes wet with tears. 'Yeah. About that last argument – I can admit that me saying what I said wasn't ideal.

Coming from a small town in the countryside, I wasn't raised in the most multicultural of neighbourhoods, and so I guess moving to London was my way to try and learn and grow and all that kind of stuff. I realise that there's still a lot of unlearning I need to do, and I can acknowledge that what I said came off as super racist. I'm really sorry.' Natalie stared directly into my eyes, leaving me no room to doubt her sincerity. This felt like a breakthrough moment for the both of us as I shrugged off her apology, feeling neither here nor there about it.

Natalie exhaled and let slip a small smile. As I made my way to leave, she added: 'By the way, your food never smelled bad, it actually always smelled delicious. I was just mad because I dunno how to cook properly, ha.'

'Oh, I knew all along, babes. You don't need to apologise!' I replied, and as I left Natalie's flat and made my way back to my own, I was left with her remarks still circling round and round in my head.

The Sisterhood of the Travelling Lace Fronts ♥
Jean, You

Jean: Soooo was she trying to call you aggressive or nah??

Artemis: No, I don't think she meant it that way, she just said that I was cold and distant to her. I've been thinking about it all day.

Jean: I mean, she was annoying. I can get why you'd be distant tbh.

Artemis: Yeah but like ... am I cold? Do you think I'm distant, and don't let people see the real me?

Jean: Sis, it's hard for me to say because we're besties so I don't get *Frozen* vibes from you, but I think you do what you gotta do to protect your peace and energy. You CAN be a little uptight or whatever, but you have your reasons, innit?

Artemis: Rah. Uptight you know, lmao. You lizard.

Jean: Lmaooo, no, but I say it with love. You protect yourself
  a lot and it comes across as you not wanting people to see
  the real you, for whatever reason. Maybe that's what led
  you to do the whole catfish thing with Ruben.

Artemis: Eugh. Maybe, idk. Can't wait for therapy tbh. Love
  u xx

The next couple of weeks were a blur. Of course, I still hadn't
heard from Ruben even though every inch of me yearned to
contact him, to hear his voice again and see how he was doing.
My body felt as if it was simply going through the motions:
wake up, get dressed, go to work, come home, cry, look at old
photos of Ruben in my photo gallery, repeat.

Meanwhile, my blog and Instagram were popping off.
I'd never been busier, in fact. I was able to channel all my
nervous, anxious, heartbroken energy into creating daily bits
of content that allowed me to shut off parts of the world in
which all the fuckery I'd caused with Ruben existed, and to
just concentrate on tending to the parts of me that needed
healing, using my own plants as a conduit of sorts. Due to my
daily uploads, I'd now very quickly amassed an audience of
over 60,000 followers, who all tuned in to my daily aesthetic
videos dubbed with me – my face finally uncovered – reciting
positive affirmations and motivational advice quotes to the
audience. It felt good to finally reveal my true self on my page
after hiding that part of myself for so long, and now that I had
become an Influencer Ambassador with three other brands,
I was able to make somewhat of a decent side hustle with
this content.

Jean had been coming over a few times a week to help with
last-minute apartment décor, as well as catching up. We spent
80 per cent of the time at the flat talking and eating, while the

other 20 per cent was spent on actual flat decorating. Today we were in the living room, painting the walls and ceiling.

'How are we doing, bubs?' he asked, dipping his paintbrush into the Farrow and Ball stone-coloured Limewash paint I'd picked out for my living room. 'When's your first session with the therapist? I promise you, it's gonna help loads.'

I'd stopped joking about it and actually found someone to talk to about all my stuff. 'It's in two days' time,' I replied, almost tearful with relief. 'I'm nervous, man. The stuff Ruben – and Natalie – said about me cut deep. But I'm still not sure about talking about all of it with a stranger.'

Jean gave me a knowing look. 'You're a Virgo, babes. Not only is it written into your DNA, but it's written into the literal horoscope for you to be a bit of a control freak. But maybe don't see it as a bad thing? The shrink will probably teach you how to convert it into something positive.'

I sighed morosely. 'I hope so, because this shit has been so suffocating.'

'I know, I can tell, babe, but when you start opening up and decanting all your anxious thoughts and emotions into another person, you'll begin to feel loads lighter. Sometimes when things get a bit too hectic for me, I just write down all my thoughts on a piece of paper and then burn it. I don't know the science behind it, but pouring all my negativity into an inanimate object always seems to clear my mind. It's like a transfer of energy or some shit, I don't know, but you should try it!'

Jean went back to painting the cabinets, but I just stared at him. My best friend. My ride-or-die pal. My chaotic other half had somehow turned into this all-knowing guru overnight. I knew that I wouldn't have been able to have done or got through any of this without him. I reached over and gave him a huge bear hug, which startled him. He burst out laughing as he dropped the paintbrush and hugged me back.

'Oh, bitch!' he chuckled. 'What's all this for? I got paint on your carpet now!'

'I just love you is all, and I wanna thank you for always being there for me. I know I've been annoying this year, and you've been going through your own shit, but your support never wavered, and I'm thankful. Also, I just love how you've turned into this wise-ass oracle overnight!'

'First of all, sis, I've ALWAYS been wise, 'kay? Secondly, I love you too. Thirdly, I'm an openly bisexual man who comes from an East African family — I've been in therapy for four years, bruv.'

Chapter 37

The last couple of weeks had taught me so much; I had some control issues, and I'd been trying to control certain situations in order to protect my heart. I controlled how I acted and how hard I worked in order to get to the top. I controlled the types of men I dated – deliberately going for guys who I knew or suspected had fat fetishes in order to be in control of their desire for me, making rejection far less frequent. I controlled and manipulated Ruben into falling for someone who didn't exist, all because I wanted to feel a sense of acceptance and romantic love without getting hurt. These were some of the issues I covered in my first therapy session. My poor therapist, Sonia, had her work cut out for her.

'So, Artemis, have you been able to tap into where this fear of rejection stems from in you?'

Sonia looked to be around fifty years old, with a sweet, wholesome face that just made you want to automatically trust her. She cocked her head to the side as she waited for my answer.

'Erm, I dunno really. I just don't take disappointment well, I guess.' I shifted uncomfortably in my seat.

'And why is that?' Sonia replied softly. A part of me wanted to respond, saying, 'That's what I'm paying you for – to tell me why I feel how I feel!' But I resisted the urge.

'I think maybe there's a part of me that constantly seeks approval. From my body, to my job. I constantly wanted my mum to be proud of me, too.'

Sonia leaned forward, hanging on to my every word. We had covered so much ground, and I was already feeling emotionally exhausted.

'I guess nothing I did was ever good enough for my mum when I was younger.' I exhaled, looking at everything in the room but Sonia. I didn't want to cry. 'To her, I was never small enough, or pretty enough. I didn't study the "right" subjects at college and uni. I didn't date the "right kinds of guys". I didn't present myself in the ways she thought I should present myself, according to her. She's just very traditional and I'm very not. I think it disappointed her, growing up.'

Sonia made a few notes in her notepad. That damn notepad. Knowing all my secrets.

'Hmm. I see,' Sonia breathed, settling back into her chair, scribbling away. 'And what's your relationship like with your mother now?'

'Oh, we're cool now. I had a discussion with her about how she used to talk to me a few years ago, and for the most part we've been able to squash it. But at the end of the day she is still an African mum, you know – the judgement comes with the job description, haha.'

That was Sonia's cue to laugh at my witty joke, but she just smiled knowingly. 'Well. That's our time, Artemis! I'll see you again at the same time next week. It's been a pleasure meeting you today.' I walked out feeling *embarrassed*, but emotionally a bit lighter.

I realised that for the longest time, I had been hiding the many insecurities and feelings of low self-worth about myself and my body under the guise of 'CONFIDENCE' and being the ★BUBBLY BIG GIRL★ who owned her body. I was confident, for sure – but not to the degree I thought I was. Talking to Jean, and being able to open up to others like Natalie and Aneni in a way I wasn't used to, had been a little hard at first, but I was going from strength to strength and, with time, I was counting on it all paying off.

I went back to waking up each day feeling grateful for one thing about myself. I managed to stop myself looking at the videos and photos on Ruben's account so much as the days went by, but I still thought about him all the time and wondered whether he really was back on the dating scene or not. I had the urge to write him a letter, to tell him everything I'd learned. To have the chance to apologise again. I guess it would be a closure of sorts, if we really were over.

'Girl, I know it hurts, but try not to think about him if you can,' Jean said one day as we were knocking back rum and Cokes in the park. 'It's your birthday week, and we can't be out here moping about him when you've got planning and partying to do!'

'But the shit hurts,' I replied. 'I'm doing better than I was doing a month ago, but I know it's gonna take time. I'm tryna do up Hot Girl Summer but I keep getting flashbacks of him. I wanna send him a letter, Jean.'

'I actually don't think that would be a bad idea, you know,' he replied, taking another swig of his drink. 'It might be the closure you need to end the chapter. If you do it though, just don't expect a reply – do it for you.'

'You're right. Maybe after my birthday.'

My birthday was the day after Beyoncé's, which normally meant that every birthday would consist of me throwing a Beyoncé-related costume party – but this year, I wanted to do something different. I wanted to celebrate *myself* instead of dedicating my birthday to my icon. This year, my birthday was going to be low-key, cute and suave, and it was going to be thrown at my flat as a little combined housewarming/birthday party. I'd put on over a stone since I came back from the States, so finding an outfit was proving a bit harder to source, but eventually I found this gorgeous Ganni bodycon floral dress with ruching up the side and a low V-neck cut. I tried it on in store and knew I wanted it as soon as the fabric hugged itself against my body. For the first time in a long time, I felt beautiful.

The Sisterhood of the Travelling Lace Fronts ❤
Jean, You

Artemis: Jean, I need your help. Should I go for the 26-inch wavy Brazilian, or the 18-inch Peruvian for tonight?

Jean: I don't know if you're talking about wigs or dicks. But I vote for 26 inches. ALWAYS xx

Artemis: After our little hospital visit, I'm surprised you can do anything over 10 inches but I digress lmaooo. I also vote for the 26 inch – oh, and can you bring straighteners too?

Jean: LMAO. I hate you, and course. I'll see you in a few hours, my love, we are gonna get turnt for your birthday, OK?? No tears! No REGRETS. It's gonna be lit.

Artemis: I cannot wait! Thank you so much for helping me organise this shit! Aight ttyl, gonna start doing ma make-up xxx

Jean: I'll see you later!!!

I wanted to feel happy and excited for my birthday celebration, but it was feeling like a bit of an act. All I really felt were nerves, given that I'd told myself I would email Ruben as soon as my party was over.

Still, I put my phone down and started getting ready for my little drink-up for this evening. Hundreds of pounds worth of leftover booze from clients at work had been delivered, and I'd tossed a few balloons around the place to make it look festive. My flat wasn't 100 per cent complete, but it felt more like home than anywhere I'd ever lived, and I loved it. With my hair cornrowed back and my make-up done, I brought out my brand-new Brazilian 26-inch lace frontal wig. She was fabulous. She'd cost me an arm and a leg, but can you really put a price on a sick slay? Tonight was going to be my night, and I was determined to feel sexy and confident.

One saving grace that I had been hanging on to was that during that fateful last conversation with Ruben, he told me he found me attractive as myself – FUPA and all. I clung to that, not because I needed a man's validation to make me feel worthy as a desirable woman, but because it was further proof of how I should have just believed in my sauce from the beginning, and that perhaps there was a sliver of hope for us after all.

Fast forward to 8.30 p.m. and it was game time. My make-up? Slayed. The hair? Served. My dress? Serving body. I looked in the mirror and stared at myself for several moments. I looked beautiful. My stomach was rounder. My cheeks were fuller. And I looked incredible. As I looked at all the parts of my body that had gained in size since going to the States, I thought about how far I'd come, and about all of the other things I had gained – confidence. Self-esteem. Accountability. Therapy was tough, but through it I was learning how to let go of my control over myself and others. I was learning how to live in the moment, and to have fun again. And for the first time in my life, I enjoyed being single. I enjoyed not dating, and just being in my own company. I enjoyed being me.

'TEMZ BABY! GET YOUR ARSE OUT HERE. YOUR GUESTS ARE WAITING FOR YOUR GRAND ENTRANCE!' shouted Jean from the kitchen.

I took a deep breath and exhaled. 'You got this, sis,' I whispered to myself, and I strutted out towards my friends and family like the bad bitch I was.

Chapter 38

A Month Later

To: info@rubenalexander.com
From: artemisprime@gmail.com
Subject: Hi (Please don't feel like you have to respond)

Hi Ruben,

I'm probably the last person you want to hear from now. I'm going to make this short and sweet, and please don't feel you have to respond.

I've been wanting to contact you for a minute now, but didn't quite know what to say. I didn't know how to articulate the feelings I've been feeling over the past couple of months, but since being on my healing journey, I've come to realise a few things and I feel as if I owe you an explanation.

Ruben, from the bottom of my heart, I apologise for misleading and lying to you. You were right all along: I was a control freak. A huge one. I was scared of letting you see the real me because I was scared that you would reject me and, at that moment, I wanted nothing more than for us to develop a friendship. I wanted to control how you saw me, because I was falling for you and I was scared that you would reject me. I had always planned to come clean, but I began to fall in love with you, and the fear grew.

Ruben, I need you to know that even if we never speak again, I still love you, and the pain of not having your friendship/companionship has been . . . difficult to say the least.

I also need you to know that my feelings for you were real. Everything I told you about myself was real. I need you to know that.

Anyway, I'm rambling now so, I'll leave it at that. I hope one day you can forgive me.

Love,

Artemis

PS I told Chantelle everything. We're cool now.

To: artemisprime@gmail.com
From: info@rubenalexander.com
Subject: RE: Hi (Please don't feel like you have to respond)

Lol. Cute email address.

Glad to hear you're on a healing journey and that you told Chantelle everything.

Thanks for your email; I appreciate your words, and for coming clean. I really do. I'd also be lying if I said I hadn't thought about you as well. I've also had some time to think, and I'm sorry that I gave you the impression that I was only into a certain type of woman – after thinking about it after our convo, I can see why I would give you that impression. So I apologise for that. I can promise you that I have/had no interest in the ladies I followed on Instagram. A lot of it was for network-ing purposes, I promise you.

Congrats on your plant stuff btw (I unblocked you). I see you now show your face, which is awesome. The content looks great.

Umm. So yeah, I don't mind you emailing, and I do forgive you.

Take care

PS You looked beautiful when we met, by the way; I had to stop myself from staring at you for too long; didn't wanna get in trouble as I was meant to be with 'Aloe', haha. You had absolutely no reason to pretend to be someone else. You're fucking stunning.

To: info@rubenalexander.com
From: artemisprime@gmail.com
Subject: RE: RE: Hi (Please don't feel like you have to respond)

Oh, wow, I didn't think that you'd respond! Um, thank you so much, I can't tell you what your forgiveness means to me. And yeah, I decided to show my face; it was time for me to stop hiding. I also accept your apology, although I wasn't trying to blame you or anything; it was my projection that caused this.

Also, you're very kind, thank you for the compliment. As if I didn't regret doing this enough . . . Xxx

To: artemisprime@gmail. com
From: info@rubenalexander.com
Subject: RE: RE: RE: Hi (Please don't feel like you have to respond)

I mean I've wanted to reach out to you for a minute so I'm happy you slid into my emails tbh. I've had a lot of time to think about what happened, and despite everything, my feelings for you were real, too. I loved talking to you – it was always the highlight of my day. I did mean it when I said I loved you at the time.

If you're ever in the Bay Area again, hit me up. x

To: info@rubenalexander.com
From: artemisprime@gmail. com
Subject: RE: RE: RE: RE: Hi (Please don't feel like you have to respond)

Well. This warms my cold, cold heart. 😊

And about the Bay Area, it's funny you mention that . . .

Chapter 39

A month later, and it was 8.30 p.m. on a brisk November evening and I was sitting in my hotel suite at the Four Seasons in San Francisco getting ready to attend a meeting with my lead clients, One Nation Athletics. It was set to be a busy week for the brand, with them filming several infomercials and launching print ads for their new campaign, and Stephen wanted me to be on the ground overseeing the project.

I felt uneasy about being back in the city again, but a client was a client, and they were a pretty easy-going client on top of that, so I had to swallow my anxieties (as well as my pills) and get the job done.

I had been on the phone to Jean, who was gearing up for his big exhibition at the Tate. He was currently at the GP after coming down with a bad case of haemorrhoids.

'Sis, I haven't been able to shit for a week. The sores are literally open. I've been scared to fart in case it sets them all off again. Can you imagine me giving a speech at the exhibition with my bumbum leaking? Nah man!'

I stifled laughter as I tried to console him. My friend. He was absolute chaos.

'Oh, Jean. I love that you can tell me shit like this – no pun intended by the way,' I added, bursting into a guffaw. 'I guess you're gonna have to be a top for the next couple weeks or so, huh?'

'First of all, Temz, I've always been a top. Let's get THAT straight, and secondly, Michael's useless – he won't even rub salve into my sores, the dick.'

'Shit, I wouldn't either! But I'm sending you all my love, and please take care, OK? I'll see you next week. Cannot wait to support you for your big night!'

'Can't wait, babes. I miss you!'

I changed into my pyjamas and took a tub of Ben & Jerry's finest into bed. The work with my client started tomorrow, and tonight was going to just be about me, this ice cream, my snacks and my incredibly shitty American soap operas.

I'd been inundated with emails from the One Nation Athletics team about me potentially moving to San Francisco part-time to help run the account. The pay package and West Coast weather was enticing, so I said I would trial it for a couple of months to see how it went – on their dime, of course.

Twenty minutes into my self-care time, I received a WhatsApp message. I picked up the phone and idly glanced at the preview – it came from an unknown American number:

Unknown: A little birdie tells me that a certain Miss Artemis is in San Francisco at the moment. Do you think she'd be open to a drink tomorrow evening with a random tech consultant-slash-singer in Oakland? X

I smiled to myself goofily as the ice cream on the spoon that was halfway into my mouth started to drip down my chin.

Ruben had added me back on WhatsApp.

I found myself messaging back:

Me: I reckon she should be available after work. As long as she gets to buy the tech consultant-slash-singer a round of drinks. She kinda owes him one. Xx

I smiled as Ruben's pending 'typing' text appeared on screen.

It was 6 p.m. the following day and I was in my hotel room putting on the finishing touches while waiting for my Uber to pick me up and take me to Oakland. I wanted to look cute yet laid-back, so I opted for my favourite square-neck orange crop top and teamed it with a blue satin midi skirt that I'd recently bought from John Lewis. I completed the look with a pair of Gola trainers. Keeping it casual, ya'know? I didn't want to look as if I'd tried too hard. I had my hair fluffed out in an Afro and finished the look with a light tint of red lipstick for a little razzle dazzle.

At 6.25 p.m., I arrived at the Viridian cocktail bar in Uptown Oakland. I stood outside the venue for a couple of minutes to catch my breath.

You've got this, Temz.

This is your chance to make a great third impression.

It's just a drink; no pressure.

I walked inside, head high as I feigned all the confidence I could muster, even though my stomach was doing somersaults. After thirty seconds or so of looking around, I spotted him tucked away in a booth by the corner. He was looking directly at me. I broke into a nervous smile as my legs threatened to buckle under me; Ruben looked more gorgeous than I'd remembered. The lights of the bar danced off his shiny, bald head as he stood up and walked towards me, beaming. As I walked slowly towards him, I couldn't help but smile too. My heart was beating a thousand times per minute as he opened up his arms and scooped me into a bear hug.

I allowed myself to slightly slump into his embrace taking in his cologne (was that a Penhaligon's fragrance I detected?), the smell of his clothes, the warmth of his skin, the quickening thumping of his heart, too.

'I've missed you . . . Artemis,' he breathed softly into my ear before pulling back and staring into my eyes. I stared back, not wanting this moment to end. It felt like something out of a fairytale.

Almost.

'I brought you a little gift,' Ruben said coyly, giving the Cheshire Cat a run for his money with a wide grin.

'Oh! I didn't know we were doing gifts, but OK!'

Ruben walked me over to the booth and there on the table, wrapped up in delicate pink foil wrapping paper complete with a bow, sat a five-inch-tall aloe vera plant.

I looked up at Ruben, who was trying everything in his power not to laugh, a mischievous smirk still plastered across his face. 'I'm sorry, Temz, I couldn't resist, I thought it would be funny!' he said, finally breaking into a guffaw.

I looked up at him, trying yet failing to hide my own giggles. 'Sir? Are you taking the absolute piss?!'

Men were exhausting. But considering what I'd put him through, he could tease me as much as he wanted. I was just glad he was there with me.

Epilogue

The Sisterhood of the Travelling Lace Fronts ♥
Claudia, Jean, You

Jean: Sis, remind me when your plane lands again?

Artemis: Uhhh, it should get there at around 8 a.m. tomorrow.
I'll dump my suitcase at Mum's and then zip straight over.

Jean: Amazing, I'm so happy you're able to make this, I'm so
excited to see you!

Artemis: Baby, I wouldn't miss this for the world! I'm so
proud of you, do you know that? You deserve all the good
things, and I know you're going to absolutely smash it.
Am I meeting you at the gallery for the opening, @Clauds?

Claudia: Yasssssss, of course, I can't wait to see your
curation, J!

Jean: Thank you, girlies, hehe! I'm gonna fucking shit myself,
man. I've never curated my own collection before – there
better be fucking alcohol. I'ma need it.

Artemis: It's going to be brilliant, babes. Don't worry. I'll see
you tomorrow!

I tossed my phone onto the sofa as I made my way towards the
bathroom to take a quick shower. I had a lunch meeting with
One Nation Athletics in a couple of hours to talk about the

marketing behind one of their new capsule collections, and I had to leave enough time to make it across the bridge to get there on time.

'Where the hell is my razor?' I sang to myself as I rooted between the shaving cream, cologne samples and random '12-in-One' body wash/shampoo hybrid products. Men could be so messy.

'Whachu looking for, babe?' came a voice from outside the bathroom door.

'Oh, never mind, I found it!' I replied, retrieving my razor and starting the shower. The bathroom aesthetic wasn't my cup of tea – I was more of a 'Mid-Century-Modern' girl myself, but it would do for now. We could work on it.

Ruben opened the bathroom door and watched me hungrily as I slipped into the shower cubicle. 'Damn,' he said, still surveying my body as the hot water cascaded down on me. 'You're so damn beautiful. I hope you know you can stay here as long as you want while you're looking for somewhere to rent. There's more than enough room.'

'Oh, I know,' I replied, attempting to seduce him with some kind of 'come-to-bed' smoulder that ended up looking as if I had an eyelash stuck in my eye. 'I'm sure work will sort out a place for me soon enough. Anyway, there are larger issues at hand.' I slid open the shower door and held out my hand. 'I've got a meeting in an hour, and I need help detangling my hair. Would you do the honours?'

A grin spread across Ruben's face as he undressed and stepped into the cubicle, embracing me from behind and planting kisses on my neck. 'The pleasure would be all mine, baby,' he replied. We kissed passionately under the cascading waterfall shower, our bodies merged into one, in sync, uncontrollable. No lies, no chaos. Simply perfect.

Acknowledgements

I will attempt to keep this short and sweet, as I tend to be a lady of many words, so here we go:

First, I want to thank my family and my parents for all their support. You were instrumental in my love and appreciation of reading, from reading to me while in the womb, to providing me with an endless supply of all the books I could ever want as a child and teenager. Your support means everything.

To my best friend of eighteen years, Uwa, who believed in me more than I ever believed in myself. Thank you, Uwa, for seeing me, for nurturing and encouraging me during the days when I would feel useless and forlorn. Thank you for seeing the talent in me during times when I could not see it myself. I love and appreciate you!

To Kevin, my very own 'Ruben', thank you for your wisdom, your unyielding, steadfast love and your unwavering support during this process, and for low-key being the inspiration behind this story, at least where the transatlantic long-distance love story is concerned. Thank you for constantly motivating me on days when I thought I couldn't finish writing. I love you.

To the anonymous person 'based in California' who I met on Myspace as a seventeen-year-old, who catfished me for the best part of two years, thank you also for being the inspiration behind this story. Uwa and I eventually found out who you really were. You've been under our noses the entire time, and we'll confront you when the time is right, hehe!

To my wonderful literary agent, Hattie Grunewald, who has been on this journey with me for years now, whose encouragement, support and PATIENCE has meant so much to me.

To Rachel Petty, thank you so much for stepping in during Hattie's maternity leave and helping me to make this book the best it could be!

To commissioning editor extraordinaire Sareeta Domingo and the teams at Trapeze and Orion Books, thank you so much for taking a chance on me, and for helping me feel seen in this field. Your enthusiasm, overwhelming support and belief in Temz – as well as the story in general – means more to me than you'll ever know. I wanted to tell a story that centred a Black, plus-sized woman being the love interest without any of the classic fatphobic tropes and jokes, and you saw the vision and believed in me. For that I am so thankful.

Thank you to my management team for being so incredibly supportive and patient with me while I got the book done. Sorry for being so annoying and having to turn down work while completing this – but we made it eventually!

Thank you to West Norwood Library for being the epicentre of where this book was written. We must continue to advocate to save our libraries – they are incredibly important.

Thank you to Crissle and Kid Fury from *The Read* podcast, who kept me entertained and laughing while writing this book. I appreciate you both!

Thank you to Samsung for creating robust external hard drives. There was a point in time when I was 70 per cent into the book and had saved the manuscript onto said device, which I then dropped from a five-storey balcony. The fact that the hard drive still worked was nothing short of a miracle.

Last and by no means least, thank you to you – the reader – for choosing to read this book. It had been a dream of mine to create characters that looked like me and to have fat, Black women portrayed positively in the literary world – to be the subjects of love, desire and all the amazing things we as human beings are worthy of. I really hope you can see that in Artemis, as flawed as she can sometimes be. Thank you for buying or borrowing this book. I love you all.

CREDITS

Trapeze would like to thank everyone at Orion who worked on the publication of *Chaotic Energy*.

Agent
Hattie Grunewald

Editor
Sareeta Domingo
Serena Arthur

Copy-editor
Donna Hillyer

Proofreader
Clare Wallis

Editorial Management
Jo Whitford
Jane Hughes
Charlie Panayiotou
Lucy Bilton
Patrice Nelson

Audio
Paul Stark
Louise Richardson
Georgina Cutler-Ross

Contracts
Rachel Monte
Dan Herron
Ellie Bowker
Oliver Chacón

Design
Nick Shah
Helen Ewing
Charlotte Abrams-Simpson
Deborah Francois

Image Research
Natalie Dawkins

Finance
Nick Gibson
Jasdip Nandra
Sue Baker
Tom Costello

Inventory
Jo Jacobs
Dan Stevens

Production
Claire Keep
Amy Knight

Marketing
Yadira Da Trindade

Publicity
Sarah Lundy

Sales
Catherine Worsley
Victoria Laws
Esther Waters
Tolu Ayo-Ajala
Group Sales teams across
    Digital, Field, International
    and Non-Trade

Operations
Group Sales Operations team

Rights
Rebecca Folland
Tara Hiatt
Ben Fowler
Alice Cottrell
Ruth Blakemore
Marie Henckel